DIAMOND CITY

FRANCESCA FLORES

WEDNESDAY BOOKS
NEW YORK

First published in the United States by Wednesday Books, an imprint of St. Martin's Publishing Group

www.wednesdaybooks.com

Library of Congress Cataloging-in-Publication Data

ISBN 978-1-250-22044-8 (hardcover)
ISBN 978-1-250-22046-2 (ebook)

First Edition: January 2020

10 9 8 7 6 5 4 3 2 1

To my mother

To my mother

PROLOGUE

"Do you want to know the secret to survival?"

Aina's eyes snapped up from the sticky wooden table and widened at the man who sat across from her. The bar's dim light glinted off his smile. Fast-playing flutes, rowdy drunks, and dancers stomping their feet across the floor nearly drowned out his next words.

"You count and you look," he whispered. "You count everything and you look at everyone. Are you paying attention, street child?"

Her frown deepened. Every underage person in this bar was a street child, but she still disliked being called one. It marked her as dirty, poor, without a future. She was dirty and poor, but the idea of a future hadn't faded from her mind yet. A high collar framed the man's pale face as he took her in. Maybe he was going to offer her a job. Something about him smelled rich, maybe the scent of cologne. He was probably one of the industrialists made wealthy by steam and steel.

"Thirty-six people were in this bar when you entered, making you the thirty-seventh." He leaned closer, his gaze fixing on her as adamantly as a noose around the neck. "The door opened once inward, and twice outward, because the wind pushed your hair around your cheeks the first time, but not the next two."

She blew a strand of wet hair out of her eyes and tried not to shiver, but she was soaked from getting pushed into the Minos River by some boys who'd robbed her. She wanted warm clothes and a bed to sleep on. She didn't want to play this man's game. Crossing her arms, she turned away to ignore him, but he continued speaking.

"That means there should be thirty-six people in this room, but did you count? There are thirty-five. Where is the missing link?" He barely paused for a breath. "You don't know. He's planting a bomb in the rafters. Don't look up; you've only got twenty seconds. I have a job you might be good at. If you come work with me, everyone here will die, but we'll survive. If you don't, you'll die without ever knowing what you could become. Do you want your life to end at twelve years, Aina Solís?"

"How do you know my name?" Her fists clenched, a chill crept down her spine. Plenty of bombs went off in Kosín, but what if this were just a lie to get her to follow him?

"Twelve seconds left."

"The Diamond Guards—"

"The Diamond Guards won't risk their lives to save a street child. Eight seconds left."

Her mouth snapped shut. The options were few, but she was cold and hungry, and this man had a job for her.

She stood on shaking legs and walked out, the man's presence behind her like a reaper waiting for its reward. In the last three seconds, they ran. The chill night wind bit her skin through her wet clothes. Her sprints elongated, and her lungs seared.

An explosion shattered the night. Aina fell into a pile of snow in a shadowed alley. Bits of wood from the building landed next to her, making her flinch and bite her tongue as her ears began to ring. Smoke, screams, and the distinctive crackle of flames sounded behind her.

The man helped her up. She took a step back, crossed her arms, and narrowed her eyes at him. He was younger than she'd first thought, hardly eighteen or nineteen. Something about him was familiar, but she couldn't figure out what.

If he meant to hurt her now, she could try to run, or fight back like she'd had to do so many times on Kosín's streets.

"Why did you help me?" she asked, trying to keep her voice from shaking. "I wasn't the only kid in there."

His smile faded slightly. "Because good things don't usually happen to girls who come from nothing."

Aina cast her eyes downward. She was already well aware of that.

He withdrew a dagger from a sheath inside his jacket. It was the sleekest blade she'd ever seen, with an onyx-black handle. A sharp breath stole through her at the sight. He waited patiently, holding it like a gift as she reached out to touch the handle with the tips of her fingers.

"Learn how to use this knife, and I'll make you into something."

SIX YEARS LATER

1

The baker's final words were smothered by a whimper.

"You know how they say you should watch out for the quiet ones?" Aina's breath fogged the blade of the dagger she held. "They were right."

She took her time with the blade, heedless of his screams. Screams went ignored in Kosín's slums. A gun would have been faster, but she preferred knives. In the hands of a trained killer, knives left less room for mistakes.

By the light of a single flickering candle, she'd waited in silence for the baker to return from the casino where he'd spent all his earnings. He'd entered and stumbled drunkenly toward his bed, where she'd pinned him.

The house smelled like salt and dough, and now blood. The coppery scent no longer bothered her like it had when she first became an assassin. The baker's screams died, leaving the house ghostly quiet as he dropped to the bed with his throat slit like a red smile. Silver moonlight reflected on his blank, glass-like stare. There was no pulse at his wrist, no breath from his lips. Another death at her hands like all the others, and while she'd grown to feel nothing after a kill, this one was different. She'd known this man.

When she was younger and begging on the streets, she'd sat in silence outside his bakery, hoping that someone would drop a piece of bread into her hands. When the hunger finally made her dizzy, she tried stealing bread from a customer. The baker had beaten her with a rolling pin until she blacked out in the snow.

He was better off dead, and she hoped every moderately hungry person in the vicinity would steal his bread tonight. She no longer needed it.

Standing, she wiped the bloody dagger on her scarf, but there was nothing to be done about the mess on her arms and torso. She pushed open the cardboard door and stepped into the street, wearing the baker's blood like a medal.

He had sold her boss's information to the Red Jackals gang, filling his pockets with kors for gambling, but guaranteeing his death by her blade. She didn't know what the information was, nor why the baker had sold it to the Jackals. Her boss, the Blood King, never told her more than she needed to know in order to slit a throat, and she wasn't stupid enough to test his patience by asking for details. Everyone in the south of Kosín—everyone but the baker, apparently—knew that crossing the Blood King was a death sentence.

The slums' springtime scents of piss, sweat, and blood filled the early evening air. Smoke from the factories spilled down the hills into this southern part of the city known as the Stacks, home of the poor and the faithful who hid their religion and blood magic practice. Houses of mud brick, corrugated metal, and rain-beaten cardboard lined the slanting roads, pressed so close together, they were nearly stacked on top of each other. Children kicked balls across the mud with scrawny dogs barking at their heels, but they all scattered when she neared them, covered in blood. Slurred yells reached her ears as she walked the curving streets and passed groups of men huddled around fires. A small part of her was tempted to return to her old ways, to buy industrial glue from the men on these corners and inhale it until she passed out on the sidewalk.

But eyes watched her from dark corners. The Jackals had been tailing her since she'd entered their territory tonight. She avoided the shadows, staying in the center of the street with her head held high to prove she was fearless even though her heart pounded in her throat.

Some of the streets of the Jackals' territory and the Blood King's pressed against one another, leaving tensions fierce whenever someone trespassed. The Jackals had tested her boss's patience by paying the baker, and she was here as a reminder that messing with the Blood King was the quickest way to get your throat cut in Kosín. The only question was whether they would risk angering him further by coming after her for walking and killing on their streets—and whether they were stupid enough to try to fight her.

Neutral territory was close, marked only by the dead end ahead with a narrow, weed-choked gap between two houses. If a lifetime here hadn't taught her which streets were safe, she'd have died years ago. A little boy sat in front of one of the houses, twisting gold and silver wires into designs to be peddled for coins in the richer districts. Aina kept her eyes on the gap, counting down the seconds until she could reach it and move on to her next job.

Ten steps away, a girl stepped out from behind a house

with a knife in her right hand and a jackal's blood-drenched jaw and teeth tattooed along her left forearm.

"Paying us a visit?" she asked, stopping in front of Aina.

Aina shrugged, keeping her features indifferent. Someone approached from behind, their footsteps quiet, but noticeable.

"Just out for a stroll," she said with a small smile. She could take out this grunt with a knife through the ribs in seconds, but that would break the tenuous peace between the Jackals and the Blood King. They could threaten and antagonize each other, but if she actually killed one of them, all hell would break loose. No, she had to find a different route of escape.

The air shifted behind her. She spun to find a gun aimed at her chest by a boy twice her size. She side-stepped him, but the girl grabbed her roughly and pushed her into the rusted wall of a house.

The pair boxed her in. Aina allowed a small trace of fear to light up her eyes so they would think they had the advantage, convincing enough that even her boss would be proud. She had seen the girl around the city, and she recognized the boy; he'd been on the streets around the same years that she had been. Once, they'd even fought over a scrap of metal to sleep under. He'd beaten her in that fight, but he wouldn't win now.

"Should I take an eye for this violation, or should we beat her and paint her blood on her boss's door instead?" the girl asked her friend. "Which do you think would leave the brighter impression?"

Before she finished speaking, Aina moved. She grabbed the boy's wrist and slammed it into the wall. The gun fell from his grasp. He lunged for it, but she kicked him in the shins with her steel-toed boots. The girl tried to plunge her knife into Aina's side, but Aina blocked the attack with her own blade and punched the girl in the stomach with her other hand.

She fled, with their footsteps pounding behind her. She reached the gap between houses, passing the little boy, who hardly blinked at the scene in front of him, and slipped through the gap to reach a neutral street. Seconds later, the footsteps faded.

Running from fights might make her look weak, but starting a gang war wasn't part of her job tonight, and she still had work to do—work that no one, especially not the Blood King, could know about.

She left the Stacks, ascending the sloped hills until she reached the city's Center. Pollution blocked out most of the stars above, but electric lights in shop windows lit the streets here. Coughing on the smoke-tinged air leaking over from the assembly plants and steel mills, Aina veered east. Men and women from the textile factories shoved past her with hands dyed purple and black, jostling against the rail workers who limped from the train station wearing dirt-covered overalls. It was a thick, sweaty mess of a crowd, but some people noticed the blood on her clothes and gave her a wide berth. Most were too exhausted and so used to Kosín's violence that they barely glanced at her.

The air grew colder as she left the crowds and entered the quieter east of the city. She passed the smudged-gray apartment buildings, their windows lit with candles instead of electricity, then checked that no one was watching as she crossed a rusted bridge spanning the Minos River.

A few miles of weed-choked train tracks and muddy fields spread toward the forest on Kosín's outskirts. Far beyond the trees, mountains edged the horizon, blue and curving like ocean waves. She walked fast, needing to get to the mines and then back into the city before all the shops closed for the night.

While the mines produced diamonds meant to be sold as jewels, plenty of the workers here were involved in the illicit trade of rough diamonds used in blood magic. Prior to the civil war fourteen years ago, many people in their country had worshiped the Mothers, two goddesses named Kalaan and Isar who had blessed the Inosen—the faithful—with the magic of blood and earth. After the war and the rise of industrialization, worship and the use of magic had been outlawed. But a few hundred Inosen were left, their faith buried in Kosín's poorest districts. Even though they hid, Aina knew they were there. They were the ones buying her rough diamonds, after all.

The sound of drills soon reached her ears. A half mile later, she approached the fringe of the forest and took in the open pit of the Hirai Diamond Mine.

With a seven-million-carat yearly production rate, it was the richest diamond mine in the world. No matter how many times she saw it, descending into the earth with different levels cut into it like tree rings, the surrounding fields crisscrossed with pale beige roads and ore-filled crates, the pit never failed to impress her. It stretched farther than she could see. Employment and production had increased dramatically ever since more rare diamonds had been discovered in it.

A few supervisors nodded at her as she approached. She waved to one of them, a man whose name she'd forgotten the minute he'd told it to her. Next to him was a large crate loaded with gray, grain-like ore.

"Miss Solís." His smile was nearly toothless. "You're back again."

"Your goods?"

He took in her blood-stained clothes with a concerned frown. "We have water if you want to wash up."

"Your goods?"

With an exasperated shake of his head, the supervisor approached a toolbox at the foot of the crate. He withdrew a small scale and worked with his back to her. When he returned, Aina slipped him coins to keep quiet about their transaction, then held out a hand.

A stream of rough diamonds cascaded onto her palm. She tilted her hand so moonlight shone on their varying opaque and translucent surfaces. The gems were fresh from the earth, still dull in sheen and needing cut and polish to be sold anywhere as jewelry. But they would work fine for magic.

"Not jewelry-shop quality," the supervisor began, "but as long as they're not entirely opaque, they'll work for your purposes."

"They're not for me," she said with a glare.

"Then they'll work for whoever you sell them to," he said with a wink.

Smiling, she dropped the diamonds into a hidden pocket of her jacket and walked away—tossing her blood-stained scarf over her shoulder as she did.

Anyone except a certified jeweler caught with a rough diamond would be executed in the street, as was the law since the war. And if her boss ever found out about her diamond sales, he'd kill her for not giving him a cut of the earnings. He'd saved her and turned her from a helpless street kid into a feared killer, but she wanted more.

This was her one way to dupe him in a city he owned through blood and bribery. He held freedom over her head. Telling her one more kill, one more bribe, one more job, until she was free to be her own boss.

"One more diamond behind your back," she whispered, her breath turning white in front of her.

When the Blood King had sent her on her first kill years ago, Aina had made a promise to herself and to all the kids without a roof who still yearned to stand on top of the world. She would be the one everyone feared, the girl who made politicians, slavers, gang bosses, and mercenaries tremble.

She would be the Blood King's equal. And one day, she would rank even higher than him.

2

Her next steps brought her back into Kosín as the sky shifted from pale blue to navy. She passed grime-covered, block-style apartments, then took narrow roads north of the Center until she reached a hill leading into Rose Court.

When dealing in diamonds, there was a pecking order not to be disturbed. She collected the goods from the mine and sold them to various vendors, who later distributed them at fair prices to magic practitioners through gangs, mercenaries, and kids with hunger in their eyes. Out of the roughly one hundred jewelry shops in Kosín, only one store at any given time would buy the uncut diamonds she carried. It rotated every one to four days, and the chosen shop was only announced through whispers spoken in dark alleys. Luckily, she was always down the right alley and knew exactly where to go.

The lights grew brighter, and laughter and gossip reached her ears as she ascended the hill, a stark difference from the whispers and shouts littering the south of the city. Between two buildings ahead, she could make out the glint of electric lights from the mansion-dotted hills in the distance. Beyond that still, the Tower of Steel stretched toward the clouds, all black spires and forbidding height under the light of both moons.

People said the Mothers had created the moons, one red for Kalaan and the other silver for Isar, to illuminate the path to happiness and light, but Aina thought they might be too shrouded by pollution to do any good.

She paused for a moment to check that her weapons and diamonds were hidden, in case she came across any guards, then joined the crowd on the main road of Rose Court.

Cobblestone streets glittered under the lampposts that flickered on at night. Floor-to-ceiling glass shop windows displayed silk dresses, leather shoes, decorative plants and rugs, boxed fruits, wine, and other merchandise for prices that could feed a family for a year in the Stacks. A stone fountain ahead was bathed in yellow light from the shops, while a couple of miles south, electricity vanished and plumbing became a myth.

Each year, this side of Kosín grew richer, and the other side—her side—fell further and further behind.

Diamond Guards patrolled the streets, the gems of their namesake studded on the buttons and buckles of their jet-black uniforms. They were an extension of the national army, reserved as a police force for the city. Aina's hand closed around the hilt of one of her daggers by habit; she suspected trouble whenever she saw the guards. Most of the people in Rose Court barely spared them a glance, but Aina watched as a pair of them approached an older woman in a tattered brown dress and patched jacket at the corner of a bank.

They asked the woman a question in low voices. Her eyes

hardened as she replied. In the next instant, one of them pushed her against the wall, pinning down her brittle arms, his diamond-edged dagger at her throat. The other guard turned out her pockets.

If rough diamonds were found on the woman, they'd shoot her where she stood.

While any worship of the Mothers was outlawed and meant a prison sentence, selling rough diamonds or using them for magic guaranteed an execution. It was considered a crime worse than faith alone, since those diamonds could be sold as jewels, and using them for magic took money away from the city.

Coins spilled out of the woman's pockets instead of diamonds, and Aina let go of some of the tension in her shoulders. The woman could have gotten the money from anything, maybe even honest work, but the Diamond Guards would find a reason to accuse her of theft. In the nicer parts of the city, they became more brutal in meting out punishment, as if to prove to the moneyed industrialists, the Steels, that they were doing their jobs properly.

Disgust crept through Aina as the guards interrogated the women. But like all the well-off people in Rose Court, she turned and walked away as if nothing had happened. Not even her boss's bribes could keep a bullet from her brain if those guards caught her with rough diamonds.

That was the way of the Steels; they'd let people like her starve in the streets without a twinge of concern, then punish them again for trying to find a way to feed themselves.

A bell jingled when she entered the jewelry shop. It was small and cramped, but warm. Aina smiled at the door attendant, then browsed under the light bulbs hanging in gold-wire cages. An elderly couple examined jade earrings on a pillow inside one of the glass cases displaying the shop's best wares. She glanced over another customer's shoulder at the exorbitant prices diamond rings sold for.

Aina approached the counter. A bespectacled, balding man measuring a gem under a microscope looked up.

"Can I help you?"

"Just looking, mostly." She shrugged, her eyes trailing over a set of emerald bracelets under the counter next to a sign that read RARE EMERALDS IMPORTED FROM KAIYAN'S DEEPEST JUNGLES! She might make more money if other gems, like emerald, could be used with magic, but only diamonds worked. "The weather's a bit rough today, so I'm trying to stay inside."

There was the code: *rough*.

"I think I've got something you might like," the jeweler said without missing a beat. He withdrew a box from under the counter.

"Those are nice." She nodded at the unopened velvet box. From her pocket, she withdrew the pouch of diamonds and unhooked one side of the box he'd presented. It detached. She quickly slipped her diamonds inside before pocketing the newly detached side. There was a set price for a set weight of diamonds. Any more or less wouldn't be accepted, and she could only sell to this jeweler once until his shop's next rotation. Any wasted time or repeat visits would draw unwanted attention.

The box of coins jostled in her pocket while the jeweler disappeared to the back room to check the legitimacy of her diamonds. Her eyes flicked to the door attendant, who shifted her jacket aside to reveal the shiny handle of a gun—a clear message. If she tried to run while the jeweler was examining her diamonds, she'd be shot.

The jeweler returned and beckoned her closer, casting a

nervous glance around his shop for any eavesdroppers. In a whisper, he said, "If you want real coin, you should bring me a black diamond next time. Very rare, very beautiful. I'll pay you five times for that."

Aina grimaced. Of course the Steels placed more value on the beauty of a diamond rather than its practical use as a tool of magic that their people had used for centuries. The value of diamonds had changed from a sign of faith to a sign of how many kors were in your pocket. She nodded, keeping his offer in mind, and left as quickly as possible without running.

In half an hour, she reached the Stacks with her pulse still pounding in her ears. She never got this nervous when taking out a target, but selling rough diamonds was different. She touched the box of coins and gave it a quick shake. Heavy. She had to return home to collect her pay for the baker's kill, then wait until morning when the bank opened and she could deposit the money. She didn't entirely trust banks, but she trusted them more than stuffing her money under a mattress and hoping that a house full of criminals wouldn't find it.

More gangs heralded her, knives glinting at belts and tattoos decorating muscled limbs. They were the men and women who paid her boss to work near his manor, and they all knew her as his Blade—his killing hand. They had any number of names for her boss: the Blood King, the Durozvy Nightmare, and, after one occasion when Aina and his other grunts had watched him rip out a man's eyes for spying on him, they started calling him the Surgeon. But she knew him better by his real name.

Kohl Pavel's manor stood on the banks of the Minos River that circled the city. He called it the Dom, which meant "home" in Durozvy, his parents' native language. The Dom was a tradehouse, the name for hidden businesses like Kohl's that traded criminal services for a price. The manor had fallen into disrepair, leftover from the times when the rich built their homes along the shore before the rumble of trains and the smell of smoke became too much for their sensitive ears and noses. Vines covered most of the wide, two-story building and its barred windows. Willow trees clustered alongside the stark white walls and narrow concrete path from the street to the oak door. It bore all the appearances of a haunted house except the monsters inside were real.

A couple of Kohl's workers were poised on the roof, keeping watch even if she couldn't see them. She paid attention to the ground. Odd clumps of dirt meant bombs. After crossing the yard, she disabled a pair of knives set to fly at her face from one of the trees, then slipped through the front door. Some voices sounded from above, but cold and quiet surrounded her in the first-floor hallway. It was the only home she knew.

She walked to the second floor where she shared a room with three others who worked for Kohl in exchange for pay, shelter, and protection: another killer, Tannis, who'd smuggled herself into the city on a boat from Kaiyan and who Kohl had picked to join him from the ranks of their old gang; a spy named Mazir who Kohl had found working in a gambling den checking for cardsharps; and a thief, Mirran, who'd handled bank and mansion heists by herself until Kohl had brought her into his ranks. But he didn't call them killers, spies, and thieves; they were Blades, Shadows, Foxes. His tradehouse, his titles, his rules.

A cool wind swept through the window. It was empty except one bed, where Tannis slept. Aina changed her clothes and washed away any remaining blood, then checked her straw bed by candlelight to see if anyone had put a tarantula or loaded gun inside the sheets while she was out, whether as a test or a joke. She sat and withdrew the box of coins.

One thousand kors were inside, engraved with their country, Sumerand's, symbol: a sword and a pickaxe crossed over a slab of rock. She counted the silver fifties and gold hundreds under her breath. Counting them made her feel safer, like she'd achieved something. As long as her bank account was full, she would never starve on a street corner again.

The door slid open, and she almost jumped. Stuffing the box inside her pocket, she deadened her expression and looked up to see the Blood King, Kohl Pavel.

After six years of living under his roof, his cold gaze still injected a mix of fear and admiration into her veins. It was easy to see him as the man who'd annihilated every contender in the city so that his territory stood untouchable, who broke necks with his bare hands, who caused grown men to scamper when he marched down a half-lit street. But he was also the man who'd made a home for orphans and outcasts like her as long as they could prove useful. She wondered if he could somehow see through her jacket to the box of traitorous coins.

"Aina," he said, his voice unreadable. "Come with me."

3

Aina lifted her hands, and the coins Kohl had given her cascaded onto the elm wood desk in his office. They bounced and rolled onto the floor, where she examined them at her feet. So few compared to the ones in the box in her pocket.

"The Red Jackals almost gutted me, and I only get four hundred kors for it," she said as she bent to collect the coins for the baker's death. She felt Kohl's eyes on the back of her head as she did. Could these four hundred kors really make up for the baker hitting her with a rolling pin as a child? He'd died by her blade, but the memory of those bruises still ached.

"The Jackals aren't stupid enough to actually kill you," Kohl said. The floor creaked as he approached her. "They know I'd come after them if they did."

He didn't use candles like everyone else in the Stacks. Instead, he used the same electric lamps that the Steels in Rose Court, the factories, and the mansions all worked under, but lamps were only in this room of the Dom. The message was clear: He had more money than any of them. He took 40 percent of the clients' pay and kept the best jobs for himself. But another message hid underneath the silk trappings of the first. He could give them all of this. He could help them rise, help them move far away from the thugs and orphans and slaves they'd all been. They all knew that if they were going to make it anywhere in Kosín, they needed him more than they needed their own hands and feet. He could keep his electricity, as long as he let them keep their jobs.

Kohl leaned against his desk, the lines and angles of his face as inexpressive and sharp as a cliffside. A high collar shielded half his pale features from view. He might have been born in Sumerand after his parents had fled the famine in Duroz, but he acted as if he'd been in the famine himself; the hunger never left his eyes. He always wanted more, even after years spent attaining everything.

At first, she'd thought the rumors must be fabricated. He was surely too young to have wreaked so much havoc. But then she'd seen it for herself outside another tradehouse whose boss wasn't paying Kohl his commission. There were multiple tradehouses, but the Dom had come first, so any others that opened owed Kohl a cut.

"Hold him up, Aina," he'd said in that low voice that always hinted he was about to inflict pain.

It was a sunny afternoon near the Center where a tradehouse masqueraded itself as a dry cleaner's shop, but Kohl never worried about starting trouble in broad daylight—he'd bribed the Diamond Guards enough to give him a wide berth. A few people stopped to watch, but most were smart enough to move on.

The boss was on the ground, where Kohl had kicked him

in the stomach and face. Aina hauled him up and turned him around. Kohl's blue Durozvy eyes narrowed as he approached.

Brass knuckles appeared on Kohl's fist, the color clashing with the silver-and-sapphire watch he always wore. Both glinted in the sunlight when his fist swung. She held steady as he struck the boss in the jaw. Bone cracked, blood leaked down his chin, he muttered something about not meaning to offend Kohl.

"Offend?" Kohl's eyes had widened in shock. "You haven't offended me in the slightest. All you've done is show me you can't count money properly."

He knelt, sweeping away the dark brown hair getting in his face. Aina couldn't help wincing a little when he pulled out a dagger in the span of a breath. He was so quick, she'd missed the moment when he took it out. The boss Aina held down whimpered.

"If you can't count, I see no reason for you to have hands." Kohl smiled up at Aina as if this were a fun game. "Which one should I remove, Aina?"

"The right," she answered instantly.

It didn't matter to her which hand he took, but she could show no hesitation in answering. She'd vowed to show her worth to the man who'd given her a home and a job, who'd saved her from a bombing in a bar when she was twelve. She had to prove she was worth keeping around.

Kohl might only be twenty-four, but the tales of his reign over the south of Kosín were enough to have spanned several lifetimes. She'd studied him over the years, learning how to be merciless herself. He ensnared children like her whom no one would miss, frightening street kids who were already used to terrors, then offered them the chance to become the frightening ones themselves. She'd latched onto that chance like she gripped her knives.

But she wasn't a scared child anymore.

"You look tired, Aina." He took a step closer, making warmth rise on her cheeks. "Late night?"

"No more than usual," she said with a shrug. The box of coins inside her jacket jostled, and her heart stopped. She shook the ones in her hand to mask the sound, wondering why he'd brought her to his office. There was always a risk he'd sent his Shadow, Mazir, to spy on her. Sweat dripped down the back of her neck.

His eyes locked on hers, and she held the stare. No one else in the Dom would dare to meet his gaze, but the unspoken rules of the hierarchy had never seemed to apply to her.

Kohl nodded, breaking eye contact, and walked around the desk. His back faced her for a moment. Did he trust her enough to turn away from her? Could she really kill him, or had she simply gotten used to calculating ways to put a knife through flesh? Did a jeweler not contemplate how to cut and shape a precious gem?

"Do you remember a few years ago," Kohl's voice broke into her thoughts, "we sat in the train station's tower, and I told you what an assassin and an arms dealer have in common?"

"It was the middle of winter and my fingers were about to freeze off, but you wouldn't let us leave." She grimaced. "Assassins and arms dealers are nothing but the providers of a service, and therefore we have no reason to feel shame for the deaths we cause." The words trailed off. Her years on the streets had wiped all sense of shame from her mind regardless, and she knew better than to question Kohl's many lessons—he seemed to enjoy giving his employees cryptic advice and watching them work it out for themselves—but something

about this particular bit of murderous wisdom still made her
uneasy.

Then he turned and smiled, making her forget all her moral
qualms. She was safer without them anyway. More deadly.

"I have a new job for you," he said. "After my cut, you'll get
fifty thousand kors."

Her breath caught. She clenched her fists to keep her hands
from shaking. This job would earn her more than one hundred times what she'd gotten for killing the baker. It would
be more money than her parents combined had ever earned
and more than what anyone in the Stacks expected to see in
a lifetime. She'd worked the past six years to keep herself off
the streets, and a job like this would practically guarantee that
she'd never return.

All she had to do was kill a person.

"That's a lot of money."

"It will be the biggest haul our tradehouse has ever seen."
His voice became smoother, in the controlled and calculated
tone he always used when speaking of money. "Why do you
think I chose you?"

"I don't care. Where is the fish? I'll gut him right now." She
spoke so fast, the words tripped over each other.

"That's precisely why." His whisper rose the hair on the
back of her neck. "You don't ask questions. You don't miss.
When you decide to kill someone, you don't stand there daw-
dling and playing with your knives. You just do it."

She shrugged. "Point me to him."

"It doesn't hurt that you're almost as good as me."

Shifting her weight to one foot, Aina tried to control her
temper. Kohl placed his hands at the edge of the desk and
said nothing, each passing second of silence putting her more
on edge.

"Kouta Hirai."

She raised her eyebrows. Few names held more weight in Su-merand, let alone the capital of Kosín. About a hundred years ago, the Hirai family had come from Natsuda and monopo-lized the trade of mining tools. Spades, shovels, wedges, pick-axes, pry bars, sifting implements, and anything else needed to mine were entirely manufactured and sold by them. Twenty years ago, they bought the mines as well and grew their fortune with diamond sales to magic practitioners and mining tool sales to Steels. After the war, once diamonds were prohibited for use in magic, the family's two young sons, Kouta and Ryuu Hirai, led the country to become the leading exporter of diamonds worldwide. They were surrounded by bodyguards at all times and lived in the most protected part of the city, Amethyst Hill. They were untouchable.

"He's high up. And the person requesting the kill?"

"Higher."

Her breaths slowed, and she grounded herself by touch-ing the hilts of the scythes strapped to her thighs. Glancing around the office to buy time, she took stock of all the items she'd seen over the years. The clock on his desk ticked down the seconds. The room had little in terms of decoration, only a few gold-wire sculptures and an iron tea kettle. There was the stain on the mats where her own blood had dripped when a mark had nearly bested her.

Kohl had bandaged her himself.

"If you're stupid enough to get stabbed on the job, maybe you shouldn't be here at all," he'd muttered under his breath, then handed her a vial of painkiller he'd swiped from a clinic.

He'd clenched his hands into fists as she took it, drawing her attention to the tattoo on his inner forearm: a marking of his original gang, the Vultures. It stood out starkly on his alabaster skin. The black bird of prey's neck was broken, hung by a string of diamonds that trailed to Kohl's elbow.

Something had softened in his eyes when she'd winced in pain. Then he'd tossed the roll of bandages on the floor and walked out.

She could never quite tell if he wanted her to live or die.

"This won't go unnoticed." Her voice finally came out in a whisper. A piece of hair that had fallen onto her forehead itched at the sweat rolling down her skin, but she refused to move it. Kohl didn't trust people who fidgeted. Kohl wouldn't flinch or hesitate. Kohl would get the job done.

He came to stand in front of her, close enough that she could hear his breaths. One hand rested on the handle of the flintlock pistol at his waist. When he looked at her like this, she wondered whether he saw her as beautiful or not. She'd prefer if he didn't—it would confirm she'd succeeded in hiding any part of her that wasn't a ruthless killer. She wanted him to see her as an equal he could respect and care for, not a pretty plaything.

Her rounded cheeks, the curve of her jaw, her narrow shoulders, had all gotten her into too much trouble as a child. When she'd begun working with Kohl, she'd made sure to cut away the softness and the curves, and turn them into sharp edges instead, so no one would ever think she was weak enough to take advantage of. Years of inhaling glue on Kosín's sidewalks had left her copper skin dull and gaunt. She kept the dark waves of her hair, a mark of her Milano ancestry, in a rigid ponytail that hung to her shoulder blades. Her weapons hid any remaining weakness—a brace of diamond daggers strapped to her chest, scythes at her thighs, her palms hardened with calluses, and a small brace of blades between the knuckles of her left hand that protruded whenever she punched someone.

But no matter how tough she looked, she knew Kohl only ever saw her as the scared girl he'd saved from a bombing and turned into a Blade. He'd never take her seriously until she was as fearsome and unwavering as he was. Maybe her dreams of being Kohl's equal were a childish fantasy rooted in the mind of a girl who'd found food, a bed, and a roof and convinced herself anything was possible. Maybe she was just a grunt who'd prided herself on selling diamonds behind her boss's back but would never amount to anything more.

Maybe he was waiting for her to fail.

"After this job, you can start your own tradehouse," he said finally. "As agreed, you won't owe me commission like the others. I trained you, so I trust you to manage it well without my help. I'll extend my protection to you until you have things running."

Her eyes widened, and she forgot how to breathe. One more kill, and Kohl would give her all she wanted. She'd been begging for this chance for years. But he'd never indicated a finish line before, had only told her that the choice to set her free was his and his alone.

Good things don't happen to girls who come from nothing.

She shook the thought away. It was time to take advantage of what Kohl was offering. She nodded once.

"Choose the best partner you can find. I'll leave you to decide how to split the payment."

Aina cleared her throat. "That's generous."

"We have to take kindness where we can find it. I assume you'll choose your Linasian friend. The client has given us a week to do the job before he takes his money elsewhere. If you succeed, you get your tradehouse. If you fail . . ." He lifted one shoulder in a shrug.

She was well aware of the consequences. If she failed, she

would just be a grunt who'd reached too high, someone unworthy of Kohl's protection . . . and then she'd be his enemy. There was no choice but to succeed.

For the only time since she was fifteen and on her first assignment, fear wormed through her at the idea of killing someone. She pushed it away as quickly as it arrived. This was her one chance to rise above what she'd been given at birth, to stake out a spot of power in the city that had tried to take her life—and sanity—from her.

She'd decorate the streets in Kouta Hirai's blood before she let this chance slip away.

"I'll get to work." She turned to leave, but Kohl's hand latched onto her wrist, a flash of silver cuff links appearing at the edge of her vision. She tensed up at first, then relaxed into his grip. "Yes?"

"This is our biggest opportunity yet, Aina. The world is our oyster and Kosín its pearl. You know how valuable certain gems are." Her blood turned cold, freezing her veins from the back of her neck down her spine, along her arm to where his hand still gripped her wrist. "Are you going to take this one or let someone else sell it for you?"

She unhooked her hand from his. "I'll take it all."

4

A loud boom shook Aina awake the next morning. She sat up immediately, all thoughts of sleep forgotten. The others were already on their feet.

"What the hell was that?" groaned Mazir, Kohl's Shadow, before pulling the covers back over his head.

Mirran, Kohl's Fox, crouched in front of the window with the distinctive bright blue hair and gold eyes of Kaiya-nis people. "Looks like some idiot stepped on one of Kohl's bombs."

Shaking her head, Aina got out of bed. She'd squeezed in a shower the night before and worn her clothes to sleep, as usual, so all she had to do was throw on her jacket, boots, and scarf, then get started on this new job.

"Well, I'm not cleaning up the mess," she said cheerfully. They grumbled in response, rolling back under their blankets as Aina closed the door behind her with a soft click.

She walked down the second-floor hall, plain white walls

and cold, gray floor surrounding her, past the other bedroom for Kohl's three young recruits. She'd spent a few years there, training until Kohl trusted her enough to take on real jobs. While they all knew the basics of combat and espionage, he usually preferred that each of them was more skilled in one area than the others—he'd decided Aina would best serve as a Blade. The recruits were already awake, challenging each other to a knife-throwing game that Kohl had surely put them up to. She paused outside the door of the training room and watched as one of them hit the center of the target and let out a triumphant whoop, then she went downstairs.

Kohl's office was empty. She slipped inside, then entered a side door into the room where they kept ingredients for poisons. She restocked on the poison darts she used, then went to the armory to replace one of the small blades strapped to the knuckles of her left hand that had gotten bent. As she searched for one, her eyes scanned the two-story, circular armory lined with guns and blades of all sizes. Her first job here, before Kohl started training her to be a Blade, had been to pick up weapons from a warehouse in the east of the city. So many arms purchases went through that place, it was easy for Kohl to buy them in bulk with no one asking questions.

After the war, gangs had risen up to turn a profit in the midst of the city's rebuilding, and Kohl had built the Dom— the first tradehouse. He kept it and all the other tradehouses in the city safe as long as they paid their commission to him on time. Hers, once she completed this job, would be the first that didn't owe him a percentage of her earnings. The thought made her nerves flutter with excitement, but she refused to let it get to her head. First, she needed to become a weapon, kill Kouta Hirai, and collect her pay. Then Kohl would see her as someone he could respect and fear. And then, maybe he'd be able to look at her and see something more between them than their work.

Most of the city still slept as she headed to her destination, tracing familiar paths up the Stacks' dirt roads. Her boots slid on streets turned muddy from an overnight rain as she ascended the twisting hills that led to the rest of the city. She soon joined a throng of grim-faced workers headed to the factories, steel mills, and textile plants with their lunches in metal boxes. At a bend in the road that led to a main street lined with tailors, locksmiths and repair shops, Aina slowed.

An elderly Sumeranian man sat in the shadowed doorway of his home, which was crumbling on one side. Blood dripped from a small cut on his pale arm onto a rough diamond he held between two grubby fingers. Her breath caught at the sight, and hazy memories came: her own parents praying to the Mothers, sneaking diamonds in their sleeves, drops of blood falling on the dirt floor.

Loud voices sounded from the top of the upward curving road. Two Diamond Guards appeared at the bend, talking casually to each other, and began walking down the hill. She imagined them spotting the man, yanking him by the neck with their nail-studded leashes, dragging him to a more public place where they would execute him.

"Hey!" she hissed to the old man, who ignored her.

Like her parents had, he practiced his faith without a shred of fear. Her heart ached when the Diamond Guards punished the faithful—the Inosen—since they had done nothing wrong. But she would run and save herself if any trouble started.

As he held the diamond, the man muttered, "Amman inoke."

All blood could be used for magic. No matter if it came from an unfaithful person, an Inosen, or a Sacoren—a priest—it all produced the same effect.

But only Inosen who had been blessed by a Sacoren could take blood, channel it through diamonds, and wield magic with that murmured prayer, *Amman inoke*.

"The Diamond Guards are coming!" she said in a low voice, her eyes flicking toward the approaching guards.

Air rippled around the man, whipping his loose clothes around him. The diamond shone with an internal light through the streaks of blood, and a moment later, the house began to restore itself. Mud brick solidified on the side wall, dry and hard-packed into a perfect corner. While the magic couldn't cause miracles, cure most diseases, or create things out of thin air, it used the power of earth and blood. It provided shelter, helped grow crops on arid land, stopped blood loss, and cured blood-related illnesses.

Her father had used it to repair a crack in the street outside their house after Aina had seen a woman trip there. Her mother had used it on a local boy who'd been stabbed in a mugging, preventing his loss of blood so he would survive.

Using magic was how people helped themselves when they had no other option.

The man wiped the blood from his arm as the Diamond Guards approached and passed them. He'd tucked the used diamond between his fingers and waited until the guards' footsteps faded away before finally looking around at her and winking.

Shaking her head, she left him to risk his own life how he pleased. Plenty of Inosen had escaped detection during and after the war, though it was still a fraction of how many had lived before. But something thousands of years old didn't die out simply because the steam engine had shown its pretty face. While the rich could afford steam and steel, bright lights and indoor plumbing, the poor couldn't. For many, magic was their best choice. They would pray to the Mothers and practice magic to their last breaths, and she'd never deny them that bit of freedom. But she still wished, for their sake, that they would be more discreet.

If her parents had been more discreet, maybe they wouldn't have been shot when she was eight. Maybe she wouldn't have grown up homeless and been turned into a professional killer. But she was proud of her few successes now, even if her parents would hate what she'd become.

They'd always believed life was precious, a gift from the Mothers. She couldn't help but imagine they'd be disappointed if they knew what she was. She wanted to shout: *You died and left me to this city; what did you expect?*

As she approached the Center of the city, a train whistle broke the morning air, and smoke puffed above the station to stain the sky gray. The streets turned from dirt to concrete, and more people crowded around her in the early rush to work.

Her mind worked through the details of what she knew about the mansions on Amethyst Hill, the privately hired guards who worked there, and how exactly she might get Kouta Hirai alone. But before she did any of that, she had to ask the only person she really trusted to partner with her and put his own life on the line for this job.

Turning up a side street that wound between apartment buildings, budget inns, and low-end shops, Aina approached a bar with a sign declaring it The Tipsy Fish. Right outside of it was a notice board with news from this morning, the letters freshly inked by the printing press.

A GEM FIT FOR A PRINCESS

The Royal Princess of Linash, Saïna Goleph, is due to arrive in Kosín in a fortnight to celebrate a new, stronger alliance between our nations.
The princess will be gifted with a five-carat black diamond jewel, as a token of our new alliance, at a reception ball to be hosted at the Tower of Steel.

Aina nearly snorted with laughter as she scanned the rest of the article, which went on about how both their countries were moving into the international sphere and wanting to make more alliances and trade agreements. The jeweler had only offered to pay her five thousand kors for a similar gem, but if it was valuable enough to give to this princess, then it must be worth much more. If she ever got her hands on one, she'd use a knife at his throat to make him pay double the market price.

Shaking her head at the article, she entered the bar. It was nearly empty except for a few early-morning regulars. A group of old men played cards in the corner with a cloud of smoke around them. A smile crossed Aina's face as she took in the person she was looking for—his broad shoulders, the dark jacket he always wore that hid the multiple guns he carried. Seated on a bar stool, he spun a half-empty mug in his hands and chatted leisurely with the ruddy-faced bartender.

Aina approached and checked that no one was behind her. Then she pressed one foot on a floorboard, making it creak, and threw herself to the ground.

The man rose and fired a gun into the space behind him.

5

The gunshot slammed against her eardrums as the bullet made a hole in the wall.

The bartender dropped a bottle of firewater in shock, and glass shattered across the floor. Amid the bartender's swearing, one of the card players yelled through the haze of smoke, "It's too early for that nonsense!"

But Aina was laughing loudly from the floor.

"You almost blasted my face off, Teo!"

Teo Matgan rolled his eyes as she sprang to her feet. She wasn't short, but he stood nearly a foot and a half taller than she did.

"You're ridiculous, Aina."

She sat on a stool and spun to face him, grinning from ear to ear. "Buy me a drink."

Minutes later, Aina was giggling into a mug of firewater larger than her head. "Let me get this straight. Someone hired you to kill a lady. You thought she was pretty, so you then proceeded to—"

"Sleep with her, yes." He nodded with a fond memory in his eyes. "And then I didn't want to kill her anymore."

"I bet your boss wasn't happy about that."

"I don't have a boss. He was just the man who hired me. But you're right, he wasn't pleased, so I killed him instead. The lady heard about it and paid me, said I'm a model citizen and I deserve to be compensated for my services. I don't know if she meant the services with my gun or my—"

"Stop, stop, stop!" Aina nearly fell off the stool laughing and covered her mouth to shield the sound. The men playing cards in the corner glared at her, so she lowered her voice when she next spoke. "I don't want to think about your little gun!"

"Aina is blushing; it's a miracle." Teo shook his head. She could see why so many people found him attractive: He was nineteen years old with clear, golden-brown skin, wavy dark hair that curled in at his sharp jaw, and eyes like copper glinting in the sun. Though he'd been born in Sumerand, his parents had immigrated here from Linash shortly before he was born. Sometimes he used random Linasian words in conversation, or took on his parents' accent in a way that made most girls line up to date him. If only they knew how many guns were concealed under his jacket. "And who said it was little?"

She hid her laughter behind the mug. "I've heard rumors."

"Rumors, huh?" He shot her a teasing wink. "Are you taking my lovely partners for yourself once I've been with them? You'd have liked her; she was quite pretty."

With another blush, she swatted at him, sloshing her drink over the rim of the mug. As she took another swig, a little creature slinking along the counter caught her eye. Pushing backward so her stool squeaked loudly across the floor, Aina gestured at the spider, trying to keep her voice from shaking.

"Kill it, Teo. Please kill it."

A grin spreading on his face, Teo focused on the spider for a moment, then lifted his eyes to meet hers.

"I still can't believe," he began, in a low, enigmatic tone, "that Aina Solís, the greatest assassin in all the world, is afraid of spiders."

She was used to people teasing her about her ridiculous fear. If that spider had a heartbeat, or flesh and bones, all it would take was some force and a well-placed slash with her knife. But instead, it crept along, its legs itching at her skin when she couldn't even see it . . . She shivered involuntarily.

"Not the whole world," she conceded, her eyes sticking to the spider as it progressed along the counter. "Just Kosín, maybe Sumerand. Kill it, already! Stop laughing at me!"

As he cupped the spider in his hands and stood, Aina leaned as far away from him as she could. "Don't you dare stick that thing in my face, or I'll put you in the hospital, Teo."

Teo carried the spider to the door, placed it on the ground outside the bar, then came back to sit next to her. "I think I'd prefer getting eaten alive by a spider than going to one of Kosín's clinics."

"Good point," she said, staring into the amber liquid of her firewater. The cheap liquor tasted like dish soap with rubbing alcohol thrown in.

"Dearest Aina," Teo began, "why are you here drinking with me instead of your usual . . . I dunno, looking angry and lurking around alleys with diamonds in your pockets?"

"Shut up!" she hissed, glancing at the other patrons, who were still engrossed in their card game. The bartender had retreated to the back room. "Because I have an offer for you.

Now keep drinking and we'll come back to it once you're nice and tipsy."

Teo continued to drink, but she knew she'd get drunk much quicker than he would. At best, this was a futile attempt at stalling. Teo was his own boss, finding jobs and carrying them out by himself. He didn't have the same protection and bribes in place that would keep him safe as if he worked with Kohl or if he were in a gang, but he valued his independence more than he feared the risks. He didn't even want to work for her once she opened her own tradehouse. He took on a wide range of work, from roughing people up for late payments, to theft, to murder. His kills might not be as clean as Aina's were, as she was trained specifically to be a Blade, but he got the job done. He was always picky about what jobs he took, though, and what the risks were. Her offer would be . . . out of the ordinary.

But then again, he was the only person she could really trust in this whole forsaken city, and the only person who believed she was worth something more than her skill with a dagger. He might have girls lining up to date him, but none of them knew how good of a friend he was.

"Okay, I'll tell you." She leaned close and whispered, "I got a new job, and I need a partner. Are you interested?"

His eyes narrowed. "A job you can't handle alone?"

Taking a deep breath, Aina knew there was no point in stalling anymore.

"Kouta Hirai," she mouthed.

It was the first time she'd ever seen Teo balk. He straightened, swallowed hard, and stared down into his mug with a creased forehead. He glanced at her a few times, trying to find the right words and apparently failing when the silence stretched between them.

"That's a death sentence, Aina," he declared in a harsh whisper. "You don't just get away with killing people like him. The Diamond Guards will hunt you for months if you take out a Steel that high up. What madness has that boss of yours put into your head?"

"I don't really have a choice in the matter."

"You always have a choice, even if he makes it seem like you don't."

She scoffed. "My job isn't like yours, Teo. If the Blood King gives me a job, I do it, and I really want to do this one. He'll let me open my own tradehouse after this."

A frown tugged at his lips at those words. He knew this was what she'd always wanted. Maybe he'd reconsider helping.

"He knows I can handle this," she continued, "but he's not taking any risks. That's why he told me to get a partner, and I agree."

"Do you really?"

Her mouth opened and closed, and for once, she didn't have a snappy response.

Just then, the door banged open. Aina turned to face the newcomer. A man stood in the doorway, practically snarling, with a gun in one hand.

"Aina goddess-forsaken Solís," he spat. "You'd better run before I put a bullet through your eyes."

Aina spun on her stool a little to the right and then a little to the left to catch Teo grinning at her.

"Looks like somebody's mad at you." He chuckled, waving over the bartender to get another drink.

The man still stood in the doorway. Weak sunlight streaming in lit up his hands as they shook around the gun.

"Well, before you shoot me, I'd like to congratulate you on finding me." Aina leaned back against the counter, hoping there wasn't another spider or else she would lose her composure and this man might actually press the trigger. The mere sight of the weapon placed a chill in her veins, but she was well-practiced at hiding her fear of guns. She felt the eyes of everyone in the bar on her back and straightened to show she had no fear. "I didn't notice you following me around at all. Maybe you should look into being a spy."

"I can connect you with the right people," Teo said in a falsely sincere voice, spinning around to join the game. The man's heavy breaths were the only sound as the whole bar watched to see what would happen next.

"Now, I can tell you've never held a gun in your life." Aina tilted her head to one side. "Let me guess, that make is from Marin and only Rolland deals in those. What did you pay for it? One thousand kors? She ripped you off well, my friend. Next time go to the warehouse near—"

"Shut your mouth, or I swear I'll blow it off!" the man snarled, fumbling the gun with sweaty hands. For a second, she feared he would locate the trigger by accident. Other patrons began mumbling and moving back, their chairs squeaking across the floor as they tried to put distance between themselves and the gunman.

"I thought that's why you came here in the first place," Teo reminded him. "But now you're saying you'll let her go if she's quiet? That's generous of you."

"It is," Aina agreed. "Let's see. You must be mad because I killed someone. Not someone you care about, no one cares enough about anyone to spend a thousand kors avenging their death. Ah, someone owed you money?" She stood, stepping closer to the man until the cold barrel of the gun graced her shoulder. "Was it the baker? That man never paid his dues. Well, I collected mine from him yesterday. You must be . . .

hmm, the baker loved gambling more than anything. You own that gaudy red-and-gold casino down Lyra Avenue, don't you? The baker won't be paying you, and that sounds like a *you* problem, not a *me* problem."

The man gripped the gun tighter, his eyes so big they threatened to pop out. Teo had gone quiet, but she could almost hear him shaking with laughter.

"So, what are you going to do with that gun?" Aina leaned forward, hands on her hips. The man's expression bounced between anger and doubt. "The trigger is that little part a few inches away from where your finger is shaking. All you have to do is press a button, and your problems are taken care of. What are you waiting for, permission?"

"Aina . . ." Teo began in a warning tone.

Good, she thought. *He needs to remember I don't scare so easily.*

The man grimaced, his finger finally approaching the trigger, but Aina shifted before he had a chance to press it. In one swift movement, she knocked his wrist to the side. The gun fell and skidded across the floor.

The man reached back to punch her instead, fist flying toward her face. She side-stepped it, pushing him roughly so his gut slammed into the counter. When he turned back around, one of her daggers met his chest. She twisted the blade under his ribs and then yanked it out. Before he could do more than gasp and clutch at his chest, Aina lifted her blade and cut through a carotid artery. A few bar patrons gasped, but most turned away and went back to their conversations.

"You like to make messes when you kill, don't you?" Teo commented, tapping his fingers along the counter. But Aina was too busy watching the man die. His blood pooled beneath him, and a moment later, he dropped to the floor.

"Idiot," Teo scoffed. "Did he really think he could get away with killing you? Kohl would retaliate in ten minutes, and then his head would be staked on a pole outside the Dom."

"That's true," she admitted begrudgingly. Though she appreciated Kohl's protection, she didn't like the idea that a lot of people would back away from fights with her simply because they knew Kohl would kill them afterward. Did she command as much respect as he did, that no one would dare come after her once she no longer worked for him?

The bartender, who'd just returned from the back room, tossed his towel in the air. "What have I told you about getting blood on my floor? Get that out of here!"

After Teo pocketed the man's fallen gun, he helped Aina carry the body outside. They left it across the street from The Tipsy Fish so it wouldn't affect business, then started walking in no particular direction.

Teo was grinning, one hand swinging freely at his side, the other on the handle of a gun inside his jacket. "You know, if anyone can kill that spoiled prick and get away with it, it'll be you."

Aina's mouth dropped open. "Is this true? What am I hearing, Teo? Are you saying you want to . . . ?"

"Join you, yes." He nodded stiffly as if he were already regretting this decision. "We've never done a job together, so it might be fun, and I'm sure this one isn't coming cheap. I need as many kors as I can get to pay for my mother's medicine. How much do we earn for it, anyway?"

Kohl's words came back to her then—she could choose her partner and pay them whatever percentage she wanted out of the fifty thousand kors.

"Twenty-five thousand each. We have a week to do it."

"When we're a team? We'll get it done in a day."

"Let's wait until tomorrow when we're both sober," she said with a slow nod. "This job is too big to mess up."

If she were with anyone other than Teo, she would be doing all she could to show off her confidence. But something about the storm-gray set of clouds behind the twisting black spires of the Tower of Steel, miles north in the distance atop Kosín's hills, stirred unease in her bones while they walked. As the seat of Sumerand's government, economy and military, the Tower reminded her that someone was always watching, even if she couldn't see them.

It was true what Teo said—it wouldn't be easy to get away with killing Kouta Hirai. Apart from how outnumbered they'd be by the guards at Kouta's mansion, the Steels in the city wouldn't rest until the assassin of one of their own was caught. If even one person saw enough of their faces to report to the Tower, they'd be at risk.

But she had to kill him. The future she'd never thought she would have was lurking in the distance, staring her down and daring her to draw near. The next step was spying on her target and coming up with the best plan.

The casino owner likely wouldn't be the last person who tried to kill her this week, but she'd make sure Kouta Hirai's blood covered her knife by the end of it.

6

The wind bit as relentlessly as a rabid dog that night. Aina peered over the rooftop, beyond the rushing silver waters of the Minos River, to the fields and mountains far away. Tannis, the Dom's other Blade, sat on the opposite end of the roof. Even knowing she was there, Aina felt alone and preferred it that way when she was assigned overnight watches. The wind brushed over only her shoulders, the navy night sky enclosed only her, and the river churned past the rusted bridges for her to admire. Kalaan and Isar's moons were bright specters beyond wispy clouds and puffs of smoke, revealing the night's darkest corners and shining on a lone train trundling northward from Kosín like a snake in the dark.

As the hours passed, she ran over various scenarios of how she and Teo could break into Kouta Hirai's mansion. They would meet tomorrow and follow Kouta to come up with a plan. She'd never killed someone so rich before. Whenever she entered a place with money, it felt like she wasn't really there—like the floor beneath her was quicksand, the expensive jewels and paintings were only make-believe. How would a smear of blood look on silk clothing?

A drop of rain hit her nose, and she cursed. It was too cold for this.

"Want to ditch?" she whispered across the rooftop.

"Very funny."

When she'd first met Tannis, she'd assumed the other girl was annoyed with her all the time due to her snappish voice, but quickly learned she spoke that way to everyone. They both moved to the center of the roof, disenchanted with the night's events. Aina almost hoped someone would try to rob the Dom just to liven things up.

Even in darkness, Tannis's gold Kaiyanis eyes pierced through the night like little suns. Blue hair draped over the ivory skin of her shoulder in pretty, tousled waves, making her look much less deadly than she really was. Throwing stars glinted at her shoulder holsters as a reminder.

"Word is, Kohl's given you a good job."

Aina pressed her lips together. Tannis had smuggled herself here on a boat from Kaiyan, a heavily forested country that bordered Linash, and then joined Kohl's old gang, the Vultures. When Kohl had opened the Dom about a decade ago, he'd plucked Tannis from the Vultures to join him. Why wouldn't she deserve their highest paid job yet? A small twinge of guilt worked through Aina at the thought. Tannis was excellent at her job and deserved high-paying opportunities. But Aina was good too—and she had an agreement with Kohl, while Tannis didn't. If Tannis didn't like it, she could take it up with Kohl.

"Kohl chose me for this job because he thinks I can handle

it." She didn't care how jealous Tannis was, but she strove to keep things civil between them since they lived and worked together, and because Tannis was pretty—she didn't want to make her too mad. To ease the tension, she said, "I'm looking forward to taking down a spoiled rich kid."

Tannis's laughter rang out in the quiet night, colder than the wind on the nape of Aina's neck.

"You're going down, street child." She never used Aina's name, and it made her bristle now. She was the Kohl's best Blade. The words repeated themselves in her mind over and over, as if she were trying to convince herself. "Kohl wants to eliminate his competition. All that nonsense about letting you go off on your own is a lie. Our house has never seen a haul as big as this Kouta Hirai one, so why wouldn't he want it for himself?"

It was a fair question, but Aina didn't reply. If anything Tannis said was true, she couldn't show fear. If anything Tannis said was false, she couldn't show concern.

"He gave you this job because he thinks it's suicide," Tannis whispered, leaning forward so blue hair cascaded down the side of her face. "The city was a madhouse when Kohl opened the Dom. Law didn't exist, Kohl could kill anyone and face no repercussions. He only wanted people who were as fearless as he was, and he got them. What do you think happened to the ones I worked with, all those men and women slashing throats and robbing mansions while you were still begging for kors on a sidewalk?"

"I bet they tripped up on a job and got shot," Aina spat out, letting her anger get the best of her. Ignoring the fact that Tannis was only a few years older than her, she added, "I hear it's harder to move around when you get old. Is that the problem? Worried you're losing your touch, so you're trying to make me paranoid? If I'm gone, you'll start getting the good jobs."

"Hasn't Kohl taught you to be wary of Blades older than you? It means we're dangerous enough to have survived." Tannis's shoulders shook with laughter. "You sure believe all the compliments Kohl throws at you, don't you? The fact you have breasts and pretty hair might be keeping you alive for now, but not much longer. Keep bragging about starting your own tradehouse and competing with Kohl. One day you'll mess up, and if he still treats you like his favorite pet killer, that'll make him look weak, and weakness is the one thing he can't stand. If you lose Kohl's protection, you'll become his enemy, and anyone who doesn't like you will have free rein to kill you. *I'll* have free rein to kill you. And no one else here will speak up for you and risk angering Kohl. If they question or betray him, they'll be dead right after you."

The wind gusted hard then, chilling Aina along with Tannis's words.

"I've never betrayed Kohl," she lied through gritted teeth. "I'm not stupid."

The next day, Aina waited for Teo in the Center, leaning against the grimy wall of a shoe repair shop and trying not to fall asleep while standing. After the overnight watch with Tannis, she'd slept until mid-morning, then spent the afternoon spying on Kouta.

For the past few hours, she'd sat in the balcony of a bookshop while he read on the downstairs floor, and tried not to pass out from boredom while waiting for him to do something interesting. His guards had sat near him or wandered around the shelves, and she wondered if they were growing as weary as she was.

Luckily, the brisk wind and the noise from the train station a block away kept her awake. Train whistles blared and people's suitcases banged along the sidewalk as they rushed to the station. Dusk was a velvety blue smear on the sky littered with streams of smoke. The few visible stars painted a revealing silver on the statue in the square ahead, making it even more macabre. It figured King Verrain, his face stretched in agony, a sword buried to the hilt in his back with its tip splintering out of his marble chest.

"Solís."

She turned to face Teo, who stood at the corner in a dark jacket with his hands tucked in the pockets—either to stay warm, or to hold the handle of a gun, she wasn't sure. The reddish-gold rays of the sun lit his face a soft amber color.

"Good morning," she said.

"The sun is setting."

With a shrug, she led the way to the next stage of their job. They weaved through soot-covered, dejected factory workers getting off their shifts, and soon reached an alley that emptied onto the entertainment district's main road, Lyra Avenue. Casinos, bars, and burlesque theaters were lined up on all sides, so locals and tourists would never run out of things to do.

Shouts and laughter in different languages flooded down to the street. Most immigrants in Kosín kept to small communities, like La Cumbre, where Aina's parents had raised her alongside other immigrants from Mil Cimas; the Linasian neighborhood near the river where Teo lived; and the Kaiyanis, Natsudan, and Marinian neighborhoods in the southeast. But Lyra Avenue housed people from everywhere. Apartments for immigrant workers were on the second floor of each building, packed with people who'd come to Kosín for jobs before the war and had gotten sucked into the fighting during it. Living close to the Stacks, most of them had fallen into poverty along with the Inosen, but some had found stability by starting small businesses along Lyra Avenue.

"Sorry I couldn't help earlier," Teo said loudly over the music issuing from a casino. "I needed to take my mother to the clinic for an appointment. How was our friend today?"

"So boring!" Aina said, as a strong gust of wind whipped her black hair in front of her face "All he's done is read. I think he's read more books than people I've killed. Shouldn't rich people be more interesting to spy on?" She stopped in her tracks. "What's going on here?"

The end of Lyra Avenue was marked with bike stands and a corner bookshop before it curved into Rose Court. Now, a gaggle of people choked the street and shouts rang out over the usual bustle.

"You're annoyingly tall," she scoffed, standing on her toes and nearly falling over from trying to see above the crowd.

"Want to sit on my shoulders?" he teased. "I can buy you an ice cream cone after."

"Shut up. What's happening?"

"They've made a circle. Some guards are there. Their rifles look extra shiny today."

"What the hell?" With a frustrated huff of air, Aina placed her hand on Teo's shoulder and pressed up, so her feet dangled above the ground and she gained a better vantage point.

A circle had formed in the center of the crowd. The Diamond Guards held the crowd at bay, rifles hoisted and used to shove unruly citizens back into line. In the center of the circle, two men knelt with hands tied behind their backs and nail-studded leashes around their necks. Droplets of blood covered the stones they knelt on. One of the guards removed rough diamonds from the men's pockets and tossed them on the ground where they clattered dully on the street.

A chill swept down Aina's spine. As cautious as she was with her diamond sales, she still feared this would be her fate one day.

She'd been a child during the war, but as if she could suddenly view it through her parents' eyes, she imagined the hundreds of people who'd met their end in the same way—the shine of diamonds the last thing they saw. She imagined her parents kneeling to pray in front of an altar to the Mothers, but then the altar disappeared and their knees struck concrete, where they waited for a bullet to strike like the two smugglers here now.

General Alsane Bautix stood to the side of the prisoners. A crisp black suit over his muscles hardened by years of military service, his red copper hair and beard bright against his ivory skin, a glittering diamond earring in one ear, and unreadable features chiseled from jagged stone, General Bautix was the last person anyone in Sumerand wanted to cross. He'd originally built a fortune through manufacturing guns and other war machinery, and then joined the military. After King Verrain instigated the war, Bautix helped turn the army against him, and became known as the hero who killed Verrain and thus ended the war. His victory gave him the highest commanding military position and a seat in the Sentinel, the country's governing oligarchy.

King Verrain, who'd been a Sacoren, hated that people had begun moving away from faith and toward an industrial future that relied on technology. Verrain found Inosen who followed his guidance, and together they began to shut down factories by force, starting with the event fourteen years ago known as the Estrel Ka-Noten—the night the stars fell. He'd demanded universal worship of the Mothers, and for all signs of industry and technology to be destroyed. The Steels fought back, forcing their employees to take up arms to fight. The Estrel Ka-Noten triggered five months of civil war.

The Tower of Blood and its monarchy fell, and became the Tower of Steel, run by the oligarchy. The ban on technology became a ban on worship and magic instead, and many believed that in the violence of the war and its aftermath, the Mothers had abandoned Sumerand and its people to suffer in the mess they'd made.

"Just kill them already," Aina said, jumping down and rubbing away the tension from her wrist.

"When heretical beliefs disrupt our workforce and put visitors to our country in harm's way, it becomes clear why such discipline is necessary," Bautix drawled, his voice never tiring, his lungs never seeming to need air as he spewed ultimatums. "Magic users violate public order and safety. Magic unchecked is magic that has the opportunity to bring our country to ruin once more. When diamond smugglers undermine the economy for their own profit, we all suffer."

Turning away, she counted down the seconds to the execution while the general's voice rang out above the crowd's whispers and murmurs. As he went on, her mood jumped between indifference and anger. She leaned against a cold lamppost and stared between the shoulders of the gathered crowd. But her eyes were drawn back to the rust gathering on the lamppost. Bathed in the sparkling gold lights of a nearby shop, the rust looked like dried blood.

Bautix smirked as he spoke the words that had become famous in the years after the war; the words he always said before a public execution: "Let it be known that our goal is to progress, not to regress."

His statement was punctuated with two gunshots, each one banging against her eardrums like an avalanche. She clenched her jaw, but tried not to react in any other noticeable way. Gunshots, whether they were fired near her or at her, brought her back to the night her parents collapsed in front of her. She could usually shove the fear aside, and it didn't bother her when Teo used his guns, but executions of diamond smugglers and magic users always brought her too close to the memories she'd tried to push away.

"All right, show's over," said Teo, turning to leave.

The crowd began to disperse. People spoke in hushed voices, some trembling as they glanced at the dead men. But as the Diamond Guards began to clear away the bodies, people returned to what they'd been doing before. Aina shook her head. She might move on from death easily, but she didn't forget it—not after her parents had died for daring to believe in a power higher than steel and the coin it wrought. Her heart ached for a moment, but she ignored it to get back to work.

"Wait." She grabbed Teo's elbow, her eyes fixed on a slim figure with a stack of books carried under his arms. "I see him."

Kouta Hirai was a tall, lanky man in his early twenties with blue-black hair that fell below his ears. He might be mistaken for a student, but everyone in Sumerand knew he wasn't in school anymore; he managed one of the country's wealthiest enterprises. Just then, he'd stepped out of the bookshop where Aina had been spying on him, cast a single glance of disgust at the execution and dispersing crowd, then turned right. His guards followed him out of the shop a moment later.

She and Teo slipped away from the scene, pushing past the spectators and following the Hirai heir to Rose Court at a slight distance so as not to draw attention to themselves. They soon crossed a street crowded with horse-drawn carriages. Benches surrounded a garden of willow trees and rose bushes that lined a path toward a pond at the center.

One of Kouta's bodyguards masqueraded as a businessman eating lunch on a bench, but through his shirt, Aina saw the outline of a gun. Two more guards stood at a corner, pretending to admire the garden, but their eyes were trained to watch for any threats. She couldn't simply throw a dagger from here and walk away whistling. Any one of those guards would jump in front of a blade to protect her mark.

Kouta sat on a bench near the center of the garden, reading a stack of documents now. She wondered at what age he'd learned to read, remembering how she'd only picked up the skill at fourteen after Kohl had thrown enough books at her to get her to learn.

"You can't be a great assassin if you're illiterate, Aina," Kohl had said when she'd finally thrown a book back at him.

"Why not?" she'd asked. They were sitting at a small table in the training room. Two other employees of the Dom sparred with each other, using techniques Kohl had taught them to take down bigger opponents. She itched to run over and join them, beat them, prove herself.

But Kohl's hard sapphire eyes pinned her in place as he tapped the book in front of him. "Because you can't be an effective assassin if all you do is swing around a knife. What makes an assassin different from any other killer?" Without waiting for her to reply, he said, "Assassins don't get caught. You find your mark and take them out, leaving the least amount of bodies behind as you can. You are efficient; you are fast; you are flawless. So you need to make people think you're something else. You're an aristocrat, a bartender, an artist, and you have no idea how that man just slumped over in his chair with a dagger sticking out of his neck. Sometimes that's the only way to reach a target. Not through a window or up a drain, but through the front door, as someone they would never suspect. To pull that off, you need to research. You need to read."

"I can read a room," she'd replied instantly. "And my marks. I know who will fight back, who will beg, and who will freeze up and wait for me to strike. That should be good enough."

Before she was done speaking, he'd opened the book to the first page and shoved it in front of her.

"Who taught you to read?" she'd blurted out, partially to continue avoiding this lesson and partially because she was curious. Had he grown up reading, or had he learned at a later age like she had?

"My old boss taught me." His gaze had flicked to the vulture tattoo on his forearm. "My parents were illiterate. After they got arrested and I was on my own, I joined the Vultures, and reading was the first thing he made sure I knew how to do."

Her brow had furrowed. "Why'd your parents get arrested?"

Instead of answering, he'd shoved the book closer to her and tapped the top of the page. "Read."

For Kouta Hirai, reading was just another thing he could take for granted, something he'd grown up with. Shoving down an intense feeling of having been cheated, she waited for him to finish. Finally, an hour later, he placed his stack of documents into his bag.

"Let's follow him home and figure out the rest of our plan," she proposed as Kouta stood. His guards immediately flanked him.

A loud, girlish voice sounded nearby, and Aina had to fight the urge to whip out a knife.

"Your scarf is really pretty!" squealed the young woman from a few feet away. She wore a silk blue dress and gems at her ears that indicated how rich she was. One of Kouta's guards turned around, so Aina put a smile on her face and pretended to be intrigued by what the girl was saying.

She'd bought the scarf as a joke when the shop had run out of red ones and only carried white, so she decided to dye it herself with blood. The redness had faded to a rust color she wasn't very fond of, but apparently this girl liked it.

"Thank you!" she gushed as the guard turned back around and left with Kouta; time to follow. "You'll never guess how it got this way."

The girl tilted her head to the side, mouth popping open in curiosity, but Teo pulled Aina away.

"Come on. Don't traumatize the poor girl," he grunted, but smiled anyway.

"Live a little, Teo!"

7

It was a short walk out of the city with the setting sun at their backs as they followed Kouta and his entourage eastward. The path curved away from Rose Court, turning from cobblestone to dirt. She beckoned to Teo, and they both stepped behind trees that lined the path out of the city.

A carriage with two horses waited ahead. The guards' voices were the only sound as they quickly confirmed with Kouta whether he would like to go anywhere else before heading home. He got in the carriage moments later, the carriage lurched forward, and she and Teo stepped through the trees, their footsteps in time with the sound of the wheels churning through mud.

At a safe distance, they followed the carriage across a bridge and through a dirt path enclosed by a small forest. The farther they walked, the less tainted the air became.

Soon, the carriage left the forest trail. Aina and Teo hid behind the trees at the fringe of the forest and watched the carriage approach the gate surrounding Amethyst Hill, the community where the rich stored their mansions and jewels. She'd heard enough stories of the people there to be disgusted by them. Last year, one of the women who lived here threw a bonfire party by burning all her out-of-season dresses, which had cost thousands of kors each.

She and Teo moved closer to get a better look, but managed to stay in the shadows of the trees. It was more of a wall than a gate, ten feet high, hewn of a pinkish stone inlaid with scattered brick that was supposed to look chic and accidental, but really just looked pretentious. Armed guards sat inside bulletproof enclosures at intervals along the wall, ready to open the giant iron gates for anyone with proper identification.

One of the guards pulled a lever from inside his glass enclosure, and it triggered the opening of the gates. The carriage rolled through at a slow pace.

"That's when we can get past," Aina said, pointing. "The other guard can't see us from his position, and the guard facing us won't be able to either. There's a blind spot when the gate opens for a carriage to go through."

Teo nodded, then pointed at a few willow trees lining the wall. "We can use that for cover too. We'll have to move fast to keep up."

They settled in to wait for another chance. In a few minutes, another carriage approached the gates, this one with white letters on the side declaring that it belonged to the Spennard Cleaning Company.

The guards opened the gate for the cleaning company's carriage to make its way through. It rolled toward the gate, gravel crumbling beneath it, and blocked the guard's view.

"Let's go now," Aina whispered.

Keeping low, she led the way toward the willow, with Teo behind her. Once they reached it, she stepped onto Teo's cupped hands to push herself up the wall, then pulled him over as quickly as she could manage. His weight nearly knocked her off the narrow ledge, but she steadied herself and jumped down. She crouched and held her breath as she looked toward the glass enclosures with the guards. Their plan had worked; no one had seen them.

They ran swiftly behind the mansions. Before leaving the Dom earlier, Aina had asked the Fox, Mirran—Kohl's best thief—where exactly Kouta's mansion was in Amethyst Hill. Mirran knew the area well from past robberies of these mansions, and told Aina that Kouta lived in the northernmost one. As she and Teo made their way to it, she tried to conceal her disgust and jealousy at all the luxury surrounding her. Who in the world needed a three-story home as wide as a city block with a backyard as big as a forest? Lattice screens surrounded windows lit by electric light from within, while children starved in the streets a few miles away.

The sun had fully set by the time they reached the Hirai mansion. It was the largest one they'd seen yet, its gardens massive and perfectly maintained, the smooth white façade of the house sickening in its luxury. Maple trees lined the sides of the house like pretty soldiers, their leaves brushing against the cream walls. Servants waited at the front doors, somehow managing not to drop dead from the boredom of standing there all day. Only two people actually lived there, Kouta and his younger brother, Ryuu. She couldn't fathom why they possibly needed so much space.

They'd arrived in time to watch Kouta, flanked by his bodyguards, approach the front doors. The servants bowed them inside, holding open the doors and then closing them tightly after Kouta and his guards entered. She and Teo waited behind the fence, searching for some way to enter the building without getting caught.

Long minutes passed. Guards stood in some of the windows and at the back entrance, all of them carrying guns. Her eyes scanned the trees, windows and rooftops, trying to find a way that could be accessible to both of them. Teo couldn't climb along a window ledge, and she couldn't masquerade as a guard since the only ones she'd seen here were men as big and bulky as houses. Even if they did manage to get through a window, they had no way of knowing what the security was like inside.

Just then, the carriage from Spennard Cleaning Company rolled to a stop, hidden behind a copse of trees at the end of the pathway leading to the house. Aina's eyes widened as she stared at the name of the cleaning company, and for once, she was grateful Kohl had forced her to learn how to read.

She tapped Teo's shoulder and pointed. A man and a woman in the cleaning company's uniforms stepped out of the carriage, carrying buckets of cleaning supplies, and approached the front doors. They waved their identification badges at the servants, who allowed them entry after a brief glance. Aina's eyes narrowed at the pair's uniforms as they passed through the wide doors.

"I have an idea," she whispered to Teo. "We'll need fake IDs."

Teo nodded in agreement. "Shouldn't take more than a couple days, you think?"

"I need to introduce you to more people," she said with a laugh. Maybe it was the fresh air, or maybe it was the sense of being one step closer to all her goals, but right now she didn't feel the need to hide her pride. "I'll get them tomorrow. We'll each be twenty-five thousand kors richer within a day, and I'll get my tradehouse."

8

"That looks nothing like me," Aina said, shaking her head at the forty-something woman with light, short-cropped hair smiling up at her from the black-and-white identification photo. She tossed it back on the table in front of the man selling it to her.

He merely took the cigar out of his mouth and exhaled, the spiced scent filling the room along with a cloud of smoke. They were in a cramped closet in the the back of one of the tradehouses near the warehouse district, this one masquerading as a run-down bar. The loud voices of patrons, local workers loosening up after the day's shift, drifted to them through the wooden slats.

"Look, that's all I've got on short notice," he said, another puff of smoke hitting her in the face as he breathed out. "If you want a better one, it'll cost you."

She had to fight the urge to laugh. Anyone from a tradehouse could go to another tradehouse and get discounts on services, but he was trying to play her. She was used to people underestimating her until she proved them wrong, and this would be no different.

"The one for my friend is good," she said, casting another quick glance at the photo of the man he'd procured for Teo, taped to a white card with Spennard Cleaning Company at the top. The man in the photo was older than Teo, but had the same dark hair and a similar cut. She pocketed that one, then said, "Come on, show me what else you've got."

He leaned back and put his feet up on the desk, his eyes roving over her once before he said, "Show me what you've got under all those clothes and maybe I can—"

Before he finished speaking, she'd jumped over the desk and placed a knife at his throat. When he gulped, the cigar tumbling from his mouth to the floor, she said, "I don't have all day."

Minutes later, he found a suitable photo of a girl with Sumeranian features—dark hair, light eyes and skin. It was hardly a match, but at least they were the same age, and the servants wouldn't notice smaller differences if she flashed the card quickly enough. It took the man a while to tape the photo to the card while her knife was still at his throat, but he managed, and then she set off to meet Teo.

Since that had taken longer than expected, she had to take shortcuts to meet Teo on time, passing as quickly as she could through the Center.

Her first year as a Blade, Kohl had kept her close on his forays into the city. At first, she'd been miffed, thinking he didn't trust her to go anywhere on her own. But it was something else. Those nights skirting authorities, discussing technique in the train station's tower, Kohl introducing her to all his contacts, were a special type of training. While the others had been left to figure out Kosín on their own, Kohl had given her a front-row seat to his mastery of the city. She'd never known why he did this for her, but she hoped it was because for some reason, he didn't want her to fail.

She entered a café, waved to the owner, and proceeded to the alley of overflowing dumpsters behind the building. She passed the receiving doors of shops, restaurants, and bars until a street opened on the right and a small huff of air caught her attention.

The alley served as a grimy courtyard where the residents of each building could hang lines of clothes to dry. Halfway down was the person she'd been thinking of: Kohl.

But he wasn't alone. Three men were with him, including their Shadow, Mazir. Kohl slammed one of the other men to the ground, his movements swift and nearly soundless. The second man lunged at him, but Kohl grabbed his arm, stretched it taut, and slammed into it above the elbow to break it.

A sliver of red moonlight flashed on the barrel of Kohl's gun. He raised it, and with one bone-shattering shot, Mazir fell to the ground before he even had a chance to defend himself. Two swift shots took out the other men. Aina had stopped breathing. Something about Kohl's kills always stunned her, as if they were an unattainable level of efficiency that would forever mark her his inferior.

"Kohl!" she whispered before ducking in case he might fire at her. But he merely looked up, his blue eyes latching onto her without any hint of surprise, as if he'd known she was there the whole time.

Once she walked toward Kohl, Aina nudged Mazir's body with her foot. Just like that, one of their own was gone. No one in the Dom would speak of Mazir again after learning that Kohl had killed him. Every time they'd ever joked or worked together evaporated into distant memory. Blank eyes stared up at her, declaring, *Screw up and you'll be next.*

"What did he do?" she whispered, pushing loose hair behind her ear and trying not to picture Mazir's body being carried on the barge toward the mass graves in the south.

Kohl pointed to one of the other bodies. "He's the one who gave the baker information. They were both at the casino together, Mazir drank a bit too much firewater and spilled some secrets. Tannis found out that it was him."

Aina briefly wondered what secrets Mazir had told the baker, and which of those the baker had sold to the Jackals, but kept the question to herself. Kohl would only tell her that if he wanted to. Too much curiosity would make him distrust her, and then he might become suspicious of her own secrets.

When Kohl holstered his gun, he bent to confiscate some kors from the dead men's pockets. He was close; close enough that she could see the crease of his shirt along the muscles of his back, close enough to smell the sweat on him and feel the heat from his body.

There was an odd tension between them, one partially fueled by the challenges of their job and by . . . something she hadn't quite experienced before. It was admiration multiplied by the competition to always be the best. Her body didn't seem to know the difference between that and the strange heat between them now. What was this push-and-pull dynamic that always kept them just inches away from each other? Did he feel it too, or was it all in her head?

She shoved down those thoughts. If Kohl could keep emotions and impulse out of his work, then so could she. If she wanted to prove herself to be more valuable to him than Mazir ever was, then she had to be flawless in killing Kouta Hirai.

"Tonight is the night," she said, meeting his gaze with nothing but confidence.

"For your Hirai hit?" Kohl nodded slowly, pride tinging his voice. "You know why I picked you, right? I see a lot of my own ambition in you. You can do this. Good luck, Aina."

He walked by her, their shoulders touching briefly. Then he disappeared down the alley without a glance back.

"I don't want luck," she whispered to the dead men.

Minutes later, after a few more shortcuts, Aina reached a burlesque theater on Lyra Avenue. Teo stood off to the side with a bag in hand, his shoulders hunched against the cold wind blowing through a gap in the buildings.

"Is this your side job?" she asked, gesturing at the theater. He rolled his eyes and led the way.

As they walked, the crowds grew rowdier. Nighttime revelers were on their way to whatever entertainment they could find: bars that never closed, burlesque theaters and brothels that catered to every taste, the casinos sucking in addicts every day. Music blared on street corners, mixing with loud, drunken shouts that kept her senses sharp and eyes peeled.

Soon, they reached a garden-lined street of Rose Court lit by purple and silver lights from the window of a shoe shop. Between a bakery and a silk clothier across the road, a curving bridge led to Amethyst Hill.

The Tower of Steel loomed to their left as they walked, a black monolith against the starlit sky. The streets became dirt, and trees soon surrounded them. She was always uneasy when walking through forests, since the concrete and stone of Kosín were much more familiar to her than grass and tree roots. She had to watch her step carefully to avoid tripping.

Teo, on the other hand, had no such problem with the terrain. His parents had been falcon riders in the steppes of Linash, using giant falcons to hunt and to spot gold in the terrain. They'd taught him how to navigate nature. He stepped with a limber gait over fallen branches and twisted roots, his hands touching cypress trunks like they were extensions of his arms.

The plan was simple. This far from the city, the guards never saw any action, so they wouldn't expect her and Teo until it was too late and Kouta's maids were screaming for help. It would be done in less than an hour, and she hoped no more blood would be shed than was necessary. The goal was to take out the mark as quickly and efficiently as possible, not to cause a massacre in a city that already leaked blood from the gutters.

Yet if someone stood in her way, it was her job to take care of them, and she would.

They soon reached the gate and waited for a carriage to arrive. If they could have sneaked onto the cleaning company's carriage, they wouldn't have had to risk being caught climbing over the gate. But they'd had to come up with a plan fast, and they would be more easily caught as frauds if they entered the company or boarded the carriage with other employees. Besides, they didn't know when the carriages were set to leave each day, and there hadn't been enough time to figure it out.

As they waited, Aina touched the hilts of her knives. Even if she lost all her knives or couldn't reach one, she had poison darts in a pouch at her waist that would paralyze a target within a minute. Kohl's lessons rang in her head: *A good assassin always has a backup plan.*

"Remember, we only kill if someone gets a good look at us. We incapacitate otherwise, unless they're trying to kill *us*.

Try to only attack guards, not servants. Do you remember the backup plan?"

Teo nodded. "If we get caught and all goes to hell, try to get to Kouta anyway—we can't risk security tightening if we end up having to wait for another day."

"Yes. But if we can't even get into the mansion, or if something else ruins our plan, then we'll wait for the weekend and sneak in with their food supplies." She hadn't believed it when Mirran had told her that all the inhabitants of Amethyst Hill had their food delivered to them every weekend, but now that she'd seen the mansions up close, she wasn't surprised. Still, waiting for the weekend would be pushing too close to her deadline, so that would remain a backup plan.

When the carriage rolled through and blocked the guard's line of sight, they ran to the line of trees near the wall, and Aina hauled herself up. Kneeling, she bent to help Teo carry himself over. It was then, as she was about to jump down, that she felt a sharp tug on her foot.

She dropped down the wall, twisting out of the grip. Whoever had grabbed her blew sharply on a whistle a couple of times, then reached down to grab her again, but she twisted his arm behind his back, withdrew one of her diamond-edged daggers, and stabbed him through the back of his neck. She pulled out the dagger and he collapsed to the ground where he bled out on the grass.

His whistle had drawn over the other guard from the gate, who ran toward them now. He saw Aina first, but failed to glimpse Teo passing through the shadows along the wall.

"Oh, good sir, this guard attacked me on my nightly walk!" she gushed, making her voice as high-pitched as possible. "I slapped him in the face before he could do anything dreadful, but I surely hope he's all right!"

The guard slowed, his eyes flicking to the guard on the ground, whose blood he probably couldn't see because of the dark grass.

That second cost him. Teo lunged toward him from the shadows. Aina glanced across the fields that separated them and the houses ahead, her nerves rising that someone might have seen them and their plan would be ruined before it even really started. But no one was in sight. A sharp crack and an exhalation of air told her Teo had effectively broken the guard's neck.

"That wasn't supposed to happen," she said, shaking her head as they hid the bodies behind a tree trunk.

"Do you think we should wait?"

What would Kohl do? she wondered.

Yes, there'd been an obstacle, but these guards were dead. They'd been too close, gotten too good of a look at her face—they couldn't be left alive. Now, they wouldn't be able to report descriptions of her or Teo to anyone.

By the time anyone even found the guards' bodies, Kouta would be dead.

"Let's keep going," she said.

They soon reached a long sidewalk that led to the mansions. Aina wiped a bit of the guard's blood on her scarf and swept her hair from her face. They needed to blend in for a while.

Teo tapped her shoulder twenty minutes into their walk and nodded at a groove in the wooden fence that surrounded the mansion. He slid into the groove and withdrew a set of clothes from the bag he carried. The clothes were cheap imitations of the actual company's uniforms, the label stitched onto clothes taken from the Dom by a seamstress who lived in Teo's apartment and had done the job for ten kors. They could only hope the uniforms would be convincing enough to fool Kouta's servants, hence why nighttime was better for the kill.

While he changed, Aina kept watch. A rustle of clothes, a grunt as he tried to fit into trousers that were too small, and he was done.

"Here," she said, passing him the fake cleaning company identification card.

Cold air brushed her shoulders as she changed next, taking off her gray jacket, blood-stained scarf, and slim-fitted shirt, stuffing them into Teo's bag and throwing on the blouse and apron he'd brought. They rearranged their weapons, stuffed the bag in the groove, and set off.

After slipping past the fence, they hid behind the copse of trees where the carriage usually parked, then stepped into view.

Lights from countless windows shone down on them as they marched up the front steps like they owned the place. They lazily flashed their fake badges to the servants, who gestured for them to enter through the tall oak doors. As they stepped into the entrance hall, Aina raised an eyebrow at Teo. Even the janitors here had doors opened for them. Then her eyes moved to the interior of the house for the first time, and her composure shriveled in awe.

It looked as if the Hirai family had robbed a museum. A glistening marble floor spread away in circular fashion with amber clusters embedded in patches. Between shimmering gold panels ahead, vases decorated with herons, cranes, and chrysanthemums stood atop marble plinths.

They had no idea where the doors led, but they had to start somewhere. As they slid one door open and entered a wide hallway, with royal-blue paint and gold leaves decorating the walls and interspersed by light bulbs in cages of silver vines,

Aina pressed close to Teo. Being near this much wealth made her uneasy. She was suffocated by marble, drowned by gold, until they entered another hallway with two people walking toward them and chatting amicably.

It was a man and a woman, the latter of whom wore a maid's uniform similar to Aina's. The man's breath caught for a moment as he examined the newcomers. Aina and Teo waited for them to make the first move.

"Excuse me, who are you?" asked the man in a voice that failed to be polite. "Did Spennard send new people again without telling me? I'm sorry, but you'll have to go home." He shrugged in a way that told Aina he was very much not sorry. "Can't afford to be paying every sad-looking girl who walks up with a dustbin and a pretty face. Go on, go home, I'll have Spennard place you somewhere else tomorrow."

Silence fell as he finished speaking. Based on Teo's shifting stance, Aina could tell they were thinking the same thing.

"Excuse me," she simpered, walking toward the bossy man. The maid beside him bristled at how forward Aina was acting. To piss her off a bit more, Aina raised a hand and placed it on the man's forearm. "Do you have to be anywhere urgently? No meetings to run off to? I'd like to chat about my schedule here, if you don't mind. I'm sure the boss wouldn't have placed me here without a good reason. You're not busy, right?"

"Sorry, miss, my wife and I are going home for the night." His words tripped over themselves, and a red flush slid up his neck. He gave a consolation nod to the maid, who glared back, unaware that Teo was sliding along the wall behind him.

"That's too bad." Aina kneed him in the stomach, then slammed her fist into his jaw so he dropped to the ground unconscious.

"No, don't!" wailed the maid. A second later, Teo placed his arms around her neck and made her fall asleep.

Aina grabbed the man's arms to haul him into the nearest empty room, debating whether they'd have to kill these two or if they could leave them unconscious. But just then, an ear-piercing screech sounded from the end of the hall. Another maid stood there with her mouth open in terror. Aina whipped out a dagger from her boot and hurled it, but the woman disappeared around a corner, screaming that there were intruders.

"I think our plan might be compromised," Teo said as thunderous footsteps pounded and shrill whistles blared from everywhere at once.

9

A door slammed open and two guards charged down the hall through the door she and Teo had come from.

Teo shot one in the chest and dodged the next shot. A volley of bullets followed, barely missing them and pinging off the marble floor.

Footsteps sounded from the other direction. Aina wouldn't stand a chance against multiple men with guns while she only had blades and darts. She rushed down the hall, grabbing the dagger she'd thrown at the maid, then waited at the corner, pulse pounding in her ears. Right before fights like this, she sensed herself, along with any guilt or softness, melting away to be replaced by the Blade that got the job done, the sharp edge that made people fear her instead of the other way around.

Someone turned the corner a moment later, and she jumped. Tackling the guard to the ground, she punched him in the throat and knocked his gun from his hands. Another guard rounded the corner, but she slammed the hilt of a dagger into his head before he got a good look at her face. He dropped to the floor with a heavy thud.

More footsteps sounded from both directions, the ceiling above shaking as boots pounded across it. The light bulbs rattled in their silver cages. Teo was nowhere to be seen, but she heard gunshots from the floor above.

Turning the corner, she ran up a staircase at the end of the next darkened hall. Sweat dripped down her neck. A clock seemed to tick in her head, counting down the time until she either found Kouta or was caught in the effort.

She edged around a landing and peered upward to see guards and servants gathered around the banister ringing the next floor's landing. Servants stood at either end, maneuvering iron chains wrapped around pulleys. Something metallic screeched. From a crack in the ceiling, a steel gate slid down to seal off the staircase to the upper levels. She couldn't slip under—the guards would shoot her on the spot. She could try to run to another staircase, but those might be getting blocked off too, and she was running out of time. Kouta would be evacuated if she failed to reach him soon.

A vent in the wall with a bronze grate caught her eye. She waited for the steel gate to fully drop, closing off the upper landing and set of stairs ahead of her. But this vent . . . if it led to the other side, into the inner halls of the building beyond the gate . . . maybe she could get in that way.

After pulling out the nails holding down the grate with a dagger, it fell to the floor. She cringed at how loud it was, then slid inside before anyone could come to investigate the noise. It was narrow, but she had enough room to pull herself along by the elbows.

The darkness of the vent closed in around her. Pinpricks of

light were in the distance, but still far away. Her breaths grew shallow; her throat closed up. She searched the dark corners of the vent as if expecting a giant spider to crawl out and devour her, or for something to grab her and pull her into the depths of the shadows. She hated the dark, but her jobs often required that she used it for cover when she had to. When she still slept on Kosín's streets, she'd had to sleep in the dark, but often kept her eyes open at night, unable to truly relax. If she couldn't be brave in the darkness when she had to with her jobs, she'd end up on the streets again. The thought chilled her for a moment, sending doubt through her at lightning speed.

Everything was going wrong. They'd been seen and had left bodies everywhere, some alive, some not so lucky. If Kohl were watching right now, he'd call her the biggest idiot alive. She swallowed hard, trying to shove down the sense of incompetence that rose up, but it clawed at her.

She crawled until she reached another grate. Cool air hit her from beyond, but she couldn't see much out of the tiny holes in the grate. Instead, she pulled out her dagger again and tugged out the nails. This grate fell to the ground two stories below.

The vent had led outside rather than farther in. She was staring at the gardens, Kalaan and Isar's moons shining down on her, illuminating the copper skin of her hands where she rested them on the edge of the vent. Taking a moment to breathe in the quiet night and let the light of the red and silver moons wash over her face, she glanced left and right.

A pipe was attached to the building with thick iron bands set every five feet or so to hold it in place. The Dom was lucky enough to have pipes, unlike anywhere else in the Stacks, but the sight was still somewhat foreign to her. Without a second thought, Aina reached over and grabbed the pipe as tightly as she could. She shifted her body out of the vent halfway, then withdrew a single leg and placed her foot on one of the iron bands, and then the next leg.

She climbed as fast as she could, her back burning with the exertion, Kohl's voice in her head screaming, *Stop being weak!*

The third floor's window came into view. Peering over, she saw an empty hallway. Freeing one hand from the pipe, she anchored herself in place, then withdrew a knife to cut open the screen so a hole appeared big enough for her to squeeze through. She grabbed onto the window ledge, removed her legs from the pipe and for one horrifying second dangled in the air before hauling herself up to sit on the ledge.

She wiped the sweat from her forehead, but before she could take another breath to calm her nerves, a hand latched onto her shoulder and yanked her off the windowsill.

Dropping to the floor, she head-butted the person behind her. Their nose cracked. They tried to call out, but she spun around and punched the guard in the jaw, knocking him unconscious, the blades between her knuckles leaving bloody marks all over his face.

She took a moment to listen. Gunshots still fired from somewhere, which meant Teo was doing fine. This hallway was less lavish than the one downstairs. The walls were a pale beige color. Detailed carved wooden panels sat above doorways with lamplight glinting off their smooth finishes.

The carpet muffled her footsteps as she walked down the hall. At the corner, she crouched and quieted her breaths. An empty floor spread away ahead, and on the right, only visible if she peered around the corner very carefully, was a door with three guards standing outside it. Just then, someone about her age was escorted into the room, and it was locked behind him. It wasn't her mark, so it must have been his younger brother, Ryuu Hirai. Perhaps they were both inside.

Careful not to prick her fingers, she withdrew a small blowgun and four poison darts. She placed one in the blowgun. She blew into it, replaced the dart, and repeated until all three guards fell to the ground unmoving with darts in their necks—the effects would last several minutes, giving her all the time she needed. Placing the last dart between her teeth, she moved forward.

A rough grunt sounded behind her. Whipping around, hands going to her knives, she saw Teo knock out a guard who'd been creeping up on her.

"You go in. I'll keep watch," he said, his hands covered in someone else's blood as he dropped the guard to the floor. "That was his younger brother who went in, so he must be hiding there too."

With a cheery wave, Aina leapt over the guards' immobile bodies and opened the door ahead, expecting a bedroom. What she actually saw made her roll her eyes. A library. Of course Kouta would be in a library even in the middle of a lockdown on his own house.

It was one like she'd never seen before. The whole library was circular with bookshelves set upon rising concentric platforms, the room so wide that the farthest bookshelves disappeared into the room's shadows. Cedar beams crisscrossed the ceiling in an umbrella-like design, meeting in the middle. A wide table sat in the sunken center of the room, but was unoccupied.

Kouta must be among the bookshelves. And what of his brother? All the guards must have been busy searching the halls to find her, not yet aware that she was already here.

A hand latched onto her shoulder.

"No one is supposed to be here. Intruder! Guards, help!"

She spun around, shooting the dart out of her mouth. It buried itself in the servant's neck, and he collapsed on the floor with a dull thud.

Aina moved forward, searching every inch of the place for Kouta and placing another dart in her mouth as she went. She kept her footsteps light. The library was so quiet, the slightest sound would give away her location and the Hirai brothers could hide. But as she passed an aisle between bookshelves, her breath caught.

There he was, at a desk, scribbling in a notebook full of figures, probably something to do with their family's mining business. Shadows encroached around the small bubble of golden light from the lamp on his desk. She withdrew a diamond-edged dagger.

For a moment, she hesitated, doubt gripping her. Success had never been so close before, never right at her fingertips and so easy to grasp.

Good things don't happen to girls who come from nothing.

Another Blade should be in this mansion, a defenseless target the only thing standing between them and their future. It didn't seem real that this could be her opportunity.

Yet she was the only one who could make it real.

Lunging forward, she grabbed Kouta around the neck and forced him to the floor in the span of a breath.

He tried to speak, but she swept the blade across his throat, blood coating her arms in a hot wave. All his money wouldn't save him now.

She never felt joy from killing, but with this one, like the baker, she felt a small sense of justice. Kouta was a Steel, the same as all the others who kept people like her poor and Inosen like her parents at their mercy. But unlike the baker, she'd just earned twenty-five thousand kors for this kill.

Before letting Kouta drop to the floor, her eyes fell to a ring on his right hand: three large diamonds interspersed with two rubies on a silver band. That would fetch a nice amount of kors.

As she slid the ring off his finger and placed it in the pouch with her darts, a gunshot fired and a searing pain reached her side, making her drop the dagger. She let go of the dead man and rolled to the side to face his younger brother, Ryuu Hirai.

He held a gun in one hand, its barrel still smoking from the shot he'd fired at her.

"You're too late," she hissed, trying to mask the fear that surged through her at the sight of the gun.

A long beat of silence passed. Ryuu shifted slightly. Candlelight caught his face—narrow with high cheekbones, a sweep of black hair, unblemished bronze skin and umber eyes that somehow reflected anger and fear at the same time. They held the shortest, but somehow also the longest, staring contest in history. He had the advantage here, his gun aimed at her face, but he wasn't shooting. She could tell he didn't intend to kill. He'd only meant to stall her.

"Who sent you after him? Don't move."

She twisted his wrist so the weapon fell, then kicked one of his knees so he dropped to the floor.

"When you yell out threats instead of acting, no one will fear you," she spat, retrieving her dagger from the ground and sheathing it into the brace on her torso.

Some of the bravery dissipated in his eyes, fear leaking through in its place. He let out a sigh that sounded like resignation, disappointment. When he looked up at her, it was clear he expected to be killed next.

One sentence in Kohl's voice flitted through her mind with the same dazzling sensation as a shooting star.

Kill anyone who sees you.

She smothered its light. This job had been accomplished through her own merit. She didn't need Kohl's lessons anymore with this success behind her.

The door slammed open and three guards rushed inside, shouting for her to step away from Ryuu. Aina bent her knees, prepared to jump behind a bookshelf to dodge any bullets they fired. Just then, two gunshots sounded from the hallway, and one of the guards dropped to the floor screaming with both knees blown out.

Teo appeared behind the second guard and put him in a headlock before he could react to his colleague's collapse. Aina stepped out of Ryuu Hirai's reach, rolled to the side as the third guard shot at her, then flung a dagger into his side as the stray bullet pinged off the floor.

They ran into the hall, jumped over the bodies—Aina grabbing her dagger on the way—and slammed the door shut behind them.

"There's an empty set of stairs down this hall and to the right that leads outside," Teo said, breathing heavily with cuts on his forehead and a bruise swelling under one eye as they ran down the hall. "You're bleeding."

She shrugged, fighting down a wince at the building pain in her side. It didn't matter if she was bleeding; it only mattered if the job was done. She needed to tell Kohl she'd done the job—collect her money, open her tradehouse, prove to him she was no longer the helpless girl he'd saved—and hope that all their mistakes tonight wouldn't come back to ruin them.

"Not as much as Kouta Hirai," she said. "Let's get out of here."

10

Aina tightened the bandage around her waist after
cleaning up the wound and wiping the blood off her hands
with a wet rag. She wished Teo's mother, Ynes, didn't have to
see all the blood, but she'd had to take care of the wound as
soon as possible. Luckily Ryuu Hirai hadn't really tried to kill
her, and the bullet had passed through cleanly. It would heal
over completely in a few weeks.

Everything in Teo's apartment seemed so normal compared
to a few hours ago in the Hirai mansion: the table adorned
with porcelain knickknacks, Ynes resting against a pile of
sheepskin blankets, and Teo standing in front of a tea kettle
on the stove. The steam from the kettle rose into the air, its
warmth reaching Aina where she stood at the windowsill.

A breeze brushed against her face from the open window,
bringing with it the coolness of a late spring evening. The air
was already humid, which was a welcome relief from the cold
winds of the past few days.

Raised voices reached her ears from the street. An alley extended between Teo's building and the one across from it, with the flickering orange light of candles in all the windows. Passing by the mouth of the alley, sometimes in groups and sometimes as stragglers, were factory workers off for the day and ready to let go of their stress at one of the nearby bars. Teo lived in the neighborhood called the Wings, which was made of roads shooting off from Lyra Avenue likes the wings of a bird. It was mostly an area of cheap apartments where immigrants and factory employees lived.

A few minutes later, Teo handed a cup of mint tea to Ynes, who muttered thanks in Linasian, and then gave one to Aina.

"I'll collect our pay from the Blood King in the morning," she said.

"Thank you. She needs medicine." He glanced over his shoulder to where Ynes sat wrapped in blankets on the floor, a cup of tea held in both hands.

She leaned forward, speaking low enough that Ynes couldn't hear. "After this job, will you have enough?"

He nodded stiffly, wringing his hands together. "She'll never have to work again. Or she could take a part-time job somewhere that won't kill her just by breathing in the fumes. I won't lose both my parents because of Steels."

His voice caught, then, and he turned back to the stove to resume cooking. Aina glanced between him, Ynes, and the Linasian paintings hanging on the walls—some of the countryside and some of Terroq, the name of the falcon god that people from their country worshiped freely.

Like so many others, his parents had immigrated from Linash in search of work in one of the many factories here. They'd been falcon riders in Linash, but border skirmishes with Kaiyan had made the country dangerous to live in, so they left when Ynes was pregnant. Once the war began, his father had thought he'd be safe working on the rail tracks on the outskirts of the city. But since rail construction sites were some of the most important projects to the Steels, King Verrain had made sure to bring his fighters there. The rail workers tried to fight back, but most were killed. After his father had died, Teo left school to work and help his mother.

While Teo cooked, Aina walked to the bed and sat across from Ynes, who coughed and clutched the necklace she wore, its amber pendant decorated with the etching of a falcon. Worry lines pulled at the edges of her eyes and mouth. It was rare to see her here, since Ynes was always either working on the textile factory floor or being treated in the clinic for the illness in her lungs.

For a moment, Aina felt out of place in their home and wondered if her life might be different if she'd somehow moved south to Mil Cimas after her parents' death when she was eight. She didn't have a family. That was what she always told herself, but maybe there were relatives in Mil Cimas who'd have been willing to take her in and care for her like she belonged with them. But the thousand-mile journey to the southern tip of Sumerand, and the boat she would have had to take to Mil Cimas, weren't cheap. And then if she had even gotten that far, she would have had to search for family she'd never met.

Thinking this way—imagining other lives for herself— never got her anywhere. All she had was Kosín and what she could wring from it. Could her parents, despite their beliefs about the sanctity of life, be proud that she was one of Kosín's most feared killers if they knew that was all she had to live for? All that their beliefs had gotten them was a death sentence.

As Teo worked in the kitchen, Ynes glanced toward him

once, then leaned forward and took Aina's hand in her weak-ened grip.

"I know Teo is always getting into trouble," she whispered. "He'll never work for a factory, and there aren't many other jobs in this city, I know that. We thought our lives would be safer here than in Linash, but . . . sometimes I can't be there for him in the ways I should."

"You can't help that you're sick," Aina said. "He knows that. He would never blame you for having to take these kinds of jobs."

A cough rattled through Ynes's throat. She covered her mouth with the blanket, then focused on Aina with watering eyes.

"You're strong, young, smart," she said. "I can't do much to help either of you, but you need to be there for each other. Promise me you'll be there for him. Please help him when he needs it, and I can't."

Aina nodded vigorously. "Always."

She hated making promises she wasn't sure she could keep, but Ynes smiled warmly at this one, so she couldn't regret it. Whenever she was around Ynes, she felt some comfort, like she had another mother caring for her when her own couldn't. She would do what she could to assuage Ynes's worry for her son.

A few minutes later, Teo brought over bowls of mutton and potatoes to where Aina sat at the edge of the bed. Ynes stood and moved to her room with Teo's help, coughing all the way there.

They ate dinner quietly and, after clearing away their plates, Teo returned and threw himself under the blankets, eyes closed. Aina tensed up, then forced herself to relax.

Who closed their eyes in front of someone capable of killing them? It was that word she didn't recognize, that sense of relationship built up between two people. It was trust. She had no idea what she'd done to deserve it.

"So, Aina. We've known each other for a few years now. I know that you're good with a knife—"

"Excellent with a knife—"

"—You like firewater, and you think diamonds are the prettiest kind of jewelry." She rolled her eyes. "I'll tell you something you don't know about me. I'm good at my job. I'm my own boss, and it pays well. But sometimes it's exhausting. You can only pull a trigger so many times before your fingers get tired. Coming home at night and taking care of my mother, it makes me a feel a little . . . less like a monster. How do you cope with it?"

"I try not to think about that," Aina said. "This is my life. If I ever deny that, or start to feel guilty about my jobs, I'll lose my touch and end up in an alley with a bunch of bullets in my chest."

He nodded, no sign of judgment on his features.

"There were too many casualties. Too many things that went wrong tonight." Aina paused, trying to voice what was bothering her. "I didn't have time to watch him die."

Teo opened his eyes and scoffed, "I know a dead man when I see one. You slit his throat completely through, Aina. He's gone. You should be happy."

With a bitter laugh, Aina said, "Happiness has nothing to do with it."

"I know." He frowned. "When you grow up starving, and someone finally hands you a piece of bread, you don't think it's real. Or you think it's a trick."

Aina nodded. "Or like I have to be extra careful. It feels like . . . if I make one mistake, I'll lose everything and end up back where I started."

"Why do you sell the diamonds behind your boss's back, then?" Teo asked. "Not judging. Just curious. It's really risky."

"I don't know," Aina said. "I suppose it feels good to have a little control. You know, it's been six years, but sometimes I can't believe Kohl saved me from that bombing. Like one day I'll wake up and still be a child freezing on a street corner somewhere, half in a coma from sniffing glue. I know it's stupid."

"No, it's not. I'd think you were stupid if you got used to the idea of being secure. But you killed Kouta Hirai. If Kohl ever regretted saving you, he won't now."

"Who knows what he thinks?" She lay down and sighed, a few wisps of black hair flying away from her face as she did. "He usually just pays me and then waves me out of his office. But this is different. I don't know how he truly feels about me starting my own tradehouse. He shows nothing."

"Sounds like you need some kind of assassin support group."

She slapped him on the shoulder, and he pretended to wince in pain.

"But really, if Kohl won't say congratulations, then I will. Congratulations, Aina. You're the best Blade in Kosín, and when I watch you cut holes in people, I think I hear angels singing."

She let out a snort of laughter and then hushed herself, remembering his mother was trying to sleep in the next room.

"So, why does Kohl's approval matter so much?" Teo asked. "You already know he respects you. He trusted you enough to do this job in the first place."

"That's true." Aina twirled a frayed end of the blanket around her finger. Even on that first terrifying night she'd met Kohl in the bar that was about to be bombed, each of his words and movements were like lightning across a bleak sky. It was an innate charisma he bore, one she either wanted to attain for herself or break down into something more human with what she might mean to him.

"Can you keep a secret, Teo?"

"Sure," he whispered. "You can tell me anything."

He blew out the candle on the nightstand, leaving them in darkness except for the moonlight coming through the kitchen window. She focused on that beam of light as she tried to voice her thoughts.

"I find him . . . admirable," she said. "He's fearless. Capable. I've never seen anyone fight the way he does. So that's it. I admire him."

There was a brief pause when she was very grateful the room was dark enough to hide her blush.

Why did I even say anything?

She could practically hear the smile spreading on Teo's face. "So, what you really mean to say is that you're attracted to him because he's good at killing people?"

With a shocked gasp, she pushed him so hard, he nearly rolled off the bed. As he laughed, she pulled the blanket up to her face and turned toward the wall so she wasn't facing him.

"No," she answered resolutely, even though her cheeks burned.

"Well, you need to start seeing that you're good enough with or without his approval. You don't need him to break out a bottle of champagne every time you kill someone, and starting your own tradehouse isn't good enough. You have to do what you can to succeed. You need to prove that you're better than him."

As if she didn't already want that. Digging her fingers into the blanket, she repeated in a small voice, "How?"

"Beat him. Take him down. Not that I advocate violence, young lady." He paused for her to laugh. "Once you do, he'll lose all of his murderous allure. Then you can see whether you actually like him or if that's all there was to it. And then you can see if there's someone better for you."

She glanced over at him at those words, her brow furrowed, but his eyes were closed and his features revealed nothing.

They fell asleep minutes later. As her eyes grew heavy, Aina imagined what it would feel like to have arms around her waist, but failed to put a face to the picture.

The following morning, Aina returned to the Dom. She slid open Kohl's office door to find him seated at his desk in the middle of writing something, the orange lamplight shining on his vulture tattoo and the sapphires on his watch. Kohl's eyes, devoid of emotion, slid up to lock with hers.

"It's done."

A smile flickered across his face. "So I've heard. The client sent a message this morning to let me know. I knew you could do it, Aina."

She fought the urge to say, *Of course I could.*

In a few strides, he reached the door, took her hand, and pulled her inside the office. He took her to his desk, then let go of her hand and unlocked his safe. He pulled out a box of money and gave it to her. It was so heavy, it dragged down her pocket once she placed it inside.

"Do you have any more big hits coming up?" she asked, keeping her voice casual. "I'd be happy to take them off your hands."

"Perhaps." One side of his lips pulled upward in a smile, but it didn't reach his eyes. "Let's say that if your Kouta Hirai hit was a diamond, then my next job is a black diamond. A once-in-a-lifetime chance."

His voice trailed off. Curiosity tugged at her, but when he didn't elaborate, she knew he wouldn't say anything else. All she wanted was for him to tell her she could be free to start her own tradehouse, but she had to wait for him to say so.

It was like any other kill. She told him it was done, he paid her, and they moved on with their lives. But there was something different now, something nearly tangible in the air that electrified when he approached. His footsteps pressed into the carpet below, somehow even heavier than the box of kors. Was she really going to leave him now? Would the others bid her goodbye, wish her luck? Would he?

Uncertainty shot through her like lightning. She'd been planning this for years, but now it seemed anticlimactic, or like perhaps she was getting in over her head. Would she be more content to stay here, living under his protection, if he would simply hold her, tell her he cared, and that he didn't want her to leave?

"You've done well, Aina. I knew I was right to bring you here." His blue eyes shone with pride, with the most praise anyone had ever shown her. "You've done enough. You've earned enough money, you have the support you need, and you're as skilled as you need to be. I won't stand in the way of your success, but you can still come to me if you need assistance. I'm sure I'll see you again."

She nodded and took a step back, one hand resting on the doorframe. But he'd already returned to his desk. Before he could look up and ask why she was still standing there, she left, surprised to find she was trembling.

What did I expect, a party?

The Dom looked so cold and bleak from the outside. She

thought of Tannis and Mirran, Mazir's empty bed, the three recruits Kohl trained. She'd kept her distance from the others most of the time, too focused on her own job and too wary to trust any of them enough to become true friends. But they'd still worked together, trained together, bandaged each other whenever someone was injured, and did their best to keep Kohl happy so they could all stay here.

She would be alone with her own tradehouse until she managed to build up a team. She had ideas of where to start, and she was grateful to still have Kohl's protection, but she would miss the sense of community and safety in the Dom.

Shaking her head, she walked away, refusing to look back. She'd gotten what she'd fought for all this time. Perhaps she would feel more confident once she got her own tradehouse operating. There were always whispers on the street of grunts at other tradehouses who didn't like working for their bosses anymore, but she had to be careful in contacting them, or else their bosses might find out she was trying to poach them and kill them before she could.

After depositing her and Teo's money in the bank, Aina tightened her blood-stained scarf and set out. Passengers jostled by her with luggage as she passed the train station. Raised voices caught her attention from beyond them.

A crowd had circled around King Verrain's statue, the sword through his chest reflecting the midday sun with a startling brightness that drew her eye like a moth to a flame.

In front of it stood a raised platform surrounded by Diamond Guards. Their rifles glinted under the sun and their wolflike gazes penetrated the crowd as if trying to find the criminals among it by sight alone. But her eyes focused on the people who stood on the platform, their chins lifted imperiously, their clothes of fine silk, velvet, and leather. Only the wealthy could afford clothes like that, and these five composed the Sentinel—the highest governmental body in the country, all Steels, and each of them even richer than the Hirai family.

General Bautix spoke while the others nodded beside him with hardened expressions. Since he was speaking, Aina assumed this was some kind of security or military announcement—he operated the prison, commanded the military and, by extension, the Diamond Guards. Bautix seemed to gain more confidence as the crowd grew, each additional spectator contributing to the volume of his voice, the fervor in his eyes, and his overinflated ego. On Bautix's right were the rest of the Sentinel, whose names decorated every government document and announcement: Mariya Okubo, the only woman in the Sentinel, and the three other men, Eirhart, Gotaro, and Diaso.

As if they'd planned it, the black spires of the Tower of Steel rose directly behind them to the north. Others might feel foreboding, a sense of power, perhaps faith restored in the Sentinel that drove their country into an industrialized future. Aina only felt the press of smoke on her lungs and a gap between herself and them.

Bautix's voice boomed over the gathered crowd. "One hundred thousand kors will be rewarded to whomever reveals the identity of the murderer of Kouta Hirai."

She froze, her eyes fixed on Bautix's face.

"Last night, a pair of unidentified persons infiltrated Amethyst Hill. One of them killed Kouta Hirai, who was among our city's greatest financial contributors, in his own home. Motive is unclear. The primary suspect is a girl roughly eighteen or nineteen years of age, of Mil Cimas ancestry with black hair and brown eyes. We have a sketch of the killer's face from witnesses that night." One of the officers below the stage passed a rolled-up piece of paper to him, and he unfurled it to reveal a sketch that made Aina's breath catch in her throat. "The Hirais are longtime personal friends of mine. I consider their late father like a brother to me, and I have given his sole surviving son, Ryuu Hirai, my personal assurance that we will bring this murderer to justice." His voice ended with a ringing finality that settled upon the crowd like dust.

She shrank into the nearest alley and pulled up her scarf to shield her face, ignoring the coppery scent of dried blood on it. She imagined eyes on her in all directions. Bautix's words had spread like fire through the crowd, provoking daydreams of buying boats and houses and jewels among workers who could barely afford to eat multiple times per day.

The drawing Bautix had held up resembled her with frightening accuracy. With a slight grimace on her lips and a cold determination in her eyes, the drawing had seemed to almost be in motion. The only person who had gotten a good enough look at her last night was Ryuu Hirai himself. She was a fool to have left him alive. Kohl would scold her for it later.

The Sentinel might have a drawing of her, but if she laid low, maybe dyed or cut her hair, she would be fine. This would blow over eventually.

The longer she thought about it, the more confident she grew. Her nerves from all the things that had gone wrong last night seeped away and left her with an overwhelming sense of satisfaction, like a balloon that had been filled to bursting.

"I did it," she whispered to herself in the alley.

She'd beaten Kohl's final test. No longer was she just a Blade doing his bidding. A girl who'd nearly frozen on the street years ago had become one of the city's most dangerous criminals. She would never fear becoming a street child again because she herself would rule the streets. Everyone in the

Stacks would respect her too much to come after her. And Kohl would start to see her differently now, she was sure of it.

She wanted to tell herself not to let the excitement get to her, to be aware that it could all change in a minute, that retaliation could come from any corner . . . but for once, she chose to be proud of herself.

Sticking to narrow side streets, she made her way toward Teo's apartment. She avoided eye contact with everyone, keeping a dagger in her sleeve to reassure herself she was far from helpless even with a price on her head. She was on her own now, but she still had Kohl's protection and everything he'd ever taught her, plus her own grit, to protect herself.

One long day of training three years ago, Aina had grown even more determined to do anything she could to survive, anything to prove herself against the people who would see her dead. She hadn't known that the next night, Kohl would tell her who her first kill would be.

She'd been shooting targets behind the Dom for an hour before Kohl said to stop. Instantly, she'd begun to lower the pistol, her face coated with sweat despite the cold winter air. They'd had targets lined up on the Minos River shore for her to shoot at, and most were fallen, but she was shaking as if she'd been in a real life-or-death fight. Every time she held a gun in her own hands, all she saw was her parents collapsing to the floor. The memory never left, no matter how hard she'd tried to push it away.

Kohl never stopped shooting practice early, no matter how much she'd used to beg before learning better.

"No, let's keep going," she said in a rush, lifting the pistol again.

Had she really looked so weak that he actually offered to stop early? Was this a trick?

Then he reached out and took the pistol from her, his eyes flicking briefly to her shaking hands before he said, "Seriously, let's stop. I want to go somewhere else."

She nodded stiffly, then followed him from the Dom, up the slanting, sleet-slicked hills of the Stacks and toward the train station in the Center.

They passed through the turnstiles without paying. One of the employees gulped nervously and waved them through, but Kohl barely glanced at him.

Passengers and suitcases jostled by them on their way to the hulking metal trains. The wheels alone stood nearly as tall as Aina. Steam and smoke billowed above the platform, making her hold her sleeve to her mouth and nose as they skirted around passengers. Her reflection in the bronze finish of the train showed her trailing after Kohl as if she were his shadow.

They reached a locked door a few minutes later. Kohl picked the lock and led the way up a narrow stairwell, down an empty hall, and to a tower on the second floor. Windows were on all sides except one, where a giant bronze clock hung.

She shivered in silence while Kohl stared out at the city with his arms crossed. It was the beginning of winter, the skies gray, frost climbing on windows. She pulled a pair of frayed mittens from her pocket and tugged them on, wishing the cold didn't bother her. Kohl seemed to not mind it at all. With a serene look on his face, he stared down at the city like a king gazing upon his subjects.

Fighting the urge to rub her hands together for more warmth, Aina asked, "Did you want to show me something?"

He gestured at the buildings, which were tinged with the purple-gold light of a cold evening. The setting sun was behind them, but there was no warmth in that sunlight this late in the year. Since she'd spent most of the past few years at the Dom, it was easy to forget that other people saw the city from different viewpoints. Most of these streets weren't anything to look at, but right now, with the city bathed in light before them, she could admit it was rather beautiful.

"When you start working, you're going to have to get to know the city better."

Raising an eyebrow, she said, "I grew up here."

"You grew up in the Stacks. You don't know the rest of the city and how it might help or hurt you in any job you take."

The last rays of sunlight glinted on his blue eyes as he turned to face her, leaning against one of the pillars of the tower.

A moment later, she realized she was staring at him and looked away, warmth rising up her cheeks.

Clearing her throat, she nodded at his tattoo of the vulture hung by a diamond bracelet and asked, "How did you learn? Did your old boss in the Vultures teach you like you're teaching me?"

All she'd known at that time was that he used to work with the Vultures, that his old boss was dead, and that Kohl had destroyed every remnant that the Vultures had ever existed except for the tattoo on his arm.

The side of Kohl's lips tugged up in a smirk. "Come on, I know you're curious. What else do you want to know?"

"How did you fall in with them?" she blurted out.

He took a long time to answer, but she didn't speak all the while. She placed a hand on a pillar, ignoring the cold that pressed through the holes in the thin material of her gloves. The fact that the Blood King had offered her a piece of his history, when all anyone really knew was that he was a violent enigma with hundreds of crimes behind him, meant something. Maybe it meant he would trust her soon, that her place here would be secure, and she'd never have to fear losing this new home.

"You know how my parents came from Duroz to escape the famine before I was born? Well, they didn't exactly come on a luxury ship. The deal was that they would smuggle weapons into the city in exchange for passage. They held up their end of the deal and got us an apartment on Lyra Avenue, but some gang found out and threatened to report them unless they helped launder money through the tailor's shop where they worked. They did it for nearly a decade before the Diamond Guards found out and arrested them."

"So, then you were on your own?" *Like I was,* she wanted to add, but stopped herself.

"For a while, but apparently my parents owed some money to the gang they were working for, and the gang decided this was now my debt. I dodged them for a while, and started taking on any jobs I could get. I even put together my own group, a few kids from the neighborhood—we mostly did small robberies together, pickpocketing tourists. Then the boss of the Vultures found me, and suddenly the threats from the other gang stopped. He offered to protect me if I started doing errands for him, and that if I did my job well, he'd put together a bribe to get my parents out of prison."

Her eyes widened. "Did he?"

"I became a spy for him," Kohl said with a dark laugh, a far-away look taking over his eyes as he told her his past. "At first, I didn't care about the details. Never get too curious in Kosín, you know. After a while, I realized I was spying on factory bosses and employees who were planning to fight back when King Verrain was threatening to shut them down. Then, the war started, and my job changed. I started smuggling weapons and money to the factory workers, and then my boss also had me bring information to the people who were working with King Verrain. He was playing both sides. I didn't care one way or the other. When the war died down, I asked my boss if it was time to put up the bribe for my parents."

His bitter tone already gave away the answer. But she asked anyway. "He said no?"

"He said bribing wouldn't work anymore, that things had gotten stricter with the Diamond Guards after the war. We'd have to break my parents out with the help of a contact he had in the Tower. We would meet at secret tunnels leading into the Tower and break my parents out together. I was stupid enough to believe him. Turns out, he thought I was a loose end that needed to be cut off. I knew too many of his secrets, especially how he was passing information to both sides during the war, and he just wanted to get out of Kosín with the money he'd earned. Diamond Guards were waiting for me at the meet-up spot and threw me in a cell. Boss was nowhere in sight. A few days later, I found out my parents died a few months after they were arrested. Some illness they got in the prison."

She was suddenly glad his boss was dead.

"How did you get out of the Tower?" she asked. "Start a prison riot or something?"

"Sometimes you have to be subtle. I used a little stealth. A little poison." His eyes hardened again, a complete contrast to the smile spreading on his face. "Things you need to improve at before I throw you back on the street."

The next day, he'd told her it was time to do her first job. She'd been frightened, but had agreed, determined to become the best at whatever would help her survive: killing, spying, brewing poisons, telling lies. Anything except firing the pistols that made her fingers shake.

Now, with the Sentinel's reward for her capture hanging over her head, she still knew there was only one option—keep going, keep fighting, keep defending herself. That was what had gotten her where she was now, with Kohl's support in opening her own tradehouse, and it was what would keep her here.

She turned off Lyra Avenue and onto one of the narrow streets of the Wings. White apartment buildings towered over her as she picked up the pace. At an intersection, she finally caught sight of Teo across the street.

She hissed his name, looking around to check if anyone was watching them. The street was empty except for a man sleeping on the corner.

Teo's eyes widened when he saw her, and he jogged across the street to reach her.

"Teo, we're rich!" she whispered.

He took a few deep breaths, like he'd been running. The sun brightened his golden-brown skin, his copper eyes, highlighting the sweat on his forehead. His gaze flicked to the street again as if expecting an attack at any moment, then he took her hand to pull her into the shadows of the nearest alley.

"Thank the Mothers you're safe," he said. "I've been looking all over for you."

"Oh, did you hear about the Sentinel?" Her brow furrowed. "They do have a good drawing of me, but I'm not really—"

"Not that. You haven't heard? Kouta isn't dead. He survived."

"What?" The word rang hollow in her ears. "No, he didn't."

Teo shook his head, a growing dread in his eyes. "Maybe the Sentinel hasn't heard yet, but news is getting around on the streets, so it's only a matter of time. This morning I went to the black market to ask around for jobs, and I heard people talking about it."

Her mouth went dry. Images flashed through her mind, uncertain and weak. Kouta Hirai falling off the chair, red blood dripping onto cedar wood, the distinctive slice of skin and arteries under her trusted dagger. That very dagger seemed to pulse under her clothes, warning that she'd messed up.

She should have known not to be too proud of herself.

"Kohl." She suddenly found it difficult to breathe.

In his office, his hands holding hers; words of praise and promises of glory; Mazir's glass-like eyes staring up at her, asking why she hadn't yelled out or done anything to stop Kohl from killing him.

Aina held a hand to her forehead and took a few deep breaths. This was the first time she'd ever messed up on a kill, but she knew that wouldn't matter to Kohl. Her future slipped out of her grasp like smoke from rusted steel mills.

"He can't be alive," she whispered. Before Teo could do more than call her name, she ran, the sun blinding her as she raced toward the Dom.

12

Her feet slammed across the pavement, propelling her past the bone-white apartments and toward the line of shops and bars that led south toward the Stacks. Pigeons darted out of the way and a girl sweeping outside a storefront yelped when Aina nearly crashed into her.

Whispers sounded from everywhere, words like *Hirai* and *assassin* and *one hundred thousand kors*, boiling a new energy through the city's veins with the price on her head. If she reached the Dom before Kohl learned of Kouta's survival, he might give her a second chance. Running in the opposite direction would only mean her death. She fled through two narrow streets choked with pedestrians and down a back road. Entrances flicked past her vision, growing blurrier the faster she ran. But as she sprinted past an alley, something yanked her roughly inside.

She barely got her hands to her knives when she was slammed

into a wall, the back of her head banging off it so hard, she bit her tongue and her vision blackened briefly.

Kohl Pavel stood in front of her, one hand gripping her arm so tightly, it went numb.

She tried to twist out of his grasp, but his fist collided into the side of her head with a hard thunk. Her legs almost gave out, but she managed to stay upright. Her head spun, everything blurred and dizzying, so she couldn't tell if he was moving toward her again or if he'd stopped in place.

Survival instincts kicked in. She jumped out of the way and grabbed the knives from her boots.

"Don't be stupid, Aina," Kohl growled, raising his gun in the air between them, a cold look on his face that made her feel like any other target. She stared down the barrel and imagined what the air would smell like as the bullet flew forth to lodge in her brain. His voice slid toward her like smoke, darkening the space around them. "Why is Kouta Hirai still breathing?"

Aina sat on the cracked cobblestones, taking deep breaths to ease the dizziness from the punch. If Kohl had wanted to kill her, he would have already. Instead, he had knocked her around a bit and was ready to talk now. Maybe she could still prevail.

"I could swear he was dead," she said, staring at her clasped hands. They didn't quite seem like hers anymore.

How had this kill been robbed from her? She'd worked every day since joining the Dom to get better, to become as formidable as Kohl to prevent outcomes exactly like this. Her kills amounted to her respect, her future, her way off the streets. She would never allow herself to forget what it was like to have nothing, and she would never allow herself to return to nothing simply by failing at a job.

Her voice grew louder, angrier, roiling with the injustice of it. "I practically decapitated him."

Kohl approached and knelt in front of her. His arm with the vulture tattoo reached out, and he touched her hair lightly. It was something icy and fiery at the same time, something she wanted to recoil from and draw closer toward and simply couldn't locate a middle ground within.

"You didn't stick around to make sure? You wanted to get out of there quickly? Were you scared?"

"No! I just . . ." She swallowed hard and moved a strand of dark hair behind her ears, brushing against his hand as she did—wishing he would take it. "I thought he was dead. I don't know what else to say."

She expected a reprimand, not for him to trail his hands down the side of her face to rest at her chin. It ached from the punch, but his touch was warm against the building bruise. He was so close, so formidable and so unattainable, she wished more than ever that she could be his.

What is wrong with me? she thought, then shook it away.

If she wanted it, there was nothing wrong with it, was there? And he might be angry at her now, but wasn't he right to be? She was the one who'd messed up on a job.

"Do you have any idea what it means that you've failed?" Something darkened in his voice, and her chest tightened in response. "This wasn't any regular job, Aina. You were sent to kill one of the richest Steels in this goddess-forsaken city, and you failed. Have you forgotten what Steels do to people like you who reach too high?"

"I can pay back the money," she said, the words blurring together in her rush to get them out.

"The money doesn't matter." He exhaled sharply, his warm breath hitting her face, and she cursed herself for leaning closer.

"People come to me because they know my grunts can get the job done. If I disappoint some angry or vengeful person off the street, that's no problem—I send one of you to shut them up. But when I start disappointing people in power, that's a problem."

She frowned, then asked the forbidden question, "Who was the client?"

"What gives you the right to know?" His eyes widened in false surprise, and her confidence slipped again. "Oh, do you think you're still my favored Blade? You've ruined that for yourself, Aina."

Shame burned across her cheeks. She swallowed against the dryness in her throat, but it didn't alleviate the cold numbing sensation in her bones.

"Does this mean you won't let me open my own tradehouse now?" She hated how small her voice sounded.

"Have you forgotten everything I've taught you?" His forehead crinkled in sadness for the briefest second, quickly replaced by indifference. "You and the others are worth more dead to me than failed. If you can't make people believe you'll hurt them, what reason would anyone have to fear you? If I protect you, if I still favor you, a contender for my position who's failed so miserably, I lose all credibility. Everything I've built would fall apart. The safe home I've made for people like you would become an open target. You've lost my protection, Aina."

He'd said the words, but they took a long while to sink in. This didn't seem real. It was too terrible to be real.

Her voice trembled as she said, "You say protecting me will make you look weak, but you're already protecting me by warning me."

He turned his face slightly so she couldn't see what was in

his eyes. In the span of one day, she'd fallen from the top of the world to the dirt at his shoes.

"Not only will you have people coming after you to get the reward for your capture," he finally said, turning back to her, "but anyone with a grudge against you, anyone whose brother or son you've killed, anyone you've injured in the line of work, will be free to come after you too."

"How do I fix it?"

"Your mark thinks he's invincible now that you've failed. Strike soon. Either Kouta Hirai is left breathing at the end of this or you are, not both. Bring his head and leave it on my desk within a week. If you fail again, I will not be so kind."

The murderous look in his eyes was enough to make her jump to her feet. She raced down the alley, heart pounding in her ears, and turned the corner.

A gunshot from behind her rang out, the bullet slamming into the brick wall inches from her face.

13

She didn't stop running until she reached the end of the street, then ducked behind barrels of freshly caught trout at a shop front. The stench was horrific, but this was the closest place to hide. Peering around the edge of the barrels, she watched the mouth of the alley. In a few minutes, Kohl appeared. He turned in the direction of Lyra Avenue and disappeared from view.

The scent of smoke from the shot he'd fired permeated her senses. Countless bullets had been fired in her direction, but this shot rang in her ears over and over. Her head still pounded from Kohl's punch. She gulped to bring some moisture to her dry throat. A heavy weight settled on her chest, making it hard to breathe, and hope vanished from her like smoke plumes into the sky above Kosín's factories; it left a stain.

She was a fool for thinking this chance to be successful was actually real. Whenever happiness seemed close, reality snatched it away. She would have been better off sticking with

Kohl for the rest of her life. At least then she'd have his protection. Whatever reputation she'd built up over the years was gone now.

It was true: *Good things don't happen to girls who come from nothing.*

She'd been a fool to think she was different. But if she, a trained killer, made into one of the most feared people in the south of the city, couldn't make something of herself, what did that say for kids still sleeping on the street with no one to help them? She'd failed them all.

And Kohl had shot at her. Kohl had nearly killed her.

He never misses, she thought to reassure herself. That had been a warning shot, nothing else.

One of her hands impulsively clenched a weed growing in the alley. The weeds stuck out of the irregular patches of cobblestone, choked and curling from green to yellow to brown.

An image as clear as a summer sky flashed through her mind: rain pounding on the weeds and flowers that had grown near her old house. Her father had knelt next to her, his thick, black mustache ruffled by the wind, and together they'd watched the lightning blaze across the sky on one of those quiet days before the Estrel Ka-Noten, the night the stars fell, when there was so much blood and violence that people said even the sky looked red and no one could see the stars. Her parents had only lived for a few years after the war.

A peal of thunder had sent her cowering under his big arms. She'd told him she wished she could be one of the creatures from a particular Milano folktale he'd told her, the magical being that could change form between bird, butterfly, insect, and any other animal as easily as breathing. Then, she could transform into a firefly and dart through all the raindrops with the Mothers guiding her until she reached somewhere dry.

She usually suppressed memories of her parents, but now her father's words came back to her clearly. In the crispest southern Milano dialect, her father had told her: *Even if a lion dresses in silk, it will always be a lion.*

She couldn't have become a firefly to escape the rain any more easily than she could cease to be the helpless girl Kohl had saved from the bombing six years ago. She squeezed her eyes shut and tried to remind herself she wasn't helpless anymore.

She replayed the events of Kouta's death in her mind, trying to figure out where exactly she'd gone wrong.

The only thing that stood out in her mind was the young heir, Ryuu Hirai.

Her thoughts fixed on him, blotting out everything else until a buzzing sound built up in her ears. She imagined the color of his blood on her blade.

Kohl's advice that she should kill anyone who saw her rang true, though this had been the first time she'd ever failed to follow his words.

The idea sent a tremor of fear through her. Without him on her side, she wouldn't just be at risk of capture or murder. She could easily picture herself sliding back into old habits. Her hand went to her nose, searching for traces of glue. Nothing, for now. If it was a choice between going back to the streets or dying, she'd gladly let Kohl stab her in the heart.

She assessed her injuries and decided she was in good enough shape to get right back to work. She'd worry about the bruises after Kouta was dead.

She could ask Teo for help, but right now, she didn't want anyone else to see how desperate she was. It had been easy enough to break into the Hirai mansion before, even without knowing how many guards would be there. But to do it without Teo's help, and likely face more security after the attempted murder, she needed to get supplies fast.

In seconds, she was off to the bank, and managed to keep her voice from shaking as she asked the teller to withdraw money from her account.

"I'm sorry," the woman said with a well-practiced, courteous smile as she looked up from the ledgers. "The account in question has a zero balance."

Aina laughed unsteadily. "Do you have the right number? Try again."

But the woman shook her head after a few minutes of renewed searching. "It looks like the funds were withdrawn twenty minutes ago. Is it a shared account?"

Without answering, she stepped away, left the bank, and drew in shallow breaths in the bright sunlight outside. Kohl had opened her account in the first place, so he had access to it. Since he'd gotten her the jobs, he'd probably claimed it all as his money now, even though half of it had been earned from her diamond sales.

She clenched her fists so tightly, her nails nearly pierced the skin on her palms. The familiar helplessness settled on her like cloying smoke, making it difficult to draw breath. She was back where she'd started, on the streets with more fear than kors. As much as she'd shoved those memories away, they returned now as easily as donning her scarf each day.

Her first instinct was to head to the mines and get diamonds to sell so she could have money, but she needed to pay the supervisors a cut and she had no kors to do so with. The drawing of her that Bautix had held up flashed through her mind's eye. Any of the workers at the mines might report her, especially since the mines were run by the Hirai family. It was too risky.

There was another option. This idea was probably as smart as walking off a cliff and hoping a cloud would appear and save her from plummeting to death. She needed to return to the Dom and get supplies without Kohl realizing she was there.

When she stepped away from the wall, turning south, she saw it—a poster glued to the side of a building, one of its edges flapping in the wind. It was the drawing of her, reproduced, with the reward amount for her capture printed in bold letters at the bottom.

She drew her hood over her head, pulled her scarf over her nose and mouth, but her breaths still came in sharp bursts and her hands still shook.

There were more posters lining the buildings along a dirt path as she wound her way down it and toward the Stacks. The posters diminished in frequency as she descended the hill into the south of the city, but there were still a few, some against the sides of cardboard houses and others strewn across the ground. Her own face stared at her from every corner. Every time someone looked at her, her hands flinched to her knives, certain that person would recognize her even with her hood drawn and her scarf shielding half her face.

She hurried now, wondering if any of the gangs or trade-houses had already heard that she'd failed at the job, that she no longer had Kohl's protection—that they were free to do whatever they wanted to her.

Before she'd joined the Dom, the Jackals had tried to jump her into their gang, but she'd kept dodging them, too scared to put her life in their hands. Once she'd started working for Kohl, they'd always sent her cold, threatening glances, but until now, they could do nothing about it.

Once the Jackals found out about her failure, they would

come after her with no fear of repercussions. She'd killed the baker in their territory, and they would want to punish her for it.

The thought frayed her nerves, making every shadow resemble the barrel of a gun. If they caught her off guard, she'd die at their mercy in an alley with no one to mourn her, like Mazir.

The lack of Kohl's protection felt nearly tangible and dissolved all the bravery she'd gained in the past six years. If she failed to fix her mistakes, she'd never have his protection again, and worse, she'd lose him.

The anger on his face, the disappointment in his voice, were engraved in her mind. Losing the one person who'd given her another chance, who'd taken her from the streets where she would have died—the thought alone was like a stake through the heart.

No one was on the first floor of the manor when she entered, but she heard voices upstairs. She felt like an intruder in her own home, sneaking along the ghost-white walls, making her footsteps quiet as she slipped through Kohl's empty office and into the side room that they used to brew poisons. She shut the door behind her with a soft click, her heart hammering out a countdown to when Kohl would reappear and kill her.

Moving as quickly as possible, she lit a fire under two of the clay pots and donned a mask over her nose and mouth. She already had enough darts filled with a wolfsbane poison that could kill a human in seconds, but she needed to make two different types of paralyzing poison: one injected by dart that would leave the victim unable to move for several minutes, which she had used to break into the Hirai mansion yesterday but had now run out of, and another that would knock anyone in the vicinity unconscious if they breathed in its fumes for longer than a few minutes.

When the poisons were done, steam filled the air with a noxious scent and sweat beaded on her forehead. As she carefully filled a vial and a set of darts with the concoctions she'd brewed, the door creaked open.

14

There was no hiding that she was in here, but she ducked behind the pots anyway and hoped to simply melt into thin air.

A young voice rang out, "Who's there?"

It was one of the young recruits Kohl was training to work for him. Aina exhaled in relief, then stood and waved as though nothing were out of the ordinary.

"Miss Solís," the girl, Johana, said slowly. "Do you know where the Blood King is? Or Mazir?"

She bit her lip, thinking of how best to answer. "The Blood King is busy." She failed to mention that Mazir was dead. The kid would figure it out soon enough, just like she would figure out that Aina was next in line.

"Oh." The girl frowned, worry lines pulling at her forehead. "He's never here lately. Do you know what he's been up to?"

Teaching me a lesson. "I said, he's busy. You don't need to know where your boss is. If you want something to do when the Blood King isn't here, or when I'm not here, ask Tannis or Mirran. And if you're really bored, you can clean the Dom. Start with this room."

With that, she tucked her new poison supplies into a pouch on the inside of her sleeve and into another pouch hooked to her belt. Part of her was tempted to take more weapons from the armory, but Kohl would definitely notice if those went missing. Leaving the girl to clean up, she left the manor.

A knife appeared at her throat the moment she stepped outside. She grabbed her attacker's wrist and twisted as she whipped around. The knife clattered to the ground. When she saw who it was, she relinquished her grip with caution.

"Someone's instincts are sharp today." Tannis smirked as she bent to pick up the knife, gold eyes sparkling with challenge. "You look nervous, street child."

About a hundred questions flicked through Aina's thoughts in an instant, but one stood above the rest. *Does Tannis know that I failed?*

"Watch where you stick your knives," she said before stepping away.

She sensed Tannis's gaze on her back the whole way down the street. She might have been able to trust Tannis before, might have liked her, but she was too loyal to Kohl. She'd gotten away without being killed for now, but either Johana or Tannis would tell Kohl about how suspicious she was acting, and then she'd be in even further jeopardy with him. The thought made her stomach twist in knots, but she had no time to let fear take her over when Kohl had only given her a week to finish this job.

The afternoon heat built up as Aina walked to Amethyst Hill. Soon, all she heard was her own blood pounding in her ears, and all she felt was the dagger she gripped under her jacket. Being cautious hadn't helped much last time, so now she would use surprise to her advantage. She wouldn't waste time nor try to hide what she was here for. If killing any guard who tried to stop her was quicker than incapacitating them, that was what she would do. Today, she wanted to make an impression, that anyone who got in her way was a target. That way, once Kouta was dead and people heard she'd fixed her mistake, they would also hear how ruthless she'd been in the effort. She would be safe for a long time.

Ryuu would tell her exactly how his brother had escaped death, what their plan was, where his brother was now—and then he would die too.

Twenty feet away from the main gate, she paused in the shade of the trees, withdrew a wolfsbane dart and stuck it between her teeth. A steady calm settled over her. Her fears and her humanity slipped away, leaving the Blade she was in their stead. Beyond the gate, mansions and manicured gardens spread toward the horizon. She approached the entrance where the two guards sat within their glass enclosures.

One of them exited his tower as she approached, whistling casually.

"Good afternoon, madam. Please show your identification."

Aina smiled and turned slightly to block the other guard's view.

"Don't have any," she said, thrusting forward to lodge a knife between his ribs. She twisted and yanked it out, catching the guard as he fell. His hands grasped at the blood pouring from his chest.

"Help, I think he's having a heart attack!" she shouted.

Footsteps pounded behind her. Spinning around, she dropped the bleeding guard and blew outward. The dart landed in the second guard's neck. He collapsed to his knees, hands grasping for the dart, but even though he managed to pull it out of his neck, the poison spread quickly. He would be dead within minutes.

She left the guards where they'd fallen and made her way down the main road. Families passed her, sending her odd glances at the splash of blood on her sleeve. Most avoided her out of pure instinct. The bruise on her temple from Kohl's punch throbbed as she walked, but she gritted her teeth against the pain and used it to fuel her adrenaline.

There were more security guards than last night at the Hirai mansion. A few were poised in windows on the upper levels. Others sat in trees, probably thinking no one could see them. She failed to remember the last time she'd climbed a tree, but there weren't many other options.

She withdrew a dagger from her boot, took aim, and threw. It punctured the back of the guard's neck, knocking him to the ground. After shoving his body behind a bush and retrieving her weapon, she climbed the tree and crawled along the branch, thankful there was only about a foot or two of space to jump between it and the open window. But first . . .

Taking out the vial with one of the new poisons she'd brewed, she lobbed it inside the open window like it was a grenade. Glass smashed on the floor inside, the sound making her wince. She covered her nose and mouth with her scarf, breathing in the copper scent of dried blood—which was still better than breathing in the fumes of her poison. A few minutes later, she jumped to the window and tumbled through it to land next to an unconscious guard. All down the hall, at intervals of about ten feet, guards and servants lay on the floor, knocked out from the poison. It had certainly been effective.

She could kill them all, but that would waste precious time—someone still conscious could stumble upon this hallway and raise an alarm. She was safe for now, so she left the unconscious bodies and moved on.

She proceeded down the hall, bounded up a set of stairs while dodging servants and guards, and then slowed. Three guards stood outside of a room around the corner, all armed with guns that could rival any of Kohl's. She crouched behind the wall, as silent as possible, withdrew her blowgun, and fired. Two guards collapsed, the poison killing them quickly. But right before she fired the third dart, the final guard jolted out of place, leapt in front of Aina and pointed a gun directly at her head.

"Turn around and place your hands above your head."

Trying not to smirk, Aina turned around and lifted her hands above her head. A second later, the guard grabbed her wrists and twisted them behind her back. Aina slammed her head back and heard the man's nose break. Whipping around, Aina cracked the guard's neck and let him drop to the floor.

She stepped over the body and opened the door a fraction. A bedroom greeted her, extending in all directions in sickening luxury—the granite floor, the obnoxiously large bed, floor-to-ceiling windows facing the endless fields and mountains east of Kosín, a broad shelf filled with books, a red lacquer desk, and a glittering gold chandelier that hung above it all.

Steam poured through a gap above another door across the room, and the sound of running water reached her ears. It must have been Ryuu inside.

An idea struck her, and she went back into the hall to retrieve the guard's corpse. Hauling it inside by the armpits, Aina left the body near the bathroom door. She locked the door to the room, then pushed over the desk from the bedroom and placed it next to the wall. For a moment, she thought she heard Ryuu singing.

She lifted the body upward and then, straining under the man's dead weight, managed to stand on top of the desk while carrying him. She lifted the body and tossed it over the wall of the shower.

A shout told her all had gone to plan.

15

Aina jumped down from the desk as the door swung open. Before Ryuu could step a foot outside, she rammed her elbow into his nose. He slipped again and nearly fell, but caught himself on the doorframe.

Stepping farther inside to block his exit, Aina examined him. He'd managed to wrap a towel around his waist. Steam and drops of water clung to his skin, highlighting a few old scars on his chest and shoulders. His nose and mouth were covered with blood from where she'd hit him. As she approached, he backed into the wall, wiping the blood off his face as best he could.

"Why are you here again? Did someone send you after me too?" He shook his head at the dead man on the floor, eyes wide in disbelief. "He worked for our family for a decade."

"Well, he clearly wasn't very good at his job."

She stepped into the shower and cornered him, ready to

strike again if he tried to call for security. He was at least a foot taller than her, and she straightened to feel bigger.

"Did you help your brother survive?"

"I have no idea how—"

"Liar."

Aina pinned him to the wall. He nearly broke out of her grasp, but Kohl had spent the past six years teaching her how to beat people who were bigger than her, and this was no different. She withdrew a dagger and placed its tip at his collarbone.

"You're going to give me answers. And if I think you're hiding something, my dagger will show you how I feel about liars."

It had been a while since she'd allowed anyone to live long enough to witness fear build up in their eyes. If she hadn't seen so many people at the end of their hope, she might not have noticed it in the first place. But his fear was slow and steady, as if he was trying his best to hide it. His breath grew shallower with each passing second.

"I know you can kill me," he said in a matter-of-fact tone, his eyes deadening as if he'd long ago accepted his fate. They were the eyes of someone accustomed to threats. "I know what you are. You're an assassin." He said her job title with the same air children used when telling ghost stories.

"Good for you. So, how do people with slashed throats get up and walk around? How do I know it was really even him that night? You were in the room with him. Tell me what happened."

"I'll tell you what I know," he said. "Just . . . let me get dressed, okay?"

"You have two minutes," she said, pressing her dagger a little more into his skin as a warning before leaving the bathroom.

A minute later, he entered the bedroom and sat on the oversized bed while avoiding her gaze. Now that she didn't have a knife at his throat, she got a better look at him. The chandelier's golden light glistened on his wet hair. The sleeves of his mauve-colored blouse were rolled up to his elbows, the color a nice complement to the bronze shade of his skin. His blouse and sleek black pants likely cost more than all the clothes she'd ever owned. His hands curled into fists at his sides. The fear she'd seen in him before was gone, but now he seemed distressed, his eyes downcast.

"Sit, please," he said after a moment. "You're making me nervous, and this is hard enough to talk about."

She stayed exactly where she was to show him who was in charge here. The seconds ticked by.

After it became clear she would do whatever she wanted to do, he shook his head and asked, "What do you know about the magic of blood and earth?"

"I know you might get a slap on the wrist or a few months in prison for it, but anyone from my side of the city will be shot with no questions asked. Isn't that how justice works in Kosín?"

He grimaced. One hand flinched toward her knife, aching to thrust it through his neck.

"All right, I'll tell you. Once you left last night, I felt for a pulse. He was still alive, but barely. So I asked an Inosen maid to use magic to save him. He was bleeding out, and the magic can save you from blood loss."

He glanced at her out of the corner of his eyes as if he were somehow ashamed. But she had no sympathy for him. Her life was ruined because Steels like him could get away with whatever they wanted. He probably had diamonds lying all over the house in jewelry and decorations, ready to use, so he wouldn't even need to risk his life purchasing rough diamonds illegally like her parents had to do.

"You Steels really can afford to be hypocrites, can't you? As soon as magic becomes useful to you, you'll use it and get away with it, but otherwise, you're happy to condemn the poor Inosen and rip their beliefs away to keep them from taking back any power of their own."

Ryuu's brow furrowed. "My parents were Inosen. They never received the blessing by Sacoren to be able to use magic, but they still prayed, worshiping the Mothers and asking for guidance. They hid their beliefs once they saw how King Verrain was stirring up trouble, but they still helped the faithful when they could. The maid who helped us, she's from Natsuda and also Inosen, so my parents took her in to protect her once the war started. They allowed plenty of Inosen to live and work here safely, so my brother and I do the same. Do you think it's impossible for someone you call a Steel to be faithful?"

"What do you mean, *call* you a Steel?" she spat. "You are one. You own the diamond mines. You're rich. All of your inheritance is thanks to the thousands you people killed during the war."

"I was a child. I didn't kill anyone—"

"Even if you didn't personally kill any Inosen during the war, you and your family sat back and watched it, so don't talk to me like you understand. Maybe your parents let Inosen hide here, but they didn't do anything to protect the people dying in the streets. My parents were killed for their beliefs because they didn't have money or high-up friends to protect them. That's why you're still breathing after using magic and they're rotting away in a mass grave with the rest of the Inosen you and other Steels allowed to die."

He opened his mouth to respond, then closed it and shook his head. "You're right. It's not fair."

She blinked. Never in her life had a Steel admitted the situation wasn't fair.

"So, do you follow Kalaan and Isar?" she asked after a pause.

It was odd to meet someone her age who was faithful. When people turned faith into money and prayers into bullets during the war, most people began believing the Mothers had abandoned Sumerand. Only a few hundred Inosen remained, and most of them were older.

Ryuu gave a half shrug, half nod. "My parents stopped praying when I was really young, once the war started, so I don't know too much about the Mothers. But I've never been against it. How could anyone in my family be? After all, most of our original fortune was first made from Inosen purchasing diamonds, before magic was banned and we turned to exporting the diamonds as jewels instead. Even people in my family who weren't faithful themselves never wanted to ban the religion."

"So, your family were Steels, but they still didn't turn against magic once the war started," Aina observed. "Did they ever ask their workers to pick a side?"

He shook his head. "They stayed neutral. Even now, there's a secret worship center near the mines. We have our private security keep the Diamond Guards' attention away from it. And while we don't aid in the illicit sales of diamonds, we also do nothing to stop it. We do favors for the Sentinel when we can, like mining high-value diamonds or selling them jewels and construction materials at a discount, to keep them from looking too closely. I can't help that I was born rich, but I'll do what I can to even things out a bit. My parents never did anything to oppress the Inosen and neither will I."

Her face twisted into a scowl as he spoke. She couldn't let a rich boy with a heart distract her. She had to get the information from him, then kill him.

"What happened after you saved your brother?"

"I reported that he'd been killed," Ryuu continued, "gave the Sentinel a sketch of you, and paid off a mortician to pronounce him dead. We didn't want anyone finding out the truth and coming back to kill him, or looking into things and figuring out we used magic to save him. The Sentinel probably thinks his body is at the morgue right now."

"So, where is he really?"

Ryuu shrugged. "When I woke up this morning, he was gone. He's nowhere in Amethyst Hill. He might not even be in Kosín anymore. If he's afraid someone will come after him again, leaving might have been the safest option. My guess is someone saw him, and the truth got out that he survived . . . which I suppose is why you're here."

"Could someone have taken him? Kidnapped him? Tried to kill him?" *Since I failed,* she didn't add.

"No, a servant saw him leave this morning with a few guards."

"Do you know who wanted him dead?" Aina asked.

"You," he said, frowning. "Apparently."

"Someone paid me to kill him," she corrected. "Can you think of any reason someone would want him dead?"

Tilting his head to the side, Ryuu thought for a long moment. Then he leaned forward, hands balanced on his knees, and whispered, "He found out something about a secret project called 'Black Diamond.'"

She frowned for a moment, wondering why he was being so open with this information. But then her curiosity took over— if this helped her find and kill his brother, she needed to know it.

"What is that supposed to mean?"

"I don't really know. But I think it has to do with our parents' murder. He's been trying to figure it out ever since they were killed."

It was common knowledge that the Hirai brothers had been orphaned at a young age, but she hadn't known their parents had been murdered, like hers. It might be one of the only things they had in common.

But showing any sympathy would make her look weak, so she kept her voice flat as she asked, "Your parents were killed? I remember the news report. I thought they died in a gas explosion during the war."

Ryuu winced. "There was an explosion, but they were both shot before it."

She blinked and stepped back. All she heard were gunshots. The sound threatened to drown out her own voice as she said, "I didn't know that."

"Neither did we until after that winter. The autopsy found bullets in . . . what was left of them."

She turned her head, feeling slightly nauseous.

"My parents were shot too, a few years after the war," she said, unable to hold back the words. Then she shrugged. "They were Inosen, and they used magic. Inosen back then were being killed every day by the Diamond Guards or anyone who worked for them. That's just how it was."

After a pause, he continued, "My parents died on a night when King Verrain's followers attacked the mining site. Everyone assumed they were killed in the gas explosion that occurred during the fighting. Other Steels rose up on their behalf and fought back harder."

Aina grimaced. Already, the story didn't add up, and she was growing suspicious too. When King Verrain had shut down the factories, the Steels retaliated, forcing their employees to fight back—the employees mostly did, many of them forsaking their faith and choosing to fight for the Steels because they needed their jobs more than they needed the Mothers. They fought with the weapons the Steels gave them, mostly guns. King Verrain and his followers, including some men from the army who were loyal to him, used guns too, but mostly fought with blood magic. They twisted it in evil ways against what the Mothers wished.

Instead of using it to heal blood-related diseases, Verrain used it to cause hearts and veins to burst inside living people. Instead of using it to build shelter, he used it to topple buildings to ash. Instead of using it to shield themselves, he took the minerals from dirt and rocks and forged them into swords. Countless people's murders remained a mystery, and apparently Ryuu's parents were included.

King Verrain hadn't been subtle in his actions. If he wanted to kill an enemy, he made it obvious. But this . . .

Ryuu continued, voicing her thoughts, "It was covered up, to make it look like an accident that happened when Verrain attacked. Which means that whoever did it was probably a Steel. I was too young to understand, and my brother didn't tell me the truth of their deaths until I was older. But Kouta . . . he was ten when he had to take over our business, and he started looking into their murders. He's been trying to uncover the truth for years. He said he'd tell me more once he found out what this Black Diamond project was, but then you came along before he could. I want to know what he discovered, and I want him to be safe."

As his voice trailed off, she stared at him for a moment, considering his words. His brother might be a Steel, but he hadn't lived a completely pampered life. He'd had to start managing a business and investigating his parents' murder at an age not much older than when she'd found herself on the streets.

But no matter what his life story was, nor why he was being targeted, his survival meant her death. She had to find and kill him.

A heavy knock sounded on the door, making them jump. Someone began shouting, "Master Hirai!" over and over.

Ryuu stood, opening his mouth to call out to the guard, but she kicked him in the knees so he fell to the floor with a huff of breath. She withdrew a dagger and placed it under his earlobe while pinning him to the floor. Leaning close, she whispered, "Try to shout, and I'll cut off your ear. Try to move without my telling you, and I'll search for more appendages to remove. How does that sound?"

He froze, then gave a stiff nod.

"Open the door a crack," she whispered, freeing him from the floor. "Tell them everything is fine. I'll be right behind you, ready to press this blade into your heart if you give them any hint something is wrong."

Gulping, he stood and walked slowly to the door with the tip of her blade at his back. She stood to the side as he opened the door and conversed in a low voice with the guard, who informed him of the bodies outside his door and the guards who'd been knocked unconscious downstairs.

"I'm safe in here," Ryuu declared, his voice surprisingly steady. "Lock down the house and post new guards outside my door. Remain calm and keep vigilant. Whoever it is, they're after my brother, not me."

The guard replied affirmatively, and Ryuu shut the door with a weary exhale. When the guard's footsteps faded away, Ryuu turned to her, and she backed him into the wall and placed her knife under his collarbone. He'd told her enough. She tightened her grip around the knife.

"Wait," he said. "There's a reason I told you all this, besides you and your knives. I want your help, and you could use mine. I'm a Hirai. My name alone can open doors."

"I don't need you to open doors for me. I got in here just fine on my own."

"I think you underestimate the situation," Ryuu said in a flat voice. "Whatever this is with the Black Diamond project my brother was looking into, it's bigger than some grudge or simple vengeance. That's why I don't want any official help until I find out what Kouta discovered. The drawing of you that I gave to the Sentinel will keep them out of my business for now. I need help from someone skilled, who preferably doesn't have ties to the government or any Steels. How much were you paid to kill him?"

She bit her lip, debating between stabbing him and hearing him out.

"Seventy-five thousand," she lied.

"Look, I can't find my brother and keep him safe on my own." He swallowed hard, his eyes cast away from her, as if this were difficult to admit. "I'll pay you double that amount if you work for me instead and help me get him back safely and discreetly. I'd prefer you to work for me instead of for someone else who might ask you to find and kill him again. We can ask one of my Inosen employees to do a tracking spell to help find Kouta."

She almost laughed in his face. He was so naive to think money was all she needed. All the kors in the world were useless to her without Kohl's protection and with a price on her head. And if Kohl found out she was working for someone else, she'd stand no chance.

But Ryuu was right. His name could open doors for her, if Kouta was really involved with something so secretive. And if his name alone couldn't open doors, his money definitely would. Since Kohl had taken all her money, she needed the help to pay for weapons, bribes, and a tracking spell to find his brother.

The minute they found Kouta, she'd kill both of them, then regain her position in the city.

"Deal. I'll help you find your brother," she said, feeling the half-truth roll off her tongue. Kohl had always said half-truths were the best kinds of lies, and if she wanted to get back under his protection, she needed to use every lesson he'd ever taught her. "Under two conditions. I give the orders, and you cough up the kors."

He sighed with relief, then reached out to shake her hand.

"Now, there's no way we're asking one of your employees for help," she said, staring at his hand until it fell back to his side. "If they recognize me or find out I'm the one who tried to kill your brother, they'll hand me over to the Diamond Guards."

"They'd never betray me like that."

"For a hundred thousand kors, they would," Aina said. "And they'd probably think they're doing you a favor by turning in your brother's attempted assassin. Besides, I don't trust you. Once you get the information you need from the tracking spell, you'd happily let them turn me in. We'll find a different Inosen to track down your brother." Her tone left no room for argument.

After a pause, he gave a begrudging nod. "So we're clear, I don't trust you either. If you try anything, remember I'm the one with the kors."

She let a small smile spread on her face. "The money is all I want, so don't worry about me."

It was so easy to tell a lie to someone who already believed it. His shoulders visibly lost tension as she confirmed what he probably thought of her—a money-hungry girl from the Stacks whose loyalty could be bought, like all the guards and servants in this mansion. She would put him in his place before this was over.

"My name is Aina. Now, how do we get out of here, since you've asked your guards to put up more security? I don't want anyone here seeing me. Even if they don't recognize me from last night, they have that very helpful sketch you made of me wallpapering half of Kosín to remind them."

With a sheepish look, he moved to a nightstand near his bed and rummaged through it for a pen and paper. As he scribbled a note, she peered over his shoulder.

"I'm leaving a note that I'll be gone for a few days," he said, straightening and placing the paper on the nightstand. "I don't want the Sentinel to start looking for me too."

"A note? They'll probably think you got kidnapped if you just leave a note. Don't your guards follow you everywhere?"

"Kouta's the one who manages the company," Ryuu said with a shrug. "They don't watch me as much. I've been going into the city alone for a few years now."

Then he gestured for her to follow him to a corner of the room, next to an armoire. He took a jacket from it and drew it over his shoulders. Then he pushed a portion of wall that didn't look any different from the rest of the wall, and it swung inward to reveal a secret passage with no light except for a slit of a window cut into the wall halfway down.

Narrowing her eyes at him, she said, "If you try anything, remember I'm the one with the knives."

She kept a short distance between them as he led her down

the hall and past a heavy tapestry into the same stairway she and Teo had used to escape last night.

Either the Hirai brothers or she would be lying dead in an alley at the end of this. Ryuu and Kouta had already had their chance at wealth and success. Now it was her turn.

16

The lights of Rose Court shone more than the stars in the sky. Aina kept close to Ryuu as they walked down the cobblestone streets lined with clothing stores, hair stylists, and high-end jewelry shops that would never accept her diamonds. Pedestrians walked leisurely past them, in and out of shops with their hands full of boxes and bags of purchases. Gold and silver electric lights hung brightly in every window, seeming to put her on display the deeper they walked into the city. Earlier when Kohl had threatened her had been like a daze, some kind of torture meant only for her. But now that she was back in the city with Ryuu at her side, she felt all the more exposed. She kept her face half-hidden within her collar, but her eyes found every wanted poster of her, and she expected a Diamond Guard to jump out and handcuff her at any moment.

Ryuu walked beside her with his hands in the pockets of

his long tweed jacket, his chin lifted but his eyes guarded. She wanted to tell him to take his hands out of his pockets, to always be alert and prepared, but then again, they were in Rose Court and not the Stacks. He was either very good at ignoring how people stared at him or he was unaware. People at every corner pointed at him and whispered to each other with curiosity in their eyes, possibly talking about his brother, or maybe they, like she, had just noticed how handsome he was under the golden lights of Rose Court.

She ignored it, mostly, until they turned a corner and a poster with her face and one hundred thousand kors beneath it stared down at her from a shop front.

"You know," she said, clenching her jaw, "if you would call off that goddess-damned reward for my—"

"I didn't put that up," he said with a frown. "I only reported the crime and gave the Sentinel the drawing. They're the ones giving the reward."

"Why would they do that?"

"Well, with the new alliance we're making with Linash and their princess visiting soon, the Sentinel wants the city to look safe. So, they're being harder on crime now." He shrugged. "You shouldn't complain, you know. No one would expect me to be walking around with my brother's killer, so if you're with me, no one will look at you and think you're the suspect."

She couldn't argue with that. And his shortcut through the mansion and out of a side door that let them slip into the neighbor's backyard to escape would have taken her a long time to find on her own. She hadn't asked what he planned to do with the bodies she'd left behind. She supposed rich people had their own ways of covering up crimes. Then again, this pampered prince seemed far more accustomed to death than she'd expected him to be.

"Where can we find a blood magic practitioner?" he asked.

"Let's find my friend first," Aina whispered. With so many people pointing at Ryuu, every word she said seemed amplified for all to hear. "We need to get out of Rose Court. Stuff your wallet down your shirt. I could have robbed you five times by now. Keep your head down when we get out of here. Well, don't stare at the ground. Keep your head down and up at the same time. I know that doesn't make sense, but do it."

"I'm fine," Ryuu grumbled, but he hid his wallet better anyway as they set off.

Aina led the way out of Rose Court, down a hill, and through narrow roads until they approached the Center. Dimly lit bars were already packed with railroad and factory workers as the sky darkened to navy. Lampposts flickered on. It was as they crossed into a small, open square that she saw Teo's head and shoulders bobbing above the rest of the crowd.

"There he is," she whispered.

"Wait," Ryuu said, grabbing her sleeve before she could move too far. "Do we really need his help? I don't want too many people knowing what we're doing."

Yanking out of his grasp, she said, "Don't grab me like that again unless you want me to punch you in the face. And don't you remember our deal? I say what we're doing. Your job is to pay for it and keep quiet. I usually stay away from people who use magic, so I don't know where to find them. He will."

When they caught up to him, Teo let out a sigh of relief.

"Aina, you're all right! I've been going around, listening to conversations to try to pick up who's heard about—" He saw Ryuu then, and his eyes slid between them, probably wondering why she was hauling around a young Steel and whether she was planning to barter him off somewhere.

"Teo, this is Ryuu," she said. "Ryuu Hirai."

Teo's mouth fell open. A moment later, he grabbed her by the elbow and pulled her a few feet away so Ryuu was out of earshot.

"Why the hell are you with him?" he asked. "What does he know about his brother?"

"He knows, but I need him around for now," she whispered. "He thinks we're helping to find his brother, so he trusts me enough. Relax, I didn't tell him you had anything to do with last night."

Teo stared at her like he'd just seen cows flying. "You think I care about that? If you go down, I'm going down with you whether you like it or not, Aina. Why would you talk to him? Has that Kohl taught you nothing?"

Her face burned. "Kohl has taught me enough. Now, we need to find someone who can do a tracking spell. This is dangerous. Can you help?"

He shook his head and cast another suspicious glance at Ryuu, who frowned at him, as if he'd just recognized Teo from last night.

"All right," Teo said with a sigh. "But once we do, you have to tell me what's going on."

As they walked, veering toward the southern half of the warehouse district and the beginning of the Stacks, Aina kept her eyes peeled for any older people who might be magic practitioners. It was that feeling of when you searched for something, it was nowhere to be found, but if you stopped searching for it, it would appear. Right now, she could swear every person over the age of thirty had decided to hide inside their homes for the rest of the night.

With mud up to their boots, an early spring wind playing in their hair and mixing with the stench of the river, she, Teo, and Ryuu walked through alleys deep in the warehouse district until they reached the back entrance of a quiet storage building.

With a furtive glance around the corner to make sure no one was watching them, Teo led the way inside and to the building's dank basement. Secret meetings and markets were often held in the basements of warehouses and factories or in the tunnels that ran beneath the city. Ryuu nearly spoke a few times, but Aina hissed at him to shut up each time. When they reached a door with the smallest of cracks near the ceiling, Teo spoke a password, then slipped a few kors through the crack. The door slid open.

Smoke filled the air so thickly, it was hard to see more than a few feet ahead. They weaved through the crowds, which mostly gathered in the pathways between the different vendors of the market. The flickering orange flames of candles spread throughout the market were caught behind silk flowing from the ceiling and blown glass sculptures that turned the light violet, cerulean, and crimson.

Along the walls, she could make out the dust-coated, crumbling altars that had been used down here to worship before the warehouse was built over it and the Inosen's lives snuffed out. The dim light lent an eery glow to the sculptures still molded into the walls and ceiling in the figures of the Mothers, Kalaan and Isar. Their faces had been smashed to the point that they were barely recognizable. Kalaan, the goddess of love and war, carried a bow and arrow, painted red, while Isar, the goddess of hope and intellect, held a silver harp. The paint had chipped over the years, leaving all the statues with a muted gray cast.

People sat upon rugs smoking, drinking, and chatting among themselves. Vendors sold their wares to any number of shady characters. Hooded Durozvy arms smugglers huddled in a group, their eyes watchful and mistrusting. Most arms in the city were sold through the main supplier Kohl had always sent her to, but some other sales made their way through markets like these. Kors were slipped under tables and within handshakes. No one looked too closely at her, so engrossed in their own crimes, they didn't seem to notice one of the most wanted people in the city walking among them. Still, she was careful not to meet anyone's eye.

Teo led them past a section of Linasian reindeer fur and velvet traders, nodded at them and mumbled a greeting in their shared language. They finally stopped in a darkened corner, and Aina smiled a little. Despite the general shadiness of the place, it was somewhere familiar and welcoming to her. It was almost like being back in the Dom.

"Is this the illegal black market?" Ryuu whispered loudly, his eyes bigger than the moons.

Ignoring him, Teo asked Aina, "How did Kouta survive? And why are you with *him*?"

She waved a hand at Ryuu in frustration. "He saved him."

"With magic? That's the only way you could stop that much bleeding." When Ryuu nodded, Teo turned to Aina, his eyes narrowing. "Have you seen Kohl yet?"

Her hand moved to her temple, feeling the bruise that was surely purple by now. "He wasn't thrilled."

Teo frowned and reached out to touch the bruise. Aina winced, not just because it still hurt, but because she knew Teo wouldn't understand.

"He hit you?"

"What do you expect?" she asked, stepping back. "I messed up. I'm lucky he's giving me another chance."

"That's bullshit," Teo said with a shake of his head. "What are you going to do now?"

She nodded toward Ryuu. "He's going to help us find Kouta by paying for a practitioner and any bribes we need." Swallowing hard, her eyes focused on anything but Teo's face, she muttered, "Kohl took my money as punishment."

"All of it?" Teo asked in a flat voice. "Everything you earned since you were twelve?" When she nodded, he said, "You can use my half of the earnings, Aina—"

"No," she snapped. "You earned that, and you need it for your mother. I'm not going to take it from you." She leveled her eyes at Teo to let him know to keep up the lie with Ryuu. "Ryuu is paying me double what Kohl did to help find his brother alive. So, who do we ask to track him down? You're friendlier with people. No one would trust me if I show up on their doorstep asking about magic, and we can't just ask anyone. You never know who will snitch."

Teo bit his lip and glanced around, checking for any eavesdroppers. "The wrong people could catch us for this at any moment, especially if we use magic. You should lie low until this blows over. Make a job for yourself. Don't let Kohl decide who you are anymore."

Her hands curled into fists. "Kohl decides nothing. He's made it very clear he's not my boss anymore. But the whole city will be after me for the Sentinel's reward now that I don't have Kohl's protection anymore."

"Not if you kill him first. That would earn you all the respect you need."

Aina rolled her eyes and stomped her foot. "Come on, Teo! I understand if you don't want to help, but please think about it."

"I could pay you to help us find him," Ryuu proposed. "What do you need?"

The idea zoomed through her thoughts, and she nearly

jumped up and down to suggest it. "Teo, what about medicine for your mom? Ryuu could pay for it."

"A lifetime supply," he added with a wide grin. "I'll pay upfront."

With a frown, Teo said to Aina, "You know I'll help. I don't like seeing you in danger, especially not because of that boss of yours. Let's get you out of this mess as quickly as possible." Then he turned to Ryuu. "I earn my money, Hirai. Maybe you look at me and see a criminal, but I keep my work as honest as I can, and I don't take handouts. Once we know where to find your brother, you'll get the medicine for my mother."

"Done."

"It's pretty easy to get you to do things once I start pressing the right buttons, did you know that?" She winked at Teo, who shook his head in exasperation, but she saw a smile tugging at his lips.

Ryuu shrugged. "It's easy to get anyone to do something if you put enough money in front of them."

She tilted her head to the side. "Must be nice to buy solutions to your problems."

"Must be nice to threaten your problems," Ryuu countered with a raised eyebrow.

She couldn't help but laugh a little at how serious he looked.

Teo led them to a spot in the far west corner of the market. Beyond a haze of smoke was an attractive girl about seventeen or eighteen years old with ochre-brown skin, soft features, black hair, and bright, cedar-brown eyes—features that meant her ancestors had come from the country Marin. There, people still spoke a version of the old holy language to this day and worshiping the Mothers wasn't outlawed. The girl sat at a table, barrels of alcohol around her, and argued with a man on the price of a jug of liquor he'd smuggled in from Kaiyan.

"Isn't that Raurie Coste?" Aina whispered.

Teo nodded. "Her aunt uses magic. Whenever Raurie's not working at her uncle's bar, she negotiates prices on imported liquor here. Helps her uncle's bar keep the best stock, and other owners pay her for her input. The people who sell to her don't expect her to be so good at it because she's young and pretty, but then she outsmarts them. She's trying to earn enough money to get her family out of the Stacks."

"Good for her," Aina said with an approving nod.

As they approached Raurie's table, she sensed Ryuu gazing around the black market with cautious eyes. She'd known most of these people her whole life. To bring Ryuu into this circle of people that he could never understand felt like she was betraying them. What did he think of the rags the women wore, the unshaved faces of the men, the people missing teeth, the grungy interior?

As the man left with his payment for the liquor, Aina took a seat directly across from Raurie.

"You've seen me around before, haven't you?" she asked as a greeting. "Have you heard anything about me recently?"

Raurie frowned and shook her head. "Nothing recently; I've been here all day."

Aina nodded, relieved that she saw no deceit in the other girl's eyes. "I know you're a busy woman, Raurie, so I won't waste your time. I need something from you. He can pay you whatever you want." She nodded at Ryuu, whose eyes widened. "Seriously, name your price."

"When did I say she could—"

"Be quiet, Ryuu, she's thinking."

Raurie grimaced, then tapped her fingers along the wooden table while she considered. People from the Stacks never heard that they could name their price, so she was smart to be suspicious. Aina considered her, wondering how much she was involved in her aunt's magic practice, if she knew how dangerous it was, if she cared.

"What do you want?" she asked while putting away the Kaiyanis man's bottles of liquor with a studied mask of indifference on her face. "Some things don't have a price."

"Nothing bad, just illegal," Aina said, waving a hand dismissively. "Teo tells me your aunt offers certain . . . services. We'd like to pay her a visit to help us find someone. So, name your price."

Raurie smiled, then. "One thousand kors."

"Come on, Raurie, be more ambitious!" Aina urged as Ryuu shook his head in disbelief.

"Is it your personal goal to watch my family go bankrupt?"

"That's just sort of a bonus for me."

"Five thousand," Raurie suggested, raising her hand as if she were at an auction.

"Done!"

As they shook hands, Raurie said, "You'll need a piece of the person you're tracking, though. A strand of hair, a fingernail, anything."

"Gross," Teo said, but Aina was already pulling out one of her diamond-edged daggers, suddenly glad she hadn't had time to clean her weapons since last night.

"What about this?" Tilting the knife, orange lamplight shone on Kouta's blood stains. Ryuu quickly turned away, looking ill.

Raurie nodded. "That will work. We'll need to be careful,

of course. The Diamond Guards aren't going easy on anyone now. Since the Linasian princess is visiting soon, the Sentinel is trying to stamp out all crime to make the city look more respectable," she scoffed. "Good luck to them. But there's so much going on in the Stacks, the Diamond Guards can't keep track of all of it. We'll be fine as long as we're careful."

As she finished speaking, a door slammed shut. Aina pulled out two knives while tucking away the dagger with Kouta's blood on it. A gun was already in Teo's hands, and he passed another one to Ryuu. Raurie stood and withdrew a hammer from under the table.

The chatter of the market died down as everyone turned to watch what was about to happen. For a second, Aina assumed some Diamond Guards had tracked down the place, and all it would take was a few well-placed bribes to keep the night going. But then, roughly twenty people wielding a mix of knives and guns parted the crowd, backing the four of them into a corner. All had the same tattoo on their left forearms of a jackal's bared jaw, stained bloodred. Nearly half of their gang seemed to be here. The two Jackals who'd nearly beaten her in the alley worked their way to the front of the group. The girl held up a single strand of black hair.

"You should watch where you leave your things," she said, tossing the strand to the floor and grabbing a gun from a holster at her thigh in one smooth movement.

A jolt of fear shot through Aina, making her take an involuntary step back. She was about to find out whether Kohl's protection truly was null and void.

One of the men nodded at her.

"Miss Solís. I hear you're no longer employed."

She said nothing, only narrowed her eyes at his challenging glare. Teo's hands gripped his gun tighter.

"What are they talking about?" Ryuu whispered, far too loudly.

Her shoulders tensed, and she bent her knees slightly, waiting for her hunter to make his move.

The man lifted his gun and fired straight at her face.

17

She ducked just in time. Screams filled the market as people crashed into each other, trying to escape through the only exit. Wild gunshots punctured the air. She skidded toward the back wall, covering her head as best she could with Ryuu running half-crouched behind her.

They reached a low table, and she flipped it on its side so it could serve as a shield. Ryuu ducked behind it, clutching Teo's gun.

Peering over the table, Aina aimed and flung one of her daggers. The blade whistled through the air, then slashed through the neck of the girl who'd cornered her in the alley a few days ago. She collapsed, her blood staining the floorboards deep red.

At the same time, Teo began firing at the Jackals, his aim flawless even with bystanders speeding past his view.

Bodies dropped everywhere in the crossfire as she and Teo fought off the Jackals. Raurie slammed her hammer into the head of a Jackal who'd tried to sneak up behind her. People leapt over bodies and ran toward the door, but Aina noticed some of them standing over the bodies of fallen Jackals and rifling through their pockets for whatever could be taken. Whistles blew and heavy boots pounded on the floor of the storage building above, probably Diamond Guards rushing toward the sound of bullets. If any of them caught her here, she'd be taken straight to General Bautix.

Ryuu rose above the table and shot a Jackal who'd been approaching Teo and Raurie from behind with a knife. The bullet hit the man directly between the shoulder blades and he collapsed, blood pouring out of his back. When shots fired at them next, leaving smoke in their wake, Aina pushed Ryuu's head down behind the table.

"Where did you learn to shoot like that?" she asked. "You never mentioned you'd be useful in a fight."

"There's a lot you don't know about me," he whispered, a tense smile tugging at one side of his lips. A shot knocked one of the wooden table legs nearly clean off, and they both winced. Aina shook her head to try to clear the sound of bullets firing at her from every direction. Ryuu's eyes blazed with a fire so different from what she'd seen until now. The change shocked her, but she wouldn't complain about having someone else to help against the Jackals.

A bullet hit a wooden barrel near them. The barrel was knocked over, alcohol pouring out of the new hole in its front. As it rolled away, brown liquid spilled into a drainage gate next to it. A small padlock was around the rusty handle, but it looked weak enough to break.

Aina couldn't believe what she was about to suggest. One of the only things she hated more than the darkness were spiders, and the city's underground network of tunnels promised both.

"See the handle in the floor there?" she asked Ryuu, passing him one of her scythes. "Take this, break the lock, and open the grate. We'll make our way out through the sewers. Try not to get shot."

Before he could say anything, she stood and faced off with a man sneaking up on them. She twisted his wrist so his weapon dropped, then sliced through the side of his neck. Just then, another Jackal swung a fist adorned with brass knuckles at her head.

He was the same boy who'd cornered her in the alley after she'd killed the baker, the same boy who'd survived on the streets like she had. She ducked to avoid the strike, but his next punch was aimed at her side. Her head spun as he hit her bandaged bullet wound, the brass knuckles sharp and hard. The wound seared with pain, the skin tearing open and bleeding as she fell back.

Then another shot fired, and the boy dropped in front of her, clutching a bleeding arm. Ryuu nodded at her from behind him and reholstered his gun.

She turned to the boy, on the verge of delivering a killing blow, but then she remembered his name: Olaf.

And she remembered the hungry look in his eyes as they'd both begged for scraps in Kosín's alleys. He'd ended up here the same way she had.

She turned away and hissed at Teo to catch his attention. He fired at another Jackal, striking them in the chest, then glanced over his shoulder. She signaled to him to follow Ryuu.

Ryuu jumped behind the next table for cover on his way to the grate. Bullets pinged against the table's surface, one blasting through and nearly piercing Ryuu's shoulder. To her surprise, he barely flinched. He moved toward the grate to begin breaking the lock.

As Ryuu and Raurie slipped through the opening in the floor a moment later, Teo backed up next to Aina, and together they faced the last two standing Jackals. He fired at one of their hands, making the man howl in pain and drop the gun.

When the last Jackal raised her gun, Aina threw her other scythe into the woman's neck. She ran to retrieve the weapon, and on her way back to the sewer opening, ripped off the broken table leg. A second later, she dropped into the sewer where Ryuu and Raurie had disappeared. Teo followed behind her after taking out the last man.

Once Ryuu closed the grate above them, Aina shoved the wooden bar through the lock, hoping it would hold against anyone who tried to break it. For a moment, they slumped against the wall to catch their breath. Aina put away her weapons, fingers shaking as she did. The Jackals had probably seen her as an easy target since she'd lost Kohl's protection. She scowled, half wishing she could have fought them on her own to prove she was strong by herself, but that was foolish. If Teo, Raurie, and Ryuu hadn't been there, she'd be dead.

Teo stood apart from the others, staring down the dark tunnel ahead, while Ryuu leaned against the wall. Raurie placed shaking hands on her knees and took deep breaths.

Blinking to adjust her eyes to the dark, Aina turned to Ryuu and muttered, "Thanks for your help back there."

He scoffed and pushed off from the wall. "You don't need to thank me. I didn't do it for you. I'm not going to sit back and let you get killed while we still need to help my brother."

His voice was harsh, but cracked a little at the end. He'd surprised her with how he'd come alive during the battle with the Jackals, how he'd been able to fight even if he was scared.

If his aim was so good, he could have killed her when she'd attacked his brother last night. But he hadn't.

She couldn't quite figure him out yet, but it was clear he'd do anything to find his brother. Even though she was going to betray him, she couldn't help but admire him for that.

"Let's go," Aina said, trying to sound braver than she felt with the darkness gathering around them. "We should look for an exit to the street."

"I have an idea," Ryuu said. "This will lead to a sewer which should pass underneath the subway tunnels being constructed. We should go out through one of those."

"How do you know that?" she asked.

"My family has been in the mining business for nearly a century. The Sentinel always wants our advice whenever they do underground construction. And whose equipment do you think they're using?" He spoke with the typical entitlement of those born rich and unable tell the difference between their accomplishments and their inheritance. It didn't help when he added, "Not so bad, having me around, is it?"

"We'll see," Aina said, fighting the urge to roll her eyes.

Ryuu led the way through the wide, dark tunnel. The foul stench of the sewers soon reached Aina's nostrils. Water trickled to their right, so they stayed near the wall of the tunnel.

Her bullet wound smarted with pain as new blood leaked out, but there was nothing she could do about it now. As they walked, she wondered why she'd allowed Olaf to live. It would have been easy enough to kill him and cut one more enemy out of her life. But she knew the answer, deep down, even if Olaf didn't remember her—she couldn't kill someone who'd spent his childhood on the streets like she had, who had few choices as it was. She'd wanted to give him another chance, even if he wouldn't give one to her, and even if Kohl would call her stupid for doing so.

Soon, the pathway sloped downward. Aina's breaths grew shallow, making it difficult to focus on where she was walking. Her eyes flicked to every dark corner they passed. Unseen animals darted around nearby, their claws scraping against the tunnel walls and floor. She knew any other Blade would love the darkness for its ability to cloak them, and she used it when she had to, but she had learned to be quiet and deadly even in brightest day.

There were many tunnels twisting underneath the city, but each one of them reminded her of when her parents had taken her to underground worship services for the Mothers.

They'd taken a new secret entrance every week, and Aina could never keep track of where they entered or exited. Holding hands, they'd walk with bated breath and jump every time they heard someone else moving around in the darkness. Sometimes it was a patrolling Diamond Guard, and they had to hide until the guard passed. Other times it was another Inosen, holding a finger to their lips as they all proceeded to where the Sacoren held services with altars so dimly lit the faithful could barely see the prayers written in the religious text. It didn't matter, since neither Aina nor her parents could read.

The prayers in the old holy language spilled from her mother's lips, memorized instead of read, and Aina had copied her even if she couldn't understand what was being said. During most of these services, her attention had wavered, and instead, she looked at the statues of Kalaan with her red bow and arrow and Isar with her silver harp embedded in the rock walls. Sometimes she'd prayed too, for the Mothers to watch over them when they risked their lives to come here. Sometimes she'd prayed for her parents to stop, to be safe, and to say their prayers in their hearts instead of out loud where someone might hear them.

In a way, her mother had been the first person to teach her how to be silent and secretive, not Kohl. Occasionally, she wondered if her mother had known they might be facing the wrong end of a gun one day, and had tried to teach Aina to be quiet, to be quick, and to escape before the gun could be turned on her too.

Raurie was a steady presence walking ahead of her, and Aina tried to focus on her instead of letting the darkness swallow her. She was curious how involved Raurie was with her aunt's faith. Did Raurie know the prayers, or had they trickled from her mind like they had from Aina's? If magic got her aunt killed, would Raurie consider it a blessing or call it a curse?

A half hour later, Ryuu whispered for them to stop and gestured to a ladder bolted into the wall. They climbed one after the other, exiting into another long tunnel one level up. The air was slightly warmer here, but dust cloaked it, making them cough as they walked. At the end of a tunnel, they reached a wide cavern with dim lights strung along the roof. The new light revealed the strange scene in front of her.

Giant, hollowed-out hunks of metal sat in a cluster. Trains. It was like a mausoleum for the metal beasts that stretched twice her height toward the lights at the top of the cavern. News reports often proclaimed how underground train travel would bring Sumerand ahead in the worldwide rush to industrialize.

They approached a ladder with its rungs dug into the wall, then climbed to another circular door. Ryuu pushed it open and light flooded through. A moment later, they exited onto a street a few blocks from Lyra Avenue.

They rushed to an empty alley between two shops, passing a wall covered in posters of Aina's face as they did. Cold night air rushed in, making Aina shiver despite the lingering heat of the battle they'd fought. She placed her hand on the bullet wound in her side. New drops of blood dotted her shirt from where the Jackal had punched her. She tied the end of her shirt into a knot near the wound to cover it.

"Wait a minute," Raurie said, holding up a hand as Aina began to turn away. "I saw those posters. You're the one who tried to kill Kouta Hirai."

Aina straightened, one hand going to the hilt of her knife, but Raurie shook her head. "I'm not a snitch. Do you think I want to help the Diamond Guards, when they've been arresting and killing people of my religion for years? I don't care what their reward is when they would just as soon throw me in jail. But people are after you, and now you want to put my family in danger."

"About that . . . ." she began, with no idea of what to say next.

Ryuu spoke before she could come up with a reply. "Please, I'm Kouta's brother. We're trying to find him, not kill him, and we need your help."

Raurie took a step back from them. "My aunt is always risking something when she takes on jobs like these, but she's not reckless. Do you think we'll be safe if the Diamond Guards find out we helped a wanted criminal with that big of a price on her head? I can't put her or my uncle in danger."

As she spoke, Aina turned slightly away from Ryuu. She didn't need him figuring out that money wasn't her main priority either. But then she remembered what Teo had said about Raurie working her whole life to get her family out of the Stacks. She hadn't spoken personally to Raurie before, but she'd seen her in the black market all the time, for years, working in the same corner. Her uncle's bar was popular with locals at the border of the warehouse district and the Stacks, but it couldn't compete with establishments on Lyra Avenue or in the Center. She was likely making progress with her goal, but it was clearly slow progress.

"Okay, what if Ryuu gave you enough money to leave the Stacks?" she suggested. "Twenty thousand kors should be enough to get you and your aunt and uncle a new place to live wherever you want. Your aunt does the spell for us, and then you leave. The Diamond Guards won't find you if you move fast enough."

She held Raurie's gaze as the other girl took a long moment to think it over, biting her lower lip. Then, Raurie let out a small, resigned sigh, desperation flickering in her eyes.

"All right, let's do it," she said, nearly spitting out the words as if she was already regretting them.

"Thank you," Aina said.

"What exactly are we up against, Aina?" Teo asked.

"I've fallen out of Kohl's protection," she said with a sigh. "So the Jackals came after me. They can kill me without any retaliation from Kohl. Anyone who's ever had a grudge against me and anyone who finds out I'm the one who tried to kill Kouta will come after me now."

"Anyone with a grudge against you or anyone who wants to make one hundred thousand kors?" Teo shook his head. "So, the whole city."

The real danger of what she faced for her mistake had finally settled. Her failure weighed on her chest, making it hard to breathe. Tears pricked at the corners of her eyes, but she fought them down. If she was going to betray and kill Ryuu once they found his brother, she refused to let him see her weak.

She glanced at Ryuu who, despite his bravery in the fight, appeared tense and shaken now. But when she caught his eyes, he fixed his face into a hard mask.

"That won't interfere with our agreement, will it?"

"Not at all," she said in a flat voice. "We should go."

Before someone else tries to kill me, she thought.

She tried to ease her nerves as they walked Raurie to where the hills began to dip down into the Stacks. They'd killed or injured half of the Red Jackals gang. That would place some fear in their bones for a while. But once they recovered from the shock and bolstered their numbers, they'd come after her, and they wouldn't mess up again. For now, at least, she'd bought herself enough time to visit Raurie's aunt and use the tracking spell to find Kouta.

She no longer had a home. She had no guarantee that she wouldn't be on the streets by tomorrow.

She didn't have Kohl to protect her. The loss of him—not only his protection, but his respect, and the hope that he might think of her as more than an employee one day—was nearly a tangible ache in her heart. Dreams of standing at his side, of no longer having to hide what she felt, trickled away, taking her bravery with them.

Her life had changed completely in the span of a day, and the mere thought of it made her head spin. Teo would say she could stay with him, but that only made her wonder how long it would take him to get sick of her; how long it would take him to abandon her, like Kohl had.

The sounds of rats skittering and quiet movements in alleys commanded the night as she, Teo, and Ryuu made their way to Teo's apartment under the light of the full moons. Halfway there, Aina paused, her eyes trailing down one particular street. If she was careful, no one there would recognize her. Only for a few hours, to clear her head, and then she'd get back to the job.

"I'll meet you later," she said in a low voice, and then left before either of them could ask where she was going.

18

Aina pulled her hood over her head and walked down the street. Voices from people speaking in Milano at a corner reached her ears. She understood some of it, but not all, and tightened her hood around her head to shield her features, her copper skin, her black hair, so no one would try to speak to her in Milano and realize she barely knew the language anymore. Milano citizens were a minority of Kosín's population, but they'd formed a small community on this street and the surrounding blocks. It was always strange returning and feeling like she both belonged here and didn't.

She soon reached a house at the end of the street, one she didn't acknowledge on a daily basis, but which was always there for her when she needed it.

There were no candles lit in the windows. The family inside must have been asleep. A lump built in her throat as she climbed to the roof—the place that had saved her while the gunman filled her parents with lead. She stared at the roof's surface and imagined the room below.

She'd hidden here the entire night and the next day after her parents were killed.

As night fell, she had woken up, flexing her stiff fingers and toes. Her lips were chapped and nearly stuck together with the cold air. Her voice ached from how she'd sobbed the night before. Her stomach rumbled for food.

Had it all been a dream?

The city looked the same. All the streets surrounding her were exactly as she'd always known them, a mix of rust and cardboard descending farther south toward the river and, in the other direction, ascending the hill toward the Center of the city. Most of the Stacks were under a dusky-blue evening sky since the sun had nearly set, its final red rays spreading over the western horizon likes the wings of a bird. The air still smelled like smoke, mixed with the scent of rice and beans cooking in a nearby house. A busker somewhere nearby played a flute. The music blended with quiet voices from beyond the thin walls of homes.

It didn't seem possible that something so terrible could have happened and not changed the way the whole world looked, smelled, sounded.

It was a nightmare, she decided. Her parents were probably looking for her. Her father would have dinner ready soon.

She scrambled to the edge of the roof and dropped to the ground, getting dirt on her pant legs. Her mother would scold her, but she was so hungry, it was hard to care.

The back door to her house was dark. At this time of night, her parents usually lit a candle. Unless they'd run out, of course, then they would eat dinner under the Mothers' moons outside.

Right before she entered, a firecracker set off in a distant corner of the neighborhood, making her jump. A dog from the other side of the road barked. A door slammed nearby. These sounds were all normal, but for some reason now, they set her pulse racing.

She pushed open the back door. "Mami? Papi?"

Darkness enveloped her as she walked inside, leaving the door open a crack. A small sliver of light from outside spread over her foot and across the floor like a trail. A foul stench reached her, like old meat, but sickly sweet at once, clinging to her nostrils and clothes in a way that made her certain she'd never be able to wash it off. Her stomach turned over as she took tiny steps beyond the threshold of the house. Flies swept past her ears, their whining buzz setting her nerves on edge.

Maybe I'm still in the nightmare.

Fear gripped her. If this were the nightmare, maybe the man with the gun was still here.

She called for her parents again and took a few more steps. No one answered.

Instead of her vision getting used to the darkness, the shadows seemed to grow until they nearly consumed her. The flies came back, brushing against her face and clothes along with the foul smell.

She took another step forward. The trail of light from outside reached past her. The buzzing flies followed the sliver of light toward the shape of a limp hand.

She couldn't breathe, she couldn't move, but the reality hit her. Her parents were here, but they would never answer her calls again. They'd been swallowed by the dark, and if she didn't leave right now, it might swallow her too.

It was just a cold roof, poor in construction, no different from any other roof in the Stacks. But it reminded her that once, she'd had people who'd protected her instead of having to do all the fighting alone. Here, she could allow herself to remember her parents without feeling weak for doing so.

Her parents had each been brought by their families from Mil Cimas when they were young, her father from the south and her mother from the north. People worshipped the Mothers not only in Sumerand, but also in Marin and Mil Cimas, so her parents had grown up with the religion.

It was odd to think of a place where people didn't have to hide what they believed in, and so easy to forget that Sumerand's view of religion was an exception rather than the rule. Only Sumerand and the north of Mil Cimas had banned the religion. People had tried to flee to Marin and southern Mil Cimas during the war, but travel was expensive, and Diamond Guards caught and killed many Inosen along the way. Her parents had considered fleeing, but hadn't had the money and hadn't wanted to put Aina at risk, so they decided to stay in Sumerand and kept up their faith even once the war began.

The cracked pavement in front of the house was still choked with weeds, but some yellow flowers stood out. Her mother had said they reminded her of her earliest memories, of the flowers that grew on the hills near where she was born in Mil Cimas.

"There was a flower in every color you can imagine," she'd tell Aina, promising to take her there someday.

She would tuck the yellow flowers into her own short hair and Aina's braids, reciting poems and singing lullabies in Milano all the while. Aina's knowledge of the language had faded over the years with no one to practice it with, and now she could hardly remember the words to those songs.

Her mother's face was a blur in her mind now, but when

she was younger, everyone had told her how much they looked alike. Sometimes when she cleaned her daggers and caught her reflection on their surfaces, she saw her own eyes, her mother's eyes, and imagined her parents telling her the Mothers' teachings that life was precious and to take one was a sin.

Then she breathed in sharply, her eyes fixed on the clock in the train station's tower in the distance. Her parents' voices disappeared. Gunshots were the only sound, and she couldn't tell if they were all in her head or somewhere in the streets beyond. She watched the dial on the clock move until the gunshots faded.

Though she yearned to escape the Stacks, something about watching the streets splayed before her, spreading miles southward, comforted her and made the gunshots ringing in her ears disperse. At night, especially in the spring and summer, she had played with the other kids on this street while the adults gossiped and passed around plates of food. Her parents usually shared rice and beans, but on special occasions when they could afford it, they brought fried plantains or sudado de pollo cooked with recipes from their hometown in Mil Cimas. As candles flickered in the windows, both moons rose high in the sky, adults reminisced times before the war, and the local gang watched every street corner to keep them safe throughout the night. Wounds were healed and mistakes forgiven. Sometimes, the lack of anything made people appreciate everything.

Had she gotten too selfish? Had she climbed too high? But if her parents' ghosts came back one day and asked if she was proud of herself, she wanted to have something to tell them.

Maybe she had climbed too high. But this job was her only chance at not falling to the bottom once more.

After what felt like hours, the creak of metal sounded nearby. Teo appeared at the edge of the roof.

"How did you know where to find me?" she asked.

"This is your favorite hiding spot, isn't it?" he asked with no sign of judgment in his eyes.

"You remember?"

"Of course, I do. The first time we met."

When she was sixteen, a year after her first kill, Aina had had more confidence than common sense. She'd learned which streets specialized in drug deals and which specialized in muggings, she'd started to get involved in diamond sales, and she'd learned all about the different types of people in Kosín: the mercenaries, the thugs, the gangs, the addicts, the pimps, the Inosen, the slavers, the thieves, and everything in between. With Kohl's training in addition to her knowledge, she'd felt invincible.

That was, until she'd entered an alley one day and watched a tall boy a few years older than her being bested in a fight by three opponents. He was clearly skilled, but his gun—strapped to his belt—was probably out of ammo since he wasn't using it, and he appeared to have no other weapons while each opponent bore knives and brass knuckles. She'd thought it stupid of him to only have one weapon, but the blood on his face and arms struck a seldom-played chord within her. He was too young and strong, like her, to die at the hands of cowards who relied on numbers instead of skill. She'd made her decision, taking out two of the boys before they even knew what was happening, but the third had plunged a knife into her side. She'd fled, leaving the boy she'd saved to deal with the third opponent. She should have returned to the Dom to have her wound treated, but her survival instincts had flicked on, and there was only one place she retreated to when that happened: her old rooftop, the one place in all of Kosín where she felt truly safe.

She'd laid there, bleeding and hyperventilating. The boy she'd helped showed up within a few minutes. He'd stared at her with a mix of anger, concern, and amusement.

"How did you find me?"

He'd nodded at her still-bleeding wound. "You left a trail."

It had taken them a while to trust each other, since he couldn't comprehend why she'd helped him, and she couldn't understand why he'd followed her. He'd helped clean and bandage her wound, and a week later, when they ran into each other at a bar, they talked as easily as if they were childhood friends reunited.

"Thanks for coming," she said now, wondering what she'd done to deserve a friend like Teo.

"I get why you still come here," he said as he walked across the roof and sat next to her. "I'm still angry about my father's death. He didn't want to fight for any side in the war; all he wanted was a good job. But then the war began, and the Steels he worked for made him fight. What choice did he have if he wanted a job? And now he's dead, and the railroad he helped build still runs, carrying the Steels who sent him to his death. You know how it was. The Steels liked to paint it as a battle between them and the Inosen. But most families were secretly on both sides. Why should they give up their beliefs for a job?"

"Or they were on neither side, and died in the crossfire," Aina clarified.

"Or neither side," Teo agreed, shaking his head. He paused for a long moment, the steadily blowing wind the only sound. "There's no war now, but I feel like I'm in one. I used to watch other kids get sucked up into gangs and smuggling, and thought I was better than them for avoiding it. My parents were falcon riders in Linash before they came here, one of the most respectable jobs in their country. I never saw myself doing any dishonorable work, or becoming a criminal, until I had no choice. But when my father died, my career options were narrowed down. At least with this job, I don't have a Steel breathing down my neck, threatening to leave my family starving if I don't follow his orders."

Aina didn't say anything for a long time, her thoughts spinning. Kill or be killed. Magic or industry. Nothing could coexist—steel and smoke never left room for nuance.

"And when you realize this type of job is your only real option," Aina began slowly, "you have to fight for it. You can't just let it go when it gets difficult."

Teo reached over and took her hand, holding it between his. The moonlight hit his face at this angle, illuminating flecks of gold in the amber of his eyes. He was close enough that she could count his eyelashes or the scars on his hands when she glanced down at them. She felt warmer and braver by that touch, protected by their loyalty to each other. In her short time away from Kohl, she'd begun to notice how sometimes Teo held her hand, touched her shoulder, or hugged her a moment longer than was necessary.

Or maybe she was imagining that. Maybe she was so accustomed to never receiving affection from Kohl that affection from anyone, even in the smallest doses, seemed to mean more than it actually did.

Perhaps every time Teo touched or looked at her, it was because they were best friends and no other reason. She didn't want to ruin the friendship they had by wrongly guessing at anything else, or by clinging to something that wasn't really there.

"You just have to decide what's important to you, and put

your mind to it entirely," Teo said, letting go of her hand, then. "Like how I do with taking care of my mother. It's what drives all of my decisions. If this job is what's important to you, then I know you'll overcome everything that stands in your way. You'll get your life back, and you'll excel where your parents never could, and in ways Kohl could never teach you. You know I'll have your back the whole time."

"And I yours," she replied.

His words repeated over and over in her head: *Decide what's important to you, and put your mind to it entirely.*

Tomorrow they'd go to meet Raurie's aunt, get back to work, and find Kouta.

While Kohl had taken her off the streets, she was the one who'd chosen to work for him, pushed addiction out of her body, and risked her life every day to rise higher through the underground ranks. She'd managed to live while so many others had died.

If she was good at anything, it was survival, and she refused to let anyone take that away from her. She would finish this job, she would live, and she would never fall so far again.

19

When Aina woke up the next morning, she pulled the blankets over her head and squeezed her eyes shut. It was so easy to get comfortable in Teo's apartment, to pretend her life wasn't at risk and forget the world outside.

Is Ryuu's softness rubbing off on me?

She scowled as she remembered how when she and Teo returned last night, Ryuu and Ynes were busy chatting about the paintings on the walls. Ynes's face had been lit up with a bright smile, and Teo relaxed at the sight, but Aina had felt a surge of protectiveness for the old woman. How could a rich Steel sympathize or bond with someone like Ynes or any of them? What right did he have to sit in Ynes's house and eat her food while he had a mansion waiting for him to return to? She knew it was best to stay here instead of his mansion where his workers might see her, but he didn't have to get comfortable with any of their hospitality.

She sat up and blinked the sleep out of her eyes. The sooner they got this job done, the sooner this Steel would stop invading their lives.

The first thing she did was check her wound. It was healing again, and the bleeding had stopped. As she rewrapped the bandages, Ryuu spoke up from the pile of blankets where he'd slept.

"Good morning!" He reached over and passed her a cup of mint tea.

She glared at him over the rim of her cup. His expression didn't change. It was too early in the morning to cope with Ryuu's smiling face and bright eyes without any caffeine. He truly thought she was going to spare his brother's life. She brushed aside a brief surge of sympathy and turned away from him to drink her tea in a few large gulps.

Teo placed his empty cup on the table with a clink. "We should head out early."

"You haven't been to the Stacks yet, have you?" she asked Ryuu. "Rough part of town. Somebody's body was found cut into pieces and thrown in a trash bin the other day." She turned to Teo. "Should we leave Ryuu behind? Give him a snack, some soft blankets, reading material—"

"I'm going with you," Ryuu insisted, keeping his voice steady despite the fact that his eyes flashed when she had mentioned the cut-up body.

Leaning forward, she fixed a concerned expression on her face. "It is dangerous; I won't lie. If you'd rather wait here, you can just give us the money and—"

He let out a short, nervous laugh. "Why would I do that? And don't forget, you might need my money for more things after this tracking spell, so you need to keep me around. We'll follow the deal we made."

She let out a frustrated breath, then smiled. "Right. The deal."

While Teo went to get ready, Ryuu finished his tea and Aina moved to sit on the floor next to him.

"Why don't you carry a gun on you? You can aim, and you don't flinch when you shoot. Fighting for your life every day might not be the way you live, but you're with us now and you could actually be useful if we get into trouble later."

Ryuu shook his head, and his bravery from the warehouse last night evaporated. "After Kouta told me the truth of how our parents died, I had one of our guards teach me how to shoot. No amount of money or protection can really help you if someone wants to kill you enough. My parents and Kouta are proof of that." His voice grew quiet, and he paused before continuing. "I won't let anyone take me out the same way. But I also never want to get comfortable taking lives with bullets. I still believe in the Mothers' teachings to value mercy over revenge, and that life is precious."

She hadn't expected such a long confession. With a grimace, she said, "You don't have to tell me not to love guns, especially after what happened to my parents."

He frowned. "Don't you shoot people for a living?"

"Wrong." She pulled out a knife and placed it on the tip of his collarbone. "I cut them."

He leaned away from her, a brief flash of fear in his eyes. A bit of guilt wormed through her at the sight. There was no need to threaten him unnecessarily.

She removed the knife as Teo reentered the room. Then, avoiding each other's gaze, she and Ryuu followed Teo out of the apartment.

The sun beat down on them heavily when they reached street level and headed south, stopping at a bank first for Ryuu to withdraw money to pay Raurie's aunt. Aina began to sweat under her jacket and scarf, but she wouldn't take them off even if she were boiling. Each hand gripped the hilt of a dagger under her jacket. She was more confident than yesterday after the fight in the warehouse, but she still had to be careful.

Every sight of a Diamond Guard made her pulse race, and every person tattooed with a gang's markings made her wonder who would try to kill her next. But she had to be out in the open and get her job done if she wanted her life back. Hiding would get her nowhere.

She led the way to a set of alleys south of the Center and the square with King Verrain's statue. Her eyes watered under the bright sun, and as they crossed an intersection, she almost missed hearing the distinctive whistle of metal cutting through air.

She dodged the brunt of the attack, but her calf seared in pain as the dagger flew past her and left a sharp cut. She dropped to her knees and rolled out of the way as a streak of bright blue hair appeared at the corner of her vision. Coming to a stand in the shadow of a building, pulse pounding in her ears, she pulled out the pair of scythes strapped to her thighs.

"Stay out of it!" she yelled at Teo, who had moved toward Tannis with murder in his eyes. He backed away reluctantly, but didn't take his gaze off Tannis as he did.

"Heard you got fired." Gold, hawk-like eyes as bright as the sun flashed at Aina.

Her lips twitched. "It's more of a suspension."

She kept her face straight as if those words weren't like broken glass in her mouth. The Jackals coming after her had been one sign that her old life was gone, but Tannis attacking her felt more personal.

"Give up, street child," Tannis said in a low voice that only Aina could hear. Pedestrians slowed and pointed, many of them stopping to watch what would happen next, some of their eyes lighting like this was a free show for them to enjoy. "Kohl doesn't trust you enough to finish this job, so he's put me in charge of fixing your mistakes. Whichever one of us does it first gets to live. So, I thought, why not get rid of the competition now?"

Teo caught her eye and nodded. If he helped her win, it would make her look weak and pathetic.

This was her battle.

Catching Tannis off guard, she feinted with one scythe and struck with the other. Tannis blocked the attack with her own blade, metal clanging while several gasps rose up from the bystanders. When Tannis thrust her blade upward, Aina fell back, gritting her teeth.

Tannis feinted another strike, and Ryuu shouted a warning. Her eyes flicked over to him, but that second of distraction cost her.

A loud thunk went through her skull as Tannis punched her. She fell back, her knees buckling with the strike, and caught herself on the side of the nearest building. Her head pounded, her vision spun, but she bit down hard on her tongue to keep focus and relied on the adrenaline from the fight to keep her standing. Squaring her shoulders and drawing a deep breath, she stepped away from the building and faced Tannis once more.

They circled each other, sun hitting them as they stepped into the street, and shadows covering them when they stood in doorways. The pedestrians watching them seemed to hold their breath as they waited for the fight to resume.

As Aina slowed, standing in the light next to a horse-driven carriage with Tannis at the mouth of a dark alley, she caught sight of the vulture tattoo on Tannis's forearm. It was identical to Kohl's. Her throat went dry as she pictured Kohl coming after her himself—would she fight back or freeze as he delivered a killing blow?

Tannis moved first, swinging at Aina's side with her blade. With a sharp inhale, Aina blocked the attack with her scythe. The clang of their weapons reverberated through her bones and gasps rose up in the crowd as people moved out of their way. Before Tannis could attack again, Aina made a fist with her left hand, small blades sliding out between her knuckles, and punched Tannis in the side.

Tannis faltered. Aina stepped back, but then a flash of silver shot through the air so fast she barely dodged it. A throwing star slashed her upper arm, in the place where her neck had been a moment before.

Hissing with the sharp pain, she threw herself behind the carriage to avoid the next star Tannis threw from her shoulder holsters.

As Tannis approached, the shadow of her boots visible under the carriage, Aina grabbed onto the window ledge and hauled herself to the roof. Tannis's eyes widened as she looked up at the last second, but Aina landed in front of her and lunged forward, her scythes swiping across Tannis's unguarded side.

Tannis stumbled back as the cut seared through her skin. A grimace from one of the bystanders caught Aina's eye; they all knew a fatal blow would come next. But her legs didn't carry her forward. Her hands didn't lift her weapons to strike.

As she hesitated, Tannis took another step backward, then turned and sprinted down the nearest side street, her blood dripping on the cobblestones as she ran.

Once she was gone, Aina locked eyes with Teo, and then with Ryuu, who was breathing heavily as if he'd been in the fight himself. People on both sides of the street skirted around her too. The smell of the blood dripping from her arm, sharp and coppery, heightened with the end of the fight. The sunlight brightened, seeming to expose her even as she stepped into the shadows.

"Let's get out of here," she told Teo and Ryuu, her voice not sounding like her own. "She'll try again, but I can't kill her, or Kohl will come after me. I have to—"

"Stop being afraid of him!" Teo's large hand fastened above her elbow. Only then did she realize her whole body was trembling. "Can't he at least control his own people from coming after you? That's the least he owes you. Show him he can't throw you out like you're nothing, Aina. Show him he's wrong!"

But she was already shaking her head so hard, black strands of hair fell out of her ponytail and waved in front of her eyes. Something broke inside her. She no longer cared if anyone, even Ryuu, thought she was weak right now.

"What if he's not wrong?" Her voice cracked as she tried to wipe the blood off her arm.

Kohl had taken her in from the streets. Kohl had helped her keep her mind off glue with endless training. Kohl had made her the best Blade in Kosín. Kohl had become her idol and her obsession. Kohl had given her their best job yet and promised her all she'd wanted. She owed him.

Kohl had hit her. Kohl had shot at her. Kohl had left her to the mercy of the city. She still owed him.

She had to kill Kouta before Tannis did. Otherwise, she'd never regain her position and respect. All of this would only stop once Kouta's heart stopped beating, and by her blade alone.

Looking away from them so they couldn't read the thousands of emotions she was going through, she said, "Let's go meet Raurie's aunt."

As they pushed through the crowd, Aina wished she were

alone. The rooftop would be safer, her favorite hiding spot, the only place that was always there for her. As quickly as she'd regained her confidence last night, it left her now.

The image of Tannis's vicious golden gaze burned through her mind. Her chance at any kind of future had fallen out of her grasp like water cupped in a skeleton's hands.

One hand trailed to the blood-stained scarf she wore and tugged impulsively at the loose strands. She should just buy glue from the nearest dealer and drown herself in it. Then she wouldn't have to think. She couldn't fear life on the streets if she were too high to even realize which street she was lying down on. She couldn't feel Kohl's bullet slamming through her brain if she was too numbed from glue to feel anything.

A warm hand touched her back, and for once, she didn't feel the need to punch whoever had done it. Glancing to the left, she saw Ryuu gazing at her with concern that was nearly palpable. Focusing on his face only, Aina's nerves eased.

She couldn't understand him. He hardly knew her other than the fact that she'd tried to kill his brother, and she'd given him no reason to trust her other than her word. She'd just shown so much weakness, yet for some reason, he was comforting her instead of taking advantage.

Such merciful people stood no chance in Kosín. The thought made her want to protect him. Yet he knew her name, her profession, and the details of her crimes. Especially now, without Kohl's protection, Ryuu could easily have her arrested. She still had to kill him and his brother to protect herself.

Aina didn't like to use guns. Aside from how they reminded her of her parents, they were too cowardly, too impersonal, too distanced from the one you were murdering. But to kill Ryuu, she might need a gun.

20

They soon reached the southernmost edge of the
Stacks. A strong stench of refuse carried toward them from
the old ports and crumbling ferry buildings lining the edge
of the river. The docks here weren't used for trading anymore,
as that had moved farther north along the western riverfront,
but the barges carrying bodies to be buried south in mass
graves near old diamond mines still docked here at night.
Some of the scent still clung to the air in the daytime.

Aina's nerves settled, and her fear of Tannis coming after
her slowly turned to anger at herself. Maybe it had been smart
to let her go and avoid Kohl's wrath, or maybe it had been stupid. She'd hesitated once when she'd failed to kill Ryuu at his
mansion, and now again with failing to kill Tannis. Tannis would
only come after her again, and more confidently now that she
knew Aina would hesitate before killing her—something Kohl
had taught her to never do.

While they walked, Ryuu asked, "I know you had to defend

yourself back there, but did you really think she would kill you? I mean, you used to work together, right?"

She raised an eyebrow. "Considering she tried to slice through my neck, I think it's safe to say she wanted to kill me. Now that I think about it, maybe I want to kill her too. She never once called me by my name, always 'street child' or something. And she always took the poisons I brewed without even asking. I should have tried to get rid of her earlier."

The words felt traitorous even as she spoke them, traitorous to the only home and family she'd really known. Besides, she'd liked Tannis and had considered her a friend even if they didn't always get along. But now Tannis was the one trying to take her job from her and kill her in the process.

Ryuu's previous look of concern turned to mild disgust. "You're a very brutal person, did you know that?"

"To you, maybe. I think I'm rather calm and gentle." Teo laughed aloud at that. "Shut up, Teo, you're not in this conversation."

As they walked the muddy streets, Aina had to give Ryuu some credit. He didn't glance around with wide eyes like yesterday, and he kept his gaze forward. But he still had that strolling gait rich people used to show they could buy the entire street they walked upon. Nascent confidence was in every casual footstep, every movement that showed how pitifully unaware he was of his surroundings.

"Come." She placed a hand on his shoulder and steered him away from a gang of heavily tattooed men who would cut his eyes out and sell them to the nearest buyer if he looked too closely. "Walk at my pace. And get your damn hands out of your pockets unless you happen to have a knife or gun in them."

After another block, Ryuu leaned toward her and said in

a low voice, "The mere fact that you have to come up with reasons to kill her means you value human life in some way. Admit it."

"You've known me for a few days, and you already think you know me well enough to judge whether I'm a good person or not," she said, shaking her head. "Do you still have some childish fantasy that everyone is inherently good and just needs a fair chance? Or are you trying to make me into a decent person, so that you can take credit for saving me?"

He opened his mouth, then closed it and sighed as if to say she was hopeless.

The next few minutes passed in silence, but then, there came that feeling when someone was watching her, their eyes burning into her back so she knew exactly where they were and could defend herself. But over time, she'd felt a certain pair of eyes more so than any other, and they'd developed a distinctive feel. These were Kohl's eyes.

She turned, both hands going to dagger handles. After a quick scan of the rooftops, she found him about two hundred feet away. In the tower of the train station's second floor, where they'd spent more hours together than she could count, he stood partially hidden behind a pillar. His eyes fixed directly on her, as if he'd been watching her progress throughout the city and could draw a map of her footsteps. Had he watched her fight with Tannis? Would he have stepped in to stop it if either of them had tried to deal a fatal blow?

Even from far away, he could find her easily and predict her next moves. She wondered if he knew she was going to see an Inosen, if he would tell Tannis. But he wasn't the only one who knew things.

In their years working together, he'd trusted her with far more of his past than he'd told most people. Apart from his crimes, his tactics, his secret passages throughout the city, she knew he couldn't sleep at night and only closed his eyes at dawn; she knew he took his coffee black with one spoon of sugar like an old Milano man; she knew he was paranoid about being poisoned and so had made himself immune to most, drinking or injecting them in small doses to become accustomed to them; and she knew that when they fought together, they were nearly unstoppable.

Shortly before she'd met Teo, Kohl had gathered her and Mirran to rob a ship of visiting Kaiyanis diplomats. Mirran, an excellent actress and Kaiyanis herself, had donned a servant's uniform—after Aina had knocked out the unsuspecting servant with the hilt of her knife—and slipped onto the ship within minutes while the diplomats had gone to a dinner at the Tower.

As it was nearly winter, Aina's breath came out in white puffs while she waited with Kohl behind the ship at the edge of the docks near Rose Court. A small getaway boat waited for them, bobbing in the black currents of the river.

But something had gone wrong. Kohl, apparently able to sense trouble before anyone else could see or hear it, was on his feet, two pistols drawn. Aina scrambled up next to him, the anticipation of a fight pushing away the winter chill.

Seconds later, the sound of light footsteps reached her ears, and Mirran leapt off the edge of the second floor of the boat. She rolled on the docks and came to her feet, but several Kaiyanis soldiers and four Diamond Guards protecting the ship were already running toward them. Aina swore. Kohl shook his head and sighed as if this were only a minor inconvenience.

"She's a dirty thief!" yelled a Kaiyanis man from the deck of the ship, his shaking finger aimed at Mirran.

"Is he one of the diplomats?" Aina whispered. "They were all supposed to be at the Tower."

"He stayed behind!" Mirran hissed. "He knew I wasn't with them, so he started shouting for guards."

Kohl said nothing. He stepped ahead of them and fired two clean shots into the Kaiyanis soldiers' heads while their weapons were still only half-drawn. Mirran leapt between the next two soldiers, dodging Kohl's bullets, and struck at them with a dagger.

The Diamond Guards converged on Aina. She easily side-stepped Kohl's next shot, which hit one of the guards, then swept her dagger across the throat of another. Whipping around, she plunged her blade into the stomach of the third guard.

Then, she heard a small gasp and spun around, her own breath clouding in front of her.

The fourth Diamond Guard had caught Mirran and held his diamond-edged dagger at her throat. Kohl took a step back and lifted his hands, looking like a child who'd been caught eating too many sweets while his mother wasn't looking. Aina might have imagined it, but for the briefest second, his gaze flicked to her.

She was already moving. The guard had forgotten about her, probably assuming his colleagues had taken care of her. In seconds, she was behind him, and flung her blade into the base of his skull. With one final exhale, blood streaming out of the back of his neck, he fell to the ground and Mirran leapt free.

"Come on!" Mirran said, jumping into the moored boat while the Kaiyanis diplomat shouted for backup.

"Wait," Aina whispered. She raced to the bodies of the

guards, searched through their weapon holsters and sheaths, then followed Kohl and Mirran onto the boat with a wide grin on her face.

"So?" Kohl asked Mirran, as if this entire ordeal had been no more eventful than a walk to the market.

From her pockets, brassiere, and shoes, Mirran pulled out different jewels—opal necklaces, sapphire bracelets, emerald rings—and waved them around. The silver light of Isar's moon caught on each of them and Kohl's satisfied grin.

"Those will match my new toys," Aina said, drawing the four diamond-edged knives she'd taken from the guards.

Kohl turned toward her, his sapphire-blue eyes hard and piercing. Her smile wavered a little. For a moment, she feared Kohl might reprimand her for taking weapons that would make it obvious who she'd stolen them from—these knives were the symbol of the Diamond Guards, and no regular street thug could afford them.

But then he'd nodded approvingly. "You're turning into a good Blade, Aina. We fought well together."

She'd nearly burst with pride and had to contain her smile the entire way back to the Dom.

They fought well together, and they knew each other better than most people knew them. She met his gaze in the train station's tower for a moment longer. While she was leaving a fight against Tannis, bleeding, and trying to lay low as the whole city searched for her, Kohl stood out in the open and unafraid, as always.

Just like that, he was gone. He turned and disappeared, and the heat of his gaze simmered away. A chill crept up her spine in its absence. They weren't so close anymore, now that she'd failed.

"What are you looking at?" Ryuu asked.

Instead of answering, she gestured toward Teo. They jogged in silence to catch up, then stopped outside of a wide, one-story home constructed of mud brick with a rusted metal sheet as the door.

As Teo knocked lightly, Aina's eyes trailed to a boy lying on the ground nearby. He was young, no older than twelve. He lay on his back, eyes half-open, one hand holding a plastic bag to his nose and mouth. The other hand hung limp in the dirt. When the boy breathed in, Aina could almost smell the vapors herself. She knew how it felt, the sensation of letting go. The boy dropped the hand with the rag to the ground and stared at his own feet for a moment. Then he closed his eyes, chest rising and falling in such slow breaths that it was a surprise each time.

Her skin itched at the sight. Even years later, her mind unhinged and craved a simple sniff of that powerful glue, the one drug street children could attain in plenty. Lying on the street, clenching a bag filled with glue, watching the world spin as her breaths grew dim . . . the eyes of the people who passed her by, the dogs that sniffed at her . . . it had made her tired, confused, weak; it made her breaths come short and quick, threatening to rob her lungs of air. But it had also been a temporary euphoria that pulled her away from the body that sensed pain and loss and hunger. It also stole memories, so sometimes she couldn't remember how she'd gotten wherever she was or what she'd been doing right before. It pilfered older memories too, until the images of her parents' faces had faded to dull blurs, and her roughest nights on the streets felt like a story she'd heard rather than something she'd experienced herself.

No matter how hard she'd tried, inhaling glue over and over again, it never cleansed her mind of the sight of her parents' dead bodies on the floor. But it could make her forget those images for a while and dull the emptiness in her stomach.

She'd known the risks. It could put her in a coma, cause her breaths to come so fast, her lungs would simply give up, or just kill her in one sudden, unlucky sniff. But she hadn't cared and had inhaled it regularly for a few years until one day when she was eleven. She'd been scouring the banks of the Minos River for dropped kors and had stumbled upon a body.

The girl was Milana, like her, but in her teens. The dead girl had kept her dark brown hair like Aina's mother had, in a short cut, waves brushing against her jaw. A plastic bag was stuck to the girl's face. Suffocation often killed glue inhalers. With a shaking hand, Aina had reached out to pull the bag away and revealed the girl's mouth and nose ringed with a rash that marked her addiction—they called it Kalaan's Kiss. Aina's hand had trailed to her own mouth, feeling the buds of the rash, picturing herself dead and forgotten on the riverbank.

After that, she'd pulled away from glue and nearly died from the withdrawal. Kohl had found her a year later, and the constant training kept her mind off glue most of the time. Becoming a Blade and working toward some kind of future kept her focused. Pushing herself in training, and later in her work, was a release.

"Is he all right?" Ryuu's voice climbed through her reverie.

"He's fine," Aina answered, hoping she was talking about herself as much as the boy on the side of the road. "Go inside."

With a shrug, Ryuu left her there and entered the house. Once the door closed behind him, Aina walked to the boy and lifted the bag from his face. Paper bags were safer than plastic, but kids like him often either didn't know that or didn't care. Maybe he was trying to forget something, like she

had. Part of her wished she could tell him that some memories were etched into you, and some wounds never healed. But
she would never stop him from trying.

He was still breathing, so she stood to get back to her job.
If she didn't, Kohl would kill her, or worse, she might end up
on the streets again with a plastic bag suffocating her. She
turned and walked into the blood magic practitioner's home.

21

Raurie's aunt's home was similar to Aina's old one, but larger. Two wooden chairs and a table stood on the dirt floor, a straw mat was in the center of the room, and lit candles surrounded a small, gold-wire sculpture of the Mothers on their table.

In Aina's old home, there had also been dirt floors, a few blankets and pieces of cardboard on the ground, spiders crawling in the corners, a makeshift stove, and little else. One image stood out: a small porcelain horse statue her mother had owned. It had sat behind the stove throughout Aina's childhood. Its glimmer in the light of the flames on the stove still recalled itself clearly in her memory, even though it had all shattered when she was eight years old.

It struck her as odd that practicing magic had gotten her parents killed, and now she was about to use it to try to save herself.

"You made it!" Raurie approached from a back room,

draping a purple shawl over her shoulders. She smiled as if they were here for a party rather than an illegal magic service. "My aunt is waiting for you. I have a shift at my uncle's bar after this, but I wanted to be here to introduce you to June."

There was a hint of protectiveness in her voice, and Aina didn't blame her. It was already a risk on her part to invite them here at all.

"Are you Inosen yourself?" Aina asked as Raurie led them to the backroom.

Nodding again, Raurie said, "Yes, I have been all my life. But I haven't been blessed to be able to use magic. My aunt says it's too dangerous." She gestured into the small backroom. "Here she is."

Her aunt, June Coste, sat in the center of the room on a pillow. Black hair streaked with gray shrouded her face, which was narrow with high cheekbones. Two candles cast golden light onto her ochre-brown skin and her yellow shawl. A black tattoo curved in the center of her forehead like the blade of a scythe. Through the black ink, three small diamonds sat in her forehead, unabashedly revealed to the world. Aina's breath caught at the sight. The diamonds revealed exactly what she was.

June was a Sacoren, a priest—they were Inosen that the Mothers came to, either in a vision or in their thoughts, and asked them to be leaders of their people and to bless willing Inosen with the ability to use the magic of blood and earth. Then, they pierced three diamonds into an arc on their own foreheads as a gesture of loyalty to the Mothers and a sign that they had been chosen as leaders. Her parents had told her to always trust Sacoren, that they were there to help— except for King Verrain. He'd twisted the power given to him for his own purposes, making it evil instead of the blessing the Mothers had intended it to be.

Ever since the war, any Sacoren who were caught by the Diamond Guards had their diamonds ripped out and these tattoos forcibly inked in their place, so that everyone would know their crime. Instead of being thrown in jail or killed, they were allowed to walk freely with the tattoo as a warning to all other Inosen that steel would always be stronger than blood. June must have restored the diamonds herself.

On June's left was a tattered copy of the Nos Inoken, the holy text filled with the Mothers' wisdom, written by Sacoren hundreds of years ago. On her right was a glass jar filled with rough diamonds. Each diamond was only good for one act of magic, so it made sense that she needed a jar full of them. She said nothing as they sat, simply straightened her sleeves and took them in. This woman made a living off performing magic for people who had never been blessed to do so themselves or were too scared to. In the Stacks, older Inosen like June Coste were venerated as long as they could manage to escape the Diamond Guards' attention.

"Amman oraske," June said in greeting. *May the Mothers bless you.*

"Amman min oraske," Aina replied, the familiar words sliding easily off her tongue and easing her nerves. These were some of the few words her parents had known in the old holy language, which had died out except for use among Inosen. Her parents had said these words in greeting to the Sacoren who had led the underground worship services. "You were a Sacoren, weren't you?"

"I *am* a Sacoren, a proper one, not a twisted one like Verrain was, and I will be a Sacoren until the day I die and my soul returns to the Mothers," June said. "Even if most of the people in this city have given up on their faith, I have not. The Mothers will protect me even while the city bleeds itself out."

Aina fought down a grimace. June, like most Inosen, would likely believe the Mothers would always protect her—until, of course, there was a gun in her face with a Diamond Guard at the end of it. Maybe Aina would worship the Mothers if they could provide bulletproof shields.

After a short pause, Raurie whispered sheepishly, "You have to pay first."

Aina elbowed Ryuu. He withdrew a box from his pocket, then opened it. Coins spilled out in front of June, gold glittering in the candlelight.

"My blood will be given willingly in service to you, through the Mothers' blessing," June began. "Raurie, if you will assist me."

Raurie stepped to the side of the room and knelt in front of a chest. From it, she withdrew a small knife. She then plucked a diamond from the jar to the right and passed both objects to her aunt.

"Raurie tells me you would like to track someone. What is their name?"

Aina bit her lip for a moment, wondering how much she could trust this woman.

Then she remembered there wasn't really a choice in the matter.

"Kouta Hirai."

"So, he's still alive?" June asked, tilting her head to the side. "Have you brought something to complete the spell's connection? To perform a tracking spell, we will need the blood of the person performing the spell, the blood of the person receiving the vision, and some piece of the person you are tracking. Mine, yours, and . . . Mr. Hirai's."

Aina handed over a small glass vial with scrapings of Kouta's dried blood from her dagger. June stared at it for a moment, turning the vial in her weathered hands so it caught the light. Weariness crossed her face, as if she'd seen so much blood that the mere sight of it exhausted her. She then looked at Aina, taking in her clothes and features.

"Dare I ask how a girl from the Stacks got the blood of one of the wealthiest men in the city? Unless, of course, she recently tried to kill him . . ."

The statement hung in the air, rife with tension. Aina partially rose, one hand trailing to a dagger, but Ryuu placed his hand on top of hers and answered June first.

"I'm Kouta's brother," he explained quickly. "I was there when he was attacked. The person who tried to kill him dropped their knife, and this was left over. I need to find out where he is."

As he finished speaking, June waved her hand dismissively, but there was a knowing look in her eyes as she turned back to Aina. "It's not my business, I suppose. I will perform this spell for you. It will show us a vision of where Kouta Hirai is. Since you brought the element we will use to track him, you will be the one the Mothers grant the vision to. You, and me."

In the dim light, June brought the silver edge of the knife closer to her forearm where healing cuts trailed across her skin, then made another small prick with the tip of the blade. Small scars circled the new wound like a macabre constellation. She caught the blood on the diamond, then nodded at Aina.

Aina took the knife from her boot and brought it to her upper arm, a memory flashing through her mind of her mother doing the same thing to heal a neighbor of a blood disease. Aina had sat in the corner quietly, watching her mother's every move.

When the man had left, healed, Aina had watched him go through the window. She'd scanned both ends of the street for signs of Diamond Guards who might have been spying on them. Over the past few years, she'd seen people disappear. She'd seen people get shot. While she didn't fully understand what was happening, she knew that what her parents did was a risk.

When the man had disappeared around the corner, she let out a frustrated breath and turned to face her mother, who was busy cleaning the knife.

"Why do you keep doing that if it's dangerous?" she asked in a rush. She'd asked different versions of this question multiple times, but the answers she got never really eased her fears.

Her mother's forehead crinkled as she turned to Aina and spoke in the same calm voice she always used. "He needed help, mijita. He can't afford to go to a hospital, and I have the ability to heal him. It's what I must do with this gift the Mothers have granted to me."

She wanted to ask who would help them if *they* got caught, but she didn't know how to voice the question without making her mother angry. So, she'd kept quiet whenever they went to underground services, recited prayers, or used magic, and she stopped searching for Diamond Guards at every corner.

Now, Aina acted almost mechanically. She pressed the tip of the blade to her skin. Vibrant red blood spilled onto the blade. June held the diamond up to her own blade, and then Aina's. Blood dripped off the metal surface and onto the diamond in minuscule red bursts to join June's own offering.

While holding the diamond in one palm, June took the vial

with the scrapes of Kouta's blood and held it in her other hand. The room fell silent as they all watched her in anticipation.

Closing her eyes, June whispered, "Amman inoke."

Though all the doors were closed and there were no windows, a brisk wind found its way into the room immediately, raising the hair on the back of Aina's neck.

As the bit of diamond visible through the blood glowed with a soft internal light, Aina wondered which jewelry store it had come from, who had sold it to the store, whom June had bought it from . . . and then a black slate fell over her eyes.

22

"What—?" The world disappeared, and all Aina saw was blackness. Her fingers twitched toward her knives.

"Shh," Raurie whispered.

The vision descended into darkness, as if she were staring into a cavern lake with no chance of light reaching in.

Then it brightened and murky images formed: a long, narrow room with numerous small windows. But even though it was still daytime, the world outside those windows was dark and ominous. Rows of seats spread along the room with a strip of floor between them. A few dim yellow lights hung on the walls. Kouta sat in one of the seats, his neck still bandaged, gaze fixed on the windows as if he we were waiting for something. There was no sign of the guards he'd left Amethyst Hill with.

The scent of blood reached her nostrils. She sucked in air from the real world, which pulled her out of the vision like a fish on a hook.

In seconds, her own vision cleared, and Aina found herself in June Coste's home again.

"Are you okay, Aina?" came Teo's voice, tinged with concern. He sat right next to her, but the words seemed to come from miles away.

"What the hell was that?" she asked.

"The vision showed you where he is," June answered simply. "A long room with many seats and windows. Do you know of such a place?"

Aina shook her head. "No. Can it show us more? His surroundings, maybe?"

June shook her head slowly. "It will only show you exactly where the person you seek is at this moment, and nothing else. We have his blood, not the blood of the walls or the floor surrounding him. You may use the information you viewed through the Mothers' benefaction as you wish."

A moment of silence followed, and then Raurie spoke up. "My aunt doesn't like being involved in politics and murder."

Taking the hint, they stood to leave. June extinguished the candles, plunging the room into shadows.

After the vision and the blood in June Coste's house, everything about Teo's apartment seemed too bright and kind. Ynes prepared bowls of soup and cups of tea for the three of them and hummed while she stood at the stove.

"Thank you," Aina said when Teo handed her a cup of tea. "So, do you know anywhere like it? A long, dark room full of windows? It doesn't look like anything I've seen in the city before."

"Perhaps not in the city," Ryuu began, his eyes brightening, "but underneath it."

"What do you mean?"

"The room you saw was dark, even though there were windows." He nodded to Teo's kitchen window, where sunlight streamed in on Ynes and voices from the street filtered in. "But it's the middle of the day. Where else could that be but underground?"

He paused as if waiting for them to light up with the realization.

"Spit it out, then," Teo said after a few seconds.

"He's below, where the subway construction is happening. I have the blueprints of the system at my house. We can look at them and try to find my brother."

As he spoke, she recalled the giant tunnels, like burrowing holes for the gods beneath the earth. The metal structures of trains waited there, so big and strange, they even seemed to breathe. The tunnels might be underneath Kosín, the city she knew better than she knew anywhere else, but they were completely foreign to her. Like monsters waiting in the dark to devour her, they were poised to strike. Like Tannis with gold eyes peering through the darkness right before a fatal attack, or like Kohl at the other end of a gun.

Ryuu would help them get through the tunnels, but once she killed his brother, he would turn her over to the Diamond Guards with no remorse. He might not want to get comfortable taking lives, but once she betrayed him with his brother's blood on her hands, she suspected he would have no qualms filling her with bullets.

"I'll get them myself," she said to break the silence.

The less time I spend with you before killing you, the better, she added in her thoughts.

Hesitating was dangerous, and the more she got to know this Steel, the more likely she'd be to stall before drawing his blood. Besides, sneaking past Ryuu's guards and stealing his blueprints would give her the confidence she needed to return to those dark tunnels.

"But how will you get the blueprints?" he asked. "They're in the drawing room on the first floor, in a locked cabinet. The key is in my room."

"I've broken into your house multiple times, Ryuu. Don't doubt me now," she said with a wink. "If one of your servants sees you with me, your brother's attempted killer, they'll think I've kidnapped you or something and send for the Diamond Guards. I'll get the plans alone and meet you both back here."

"Be careful, Aina," Teo said as she stood. "More people want to kill you than usual."

One side of her mouth tilted upward in a smile. "They'll have to get in line."

23

After jumping over the fence into the backyard of Ryuu's mansion, Aina crouched behind a row of bushes and watched the side door. The bright afternoon sun made her eyes water, but she had to stay in this position. A maid was doing laundry, leaving through the side door while carrying clothes to hang on wires in the backyard. She'd just gone back in for more. While waiting for the maid to come out again, Aina withdrew her blowgun and loaded it with one of her few remaining paralyzing darts.

The door creaked open a minute later, and the maid exited carrying a load of sheets to hang. She moved toward the wire while humming, her back turned as Aina slipped by her and into the mansion. No one was in the laundry room, but when she entered the next hall on the first floor of the mansion, a servant was walking toward her. He stopped in his tracks, brow furrowed in suspicion.

"Excuse me, miss, do you—"

Her dart met his throat before he finished the sentence. She pushed him into a pantry, then made her way to the third floor, keeping her footsteps light on the staircase. If she was quick, she could get the blueprints and be gone in ten minutes, so she would do her best to only incapacitate rather than kill anyone who saw her.

There were fewer guards now with both brothers away from the house, and so the little security she saw was easy to pass by hiding in the shadows and waiting until the path ahead cleared. When she reached the third floor, she breathed more easily.

Since Ryuu wasn't here, there were no guards posted outside his room like there had been last time. The door opened with a creak. The room was the same as before, with granite flooring, the floor-to-ceiling windows, antique and lacquered furniture, and the chandelier that twinkled with golden light over the center of the room.

She searched a chest near the bookshelf for the key first, sifting through maps and drawings of buildings that Ryuu kept there. No luck. She moved to the nightstand near his bed. The first drawer contained only a notebook and pen, but the second drawer held a small set of gold keys, and next to it lay a photograph.

She picked it up, carefully as if it would fall apart in her fingers, then turned on the nearest lamp to get a closer look. The only photographs she'd ever seen before were printed in newspapers occasionally or on fake IDs she used like the ones for the cleaning company, but the technology was still new enough that it took her a moment to differentiate it from a painting.

There were no streaks of paint here, nor use of any colored pencil or charcoal. This was a real photograph, mostly yellowed, with the subjects of it captured in degradations of neutral colors. She immediately recognized the entrance hall of the mansion in the background. Four people stood staring into the camera, parents and two young boys.

Kouta was tall even as a child, his hair dark and long, his face narrower than his brother's. He had one arm around Ryuu's shoulders, and the two brothers leaned into each other with wide smiles. Ryuu was so young that, though she recognized his face, the happy expression he wore was foreign to her. His parents were still alive, and he hadn't yet discovered the burdens life would hand him. He looked no older than four or five here, the same age she'd been at the time of the war when violence leaked into the Stacks. At least then, she'd still had her parents for a few years to shield her from the worst of it.

As she returned the photograph to the drawer, something in its background caught her eye.

A small statue sat on a plinth in the entrance hall instead of the vase she'd seen when she and Teo had entered through that part of the mansion. It was a depiction of the Mothers, Kalaan and Isar, holding hands and staring down where instead of their feet, the sculptor had crafted clouds. It was a rendition she'd seen in other artwork, of the Mothers gazing with love at all the worlds and lives they'd created. His parents must have removed the statue when they decided to hide their faith, when tensions between Inosen and Steels began to grow.

She placed the photograph back into the drawer and let out a frustrated huff of air. She had no photographs or paintings of her parents. If she hadn't tried to erase their deaths from her mind by inhaling glue every day for years, maybe she would remember them more clearly, with or without a photo.

Ryuu had the luxury of his parents never fading from his memory because they were captured in a photo. But even so, they were still dead because of the war and the violence it spawned.

They had more in common in this, and their lonely childhoods, than she could have guessed before.

She picked up the set of keys and left the room. In a few minutes, she reached the first floor where, after having to hide in an alcove to avoid a pacing guard, and checking a few doors, she finally found the drawing room.

A large oak desk stood in the corner next to a standing clock. Cream-colored armchairs and sofas dotted the rest of the room, which ended in a broad fireplace. After searching for a few minutes, she found the cabinet underneath the desk. She tried a few of the keys and eventually got the right one to open the cabinet.

Rolled-up sheets of paper lay stacked on top of one another inside. She withdrew them and placed them under her arm, then relocked the cabinet and stood to leave.

When she opened the door a crack, she heard footsteps beyond it. Peering through, she saw a maid retreating down the hall.

The whole house was quiet now, and for the first time since tracking down Ryuu here, she wondered how many of his servants and guards were Inosen, and how many among them used magic. How many could he expect to harbor before someone finally caught him?

Being rich wouldn't protect him forever, as the hit on his brother proved. Shaking her head, she decided it wasn't her business what he did with his life. She'd be cutting him out of it soon enough. She shoved away her guilt at the thought and left the mansion through the back door once more.

24

As the setting sun painted a reddish-orange glow on the grimy white buildings of the Wings, Aina returned to the city with the subway blueprints held under her jacket. She watched the shadows of Kosín's streets as she neared Teo's apartment, avoiding the corners where she'd seen posters of her face hanging earlier. Though she'd made it all the way to Ryuu's house and back without getting caught, now that she was in the city, her senses were alerted to every movement. Each corner she turned, she expected a flash of blue hair and gold eyes before her throat was pinned through with a throwing star.

The moment she entered the apartment, she knew something was wrong. Ynes was the first person she saw, weathered hands clenching the blanket she rested under. Ryuu placed one hand on her shoulder in comfort. Raurie was there, sweat on her face and her breaths ragged as if she'd run here. Bruises covered her face and arms, bruises that hadn't been there a few hours ago.

"How did the Diamond Guards know it was us?" Teo asked Raurie, seated across from her at the table.

"Someone must have seen Aina go into my aunt's house and then tipped off the Diamond Guards. It was too risky; we shouldn't have . . ." Raurie let out a shaky breath, then said, "They came a few minutes after you left. They saw all of June's diamonds, and they caught me putting her knives away. It was obvious. At first they were going to take us"—she broke off, one hand trailing to a dark purple bruise on the side of her head—"but then they told my aunt they would let us go if she did a tracking spell to find Aina, since she's Bautix's priority right now. We used some of her blood that dripped on the floor during the spell. We had to, or they would have—"

"We know," Teo said, biting his lower lip. "You didn't have a choice."

"I knew Teo lived in the Wings, so I came here as soon they left, and Ryuu saw me from the window. My aunt went to a safe house for Inosen in the tunnels, and she'll get a message to my uncle to join her. She wanted me to go with them. They've kept me safe my whole life, and I would do anything for them, but I wasn't just going to hide underground and let you die. I had to come warn you, so you'd have a chance to get away. If someone had warned my parents, maybe . . ."

"So, the Diamond Guards will use magic when it's convenient for them," Aina scoffed. "Let me guess, they can use magic because they're good Diamond Guards who protect the Steels and any other use has to be punished. How long ago was this, Raurie?"

"They left less than thirty minutes ago. In the vision, my aunt saw you entering the city near the Wings. They could have followed you here. You all have to leave now."

Aina raced to the window. Holding her breath, she peered

around the edge. Her hands curled into fists at the sight of a group of Diamond Guards approaching the building, candle-light in windows flashing on the silver badges of their uniforms. Pedestrians scattered out of their way, then stood back to watch what would happen next. Aina jerked her head behind the window.

"There are ten Diamond Guards surrounding the apartment entrance," she said, her jaw clenching. "I'd fight them, but we're so close to finding Kouta, we can't risk getting thrown in jail. We need another way out. What about the roof?"

"There's no roof access," Teo said, shaking his head as he peered out of the window and to the building across from them. He turned to her, his eyes pleading. "You're the one they really want, so you need to get out, Aina. Scale the building. You're the only one of us who could manage that. Get out, and we'll deal with the guards."

"I'm not leaving you. They know I was here. The minute they see Raurie, they'll know she came here to warn us, and all of you will be shot or thrown in a cell. We need another way out."

"What about this?" Ryuu called over. He'd removed the knickknacks and cups of tea from the makeshift table, then lifted one of the two wooden planks that made it up. Carrying the plank over his shoulder, he brought it to the window and nodded to the building across from them, where a window was open. "Maybe we can't scale buildings, but we can lay this plank between our window and theirs. It should be long enough—"

A door slammed below and they all jumped. Heavy boot steps sounded on the floors below.

Teo's eyes flicked to Aina, his face paling. "No other choice." Then he glanced back at his mother, who gave him one resigned nod.

He laid one end of the plank on their windowsill, then allowed it to fall so the other end landed on the opposite window ledge with a loud clatter. They all cringed at the sound, but apartment doors were slamming open inside the building as the Diamond Guards searched and would block out the noise of their escape.

"You go first, Aina," Teo said, his hands shaking as he stepped away from the window. She never saw him so nervous, not even in shoot-outs.

"No, people who can't fight should go first," she said. "Your mother—"

"I'll go last with her. We'll slow everyone down if we go now. Raurie, Ryuu, get out of here," he called to them, his voice shaking slightly. She placed a hand on his shoulder to try to calm his nerves, but he jumped when the Diamond Guards' shouts increased in the hall outside. Their footsteps pounded up the stairs, reaching the second-floor landing and coming ever closer to the third.

Raurie went first, shaking as she crawled across the plank. Each passing second frayed Aina's nerves. Ryuu approached the windowsill next, and Teo handed him a gun that he took with a reluctant nod.

The moment Ryuu reached the other building and slipped through the window, Aina crawled onto the plank. It shook a little with her weight and the breeze blowing through the narrow space between buildings. She glanced over her shoulder once, but Teo waved at her to keep moving.

The wind swept her hair in front of her face, threatening to block her vision, but she pushed through and crossed to the other building as fast as she could.

"You're okay?" Ryuu asked as she climbed off the plank and

landed inside. An old man slept in an armchair, his snores breaking the tension in the room.

But before Aina could respond, Raurie let out a sharp cry, pointing to Teo's apartment across the alley.

Aina whipped around. The Diamond Guards had burst through the door and aimed their guns at Teo.

Aina nearly shouted at him to get across, one hand flicking to her knives to throw them into the Guards' throats. But Ryuu's hand clamped down on her mouth, and he pulled her behind the wall.

She pushed him off roughly, then peered around the edge of the window. Just then, Teo knocked down the plank in one smooth strike. It fell through the air with a sharp whistle and clattered to the ground below.

"Run!" Teo called over before he spun around and fired his gun at one of the Guards, trying to keep Ynes shielded behind him. The sleeping man jerked awake and yelled at them to get out of his apartment.

Ignoring him, Aina hissed, "Shoot them!" at Ryuu. She grabbed his hand that held the gun Teo had given him, but he jerked it back.

"Aina, we have to leave," he said in a low voice. "You're the one they want. They'll keep Teo alive as long as they can—"

A shot rang out. Raurie stifled a scream by biting down on her fist. The world screeched to a halt in front of Aina, and blood chilled in her veins.

Not Teo.

She looked out of the window. In the other apartment, Teo's mother lay on the floor, blood spilling from a wound on her head. Teo knelt, one hand cradling Ynes's head, the other arm wrenched behind his back by one of the Guards.

They forced him to his knees, tears coating his cheeks as he watched his mother bleed out. But as he tried to reach toward her again, the Guards jerked him away, handcuffing him and pinning him down.

Aina moved to grab the gun from Ryuu's grasp, but the moment she touched it, she flinched away as if the barrel itself would burn her fingers. All she saw was her own mother's head covered in blood, her father's chest riddled with holes, the gunman's face hidden by the metal he wielded. She couldn't move.

One of the Guards shouted, "She's in the building across!"

A shot fired at the window as Ryuu pulled her behind the wall again. The bullet slammed through the cheap plaster, missing her by inches, but she hardly blinked, hardly even breathed.

"We have to go," Ryuu said. Though his voice was steady and brave, his hands shook. One clenched the useless gun, the other held her. She peered around the edge of the window once more. Two Guards hauled Teo toward his door, away from his mother who bled on the floor. "Now!"

He pulled her toward the door, Raurie right behind them with the old man's shouts following. Aina looked back again, but another Guard raised his gun and fired. The bullet smashed into a clock on the wall next to the door. They fled, gunshots ringing in their ears.

25

They raced out of the apartment and in the opposite direction of Teo's building. Aina led the way through the narrow streets between the apartments that brought them out of the Wings and onto Lyra Avenue within minutes. Pushing through the evening crowd, they reached an alley next to a casino, near the storm drains set into the curb. Leaning against the wall, they paused to catch their breath. Evening gamblers gathered in front of them, waiting for the casino to open.

Fighting down the urge to run back and save Teo immediately, Aina scanned the crowd for a sign of any Diamond Guards chasing them. The red and silver lights from the casino flashed in her vision as she searched. Her chest tightened each time she recalled Teo's hands tied behind his back and how he was dragged away from his mother's body, all so Aina could get away. The image of her parents standing in front of her while bullets were fired at them seared through her thoughts.

"We have to save him somehow," Raurie said, her voice cracking as she spoke.

"Of course, we have to," Aina snapped. "I am not wasting another minute looking for Kouta until we get Teo away from the Diamond Guards. He saved our lives by staying behind. Now we have to save his."

She pushed away from the wall, ready to run to the Tower's prisons and massacre every guard who stood in her way.

"We know that, Aina," Ryuu said, placing a hand on her shoulder to hold her back like he had in the apartment. She jerked away, sending him a murderous glare, but he didn't step aside. As if he were making some kind of decision, he took a deep breath, then said, "But we won't be able to help him if we get killed in the effort. They want him alive to interrogate him about you, don't they? We have time. We can still save him and find Kouta, but charging after the Diamond Guards with a few knives is not smart, and you know it. That would only get you killed. We don't have time to figure out some elaborate, foolproof prison breakout, but I think I have a plan."

The thought of Teo being interrogated, and holding out on revealing any information, made her nauseous.

Because of her, his mother was dead, and now he was alone in his grief. She knew too well what that was like.

Her parents would have told her to take comfort from faith in the Mothers, but the Mothers hadn't done anything to stop them from being killed, and Aina didn't trust them to help Teo either. They had to help each other. They were all they had left in this world, and she couldn't let brashness and recklessness ruin that too.

And she had promised Ynes she would be there for him.

"So, what's your genius plan?" she asked Ryuu, trying to inject venom into her voice. It came out shaking instead.

"First, we need to get out of the open. Let's go to the mines. We can use the warehouses there to look at the blueprints."

The buildings seemed to grow taller on both sides, hard-packed concrete closing in as they neared the edge of the city. After crossing a bridge, they soon entered the forest, their footsteps and breath mixing with the sounds of birds chirping overhead. After a few miles, they stepped out of the forest into the light of the moons, and the Hirai Diamond Mine spread out in front of them.

Smuggling diamonds from here seemed so long ago, as if it were a part of someone else's life rather than her own. Even the fear of Kohl discovering her diamond sales had faded away completely, replaced by the fear that he'd kill her if she didn't get back to her job soon.

Ryuu led them to a small warehouse off to the side of the giant pit, about a half mile around its edge. On the way, Aina saw the supervisor she usually bought diamonds from.

Quickly, she tugged her scarf over her nose and mouth, so he wouldn't recognize her if he looked over. It had been stupid of her to let her face be seen in public, with the wanted posters hanging all over the city. Anyone could have seen her, from the fight with Tannis in the alley, to walking through the Stacks, to leaving June's house.

When they entered the warehouse, Ryuu pulled a string on a dusty light bulb. Fluorescent light flooded the cramped room. There were mostly boxes, tables, and chairs piled together. After stepping around the clutter, Aina spread out the blueprints on a table with free space.

There were so many numbers, measurements, and intricate drawings that she had no clue what she was looking at, but Ryuu traced his hand along the drawings without hesitation and muttered under his breath. He began to sketch in the margins of the blueprints, shading in details so quickly and clearly, it was obvious he was accustomed to this. For a moment, Aina wondered why he had so easily agreed to help her rescue Teo when his priority was to find his brother, but then decided not to question and risk him changing his mind.

She and Raurie stepped back to give him room to work. As Raurie sat carefully on the edge of a box and drew her shawl tighter around her shoulders, Aina searched the small room for anything that could work as a bandage. The blood from Tannis's throwing stars had mostly dried, but she couldn't risk any infection. After a few minutes of searching, she found alcohol to clean the wounds and a few workers' shirts that she tore strips of material from to bandage herself.

After, she perched on another box near Raurie. It struck her, then, how odd this was—Ryuu, someone who stood in the way of her goal, was helping her, while Kohl, the person she worked the most to impress, had abandoned her. Teo was in jail, and there was a one-hundred-thousand-kor price on her head. A week ago, she never could have imagined this scenario.

The steady scratch of Ryuu's pencil against the paper helped calm Aina's nerves at first, but the sight of stars gathering in the sky through the window put her on edge again.

Is he in chains? Is he being tortured?

Would they ever sit on a rooftop again, holding hands and speaking of things only they could understand together, their hearts beating as one? And what did it mean that she wanted to?

She tapped her fingers nervously on the windowsill, trying not to imagine every terrible thing the Diamond Guards would do to Teo if he withheld any information on her.

To distract herself, she cleared her throat and said to Raurie,

"You don't have to come with us, you know. It's dangerous. You saw what happened to Ynes just for being around us."

Raurie shifted uncomfortably, holding tightly to her shawl again. "It's more my fault than yours, isn't it? Aunt June and I agreed to do the tracking spell for the Diamond Guards."

"I'm the last person to judge you for doing what you had to do to survive," Aina said with a long sigh. "They would have killed you if you didn't do the spell. You shouldn't come with us just because you feel guilty."

"I'm not going with you because I feel guilty. Teo doesn't deserve to be in this mess, and I want to help him, but that's not completely the reason either. Let me ask you something, Aina. Did you have family or friends who died because of their beliefs?"

"My parents," Aina said instantly. "You said yours did too."

Raurie nodded. "Did your parents hide, or did they worship out in the streets where everyone could see?"

"Only in our home and at worship services underground."

"Then you know that hiding didn't help them."

Before Aina could reply, Ryuu cleared his throat and looked up from the blueprints.

"Here, a section of the subway tunnel abuts the lower corridors of the prison in the Tower," he said, tapping to a drawing he'd made. It was of a corridor juxtaposing the tunnels still under construction, with another sketch of a grate halfway down the corridor. "That's a ventilation shaft they installed recently. We can go through the vent into the prisons."

"So, there's an unlocked entrance from the prison into the subway system?" Aina asked. "I thought Steels were supposed to be smart."

"Not unlocked," Ryuu said with a smirk. "But unlockable. We can get explosives here to blow up the grate blocking the vent and enter the prison. Hardly anyone else even knows the subway tunnels are being built so close to the prison, so they won't see us coming until we're already there."

"But won't someone notice an explosion?" Raurie asked.

"Good observation," Ryuu said with a quick nod, "so we go now while construction is off for the night. In the morning, it'll start up again, and the noise from the drills will cover the sound of the explosion. We can't wait longer than tomorrow morning in any case. As soon as the clock in the Tower chimes noon, they'll start interrogations of any new, valuable prisoners. We'll break in at dawn and get Teo out before then."

"How are we going to get into the subway tunnels?" Aina asked.

"We could go through one of the old tunnels used for secret worship services," Raurie suggested. "The Steels think they managed to close them all up, but they haven't, and some of them run close to the new subway tunnels. I know of one that we can access through a sewer entrance."

They worked fast as night fell outside the windows, smuggling explosives and emergency flares into packs that Ryuu split between them. Aina made sure to grab extra weapons, as well as grappling hooks and rope. If she had time, she would have brewed a poison to use on the guards in the Tower, but every passing second might be a countdown to the end of Teo's life. There was no time for extra precautions.

Once both moons had risen high in the sky with midnight's approach, they set off.

Teo's words came back to her as they walked: *Decide what's important to you, and put your mind to it entirely.*

Aina was deviating from her plan to find Kouta in order to save Teo. She didn't know what to make of that, since looking after herself had always been her priority. Setting aside her own goals was anathema to every step she'd taken for years and made her feel like she was walking blindfolded on a tight-rope.

Tannis might kill Kouta before she could. Kohl might kill her for all her failures.

But none of it mattered if Teo died because of her. Nothing would matter, then.

26

In the shadow of the Tower of Steel, they walked quickly to the eastern shore of the Minos River. Under the gravel that fronted the river was the handle to a sewer opening, the country's sword-and-pickaxe seal engraved on the metal.

Ryuu pulled on the handle and lifted to reveal a black pit in the ground. Aina's shoulders tensed up at the sight. The moons' light failed to reach the bottom. She gestured for Ryuu and Raurie to go first, then stood alone, breathing in the cool night air for a moment to gather her composure before descending into the dark. The memory of her parents' bodies lying in the dark with only a thin strip of moonlight revealing them filled her thoughts.

She held her breath as she descended the ladder, double-checking her grip on the rungs each time she took a step farther down. By the time her feet reached solid ground, sweat coated the back of her neck and her hands shook. Ryuu lit one of the flares, flooding the tunnel with a circle of orange light, and they began to walk down the sliver of concrete running alongside the stream of water in the center.

Ryuu and Raurie kept up a conversation about their knowledge of the tunnels and the prison. Aina trailed behind them, trying not to imagine what the Diamond Guards might be doing to Teo right now.

They soon veered off the path, down a service tunnel with a concealed entrance to one of the passages the Inosen used. After another half hour of walking north, Raurie leading the way through twisting tunnels, the path widened ahead of them like the one they'd used to escape the shoot-out with the Jackals. But it seemed more stable, the construction closer to completion than the tunnels in the south of the city. The ceiling curved, dome-like, and rectangular pits were dug in the center with a half-completed rail track.

Their footsteps echoed as they traversed a narrow ledge running alongside the tracks. Doors lined the wall. Most were locked, but after a few minutes of trying different doors, Raurie grabbed the handle of one and managed to pull it open.

With bated breath, they entered the new corridor. Aina coughed on the dust and the stale air of the narrow hall. The only lights apart from Ryuu's flare were flashing dots on electric panels set in the walls. Fuel tanks stood behind shining silver grates.

"Here," Ryuu whispered a few minutes later.

They slowed to a stop under a wide, circular ventilation shaft in the ceiling, which was covered with a steel grate. Aina gulped at the sight.

The vent extended upward with no sign of light reaching down. It stared at them like the mouth of a giant snake that would eat them alive were it not for the metal blocking it.

Ryuu had mentioned a ladder, but she considered that an exaggeration on his part. The ladder was merely handholds dug into the wall that led upward beyond the grate. A section of the grate was made to slide away for maintenance in the vent, but it was currently locked with a heavy iron bolt.

"We should have about five hours before construction starts again," he said.

Aina and Raurie lit candles to create a small circle of light, and Ryuu extinguished his flare. Aina sat close to the light. Water dripped somewhere nearby, the sound like a ticking clock counting down the time until it was too late to save Teo. The thought made her chest clench painfully and her breath shorten. She wished they'd had time to come up with a backup plan—a Blade never worked without one, after all—but they'd had to work with the little preparation time they'd had.

She was veering off course by choosing to rescue Teo instead, and was working with Ryuu, someone she should have killed the first night she'd met him. Everything about this situation went against what Kohl had taught her. But he'd left her to die, so she had to do the best she could to fix that. For a moment, she felt completely out of place here. She imagined how Kohl would forgive her once this mess was resolved.

After a brief silence, Raurie spoke, breaking into her reverie. "Did you know the entire seventh, eighth, and ninth floors of this prison are all Inosen inmates? Three whole floors to try to hold us in. It's an odd feeling to willingly be breaking into the prison most Inosen try to avoid."

Aina laughed a little. "I never thought I'd be doing this either."

"I wonder what King Verrain would say if he knew the Steels were building tunnels and trains right next to his old Tower."

"Maybe he could have negotiated with them on it." Aina shrugged. "He could have avoided a war if he negotiated instead of just attacking the Steels' factories."

"I'm rather happy I was a child, then," Raurie said, wrinkling her nose. "Most of my memories of the war have faded away, but sometimes they come back."

"You said your parents died in the war too," Ryuu said. "Were they Inosen?"

"It was a few years after the war, actually. And yes, they were. They helped build some of the underground worship centers in and around the city. They even went to the mass graves and found the bodies of some Inosen they'd known. They burned those they could find and put their ashes in the cellar of an old worship center near there, but then they got caught and killed. My aunt and uncle and I might have tried fleeing to Marin, where my great-grandparents immigrated from, but June thinks she's needed more here, and I agree. It's a risk, but . . . people die in this city every day no matter what their religion is, and Inosen die whether we hide or not. If your life is at risk no matter what, then you have a choice of either hiding or doing something about it. I'm done with hiding and saving myself while other people suffer. I'll die one day anyway, so until then, I'm going to take freedom where I can, and I'm not going to hide what I believe."

Aina went silent after Raurie spoke, thinking of her own parents. They'd known death stalked them at every corner in the violent years during and after the war, so they'd done what they'd wanted anyway by following their faith.

"What do you think your lives would be like if Verrain had never shut down the factories?" Raurie asked after a pause. "If there had been some kind of truce between magic and technology?"

"Well, my parents would still be alive," Ryuu said. "If it were still legal to sell diamonds for magic, then we would have been able to keep building our fortune that way. That's what we did before the war. Now, most of our business comes from selling diamonds as jewels."

"I'd use your diamonds, then, to design and sell jewelry," Raurie said, lifting the sleeve of her shawl to reveal a hand-made beaded bracelet she must have made.

"I'd probably be a baker," Aina said wistfully.

Both Ryuu and Raurie laughed.

"What? Make little cakes all day?" Ryuu asked. "The Bloody Baker. That's my new nickname for you."

They all laughed, the sound echoing a little in the tunnel surrounding them and making the night less frightening as time went on. For a moment, if she forgot where they were and what they were about to do, she could imagine they were all normal eighteen year olds, who could talk and laugh together without fear plaguing them at every step.

"My mother used to make flower cakes once a week," Aina said, her voice softening. "We'd pick these edible white flowers in the fields outside Kosín and put them on little cakes. I haven't really eaten any since she died, though."

Her voice tapered off at the end, and she sensed Ryuu's eyes on the side of her face. She should have known better. Picking flowers in a field and eating them was something poor people did. Ryuu had probably had private chefs since birth.

"That sounds delicious," he said, while pulling out dried meat from his pack.

She watched his face for some sign of pity, but he wore a simple, kind smile as he held out the food to her. Raurie took the meat from him, then warmed it on a stick above the flames.

Ryuu held out the food to Aina, but she shook her head. She couldn't eat if Teo might be going the night without any food.

"Don't you ever eat anything?" Ryuu asked.

She shrugged, but then her stomach growled and gave her away. Reluctantly, she took the food from him and chewed slowly while staring into the flames.

She wished she could count down the time it took for the candles to burn to nothing, but that would only fray her nerves to stubs. She needed some other way to distract herself from thinking about Teo alone in one of those cells.

After they finished eating and Raurie fell asleep, her shawl pulled up to her chin, Ryuu said in a low voice, "Sometimes I can't even remember my parents' voices. Sometimes I'm jealous that Kouta was older, so he has more memories of them than I do."

A dull pain ached in Aina's heart when he said that. Maybe Ryuu had a photograph, but he had been younger than her when his parents died. Inhaling glue every day had leeched away many of her memories, but she still knew more about her parents than he did. Maybe he needed that picture in his nightstand. She recalled how serious Kouta had looked when she'd spied on him, how every time she'd seen him, he was working away at something. So different from his broad smile in the photograph.

"Your brother . . . He really took over your parents' business when he was ten?"

"He had help, but yes. He became very good at running the business—selling tools, mining diamonds—and always made sure our workers were treated fairly. We would have lost everything if he hadn't put on a brave face and taken over. Whenever it got overwhelming, he would shut himself in the library and devour book after book. I remember once, when I was six, it was the first anniversary of our parents' death. Kouta was working all day, probably to avoid thinking about it, but I think he heard me crying. I was alone. He asked a maid to bring me sweets, and a while later, he came down and read me my favorite stories until I fell asleep."

His eyes brightened a little at the memory. "When I got older, he told me he wanted me to pick my own path in life instead of feeling obligated to work for our parents' business like he'd had to do. But I've always loved drawing and designing, so I began to sit in on meetings whenever the city consulted us on construction or ordered large shipments of tools. I've apprenticed with architects before too. That's how I got access to these blueprints. Do you see why I have to help Kouta? My brother's the strongest person I know. When he was still a child, he had to learn how to run a business, start investigating our parents' deaths, and he kept me out of it so I could have more freedom in my life than he did. He'd go through hell to save me if our positions were reversed. Now it's my turn to do the same for him, no matter the risks."

"So, then . . ." Aina began, unable to hold back the question anymore. "Why did you agree to break out Teo with me? I thought you'd insist on finding your brother first."

He gazed off into the tunnel, the candlelight shining on his dark hair as he thought. "Teo has been helping us, and he's in this situation because of this job. Besides that, he's a good person and doesn't deserve this fate. I can tell he means a lot to you, and I know how it feels to almost lose someone important to you."

He gave her a pointed look, then, and guilt at how she still intended to kill his brother wormed through her. But while Ryuu's words were admirable, she still found it hard to believe he was helping her. She couldn't really trust him while their goals were so different. Yet here she was with a Steel who stood in the way of her job, and he was helping her break Teo out of prison. If she still worked for Kohl, would he help her break out Teo like Ryuu was now? She wasn't sure if she wanted to know the answer.

"So, what happened to you after your parents died?" he asked. "How did you end up as an assassin?"

"Well, the next night after they were killed, I saw people carry their bodies away from across the street. They moved in and made it their house. I was eight, I didn't know how to tell them to leave, and I didn't really want to be there either. So after that first night, I slept in alleys, on sidewalks, on fire escapes. Anywhere that people might leave me alone."

He swallowed hard and avoided her gaze. "Did they? Leave you alone, I mean? It's kind of surprising—"

"That no one kidnapped me? Yes, I was surprised too. Some tried. Others tried to jump me into their gang. But they mostly left me alone. They figured I would waste away to nothing anyway. How could I work for anyone if I was too high to stand without falling over? So, you had your money, your bodyguards, your mansion, and your brother's company after your parents died. I had the streets, glue, and the fact that I was too scared to stay in the house with my parents and die like they did." She paused and took a deep breath before adding, in a bitter tone, "My cowardice kept me alive."

Her hand moved toward her nose and mouth as if expecting to find traces of glue there.

Ryuu shook his head slowly. "I wish the city didn't allow orphans to suffer like that. Who knows what your life would be like if you had more opportunities? You still have a chance to do good in the world, Aina. You're not a lost cause."

"When did I call myself a lost cause?" she snapped, anger at his assumption rising through her. "What was I supposed to do when I was twelve years old and starving, and the Blood King walked up to me with a job? You're not going to make me feel bad about being an assassin, Ryuu, because that is what I am. I went from less than twenty kors in my pocket to fifty thousand in savings. I know that's probably what you spend in a day to maintain your backyard, but to me, it's a damn load of money, and I'm proud of it, however I got it. Even though my boss took it all back." She let out a frustrated huff of air, then asked, "What did you do to earn your money? Be born?"

Suddenly the little fortune she'd prided herself on seemed pathetic. No amount of money would erase the addictions, the crimes, the murders, and the fact that Kohl now considered her worth less than dirt. But what more was there to yearn for? Her throat closed up when she realized she didn't have an answer. Teo's words, telling her to decide what was important to her and put her mind to it entirely, rang through her mind again. She'd always thought she had a clear answer to that, but with Teo gone, and Ryuu telling her to do something else with her life, her future took on a blurry, confusing quality.

"I don't imagine your life was easy growing up," Ryuu said, ignoring the calls on his own character. "But you're smart. I'm sure you could do anything you put your mind to. Now that you're older, can't you find something else? Can't you reach higher?"

"Because it would mean I'm not a failure. If I can open my own tradehouse, it means I did the best work with the little that I was given. Don't take that away from me by telling me that I can reach higher, that the sky is the limit. My sky and yours are not the same. Let me touch my own sky."

After a pause, he said, "You're right. You do that a lot, you know? You always make me see your side of things. I hope you can see mine too. To you, my brother is the reason you lost your job and the reason your life is threatened by the people you used to work for. So, I guess I'm trying to say that I'm grateful you chose to work for me instead. I'm sorry the sketch I gave to the Sentinel helped make it easier for people to find you. I'm sorry you have to be afraid."

Her stomach squirmed uneasily as his words faded away. Kouta was a good person who had continued his parents' tradition of helping Inosen, and his only crime was trying to find the truth behind their murder. But Kohl had ordered her to kill him. If she succeeded, she would get everything she'd ever wanted. If she failed, she'd die at Kohl's hand. She would accomplish this job no matter what.

But she could no longer kill Ryuu simply because it was what Kohl would do. After all the help he'd been in rescuing Teo, she just couldn't. Maybe he was rubbing off on her.

She didn't belong in Ryuu's world. She belonged in her own, where there was no strife with Kohl and where she could walk freely through the city and know she was safe. Only killing Kouta would fix it all and return her to where she was supposed to be. And it would return Ryuu to living far above—and indifferent to—her. Nothing Ryuu said would change her mind on that. Not even the warmth of his eyes or the way he smiled in her direction would sway her. Those were the things she wanted Kohl to give her once she fixed this.

Despite that, there remained a simmering tension between them as silence descended in the tunnel. Their shoulders touched, connecting them. He smelled like the forest after a spring rain. Without meaning to, she found herself leaning closer, hoping he wouldn't move. She glanced at him out of the corner of her eye and caught him looking at her.

Her heart pounded, and between the beats, she told herself over and over that Ryuu wasn't Kohl. Ryuu wasn't the person who'd given her a way off the streets and a chance to reach for more than what she'd been given.

She shoved aside the doubts and steadied her breaths to fall asleep. She looked away from Ryuu and closed her eyes, but didn't move her shoulder away.

Tomorrow they'd break into the Tower's prison and free Teo, and then go back to searching for Kouta with the threats of Kohl, Tannis, and the Sentinel's reward for her capture hanging over them.

But for a few hours, she could pretend they were the same in their loss and loneliness, and that this warmth between them would persist even after they found his brother. For tonight, at least, that warmth would drive away the darkness surrounding them.

A loud, intrusive sound woke Aina after only a few hours of sleep. For a moment, she was back in the alley, Kohl's fist slamming into her skull with a jolting thud.

But the noise was just a drill being used in the subway tunnels parallel to this corridor. Raurie had already stood and put away their candles as Ryuu rose. He withdrew from his pack a paper bag carefully taped closed. With a small knife, he cut the tape and unrolled the paper to reveal a handful of black sticks tied together. A long black string hung out from the end of them and unfurled as he held up the dynamite.

"We need to tie this to the grate," he said, tilting his head back to look at the wide grate blocking off the vent. "There's a thin rope in Raurie's pack we can use for that. When I light the string with a match, it'll burn up, giving us enough time to get away before it blows. The construction should cover the noise."

"I'll do it," Aina said in as brave a voice as she could manage, but the drills and the shouting from the subway tunnel nearly drowned out her voice. Squaring her shoulders, she approached the handholds in the wall and stared up into the ventilation shaft.

She hated the darkness. People could sneak up on you in the dark and snuff out your life with the press of a trigger. She preferred to navigate Kosín by the grit of its streets and the height of its roofs than the depths of its shadows. Now she had to crawl into the darkness above, deep into the ventilation shaft and into the prison cells that she'd tried to avoid since she was a child.

Noticing she'd frozen in place, Ryuu tapped her shoulder. "Are you okay? I can do it instead."

"I'm fine," she said in a slightly high-pitched voice.

In her memories, she heard her father's gruff voice as he told her to be strong, that the lightning flashing across a gray sky was hope in darkness, that there was no need to hide from a coming storm because the harder it raged, the closer it was to moving away.

She'd faced plenty of dark places before, and she would face all of them at once if it meant saving Teo.

Ryuu handed her the dynamite and Raurie gave her a short length of rope. She gritted her teeth and climbed up, using the handholds and footholds cut into the wall.

With one hand, she slipped the rope through the openings in the metal grate, then fastened the ends of the rope tightly around the pack of the explosives.

Once she reached the ground again, she and Raurie stepped back while Ryuu struck a match. The flame glowed bright orange in the dimly lit tunnel. He placed the flame to the end of the string. It sizzled and crackled, traveling fast up the string toward the dynamite. They ran back down the hall and around a corner.

As soon as they took cover, the dynamite exploded. The sound crashed through the corridor like thunder. She winced and clenched her hand around the edge of the wall, expecting someone to come running at any moment. But the sound of the explosion blended so well with the ever-present thrum of drills in the tunnels beyond that no one else listening would be able to differentiate them.

When silence fell once more, they walked back to the site of the explosion, ears ringing, and stared up into the ventilation shaft. The metal grate had been obliterated, bits and pieces of its shattered frame strewn across the floor. Some of its foundation was still lodged into the wall, but they'd be able to move around it.

"You know," she said to Ryuu with a small smile, "when you said you would open doors for me, this wasn't what I had in mind."

He smiled back at her. "Ready?"

She nodded and climbed first, with Ryuu and Raurie following at a steady pace. She brushed away a few cobwebs that got in the way, hoping no spiders would appear, or else she'd probably panic and fall right off the ladder. Thankfully, none did, and she reached the top of the ventilation shaft in one piece.

Once all three of them climbed over and into a new corridor, they proceeded with the light of one flickering, white bulb halfway down. Fifty feet away, more light poured through a small window set near the top of a door. Aina placed a finger to her lips, then gestured for them to follow her to the door.

She'd heard how the Tower's prison held ten stories of cells in the central pod, with only two of the floors above ground. It was rumored to be dark enough that after one day, you craved the sun, and after a week, you forgot what the sun felt like. It made her wonder once more how Kohl had managed to get out after his boss's betrayal had landed him in prison. After all, no prisoner was allowed outside for even a minute unless General Bautix himself allowed it. Families scrounged together whatever kors they could, or took out loans from gangs, to try to bribe Bautix into releasing their loved one. Once a year, he freed a prisoner, just often enough to keep families' hopes high and their wallets open.

They reached the door. Standing on her toes to peer through it, Aina looked out into the prison for the first time and couldn't help the shudder that stole through her.

They were on the fourth level. Six stories extended above, but their heights disappeared from the view out of the small window. The three floors below were visible but mostly hidden in shadows with dim orange lights hung at intervals between cells. This center of the prison was set in a square fashion, with four walls of cells facing each other. A narrow walkway lined the four walls.

From her position, she saw the edge of the walkway beyond her door, then twenty feet of empty space separating them from the opposite wall. Staircases were set in two of the corners, and a few doors leading to other parts of the prison were at the other corners.

No guards were visible, but footsteps sounded nearby beyond her line of sight. Though there was minimal lighting on each floor, a pair of floodlights shone down from above, high-lighting parts of the prison structure. She watched for a few minutes, noticing the lights moved in a random pattern, but that they changed roughly every three to five seconds.

"Nothing but to go for it," she whispered to the other two as the footsteps faded away. Fear flashed through Ryuu's eyes for the briefest second, but he smothered it and tightened his grip around the handle of Teo's gun. Raurie's expression was unreadable, but judging by the sharp dagger she'd withdrawn from her pack, she was ready to fight.

Without wasting another word, Aina pulled open the door and stepped onto the walkway.

A sharp intake of breath to her left. She spun, but Ryuu had already grabbed the Diamond Guard who stood next to the door. He slammed the guard into the wall of the corridor they'd just left and placed Teo's gun to the back of the man's head.

"Someone gag him," he hissed while fighting to keep the guard in place.

Raurie worked quickly, as if this weren't the first time she'd ever made a gag in her life. She tightened the cloth in the guard's mouth and around his head. Aina peered around the door again, checking the ends of the walkway where it turned the corner and curved along the other three walls of the prison structure. In seconds, Raurie had finished tying ropes tightly around the guard's hands and feet.

"There are a few guards posted along the walkway between cell doors," Aina whispered to the others. "If we're quiet, we should be able to sneak along without being seen. But if those floodlights land on us, we're as good as dead."

"Sounds just as risky as any other day with you," Ryuu said.

She glanced at him sharply, about to retort, but then noticed the slight upturn of his lips.

Leading the way, Aina measured her breath in time with her steps to stay calm. As soon as the two bright floodlights whipped their beams in a different direction, she moved, in that split second between each change. With a steady rhythm, they made their way across the narrow balcony, past darkened cell doors, and reached the shadowed corner.

Peering over the balcony as they went, Aina noticed something shining far below, a crystalline surface in the prison's courtyard with several guards walking across it. It offered a shred of light in the prison's overwhelming darkness.

Noticing her gaze, Ryuu whispered, "Do you see the courtyard floor? It's made out of rough diamonds confiscated from magic users during the war. There's thousands of diamonds under that glass floor. The Tower has a lot of floors like this, but General Bautix insisted on keeping one here too, to remind inmates why so many of them are here."

Aina's first thought was how much money she could get for selling all those diamonds, but then the floodlight positions switched, and a bright circle illuminated the cell door inches from where she crouched. Jerking away, she nearly bumped into Ryuu, who grabbed her shoulder to pull her back from the light.

The lights switched again. They continued along the next wall, Aina trying to calm her nerves. Though this was the only way to proceed, she still hated being in the dark. Her throat began to close, and her breaths turned shallow like she was inhaling glue again, but she kept going.

Halfway down the balcony, she paused, then beckoned Ryuu and Raurie closer.

"Two guards are there. See them together near the door at the corner?" When they nodded, she took a dagger from inside her jacket. "I'll be right back."

Leading the way, Aina measured her breath in time with her steps to stay calm. As soon as the two bright floodlights whipped their beams in a different direction, she moved in that split second between each change. With a steady rhythm, they made their way across the narrow balcony, past darkened cell doors, and reached the shadowed corner

28

Before they could try to stop her, she continued down the walkway, keeping her footsteps quiet. The guards faced away from her, chatting casually, but as she approached, one of them stopped talking. He turned and raised his gun when she stepped out into the center of the balcony.

"Stop where you are!" he said, then blew on his whistle sharply.

Leaping out of the way, she threw a knife into the man's throat at the same time that he fired the gun. She slammed into the railing of the walkway, inches from sliding off to fall two stories down. Her heart pounded in her chest. The bullet had banged into the bars of a cell.

The inmate inside yelled out, and other prisoners rushed to the doors of their cells to see what was happening, all of them shouting out taunts to the guards. The floodlight shifted and landed near her. She scrambled away from it and clung to the edge of the balcony.

The other guard lifted his gun. The light moved again. In the chaos of the shouting prisoners, footsteps rushing nearby and whistles blaring above, Raurie had sneaked up behind the second guard and stopped him in place with her dagger at his throat.

In seconds, Aina retrieved her knife from the other guard's body and took Raurie's position, allowing Raurie to bind his hands.

"Thanks," she whispered as Raurie finished and stood back with Ryuu.

"I grew up in the Stacks," Raurie said, her hands trembling a little, but her voice steady. "Cowering and letting other people do the hard work are not among the skills you learn there."

Aina pressed the tip of her dagger into the guard's flesh, making him gulp. "Lead me to Teo Matgan's cell," she whispered. "He was brought in last night to be interrogated. Utter a sound or take us to the wrong place, and I will rip your throat apart. Move."

He nodded at a door near the corner. Ryuu opened it, peered inside to make sure no guards were waiting there, and waved for the others to follow. As they slipped inside, guards ran down the staircases lining the center of the prison, missing them by moments as the door swung shut behind them. They ran down two flights of stairs to the second lowest level of the prison.

The guard nodded at the door on the second-floor landing. Aina gestured at Ryuu to check outside it. Holding his gun ahead of him like a shield, he peered through the door, then gestured for them to follow.

They exited the stairwell two levels above the diamond floor of the courtyard. Shouts from guards running to the sounds of the gunshot returned in full force, but most were from above, where they'd left the body of the other guard. This floor was now empty except for the cells.

"Go," she hissed as the guard hesitated, making a small nick on his jaw with her knife. He winced, then moved.

Ryuu and Raurie walked slightly behind them to watch for any guards who might come their way. With Aina forcing the guard forward every few feet, they soon reached the cell.

Her chest tightened as Aina took in Teo through the bars, his wrists shackled to the prison wall behind him. His hair had fallen in front of his eyes and the top half of his face. Cuts and bruises lined his jaw and shoulders.

She elbowed the guard hard in the back. He glanced down to his belt, where a set of keys was attached. She unclipped the keys and rifled through them until he nodded at the correct one. The cell door creaked open inward after she inserted and turned the key.

Her grip tightened around the handle of her knife. Every instinct in her body told her to slice through this guard's neck so he would never speak.

She'd made too many mistakes, hesitating before kills, letting people like Kouta and Tannis get away. Kohl's voice shouted in her head, telling her to never waste a single moment. An unsteady breath left her, and she watched the hair rise on the back of the guard's neck as he trembled in her grip. He knew what was coming next.

But she also heard Kohl telling her to be judicial in her kills. Only the target mattered.

Assassins were a means to an end, a way to avoid massacres in a city where blood was so valued. Fury could never get the best of her. Neither could revenge or fear.

Frustration prickled through her at the thought. She could kill this man, or not. Either way, Kohl's voice was the one telling her what to do. No matter what she did, her actions followed Kohl's will somehow. She bit her lip so hard, she tasted blood.

Without another thought, she knocked out the guard with a slam of the hilt of her knife to his temple. He dropped to the ground, and she stepped into the cell.

The guards had only had Teo for half a day, but blood matted his hair and face, with dark bruises underneath. Gulping, she began unlocking him from his chains.

"Why are you here?" he asked in a harsh rumble of a voice.

"We came to join you. Prison's more fun with friends, don't you think?"

When the chains came loose, he pushed away from her, back into the wall.

"Teo, it's me!" she hissed, holding up her hands.

"Get away from me," he said in a ragged voice.

She stepped back immediately, her heart clenching in her chest. After a few seconds, Teo pushed the hair from his face. His hand came away bloody.

She squeezed her eyes shut for a brief second, trying to calm the anger that swept through her. If Teo had been a Steel, they would never do this to him. If he'd had Ryuu's privilege, he could get away with so much more than simply helping a fugitive escape.

"We're getting you out of here."

"I said, 'get away,'" he hissed, and for a second, she thought he was going to lunge at her. But while he looked too weak to even swing a fist, his eyes were fierce and full of hatred—a venomous look directed at her.

The sight of it made her nauseous, made her wish she was anywhere other than here. But she deserved his anger. She was the reason his mother was dead.

When she next spoke, the words tasted like bitter poison in

her mouth. "When we get out of here, you can hate me as much as you want. But if you don't get up now, I'll drag you out."

"What is the point?" he asked, turning his head so she could hardly see his face.

"Please," she said, reaching out to help him stand, but he lifted his arm to block her from coming any closer.

"I can walk," he spat out as he used his other hand to help push himself up the wall, knees shaking.

Fighting the urge to raise an eyebrow, she gave him distance, but stayed close enough to help if he needed it. They left the cell to rejoin Ryuu and Raurie on the walkway. Both of them instantly moved toward Teo, but he shook them off.

"I'm fine," he insisted. "If you help me too much, we won't get out of here at all. What's the plan?"

"No idea," Aina said. "Ryuu, could any of these other corridors lead to the subway tunnels again?"

He gave a half shrug, half nod. "They might, but if we have to blow up another vent, the sound of the explosion could draw the guards toward us. They're on the lookout for intruders now."

"Then how about we use an explosion to draw them away?" Aina whispered, her gaze moving up the walls of the prison that twisted narrower and narrower like a bottleneck the farther up they went.

Whistles still blared, but the most activity was on the floor they'd come from. Both floodlights were trained on that floor, so everywhere else was left in darkness. Prisoners were still shouting, taunting the guards and each other, their voices echoing and causing even more confusion. The prisoners on this floor had gathered at the doors of their cells, shouting for her to free them too, but their voices soon blended in with the din.

"Ryuu, give me the rest of the dynamite. You three head back to where we entered the prison. I'll make a distraction to lead the guards somewhere else."

"I'll stay with you," Ryuu said as he withdrew another set of dynamite and a pack of matches.

"Sorry, this distraction is a one-woman job."

She took the explosives and the matches, then waved him toward the stairwell with Raurie and Teo. He looked back once, like he was considering staying with her, but she shook her head and mouthed at him to hurry.

Once they disappeared, she ran down the hall and turned the corner until she was certain she stood exactly two floors underneath the door where they'd first entered the central prison. If she failed at this, at least she wouldn't have to worry about prison. She'd likely be dead.

Counting in her head the time it would take the others to reach the fourth floor, she tied the pack of dynamite to the railing of the walkway. She struck the match. The flame touched the wire.

Her breath came in quick, shallow intakes as she pulled out the grappling hook from her pack and threw it upward. In her head, she said a quick prayer to the Mothers that it would land, the first prayer she'd thought since her parents' death.

Maybe the Mothers listened, or maybe all those times she'd thrown knives at people's throats had really sharpened her aim, since the grappling hook latched itself onto the edge of the walkway two floors above.

Footsteps sounded behind her. She shifted as the light did, leaving her in darkness as an arm wrapped around her throat and the tip of a gun met her back.

She spun out of their grasp, her neck twisting dangerously.

Dropping, she rolled out of the way. As she came to her feet, the Diamond Guard she'd knocked out earlier faced her.

At the sight of the bruise on his head where she'd hit him, she smirked. He blew into his whistle to call for backup, the shrill sound making her hair stand up on the back of her neck. Before he could do anything else, she lunged forward, ripped the whistle out of his mouth, and wrapped her arm around his neck to put him to sleep.

But he twisted to escape her grasp. Footsteps pounded on the walkways above; guards responding to his whistle. He stepped back to the railing, then raised his gun and aimed at her.

The shot pinged off the bars behind her, making her grit her teeth as she pivoted away. From the corner of her eye, she saw the flame she'd lit under the dynamite draw closer to its mark. Was she imagining it or could she already smell the smoke?

Dodging the guard's next bullet, she jumped onto the grappling hook's rope and climbed as fast as she could.

The rope rocked wildly, nearly dislodging her. Looking down, she cursed. The guard had jumped onto the rope too, and climbed toward her just as the flame struck the dynamite.

The explosion went off, sound shattered around her. She froze, ears ringing, her muscles bunching up as she clung to the rope. The booms echoed off the walls of the prison, grating against the guards' shouts to each other and their footsteps pounding down the stairs—down, away from the fourth floor, where Teo, Ryuu, and Raurie were meant to escape. At least that part of the plan had worked.

The force of the explosion had rattled the hinges of the walkway and the next two above, if their sudden shaking and bucking was an indicator. The balcony her grappling hook hung to swayed dangerously. Her pulse pounded as loud as the explosion, but she forced herself up the rope. If she didn't reach the balcony before it collapsed, she'd fall two stories to the diamond courtyard below.

But as she climbed, the rope swung again, making her legs and arms clench around it as if the rope alone could save her. It wouldn't support the weight of both her and the guard for long. Kohl's voice rang through her mind, telling her to do whatever needed to be done. She'd already failed one job. She couldn't fail this one too.

When the guard was a foot below her, climbing hand over hand at a rapid pace, she let him reach up to try to grab her ankle—and then slammed her steel-toed boot into his face.

He slid, losing several feet before catching himself on the rope, making it sway drastically once more. Shouts rose up around them from guards and prisoners. A gunshot, probably fired in her direction, pinged off a wall. There was no choice but to get rid of the guard now.

She slid down, hissing as the rope burned her hands.

He tried to shift out of the way, probably expecting her to kick again, but this time she reached into her boot with one hand, grabbed a dagger, and sliced through the back of his hand. He let go of the rope, his screams joining the din as he fell toward the courtyard below.

She turned back to the rope, her back and neck clenched with tension, but while she didn't watch the guard's body slam onto the courtyard floor, she heard it. She imagined Kohl nodding in approval.

Resuming her climb, she reached the edge of the fourth-floor balcony just as it swayed.

Teo, Ryuu, and Raurie raced along the walkway, their weight

shaking it even more. Raurie flung open the door to the corridor, and Ryuu followed her inside.

For a moment, she feared Teo would run after them without looking back for her.

But then he reached over the railing, grabbed the rope of Aina's grappling hook with both hands, and hauled her up as the walkway lurched one final time.

They jumped into the safety of the corridor at the last second, Aina letting the grappling hook fall along with the walkway.

As they sped down the corridor, they heard the walkway crash against the diamond floor of the courtyard. The sound reverberated so loudly, Aina failed to hear Ryuu shout something. He gestured for them to follow him.

They raced down the hall and reached the vent in the floor. Aina went last, her hands flying over the holds in the wall until she landed in the hallway below. They ran for it, back toward the main tunnel of the subway, and slammed shut the door to the corridor.

Since it was only midmorning, construction was still underway with workers gathered around the platform. A few glanced over at their sudden appearance.

Ryuu took a deep breath and called over, "Just doing a quick site inspection. Continue working."

They nodded and turned back to their work, while Aina, Teo, Ryuu, and Raurie walked as casually as they could manage, as if they hadn't just collapsed multiple floors of the prison.

"You can go home after this," Aina whispered to Teo as they walked. "I don't want you getting hurt any more because of me."

He kept walking as if he hadn't heard her. Fear hit her,

almost as strongly as her fear of Kohl coming to kill her if she messed up the Kouta job again.

But unlike with Kohl, she couldn't simply kill Kouta and make things better.

She didn't know how to fix this, how not to lose Teo, and the idea that she might fail at this hurt more than any punch or threat Kohl had sent her way.

29

While a nurse took care of Teo's injuries, Aina waited
in a first-floor study room of Ryuu's mansion, so that the nurse
wouldn't see her and recognize her from the posters around
the city. She held a pack of ice to the back of her neck, which
ached after the guard had twisted it.

Teo's face loomed in her thoughts, in the cell when he'd
told her to get away from him, and on the balcony when for a
moment, she was terrified he would let her fall to her death.
He'd come back for her, but he also hadn't said a word to her
on the entire way back to Ryuu's mansion.

A steadily falling rain painted the Hirai gardens a nearly
black color and pattered against the floor-to-ceiling window
she stood in front of. In her parents' home growing up, there
was no glass on the windows, and rain only meant floods. The
Dom grew chilly when it rained, as there was barely any insu-
lation in its old walls. The cold usually kept her senses sharp,
but right now, she preferred the warmth.

An hour after escaping the prisons, they'd reached Ryuu's house just as the rain began to fall. Before going inside, he had his guards clear out the first floor so no one would recognize Aina or Teo, and reassured her they wouldn't disobey the order. Then he'd had a nurse called in from the city to tend to Teo and had sent two servants to retrieve Teo's mother's body. But when they returned, they reported that the body had already been removed.

Though Aina had seen plenty of bodies thrown on the barges to be taken to the mass graves outside the city, this was the first one since her parents' deaths that sent a chill through her. Teo never even had the chance to say goodbye.

She knew that nothing could have saved Ynes's life once the bullet met her brain, but part of her was convinced that if Ynes were rich, she might have been spared. At least she would have been buried in the cemetery behind Amethyst Hill, which was reserved only for the wealthiest corpses. She recalled Ynes's smile, how she'd always welcomed Aina to their house with a cup of tea while Aina recovered from injuries or spent time with Teo, how she'd treated Aina like a daughter, and how she'd pleaded with Aina to always be there for her son.

She'd always thought the fact that she was a child had been the reason she'd been unable to help her parents, but Teo hadn't been able to save his mother either, even with all his skills. Perhaps she'd placed too much blame on herself.

But if they both were truly powerless to save the ones they loved, then what hope was left at all? She pressed her nails into her arms, afraid to meet her own eyes in the window reflection.

The door creaked open. By the light tread of his footsteps, she could tell it was Ryuu before his reflection even appeared in the window next to hers. A beat of silence passed. She kept her gaze forward, not meeting his eyes as he turned to face her.

"The nurse is almost done tending to Teo," he finally said. "His injuries are mostly superficial, so he'll recover after a night of sleep. It'll be safe here; Amethyst Hill is the last place the Diamond Guards would think to look for either of you. I'm glad we got him out of there today, though. Any longer and he would have faced a real interrogation."

She nodded, not knowing how to voice her real thoughts. If Teo hated her now, and he'd been interrogated, would he have given up everything he knew about her crimes?

Instead, she changed the subject to something she did understand. "You were good back there. You acted like you break into prisons and beat up guards every day."

Ryuu let out a small laugh, one of his hands tapping an uneven rhythm on the windowpane. "You underestimate me, don't you?"

A smile tugged at her lips. "Not as much as I did when we first met."

"I understand that. Being brave is . . . something I'm trying to learn. After my parents died, we were afraid every day. Kouta hardly let me leave the house, he was so worried for me. And he fully invested himself in his work to get away from it all. After he told me how our parents really died, I was afraid to walk down the street because I thought I would get shot for having the name Hirai. Being a Steel didn't keep my parents safe."

"And then you learned how to fight back," she said quietly. In their reflections, she noticed their hands, hanging at their sides, were just a few inches apart. If she shifted slightly, they'd be touching.

"I realized the fear itself was worse than the thing I feared."

His other hand trailed to the handle of the gun Teo had given him before getting arrested. "I refused to let fear and not knowing how to defend myself force me into hiding. Force me to stop living my life. My brother has protected me his whole life, even when he was scared too. It's my turn now, even if it's terrifying." He cleared his throat and looked away from her before adding, "That's why it's good to have you on my side. I don't feel as scared knowing I have an actual assassin helping me."

See, Kohl? I'm still a useful Blade.

As if he'd noticed their proximity too, his hand moved slightly—close enough that they touched for a few brief seconds—and then dropped away again. Maybe he thought of her as a cold-hearted killer, but he didn't know how similar they were, how she felt like a coward too, and how often she tried to convince herself she wasn't helpless.

Yet, just last night, he'd tried to convince her she might be something more than a Blade. He'd told her to reach higher. But what would she even reach for, when the only thing she could do now was try not to be killed?

She still had to kill his brother, and it would end this new connection between them. The way his eyes darted to her face in the window reflection, how her cheeks burned with the hint of his gaze, and how the few inches separating them seemed to be charged with electricity, would all screech to a halt once Kouta stopped breathing by her blade.

"So, after Teo recovers, we'll get back to the job," Ryuu said, watching her through their reflections.

She nodded. "We'll find your brother."

"Do you want to go see Teo now?"

She nodded again and followed him to a lounge. She expected to find Teo resting, but he was already sitting up on a divan, with much less bandaging than she'd expected. Raurie sat in a chair across from him, holding a cup of tea.

"You look much better," Aina said, sitting on the arm of Raurie's chair and folding her hands in her lap.

"You don't need to talk to me like I'm fragile, you know," he said with a weak smile, but the movement pulled at some stitches on his jaw. She winced at the sight, wishing she could help him, but fearing he'd push her away again.

"Teo, I'm sorry," she said, and let out a relieved sigh when he finally met her eyes. "It's my fault your mother—"

"No, Aina, it's not." He shook his head, but stopped quickly, as if it was painful. "You could say it's your fault, or mine, Ryuu's, Raurie's. But I wasn't thinking right, when I put it all on you. More than us, you know who's to blame? The Steels. The Diamond Guards are the ones who killed my mother, and they did it because Bautix puts them up to it. They don't care if my mother committed a crime or not. To them, she's just someone who got in the way." His voice turned to a fierce whisper. "I'm not letting my mother's death be in vain. We're going to show these bastard Steels they can't do whatever they want to us. That they can't villainize every person who isn't like them. I'm not going to sit on the sidelines anymore while others die for daring to have a little freedom."

A chill swept through her, half-empowering and half-cold with the possibility that he was willing to start a new war. The idea of standing up against the Steels seemed like certain death. She agreed the situation was unfair, but she'd never considered actually doing something about it. How could she, when she'd spent her whole life simply trying to survive the unfairness?

You have to decide what's important to you, and put your mind to it entirely. His words came back once more. Teo had always seemed so steadfast in his sole goal of protecting his mother, so much so that she feared he might forget about himself. But now that he was alone, he envisioned some new purpose, and it was something she couldn't imagine for herself yet—perhaps not ever.

But maybe Teo just needed assurance from her, for now. He'd given her all of his dedication. He deserved some of hers.

"We will," she said, in a voice so quiet, she wasn't sure if anyone heard her.

"I agree," Raurie suddenly said, the certainty in her voice breaking the silence. "My whole family suffered because of them. I can't be afraid of them anymore. If I want to honor my parents who died for their religion, and my aunt who risks her life every day to help anyone who comes to her, then I need to stand up instead of hide."

"I know a good place to start," Ryuu said from where he leaned against a bookshelf. "We find my brother and figure out what he learned about our parents' deaths."

"You're right, let's start there," Aina agreed. *This* was something she could focus on; something that wasn't confusing. "We should all rest tonight, though. Is there a room available for Raurie?"

He nodded. "Of course. I'll have guest rooms set up for you both."

But she was already shaking her head. "I'll be fine here."

Once she and Teo were alone, she moved to sit next to him. The room grew so quiet, she heard each press of her fingers on the divan as she placed her hands down.

"I still feel like it's my fault . . ."

"I've always agreed to help with this job," he interrupted, shaking his head. "I meant what I said about wanting to fight the Steels, but we'll finish this job first. I'm not going to let your life continue to be in danger when I can do something about it. I said I'll be there for you, and I always will be."

She opened her mouth again to argue, but he reached over and pulled her into a hug before she could say anything else. When he pulled away, she wiped away the tears that had built up, and saw that he did the same.

"Ryuu tried to pay me for helping him, though, saying I'd done enough," Teo said in a strained voice, then nodded toward the bookcase. "When he went to get you, I stuffed the money between the books on the middle shelf so he can find it later. I don't want to take his money for this."

She nodded as he spoke, guilt twisting her stomach into knots. "I don't want to either. I'm only pretending to want it so he doesn't doubt me. I don't want to hurt him, but I need to do this job. And once I start working for Kohl again, neither of us will have to worry about money."

Lowering his voice, Teo said, "I know you have to finish the job so you'll be safe, but I want you to get away from Kohl. If the job doesn't go as planned, end him before he comes after you. He's the one who got you into this mess."

She shivered involuntarily and sat up straight, pushing her hair out of her face with shaking fingers. It was easy for Teo to sit there and tell her to write Kohl off, but if anything, these last days had proved how much she needed him. Between the Jackals and the Diamond Guards, it seemed everyone in the city was after her now that she lacked Kohl's protection. She had to get it back and return to the life she knew, the life that was safe for her. She had to kill Kouta.

"I heard some things while I was being processed in the prison," Teo said. "Did you know people still talk about Kohl's escape even though he's been out for more than a decade? They all disagree on how he did it, but whatever he did, it must have been good. How else would he get away with everything he does?"

"He has a lot of bribes," Aina said with a shrug. "A lot of friends, a lot of people he threatens. He seems to conflate the two."

They both laughed, then, and Aina was grateful to have him back. He and Kohl were so different to her. She and Teo had always been friends, and she would never want to risk losing that. Occasionally, though, she wondered if there was more between them. But something still held her back from seeing him the way she saw Kohl.

Teo had saved her life more than once, as she had in return, but he had first met her when she was already strong. She'd constantly proved herself to him even if she needed help sometimes. She'd spent so long building up an invincible image of herself that she was frightened to show him more of her vulnerable side.

But Kohl had seen potential in her when she was nothing and no one, and he'd saved her then. Perhaps Teo might have done the same, or maybe his eyes would have passed over her, nothing special, like they did every day when they walked past people sleeping on the street.

Until he saw her starving, homeless, and desperate, and decided she was still worth saving, she would never know.

Aina fell asleep within the hour on the armchair, her bones weary with exhaustion. A clock ticked somewhere, the sound reminding her of the one on the desk in Kohl's office. She woke up a few times throughout the night, certain she was at the Dom and that Kohl would kill her for daring to return. She shook off the nightmares as well as she could, but they returned every time she closed her eyes.

In the middle of the night, she woke with a start—another

nightmare that flitted from her mind the moment her eyes opened in the mansion's dark room. Something soft and warm covered her. It was a blanket that smelled like Ryuu's forest scent. She pulled it tighter around herself and fell asleep.

When she woke in the morning, her neck was stiff, but she was well-rested. Opening her eyes and sitting up straight, the blanket slipped off her shoulders and fell to the floor.

The door creaked as Ryuu opened it and entered carrying a tray with cups of tea. He brought Aina a cup with a warm smile, and she murmured thanks, hoping he caught on that she also meant gratitude for the blanket.

Once Teo was awake and Raurie had come downstairs, they waited for a nurse to check on Teo. While the nurse looked him over, Aina stood in the corner of the room, careful to put up her hood and shield the lower half of her face with her scarf.

"You should rest for another day," the nurse muttered while removing his bandages. "Don't want to overexert yourself."

But as she left, the door clicking shut softly behind her, Teo said, "I've rested enough."

"Are you sure?" Aina asked.

He met her eyes once, then turned away with a slight blush rising up the back of his neck, as if he were embarrassed.

"If I'm working, I'm not thinking about my mother."

"You're right. We should get back to the job." Avoiding Ryuu's gaze, she locked eyes with Teo so he would know the real job she meant. Killing Kouta while using his brother's money to do it.

Ryuu walked to the side of the room and retrieved a large, rolled-up poster from between two bookshelves. Bringing it over, he unrolled it on the floor and placed a few books at the edges to hold it down.

It was a map of Kosín, drawn in charcoal and filled in with

colored paint. The edges of the map were green smudges of forests and fields. The Minos River was a white-blue ring around the city with tributaries winding their way north and west. The Stacks were inked in gray and brown, little detail given to it except for main roads, bridges, and docks. The north and the Center had clearer buildings and landmarks, especially Rose Court. Amethyst Hill was in the northeast corner of the map, each mansion given specific detail down to the color of the paint on the outer walls.

Aina couldn't help but scoff. Even in mapmaking, the rich neighborhoods got more resources.

Ryuu pointed near the Tower's top-center position. "This is where we went to find you, Teo. There was a train yard near there and also here," he continued, pointing to the west of the city where the black market was located amid the warehouses. "But we didn't see Kouta in either of those places. If he's in one of the trains, like the vision showed, then there's one last train yard he could be." He tapped a southern corner of the map, easily able to pinpoint the location even without many details inked in.

Aina and Teo locked eyes. She would recognize that part of the city on any map.

"Can't go there," she said in a stiff voice. "That's Jackal territory. They might still be recovering from our fight, but if I walk right onto their streets, that's a death sentence. Without Kohl's protection, they can do whatever they want to me, like we saw in the market."

With a frown, Raurie asked, "What if we made our way there underground instead?"

"Is there another way?" Aina asked quietly. Going underground meant returning to the darkness, and though she'd have to do it to get to her target eventually, she wasn't eager to return to the tunnels any sooner than she had to.

"Not if you want to avoid the Jackals' territory," Raurie said. "We can go through the sewers from anywhere in the city and come underneath their territory to reach the train yard, instead of going above ground where they'd catch you. The sewers are one level down from the subway tunnels."

"They cross under the tunnels here," Ryuu said, pointing at the map, "and there's a maintenance shaft we can use to go up to the train yard where Kouta should be."

"It's a good plan," she said, trying to push away the fear, "but we need more supplies. Smoke bombs, poison darts, knives, grappling hooks, flares."

"I need guns too," Teo said. "Lost all my weapons when they arrested me. We can go to the black market to stock up. And in case anyone forgot, we just broke out of prison. More people will be looking for us. Did any of the guards see you clearly?"

"One did," Ryuu said, biting his lip. "But I don't think he knew who I was. We'll have to stay out of the open, though, since they'll recognize you or Aina."

Aina nodded. "Let's get to work."

30

The cool morning air helped Aina's senses stay sharp as they weaved west through the seedier parts of the steel mills, warehouses, and textile factories, away from where the Diamond Guards usually patrolled and far from any posters of her face.

A steady rain fell as they walked, leaving the sky a deep gray. Aina's eyes trailed to the people who slept on the sides of roads, remembering how difficult it was to survive whenever the streets were covered in snow or flooded with rain.

Now, she drew her jacket closer as if to remind herself she'd slept in a warm house last night. But the fear that she'd end up on the streets again never left.

Her eyes kept flicking to Ryuu. Each time, she had to push down the growing sense of guilt she felt for still planning to kill his brother. It had been easy, over the past few years, to always shove aside morals where her job was concerned and to become the Blade she needed to be. All she had to do was remember Kohl's words the night after her first kill.

She'd been fifteen. She'd thought Kohl had sent her on the assignment without any backup or supervision, but after the deed was done, she'd left the house of the first body to die at her hands and stepped into the alley behind it to find Kohl standing there, peering into the window.

"What?" she asked, digging her hands into her pockets. Despite the early winter bite in the air, she was still sweating and breathing hard. "You didn't think I could do it?"

She cursed herself at how much her voice shook. Though Kohl stood in front of her, sharp eyes examining her, all she saw in her mind's eye was the man who'd bled out under her knife. She wished Kohl would do something other than stand there. Maybe hold her or tell her she did a good job. Or at least take her to get a drink so she could forget what she'd done.

"I follow everyone on their first few jobs," he said with a shrug. "You wouldn't be here now if I didn't think you could do it. I'm just making sure you did it right."

Leaning against the wall, she let out a nervous laugh. "Sure, I can put a knife through someone, but is there really a right way to do it? I'll do the jobs, Kohl, but after three years here, I still can't be convinced there's any *right* way."

She'd spoken in a rush and had to take a moment to control her frantic breathing. Her eyes flicked to his face to gauge his reaction; she'd called him Kohl out loud for the first time. It was an unspoken but obvious rule in the Dom that all the young recruits called him "boss," or "Blood King." She'd heard the older employees call him by his name and began to imagine the day she could as well. His face was unreadable, but at least he didn't seem angry.

"I can tell you one way you're screwing up." When she raised an eyebrow, he continued, "You're standing right outside the murder scene, laughing and debating morals about the body I can see through this window. Let's go somewhere else."

In minutes, they returned to the Dom, and Kohl led the way to the armory without speaking. Once inside, he sat at the small wooden table in the middle of the room and began cleaning one of his pistols. Aina leaned between two racks of blades and placed her hands flat on the wall behind her to stop their shaking.

What if her target had children and they found his body first? Nausea rose through her at the thought.

"It's hard to . . ." She took a deep breath. "My own parents were shot, Kohl. How can I be someone who takes away other people's parents, their children, their friends? I know I agreed to the job, but—"

"Why would you blame the person who pulled the trigger? Blame the person who told them to do it." He looked up at her from his task and swept his eyes over her incredulous face. "Here's an easier way to think about it. Imagine you fall in love, and then one day you find out your handsome prince starts—"

"Prince or princess," she muttered as a blush climbed up her cheeks. To avoid looking at him, she tilted her head up and stared at the walls of weapons circling them, each glimmering silver under the weak winter sun shining through a window near the ceiling.

"Right," Kohl continued, "so, your charming prince or princess starts sleeping with someone else who doesn't even know that your sweetheart is in a relationship. Which of them do you think deserves your scorn?"

After a short pause, she said, "The person who cheated on me."

"Exactly. So why would you blame the hired gun? Blame the person who bought the bullets and told the gun where to point. If there's any lesson of mine that you remember, Aina, remember this: You are not a person behind your weapon. You are simply the blade itself. Do not make the mistake of thinking you're anything more important."

Her eyes snapped to him, but he'd already turned back to his cleaning.

"Is that how you live with it?" she whispered, wondering how much it weighed on his shoulders to give his employees these jobs—if at all. "The guilt?"

"It's not how I live with it." He placed his gun down with a clink of metal on wood. "That's simply the way it is."

She nodded slowly, tapping her fingers against the wall as she tried to embody his words. Maybe he'd taken her to the armory on purpose, to be among all the scythes, axes, daggers. Blades, like her. The image of the man bleeding out in front of her had faded a little. Distraction was good—from glue, from the lives she'd take. Distraction was what she needed.

"So, who was the first person you killed?" she asked. When he frowned at her, she said, "What? That's not a normal topic of conversation for people like us?"

"Do you mean my first kill on purpose," he began, "or by accident?"

"Either. They both end the same."

For a long moment, she thought he wasn't going to reply. Then he'd stood from the bench and walked toward her. Her breath had caught as he approached and leaned on the wall next to her, still holding his gun and running a finger over the shiny barrel.

He stood so close, but his eyes were averted from her.

Whenever he did look at her, she felt a sense of being examined, like she was one of his guns.

Was that all he would see her as? He was six years older than her, infinitely more accomplished, and she was just another grunt he'd picked up off the streets. What else could he ever want with someone like her?

Finally, as the silence grew suffocating, he spoke. "Remember what I told you the other day? How my old boss sold me out to the Vultures when he wanted to cut off his loose ends and get out of the city."

When she nodded, her eyes flicking to his vulture tattoo, he said, "Before I went to meet him that night, I thought I'd better get some extra money so my parents and I could start a new life once we broke them out of prison. So, I got a few friends together and sent them to break into one of the Amethyst Hill mansions. They'd all get a cut, so of course they went. When I went to the Tower to meet my boss, and found out he double-crossed me, I thought maybe I could get out of it by telling the Diamond Guards about the robbery. Surely if they knew one of the Steels' mansions was about to get robbed, they'd let a kid like me go?"

After a pause, Aina said, "They didn't."

"See, you're smarter now than I was then," he said, turning to her with a small smile. "They threw me in a cell and caught my friends too."

"I bet your friends weren't happy about that."

"Not at all. One of them was a Milana girl named Clara. You sort of look alike, actually. She hated me the most after they all got caught. A few months in, they all cornered me and started kicking and punching me. I fought back, and in it all, I . . . I pushed Clara. She fell off the balcony into the prison courtyard from six stories up."

Aina let the words sink in, imagined a girl who looked like her bleeding out on a prison floor. "So, what about her? No one told you to kill her. Do you blame yourself for her death?"

Instead of answering, he'd reached over and tucked a strand of hair behind her ear, his hand hot on her skin.

"Keep doing a good job like you did today," he'd said, making her beam with pride, until he added, "Unless you want to end up like her."

Kohl's lessons were easy enough to remember. But now, her gaze still drifted to Ryuu walking ahead of her in the rain, and her heart clenched once more.

When they finally reached it, the storage building was dark, with a chill that seeped into Aina's bones. Rain still lashed the windows in a steady torrent. Water leaked from the holes in the ceiling, and rats skittered across their path, but at least it was dry in here.

Down the stairs and through a musty corridor, they came to the door leading into the black market. Aina slid a few coins through the slot, spoke the password, and stood back as someone opened the door. With a quick nod to the greeter, they passed smoke rings and blown-glass sculptures on their way to the back corner of the market. Even this early, people still gathered to trade goods and secrets.

While Ryuu purchased their supplies with Teo's help, Aina stood off to the side near a large quilt spread on the floor where people smoked from tall, colored-glass tubes. The different scents of smoke reached her: peppermint, black licorice, pomegranate, coconut. The smoke covered her a little, making her feel safe and hidden.

She caught Teo's eye while Ryuu slid some kors to a vendor. He smiled, but it didn't reach his eyes. Maybe he was beginning to feel the same guilt she was for continuing to betray Ryuu.

Raurie, who stood a few feet away, nodded toward the corner of the market where she usually worked. "You know how I've been buying smuggled liquor here for the past eight years? I started when I was a kid. But it's still not enough. It's never enough. They want us to stay poor."

"Of course, they do," Aina said in a flat voice. "How else would the Steels stay rich? They wouldn't be elite anymore if we were all on the same level."

Raurie crossed her arms and tilted her head to the side. The light from an orange blown-glass sculpture highlighted the brown skin of her cheeks.

"I don't know about you, but I'm tired of playing by their rules. They'll try to put us down no matter what we do, so what choice do we have but to fight back? Teo has the right idea, you know."

Aina paused, wondering if she should tell Raurie what she and Teo really intended to do once they found Kouta, but decided not to—the less people who knew the full plan, the better.

But she knew that Teo would still want to fight the Steels even after helping her with this job, so Raurie might not be alone in her goals after all.

"I admire you, Raurie," Aina finally said. "Your parents were killed for their beliefs, yet you're still faithful to the Mothers, and you're ready to fight for what you believe in. I've always looked after myself first."

"Well, I still had my aunt and uncle to take care of me, didn't I?" Raurie asked. "You had no one, so surviving was the only thing you could do. Besides, I'm not really someone to admire. It took Ynes's death for me to really start thinking bigger than myself. I'm glad my aunt and uncle are in hiding, somewhere they'll be safe, like I've always wanted them to be. Now, I can try to do something my parents would be proud of. I can try to make a difference, and I think we're on the right path to doing that."

Aina struggled to think of a reply, slightly unsettled by how easily Raurie voiced her faults and her plans for the future. Maybe her faith helped her see so clearly, and maybe that was something Aina had lost after her parents' death. Was there something wrong with her for not being anywhere near as sure of herself?

She was saved from having to answer when Ryuu and Teo walked over with packs of newly purchased supplies and weapons for all of them. She took hers from Ryuu without meeting his eyes.

They set off toward the south of Kosín under the pouring rain. A half hour later, as the hill began to dip down into the clustered homes of the Stacks, they stepped into an alley. There was a bar next door, packed with people even though it was barely noon. Aina shivered in the cold as Teo bent down next to a storm drain. He used a wrench from his pack to pull up a manhole covering the entrance to the sewers. It lifted, and he went first, descending a ladder into the darkness.

Aina lit her flare before even touching the ladder, unwilling to take her chances in the dark. Covering her mouth to block the wretched scent, she followed Ryuu down the ladder with the flare tucked under her arm.

They walked along a pathway parallel to the central flow of

the sewer water, Ryuu leading with Aina's flare lighting the way. The rushing water was the only sound, apart from their footsteps and the scurries of rats passing by the edge of their vision.

She almost sensed the change in the air as they walked deeper under Jackal territory, as if they might notice her presence through the heavy earth packed above them and come down to end her. Her hair stood on the back of her neck every step farther they took.

"Down here," Ryuu said as they turned a corner.

She moved closer to him, lifting her flare to bathe the path ahead in reddish-orange light.

Something scuttled in the new tunnel ahead, the sound of many legs scraping across metal.

Aina shifted the light of her flare, then gasped and jumped back so quickly, a jolt of pain went through her sore neck.

Giant, cottony webs as large as blankets draped the tunnel ahead. Falling in curtains of intricate designs, many were empty, but others were not. One web nearby held a body inside, stiff and mummified in the tight white grip of the silk. The dead creature had a long tail, short legs, and a diamond-like face.

"Is that a cat?" Teo asked incredulously, stepping closer to it in the small circle of light.

She wanted to yell at him to come back, to get away from those webs, but her voice refused to come out.

"That's the work of cave spiders," Ryuu said in an awestruck whisper. "They're from the mountains, but they started coming to the city when we built the tunnels. They're as big as wolves."

"No, I'm done." Aina turned around, one hand gripping her flare and the other finding her knife. "I'll take my chances with the Jackals."

"Come on," Teo said with a teasing smile, holding out his arm to stop her from leaving. "You think I can't handle a little spider? We can do this, Aina."

"They're not little!" she said. When he smirked at her, she sighed and turned back around. "Fine. But I'm not cutting the webs down. That's your job."

Ryuu and Raurie walked ahead, but before Teo could join them, Aina stopped him by placing a hand on his shoulder.

"Try to keep Raurie out of any fighting we do," she whispered. "She shouldn't be in danger because of us."

He nodded, then moved to join Ryuu and Raurie in hacking at the webs that blocked their path. Aina cringed away from each one, wondering where the spiders had gone. Probably to hunt.

She held the light between the others as they worked their way through the tunnel, the floor of which grew steadily wetter. Each spider web was so large, they could wrap around her and swallow her whole if she got close enough.

After what felt like hours, Ryuu stopped in front of a rusted ladder leading up to a door set in the tunnel ceiling. About halfway up the wall was the outlet of a storm drain, with the piping system covered by a grate. Water poured through it in a steady stream to pool around their shoes and flow down a depression in the floor.

Craning his neck to look up, Ryuu said, "That will lead to the subway tunnels."

The air was humid and putrid, making her hair stick to her face as they climbed. She wrinkled her nose and pushed onward, simply glad to be leaving the tunnels with the spiderwebs.

Maybe she hadn't encountered any spiders, but she'd gotten through their webs unscathed, and she hadn't run away from the dark enclosure of the sewers. She tightened her grip around the ladder rungs and ascended, feeling bolder than before. Light shone through small air holes in the door above, illuminating the thick clouds of dust from all the construction in the tunnels.

When they were nearly twenty feet above the sewer floor, the sound of the rushing water picked up, stronger and faster.

Ryuu froze above her and Raurie, then called down, "I don't think that's a good sound."

Aina cringed against the ladder as water flooded through the grate above in torrents on its way down to the sewers. She covered her mouth and nose with her sleeve, but the water still soaked her head and clothes. She tightened her grip on the ladder rungs, but already, her hands were slipping under the falling water.

They kept climbing, pausing to wipe their wet hands on their clothes every few feet, but soon they were completely soaked, and there was no use.

As they neared the top of the ladder, Aina lifted her hand to push hair out of her eyes.

Then a scream sounded from above. Aina immediately clung to the ladder, her only thought that one of the giant spiders must have found them and was clawing its way down to devour them.

But when she glanced up, she saw that Raurie's foot had slipped. The water continued to pour down, and when Raurie tried to get a better grip on the ladder, she fell.

For the briefest moment, Aina hesitated, frozen on the ladder. As long as she clung to the ladder, she could avoid the darkness of the tunnel surrounding them.

But at the last moment, she moved. She reached out and

latched onto Raurie's wrist, both their hands lost in the shadows. She cried out as the weight nearly pulled her arm out of its socket, but she used the momentum to swing Raurie back toward the ladder where she could grab onto it. She was suddenly grateful Kohl had made her practice scaling buildings one-handed, or else she and Raurie both would have fallen twenty feet to the sewer floor.

As Teo helped Raurie resettle herself on the ladder rungs below, Aina's hands shook so badly, she nearly lost her grip.

She rubbed her now sore shoulder and looked upward again, letting the rainwater hit her face. Then, her eyes moved to the darkness on both sides.

Her parents believed life was precious, and for once, she'd saved someone instead of doomed them. A twinge of pride worked through her at the thought, and some of her fear ebbed away.

Ryuu had reached the top of the ladder. He shook the wet hair out of his face, then pushed open the door that would lead into the subway tunnels.

She was almost there, one step closer to killing Kouta and getting her life back under control.

Ryuu held out his hand to help her when she reached the top of the ladder. Taking his hand, some of her sense of triumph faded.

"Almost there," he said with a small smile as he pulled her over the lip of the door into the new tunnel. Somehow, even after they'd been drenched in rain water, he still smelled like a forest.

Giving him an awkward nod, she turned to help Raurie and Teo up the final rung and over to solid ground.

She couldn't let Ryuu's kindness deter her. Steels like Ryuu always said they would help you—then they gave you a job and got you killed while doing it. She refused to let this rich boy with a heart change her mind or do the same to her.

But he's not just a rich boy with a heart, she told herself. *He's been hurt by this city nearly as much as me.*

He helped me rescue Teo when he could have insisted on abandoning him.

He laid a blanket on me while I slept.

And he believed she would have been a good person if she'd had another childhood, when she'd never seen the point in wondering that herself.

As they sat to catch their breath, shivering in soaking clothes and in the cold air of the new tunnel, she remembered the promise she'd made to herself and to kids like her years ago.

She would rise up. She would prove that good things could happen to girls like her, girls from nothing. For all the children who froze on Kosín's streets at night in the rain and snow, who didn't have a mansion, servants, and an older brother to protect them while they mourned.

She'd never allow a Steel to take that goal from her, no matter how kind they proved they could be.

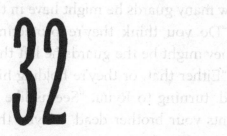

32

After walking half a mile through the subway tunnel, a new cavern opened ahead.

The train yard spread away in front of them. Hundreds of train cars gathered in clusters, some sitting far back near the curving edge of the cavern where they were shrouded in shadows.

This place was similar to the train yard near the Tower, but without the noise of construction. No platforms had been built here yet. For a few minutes, they stood at the edge of the cavern and searched for some sign of Ryuu's brother.

"That one has lights on inside," Aina said after a minute, pointing through a gap in the train cars ahead.

Golden light poured through the windows of one train nestled in the center of all the others. It was composed of three cars, each one lit up. Other train cars were poised around it like scattered dominoes.

Raurie took a step forward, but Aina put a hand on her

shoulder and leaned close to whisper, "There are guards around it, see? It's hard to tell with all the other cars in the way, but I think I see three. Maybe more behind the train. The vision only showed him sitting alone in the car. It didn't show how many guards he might have in the surrounding area."

"Do you think they're protecting him?" Teo whispered. "They might be the guards he left the mansion with."

"Either that, or they're holding him against his will," Aina said, turning to Ryuu. "Seems like someone powerful really wants your brother dead. Maybe they brought him here for some reason."

"I don't know," Ryuu said, squinting at the guards with an uncomfortable expression on his face. "We should be careful. I can't tell from here if I recognize these guards or not."

"So, our best chance to get to him . . ." she began, drawing out her voice to prolong the time until she betrayed him, "is to take them out."

But Ryuu was still peering ahead at the guards. He took a couple steps forward, frowning.

"I'll take the three in front of the train," Teo said, already pulling out his gun.

"Wait." Aina pulled out the blow guns they'd purchased at the black market, along with some paralyzing darts, and distributed them.

One step left to convince Ryuu she was on his side.

"If they really are holding him against his will, then we can keep them alive with these instead of killing them outright. You'll want to ask the guards questions in that case, right?" she asked Ryuu, who nodded. "Good. You three go to the front. I'll head to the back."

"Wait," Ryuu said, placing a hand on her shoulder to stop

her. "Why would you go alone? You don't know how many guards are back there. I'll go with you."

She shrugged off his hand and rolled her eyes. "If you think I need your help, Ryuu, you clearly don't know me very well. You two go with Teo. I'll stand my best chance fighting alone instead of worrying about you getting in the way. Wait for my signal."

The words tasted bitter on her tongue, but they made him stop insisting. She had to go alone. Killing Kouta was her job, not Teo's or Raurie's, and she wouldn't let them face the blame for it.

The only thing she could do for Ryuu at this point, as she was about to kill his brother, was prevent him from witnessing it.

He opened his mouth to say something, and she stopped in place, half hoping he would hold her back. A tense silence passed before she remembered why she was here: the job of a lifetime, regaining Kohl's protection. Ryuu and his brother were the reason she'd lost it all.

She held a finger to her lips. Her eyes flicked to meet his as she walked away, hoping she projected a silent apology in them.

Maybe she watched him for a second too long.

Maybe he noticed a change in her features, or maybe he realized how she'd avoided meeting his gaze ever since they'd left the Tower's prisons and now that she had, she'd given herself away.

Or maybe he'd been planning to do this all along.

"Help!" he shouted to the guards standing around the train. "They've come to kill him!"

The guards responded immediately as Ryuu sprinted into

their view. At the same moment, Teo pushed Raurie out of the line of fire. Bullets flew, and Aina rolled to the side behind another train that ran perpendicular to the one Kouta must be inside.

She scraped her hands and knees bloody rolling on the rocky ground, but got to her feet immediately once she reached cover behind the train. She ran down its length, peering through windows as she went. Her pulse pounded in time with the shots being fired, but she couldn't tell who was being hit.

As she reached the end of the car and crouched there, she caught sight of two guards who'd taken up posts behind the train.

All of Kohl's lessons ran through her mind. Speed, decisiveness, and skill were what she needed. She would become a weapon, take out the target, and reap the reward. Her guilt and doubt melted away, leaving her as the Blade she should be.

With quick, practiced motions, she took out both guards with her blowgun one after the other.

Then she darted out into the space between the cars, checking the fight ahead quickly to see that Teo and Raurie were still standing, then disappeared behind the train.

Boots crunched into the rock behind her and she flung herself to the side. A bullet pinged off the train exactly where her head had been.

The guard who'd fired the shot stepped out of the cavern's shadows and raised the gun again. She jumped to the right, but the shot hit her thigh this time.

Biting hard on her tongue, tasting blood, she glanced down quickly to check that it was just a flesh wound, then moved out of the way. Her vision swayed, but she managed to kick the guard's wrist to the side. The gun went skidding across the ground. Her next strike was a punch to the throat.

As he fell back, Aina moved. She smashed through the back window with a strong kick. Pushing her sleeve down to cover her hand, she cleared away the glass until there was a space big enough for her to slide through.

Lifting herself up, she tumbled through the window, hissing in pain when the glass shards scraped against her. One of the shards cut into the new bullet wound on her leg, but she was a Blade; she had no time for pain when there was still a job to be done.

Pushing herself off the ground, she saw this car was empty except for the wooden seats arranged in rows. Bright lights were spaced along the wall, casting the room in a yellow glow. A small gold chandelier hung in the center of the tapered ceiling.

Kouta must have been in one of the next two cars. Withdrawing a dagger, Aina ran down the length of this car to reach the next one, the small windows flicking past her vision. She'd find him in seconds, slit his throat, and—

The door on the other side of the car was forced open with a piercing screech of metal. Ryuu appeared at the opening, and for a moment, she froze in place, every bit of her training falling away.

Then she fled into the next car as he called her name behind her.

She slammed the door open, panting heavily as blood trickled in a hot wave down her leg.

This car was empty too. A bullet pinged off the wall next to her, and she jumped out of the way, speeding down the aisle toward the next door.

She reached it, pushed aside the door and ran into the car.

A gasp left her throat. She fell back to the wall, dropping her dagger, as Ryuu reached her.

His breath caught when he saw the scene, and he gripped the doorframe for support.

Kouta Hirai lay on the center of the train floor. Yellow light reflected on his open eyes. A bullet was lodged in his forehead, blood trailing down the side of his face and pooling around his hair like a halo.

Time slowed, until she was certain they'd both stopped breathing. Hands shaking slightly, she glanced at Ryuu. With his mouth half-open, eyes wide, and the crease on his forehead, he looked confused, as if the scene in front of them might not be real.

She took in Kouta on the floor. Only a very skilled assassin could have made their way through the train yard and killed him without his guards even noticing. The blood hadn't even dried yet, so whoever had killed him must have come here very recently.

"Too late," she finally whispered.

Anger, then disappointment, coiled through her, and she ached to release it in a scream.

Her next words shook on the way out. "Tannis got here first."

And all her chances at redemption filtered into the sky like smoke from a pistol.

33

Every shadow looked like Kohl. Every glint of the set-
ting sun on a window looked like the flash of a blade. Aina
tried to quell her fear as she weaved through the crowds of
Lyra Avenue, every bright light of a casino or bar exposing
her, but it only grew.

She veered off the main road, leaving behind the lights and
letting out a tense breath. One of the posters with her face on
it had fallen into a puddle. She made sure to step on it, then
descended the hill into the Stacks.

Was she imagining the cold, the painful blisters on her feet,
the dull ache in her empty stomach, the holes forming on her
clothes, or had barely a week of being back on the streets already turned her into the pitiful girl she'd been when Kohl
had found her?

She slowed down at a shadowed corner, taking stock of
her weapons before going any farther into the Stacks. Opening the pouch of poison darts at her belt, she riffled through

it, counting them. Her fingers brushed against something hard. Frowning, she pulled it out, then gasped and replaced it quickly before anyone saw and tried to mug her.

After glancing around to make sure no one was watching, she stared at it within the pouch: the diamond-and-ruby ring she'd stolen from Kouta when she'd first tried to kill him. It stared up at her, twinkling like little stars. In the madness after her failure to kill its owner, she had completely forgotten about it.

It had, of course, been too dangerous to go to the mines or jewelry stores to try to sell it since anyone there might have reported her to the Sentinel if they recognized her from the wanted posters. Now, she might be able to sell it, and then at least she wouldn't starve.

But it wouldn't matter if she sold the diamonds. Kohl would still come and kill her. She couldn't do anything with money if she were dead.

Maybe she could hold onto it. It reminded her of Ryuu, after all. She knew it wouldn't make up for his brother being dead or for how she'd betrayed him, but if she found a way to give it back to him before Kohl killed her, she would.

The day they'd found Kouta dead on the train played in her head over and over as she walked deeper into the Stacks.

After those long, tense seconds when they'd stared at his brother's body, Ryuu moved to the train window and thrust it open.

"Stop!" he shouted to his guards.

They stopped firing. Aina ran to the window and peered out, searching for Teo and Raurie.

They walked out from where they'd taken cover behind a train, their own guns still half-raised toward the remainder of the guards. Raurie must have fought even after Teo tried to hide her. Only three of the guards still stood, while the others' bodies lay scattered across the train yard.

From the corner of her eye, Aina watched Ryuu's gaze flick to each body, as if he were taking them in and blaming himself for their deaths.

"Get out."

His voice shocked her into stepping back. It wasn't harsh or sad. It was cold and flat, entirely emotionless, something she'd never heard from him before.

She began to back out of the train car, her eyes flicking to Kouta's body a few more times—at the perfectly placed gunshot in his forehead, the spreading circle of blood around him, and how fresh the wound was.

Ryuu, on the other hand, didn't even glance at the body. He seemed incapable, at that moment, of doing anything other than watching her retreat. He still held a gun, and she wondered if he would finally, truly use it on her.

"Ryuu, I'm . . ." She thought about saying she was sorry, then stopped herself.

Was she only sorry she hadn't gotten here before Tannis?

"How stupid do you think I am, Aina?" he finally forced out, his voice cracking a little. "I admit, I really thought all you needed was the money at first. I even felt bad for you. I knew you didn't have anything personal against my brother. It was your job, and sometimes we get forced into doing jobs we don't want, so I thought offering you the money was a way out for you. There were times when I doubted you, but I really needed your help, so then . . . I truly thought that helping you break Teo out of prison would keep you on my side. You almost lost him, and I helped you get him back. You know I almost lost Kouta. All you did was try to take him away again."

She cringed at his words. She had no excuses that he would understand—how her life depended on her own ability to take out Kouta, and that her survival was the only thing she'd been able to worry about for so long. Kohl had taught her to be a Blade: to rationalize murder, to blame it on someone else, to put it in boxes in her mind so that guilt and morals could never consume her.

But to Ryuu, murder was murder, and maybe that was the only reason he hadn't shot her in the head already.

"Get out," he repeated, before finally looking away from her and toward his brother.

This time, she listened. She left with Teo and Raurie, none of them speaking to each other as they traversed the tunnels northward out of Jackal territory and finally climbed out onto a sunlit street. The rain had cleared, leaving the day blindingly bright compared to the tunnels.

That night, she started seeing the shadows. Sometimes she wondered if Kohl was taunting her, watching her from dark alleys and rooftops like a vulture, trying to place fear in her bones before he'd finally strike. Was the long wait before he killed her simply part of her punishment?

She'd always been careful walking around the Stacks, but now she was even more so. The Jackals might have regrouped by now and could come after her at any moment. Diamond Guards could find her and haul her off to the Tower. Kohl might shoot her in the middle of the street. Her body would be thrown in a mass grave and forgotten about.

For two days after Kouta's death, she, Teo, and Raurie had stayed in the safe house where June had been hiding. The Diamond Guards would be watching for Teo to return to his apartment. June's old place was still at risk, and June and her husband wanted to lay low for a while longer before searching for anywhere new to live. At first, Raurie had been confused and angry that they'd actually been planning to kill Kouta this whole time instead of save him, but then she'd taken it in stride the way one only could if they'd grown up around crime, betrayal, and desperate moves.

The safe house was in a tunnel dug far underground, below the sewers even, along the western edge of the city. Statues and carvings of the Mothers surrounded them in the small, hollowed cave.

When she'd woken up the first morning there, a Milana woman was leaning over her with a diamond in her hand. For a moment, she was convinced she was dead and that this was her mother greeting her in some kind of afterlife. Then she'd blinked and the world came in clearer around her. The wound on her thigh had started bleeding, and the Inosen woman was tending to it.

The prayers of June and other Inosen who hid there filled her ears. She heard her parents doing the same and reminding her that life was precious. The cave soon became suffocating. All she could think of was how her parents died and she'd fled to save herself.

As long as Kohl was after her and the Sentinel still had a price on her head, Teo and Raurie were in danger simply by association with her.

When they fell asleep that second night, she left a note that she was leaving, slipped out of the safe house, and for the next five days slept in her old spots: an abandoned warehouse, a supply shack near a bridge, the fire escape of an old apartment building. Anywhere empty and quiet.

Now, she was sick of waiting and hiding. If Kohl wanted to kill her, he would do it. Prolonging the inevitable would hurt more than simply facing it.

A block away, a man stood at a corner wearing an oversized jacket and whispering at passersby what drugs he could sell them. Without hesitation, Aina walked up to him and passed him enough kors for a paper bag coated in glue and a flask of deep brown firewater, then walked to her parents' old house.

34

Aina had thought that, if at any point in her life, she decided to go back to the drugs she'd used as a child, something would rise up in her, protest, and remind her how proud she'd been for having quit in the first place.

But as she sat on the roof of her parents' home with a bottle of firewater and clutching a glue-soaked paper bag with only the cold night wind surrounding her, she realized that nothing had ever been easier.

The only other time she'd fallen back to glue was one day four years ago.

Kohl had pushed her harder than ever in training. Afterward, she'd bought glue for the first time in years and planned to put herself into a coma on the Dom's roof. She'd known there was a chance the plastic bag she inhaled from would suffocate her like the dead girl she'd seen in the river, but she saw no point in being conscious anymore.

She was there for an hour, and the sun had set by the time

Kohl found her. She watched him with blurred vision, her pulse pounding faster than it should and her breaths growing short. He pulled the bag away from her face and yelled at her to move.

When she'd stared at him listlessly, he helped her sit up and stayed next to her until she recovered. Though all her senses had been fuzzy and unclear that night, she remembered the exact pressure with which his arm rested around her shoulders, the taut set of his jaw, and the way the moons shone in his eyes as he never took them off her.

His voice replayed in her head, whispering that she should never have done this, that he was trying to help her and she kept destroying her chances. He said he would stay next to her the entire night if that was what it took. By the time she finally recovered, he straightened and muttered that he was glad she hadn't died.

The next day, she went to him and asked, for the first time, if she could one day be free to run her own tradehouse in the city. He agreed without even looking up from his desk.

"I'll tell you when," he simply said, and she left the office feeling like she finally had a purpose.

To avoid thinking of her failure, she stared out at the city. Kosín resembled a painting more than ever in her blurred vision, and she wondered from where the artist had drawn the inspiration to paint such a place that dulled sensitivities with its bleak gray shadows yet also attracted people like her, like Teo, like Ryuu, to stay there even when the city made them choke on its fumes. She imagined what this place might have looked like in the past, draped in fine silks, coated in blood, and studded with diamonds. Her gaze trailed over the Stacks, where she knew every corner, every speck of dirt, every boarded-up house, and every rumbling stomach far better than the painter ever would.

If Kohl was going to come after her anywhere, she'd prefer for him to kill her here where her parents had died. At least maybe inhaling more glue would leech away all her good memories of Kohl and leave only the bad, so maybe dying by his hand would hurt less.

She'd chosen a paper bag rather than plastic. It was less likely to suffocate her. She hoped to at least be conscious when he came, so she could ask him if she'd ever been anything more to him than a Blade.

Just then, a creak came from the other side of the house. Her head rolled to one side and her vision spun as she took in Teo. She tried to wave, but her hand tingled with numbness and fell limp.

"Should have known I'd find you here," he said, standing and walking toward her.

But instead of sitting down, he stopped a few feet away. The cool spring wind pushed his hair in front of his face. Dark brown strands brushed against the stitches on his jaw still healing from his time in the Tower's cells.

"Where else am I supposed to be?" she asked, her voice sharper than she'd intended.

"I've been looking for you," he said, sticking his hands in his pockets and gazing out at the close-pressed houses of the Stacks and the constantly hovering smoke carried down the hill from the factories. He hadn't even looked at the bottle of firewater and the glue-soaked bag she held, though he must have noticed them by now.

"Congratulations, you found me," she said, waving the bottle as if in celebration. "What do you want?"

Instead of answering her question, he sat next to her with his legs hanging over the edge of the roof. Her head drooped a little to the side, growing heavier each passing second, but Teo caught her before she fell over.

As he helped her sit up straight again, with one arm around her shoulders, his other hand moved to her chin and turned her face toward his. Her vision spun again, so she wasn't entirely sure what she saw in his eyes now, but it reminded her of a long night last year when neither of them had to work.

They'd spent hours at a bar, drinking firewater until she had no clue what she was saying or doing. Her memories of the night had always been spotty at best, but one thing she remembered was sitting in a booth next to him and how he'd brushed her hair away from her neck where it clung with summer heat.

She'd moved away, wishing it had been Kohl.

Maybe she should have stayed in place and seen what would have happened. Now there was no point.

"Your heart is beating really fast," Teo said in a soft voice as his hand fell away. "You should stop using that."

In response, she gripped the paper bag more tightly.

He raised an eyebrow incredulously. "I know you're high out of your mind and scared, but please stop and think about what you're doing for a second. My mother was shot in front of me because of this job with Kouta, and now that job is ruined." He paused, then forced out the next words. "You owe—"

"I don't have any money, Teo." She shook the paper bag in his direction. "Spent my last kors on this. Sorry."

"You thought I was going to ask you for money?" He let out a bitter laugh.

"What else would you want?" she snapped. "I have nothing

left that I could possibly owe you or anyone else. I can't fix things so that Kouta dies by my hand, and I wouldn't even do that if I could. I can't join any fight against the Steels, so give up on that fantasy. And I can't bring your mother back from the dead."

She bit her lip, almost about to take back those words, but the numbing sensation from the glue coursed through her and held back the apology. A chill spread between them, cold as winter.

When Teo next spoke, he already sounded far away.

"I was going to say, 'You owe yourself more than this.'"

Keeping her gaze on the city ahead and gripping the bag of glue with the little feeling she had left in her limbs, she heard him stand. She didn't look back to watch him go.

But once his footsteps faded away, tears fell down her numbed cheeks. She only noticed them when they dropped onto her hands and she watched them dry on her skin.

Good things don't happen to girls who come from nothing.

What could Teo possibly think she owed herself? She was an idiot to have ever thought she could reach higher. Kohl had lifted her off the streets, and she should have stayed with him instead of trying to achieve something more. She should have known she'd only get knocked down, back to being nothing but the burdensome, starving kid he'd had to save. The suspicion demanded resolution: *Am I only strong when Kohl stands behind me?*

Burying her head in her hands, she pressed her palms against her eyes until green and black stars exploded in her vision. She dug her fingernails into her forehead, hoping to draw blood. If she drew blood, she was still human, not just a failed Blade. If she drew blood, she couldn't be a useless thing to throw away.

Suddenly, a bitter taste grew in her mouth. She heard Kohl's voice pounding in her head, telling her what to do—

She stood, grabbed the bottle, and threw it. Glass shattered on the street below, brown liquid spilling everywhere. She wanted to scream, but there was no one to listen.

Kohl had kicked her out of the only home she'd ever known, taken every Kor she'd earned, threatened her, and left her to die. All the while, he'd told her it was best for her. He'd told her what she needed to do, who she needed to become, how to save herself, and in the end, he abandoned her anyway. When they were close, she'd aimed to be exactly like him, had thought no other person in the world could compare to him, and had found herself drawn to the side of him that praised, cherished, and protected her despite her faults. He'd constantly clung to the back of her mind, so that escape seemed a myth and the only option was to remain close and never disappoint him.

When love was the last thing given on Kosín's streets, it was hard to tell the real thing from something toxic. Maybe she'd clung to his version of love, telling herself it was good for her—after all, it was far better than her life on the streets—when in reality it only ate her alive. It drew her in, telling her she was nothing without it. Like the glue, her addiction to Kohl was dangerous, a tightrope she balanced on in swift wind, a call to darkness masquerading as a lullaby.

Ryuu's voice broke through her clouded thoughts: *Fear itself was worse than the thing I feared.*

Killing Kouta, completing this job, opening her own tradehouse . . . that wasn't what she needed.

No, she needed to cut Kohl off. Unchain herself from him and the fear he stirred in her veins.

She stumbled down the roof, her hands numb on the rusted

metal surface, then made her way back to the Dom. The cold breeze passing through narrow streets cleared her mind a little as she walked.

A block away from the Dom, where the stench of the Minos River grew strong, she remembered a night two years ago when a target had fought back and nearly killed her. She'd slit his throat, but barely escaped with her life. Bleeding, she'd returned to the Dom and passed out on the floor in Kohl's office.

When she'd woken up, her wounds were bandaged, and his arms held her upright. If she could go back to that night and—

What?

Kiss him? Yell at him?

Stab him, she decided, and picked up the pace.

The Dom stood tall, the willow trees shadowing the entrance as she approached under the soft silver and red of the waning moons. Candlelight shone between the bars on the upper windows.

Ten feet away from the door, she slowed to a stop. They already knew she was here. There was no point in hiding. For a few minutes, the only sounds in the night were the wind and her rapid pulse.

Straightening her shoulders, she shouted, "Kohl! We need to talk."

A few more minutes passed. Her vision wavered, blurring momentarily and then clearing, over and over.

Finally, the door creaked open. Shadows spilled onto the sidewalk. Kohl Pavel stepped outside, his eyes and the sapphires on his watch brightening the dark street.

35

Silence fell as Aina and Kohl stared each other down. The glue helped dull her fear of his calculating expression and the shadows surrounding them. She tried to focus on him, but swayed slightly in place as a wave of dizziness hit her.

"I'd ask if you have Kouta Hirai's head behind your back," Kohl said after a few long minutes of silence had passed. "But we both know—"

"If you're going to kill me, stop stalling," she said, her lips numbing as she spoke. "Don't hide behind your gun or your taunts. Fight me and we'll see who's left alive."

His footsteps echoed down the quiet street as he approached her, the sudden movement making her take a few involuntary steps backward and curse herself for doing so. His eyes lit up as if he were amused by her state.

She gulped when the sliver of metal visible under Kohl's jacket flashed under the moonlight. He probably had his new favorite Blade, Tannis, waiting in the shadows to take out

Aina with a throwing star to the throat. Was that a shadow passing along the window of the manor or did she imagine it? Nausea swept through her, but she forced it down and tried to still her trembling hands.

"You never wanted me to win, did you?" she asked. "You never wanted me to open my own tradehouse."

Another long silence passed before he said, "I wanted it very much, actually. We could have started a partnership, and none of the other fools in this city would have stood a chance against us. But then you failed."

"And then you threatened and abandoned me. You left me open to be killed."

"You know how the job works. You were a Blade. When a weapon can't do its job anymore, it needs to be discarded."

She swayed on the spot and stumbled, but caught herself before she could fall over. Then, she threw away all the rules of being a quiet Blade who didn't question her boss.

"Who paid you for this job?" she asked through gritted teeth. "Whose money is so important to you that all the years I've done my job right don't even matter anymore?"

"You knew the risks going in," Kohl said in a slow voice, as if he were speaking to a child. "You knew this would be the biggest job you'd ever taken on, and you knew I trusted you to do it, but you still failed. Don't you understand that the more you have and the higher you stand, the more someone will have to fight to knock you down? Everything I do is to raise our place on that pedestal. I got that job for you, for me, for everyone here, and your failure put us all in jeopardy. I won't risk my life's work for the sake of one disappointing Blade."

Just then, Kohl reached inside his jacket. Aina flinched, then realized he wasn't withdrawing a gun.

It was a small, porcelain statue of a horse with a pink ribbon around its neck—one that had reflected the glow of burning coals, one that the spiders in her house had never seemed to touch, one that had been the last thing she'd seen before fleeing her parents' murder. One that was all too familiar to her. One he could not possibly have.

Her whole body stiffened. The world collapsed in front of her, the cold night air and the reason she'd come here and the shadowed figures on the Dom's roof all disappearing until nothing remained but her, him, and the small statue he held.

"It's been a bit of a good luck charm to me over the years," he said, turning it over in his hand. "If you came here to die, you should probably know the truth."

"It was you," she finally whispered, the words like crushed glass coming out of her mouth.

She'd thought she'd known the worst of what he could do, threatening her, abandoning her, shooting at her, convincing her she needed him her whole life.

But there was one thing worse he could have done, and he'd already done it ten years ago.

When she spoke next, uttering the truth that seemed so impossible she'd never imagined it before, her voice sounded like it came from someone else, far away.

"You killed my parents."

She'd tried so hard to wipe away the memory of that night by inhaling glue over and over. It had worked to an extent, blurring out some things, like the gunman's face.

The memory returned now, as clear as if it had happened yesterday, and suddenly she was a small child again watching her parents die the first time.

That night, she'd been playing with a cat that had wandered in from the streets, right next to the coal stove with the porcelain horse behind it.

A soft sound had come from outside. Aina hadn't known what it was, but her parents sent a furtive glance at each other and then mouthed at her to hide.

Panicking, Aina shrunk into the shadows under the table, spiders crawling all over her sandals. She yearned to flick off the spiders, but forced herself to stay utterly still like her parents did whenever a Diamond Guard patrol passed near them in the tunnels under the city. She focused on the copy of the Nos Inoken that had fallen to the floor next to the table—the Mothers would help, wouldn't they?

Her mother wore a blue robe, her hands wrinkled from washing other people's clothes all day for meager pay. Her father, wearing the overalls prescribed by his factory job, stood to face a third person who shoved aside their scrap-metal door and walked in.

Her gaze fixed on the man with the gun.

Shadows hid most of him, beyond where the single candle's light failed to reach.

The man wore a disturbing scowl, one deep-set into him like he'd been born that way, with eyes like ice as he raised a gun.

A shot broke the silence and Aina gasped, her back slamming against the wall as her mother fell to the floor with a red mess instead of a head. A smattering of four bullets made her jump with each shot. Her father's body swayed wildly. As he hit the floor, Aina slipped through the back door on shaking legs. She hauled herself up to the roof and spent the rest of the night with her eyes wide open. She'd never wanted to move from that spot.

Four years later, she accepted a helping hand from the man who'd made her homeless in the first place.

"After I got out of prison, I found out my old boss from

the Vultures had been killed," Kohl said, his voice breaking through her memory. "So I took his gang and his businesses. I started the Dom. It was only a few years after the war, and there wasn't a clear law on what to do with Inosen and diamond smugglers, but anyone who took one out or brought them to the attention of the Diamond Guards was paid handsomely. I got paid to spy on a worship service underground, then track down and take out the Inosen who'd attended. I saw a little Milana girl there with her parents, and you reminded me of the friend I'd betrayed and pushed to her death in the Tower prison. I thought if I could kill you, who looked so much like her, and your parents . . . it would prove that I'd finally let go of my guilt for killing her, and that I was ready for this new life. I was fourteen. I could have gone after you when you fled, but . . . you reminded me of me, with how quickly you slipped away from danger. Maybe I was a killer, but I allowed one small act of mercy in letting you live, and that made me feel like I still had some kind of choice in the matter. Isn't that what people in this city do every day? They take freedom in the smallest places they can find it, and they hoard it, knowing it might ruin them one day."

She wished he would stop talking, but she could hardly move, let alone speak. What he was saying made her want to rip the last six years off of her, claw out her memory of them, throw them away, burn them. Her fingers twitched as if reaching for the bag of glue. Anything to banish the truth.

"Four years later," he continued, "I saw you enter a bar that I knew was going to be bombed. Some feud a gang had with the owner. He wasn't paying them fees for running his business on their territory. I knew I'd ruined your life as a child, but thought maybe I could fix it by recruiting you, and later by offering to let you open your own tradehouse. But then you failed, and if I didn't cut you off, I'd lose everything I've built up to protect myself and all the people I employ here. I had to, Aina."

Each new word he spoke cut into her like a blade, taking every memory she had of him—training by his side, going to him when she was injured or frightened, learning to remake herself into a weapon with a map of the city imprinted on her brain—and adding to it the knowledge that he'd killed her parents. Disgust rose through her and her head spun as she remembered all her hopes; all the nights they'd both stayed up, lost in their thoughts in the train station tower; how she'd wished he would lean closer, or take her hand, or kiss her.

Had he taken the guilt for killing her parents, stored it away in his mind, blamed someone else, and thought that teaching her to kill, too, would fix everything? It fixed nothing.

Though her vision still wavered and her hands shook, she raised her eyes to meet his and put as much venom as she could into her glare. His jaw tightened, and though it was a small reaction, it bolstered her to take a step toward him. He stepped back. All the years he'd never shown her anything, had kept his face as impassive as a wall of rock, made this a victory.

"I don't care what your twisted reasons are," she spat out. Some of it landed on his face. "You tell me you killed my parents, and then you try to explain yourself? It doesn't work like that, Kohl. You don't own me anymore."

"You'd still be on the streets or dead from an overdose if it wasn't for me," he said, wiping the spit away. His blue eyes hardened to shards of ice. "Of course I own you."

"I will never be yours." Her hands curled, trying to make fists, but her grip had weakened, so they fell back to her sides. "I'm glad Tannis beat me to Kouta. I'm done doing your work."

With some demented kind of mirth in his eyes, he said, "Once again, you're wrong. Do you really think I'd give Tannis the job after you failed?" When she frowned, he continued, "I did my own damn work. I killed Kouta Hirai."

She stepped back in shock as Kohl whistled.

Like the sleek bodies of spiders sliding down webs, the Blood King's killers and spies and thieves, all the people she'd worked and lived with, descended from the roofs and windows. He must have brought on people from other tradehouses or from gangs nearby, as a show of strength; there were far more people than those who lived in the Dom.

The rest of the street was empty. It was her against them.

She would fight back and kill them all where they stood.

But when her hand flinched toward her knife, she couldn't even grip the handle properly. All her bravery vanished.

As she turned to run, blue hair flashed at the corner of her vision.

She swayed wildly, as if the whole earth had been tipped on it side.

A moment later, she tripped. The ground flew toward her face.

Everything went black.

36

When Aina next woke, she sat up straight immediately, surprised to find she was still breathing. Thick, crimson blankets surrounded her in a large bed. Her panicked breaths slowed as she checked her surroundings.

A broad window was behind the bed, revealing manicured gardens, a dark gray sky, and heavy rain lashing the window. A gold chandelier hung above. To her right, a crystal glass of water sat atop a mahogany desk with a newspaper spread out next to it.

Her thoughts were still scattered, but at least her vision was no longer blurry, and her limbs weren't numb. She checked to make sure she had all her weapons. As she reached for the glass of water, the door opened with a slight creak, and Ryuu, Teo, and Raurie entered.

"You're awake!" Teo said with a sigh of relief.

Guilt twinged through her as memories of last night returned and made her head spin. She'd said some terrible things to Teo, but he walked over and pulled her into a hug. She rested her head on his shoulder for a moment, hoping he could sense an apology, then straightened.

"How did I get here?" she asked in a hoarse voice. Her mouth tasted like all the firewater she'd drunk last night.

While Teo and Raurie had gathered around her at the edge of the bed, Ryuu hung slightly back, leaning against the desk with his hands clenched over the edge of it. She wondered why he wasn't yelling at her to get out right now.

"What did you do?" Raurie whispered. "We were really worried when we got Ryuu's note."

When Aina hesitated to answer, Teo asked, "Did you go to Kohl's?"

She nodded, but only once, because her head ached if she moved it too much. Before Teo could do more than muster a look of surprise, she added, "I wanted to fight him. Then he set all of his people on me at once. I don't know how I'm still alive."

A silence fell on the room, broken only by the rain pounding on the window. She could remember nothing after falling in the street outside the Dom. How had she arrived here unscathed?

"How are you all here? Did you find me, Ryuu?" she asked, hating the bit of hope that leaked into her voice.

He nodded once, the smallest movement out of the corner of her eye. "Last night, I went to the kitchen to get some water. I saw you passed out on the floor. You don't remember how you got there?" When she shook her head, he continued, "Well, I couldn't let you stay there. Plus, I found something I wanted you all to see, so I sent a message to Teo and Raurie to come here."

Still refusing to look directly at her, he withdrew a long

piece of paper from a folder inside the drawer at the desk. "I held Kouta's funeral a few days ago. Kept it quiet, only invited a few families from around here. Before we buried him, I found a note in his pocket. On it was an address and a code to open a bank security deposit box. Inside the box was this folder."

He approached the bed and handed her the folder, his fingers flinching back from hers as she took it. Trying to hide how much that hurt, she focused on the folder.

All the pages inside were typewritten, which narrowed down the possibilities of where it could have come from. Only people with money could afford typewriters. Each page inside listed names, dates, and details. Many of the names seemed familiar to her, but it took her a while to figure out what connected them.

She'd seen them all in newspapers. These were Steels who'd lived in Kosín in the past two decades. Every one of them was dead. Reports flashed through her mind, blurred by the time that had passed since she'd seen them.

Train accidents. Gas explosions. Faulty electricity burning down houses. Her hands shook the more she read, and when she saw the names Hiroe and Masato Hirai, she nearly dropped the folder.

It explained that Ryuu's parents had died in a gas explosion, but it also detailed that they'd been shot prior to the explosion, along with a codename for the hired killer who'd done the job.

This was documentation of hits on some of Kosín's highest-earning residents. Her time spent spying on Kouta, and how he was reading all the time—had he been reading these documents that day she'd followed him home?

As she read the rest of the pages, she frowned with suspicion. All of these kills had been covered up or blamed on someone else. She recognized the name of a businessman Tannis had been sent to kill once. She'd had to lie low for months afterward, as there were rumors that a Kaiyanis woman from the south of the city had been the culprit.

It was clearly done to divert attention from whoever was truly behind the kills. There was nothing new to her about hired murder in this city, but to see that other people from the Stacks like her were being used as weapons and scapegoats for someone higher up than them engineering these kills, made Aina's stomach squirm with unease. When she saw Kouta's name, her heartbeat slowed. She was a part of this operation even if she hadn't known it.

The final page simply said *Black Diamond* in in the center. No names, dates, or details were given. She frowned, staring at the words for a while, but couldn't understand what they meant.

She flipped through the pages again, and as she neared the earlier kills made during and after the war, something caught her eye. In the paragraph that detailed the murders of Ryuu's parents was the sentence: "Let it be known that our goal is to progress, not to regress."

She stared at the words for a few moments, trying to recall where she'd heard them. When the realization hit her, she tossed the paper aside as if it had burned her fingers.

When she next spoke, Teo and Raurie both nodded. Ryuu must have shown it to them already. "General Bautix. He's the one who got your parents shot and made it look like it happened during the Inosen's attack on their mines."

Ryuu ran a hand through his hair, making it fall over on one side and block part of his face so his expression was nearly impossible to read. "I don't know if he figured out my parents were Inosen, but I don't think it mattered. Nothing they did could have saved them. He's been hiring assassins to take out prominent Steels for years, ever since before the war, regardless of their faith. I don't know why, but Kouta figured out that it was him. And now he's dead too."

As he spoke, a sharp pain struck the center of Aina's forehead. She leaned forward and tried to take steady breaths, but that only made her nauseous.

Memories of last night came back in piercing jolts, flashes of words, a sensation of the world falling away beneath her feet.

Kohl's the one who killed my parents.

Her chest tightened and her breaths grew shallow, like she was using glue. This knowledge of what he'd done struck her with fresh force, as if she were hearing it for the first time all over again.

"Can we talk later?" she asked, trying to keep her voice steady. "I feel like a train ran me over."

Ryuu nodded, already making his way toward the door. "We'll talk tomorrow."

Once they left, she lay back down and closed her eyes. She didn't know what to do with any of the information she'd learned, or how it even mattered since those people were already dead. She'd probably join them soon if Kohl found her again. Her head ached when she wondered, once more, how she could have survived last night.

It hurt too much to think of it, so instead, she ran one phrase through her thoughts over and over as she fell asleep: *black diamond.*

37

The sun woke Aina the next morning. Her head no longer ached, but she was parched. She reached toward the desk for the pitcher of water, but it was empty.

Next to it, however, lay the newspaper. Her head had ached too much to notice anything particular about it last night, but now a headline on the front page caught her eye.

PRINCESS OF LINASH VISITS SUMERAND FOR THE FIRST TIME, TO RECEIVE RARE BLACK DIAMOND AS GIFT.

Black diamond. Kohl had mentioned something about it too, when she'd collected the money for the Kouta hit. Now the Linasian princess was to receive it as a gift to mark the new alliance between their countries.

Then there were the documents detailing General Bautix's crimes.

She sucked in a sharp breath as she recalled the pages of names and how Bautix had arranged Ryuu's parents' deaths.

A new suspicion hit her. Clenching the newspaper in her hands, she reread the article a few times.

Minutes later, the door opened and Ryuu, Raurie, and Teo entered with breakfast and tea for her.

"I think I know what Bautix's next step will be," she said, pushing back the blankets. "I think I know why he killed your parents and your brother, Ryuu."

"Why?" Raurie asked in a soft voice, as if Bautix might hear them through the walls. "He's been on the side of the Steels from the beginning. He is one. What does he gain from killing them?"

"Everything," Aina said. "Ryuu, wasn't your family wealthy before they even began mining diamonds? That's not what their original fortune came from, right?"

"That's true," he said with a slow nod. "My great-grandparents first got rich by selling mining tools, and then my grandparents finally bought the mines."

"That's how you make money, right? Sell the tools, the thing that makes the rest of the country work, and get paid for it. General Bautix used to run the arms manufacturing in the city. He basically had a monopoly on it until he gave it up to become the general. But what if he never really gave it up? Most of the city's arms sales still go through just a couple of places. There are only a few smugglers who manage to get in more and sell them, but Bautix keeps the Diamond Guards on top of that, probably to prevent as much competition as possible. What if he's still earning money from his old business and hiding the profits somehow? And if so, what better way for an arms dealer to make money than to make other people want to kill each other?"

The more she thought about it, the angrier she became, and she slammed her fist on the bed. "Now he's the one who pays the Diamond Guards, so they're loyal to him, and the Sentinel has grown to rely on him to protect the city from conflict, so no one would think to blame him. But *he's* the one who stirs the conflict. He's basically tricked the entire city into paying him for weapons to fight, and then paying him again to end the fighting so he looks like a hero. When one conflict ends, another one springs up. Teo, what's one thing you never ask when you're paid to kill someone?"

"Why they want the target dead," Teo answered mechanically.

"Exactly," Aina said as Ryuu grimaced. "But what if their goal isn't to kill the target? It's not about who gets killed, it's about who gets blamed. You always let someone else take the blame when you can. It's a sort of backup plan to keep you safe."

Silence settled through the room as her words sank in. Her stomach tightened as she recalled what Kohl had told her years ago: *Blame the person who bought the bullets and told the gun where to point.*

With a deep breath, she continued, "Publicly, Bautix sends the Diamond Guards to kill Inosen. In secret, he puts hired men to the task of killing Steels—and most of them probably purchased his guns to do their jobs—and then pins the blame on people like me. Why do you think he wanted so badly for someone to turn me in and pulled that sob story about being friends with Ryuu's parents? So that he could garner sympathy, then pinpoint an enemy, someone for the other Steels to hate and fear. I was the perfect scapegoat. That's what he did with killing your parents, made it look like it was because of the Inosen attacking the mines. He wanted to stir up trouble. I don't know how much Kohl knows about it, but I bet Bautix wasn't happy that Kouta survived, so he kept up the hunt for me and put pressure on Kohl to get the job done." After she let her words sink in for a moment, she asked, "Ryuu, how did Kouta get this folder?"

Ryuu shrugged and leaned against the desk, his hand resting near the newspaper. "The note in his pocket just said that the folder was left in his deposit box anonymously."

"Were you invited to the reception ball for the Linasian princess tonight?" Aina asked.

"Yes, they want me to officially present the diamond to her since it came from our mines," he said with a frown. "Why?"

She grabbed the newspaper, scanned the details below the headline, then unfolded the paper and showed them the front page, her hands shaking a little. What she was about to propose was bigger than any job she'd ever taken from Kohl.

"Bautix must be tired of frying small fish. What's the only thing that could be more profitable to him than sparking conflict between Sumeranians?" When no one answered, she said, "If he kills the Linasian princess at this reception ball, where there's supposed to be so much security, it will look like it's something our government orchestrated, and that's cause for war. Sumerand has been out of the international arena since the civil war, and Linash has had its own problems. They barely trust anyone outside of their country. We're both trying to make allies now, but Bautix is going to use this opportunity to turn more profit than he ever has before. It's called the Black Diamond Project, right? The news article said she'll receive the jewel at midnight. I bet that's when he'll strike. He wants to make a scene, and this is his best opportunity."

"Do you think the rest of the Sentinel knows?" Raurie asked. "Would they be in on it with him, or do you think we should warn them about what he's planning?"

After thinking for a moment, Aina shook her head. "I don't think the general of any country's military is supposed to have a side job selling guns to anyone who pays. I know the warehouse where a lot of the sales go through. Most of the city's criminals get their stuff there. But its operations are so big that no one knows who really runs it. If it's him, and he's arming all the city's gangs and tradehouses as well as the army and Diamond Guards, don't you think that's a conflict of interest? But whether they know or not, we don't exactly have time to set up a meeting with them and find out. The reception ball is tonight. I say we stop the assassination and then see who in the Sentinel is on our side."

She rushed her words near the end, adrenaline pounding through her as fiercely as during any fight. If they let the princess die and risked a war starting, only more people would die, and the person orchestrating it all would get away with it. Her head cleared, her mistakes of last night momentarily forgotten. Maybe this was something she could do right.

Instead of being a blight on this city, she could be a cure. Instead of being a tool to men like Kohl and Bautix, she would knock them down and put them in their place.

This was something she could claim for herself.

She took a deep breath and locked eyes with each of them. A spark of anticipation flashed through Ryuu's eyes when he met hers, as if he could predict what she was about to say next. Teo's words came back to her, telling her to decide what was important to her and put her mind to it entirely. These were her allies now, people who wanted to believe in something and fight for it. Not Kohl—not anymore.

As she opened her mouth to tell them her plan, Teo reached out and swiped the biscuit off her tray of food. She glared at him.

"Sorry. Hungry," he said while chewing on the biscuit.

"I was going to eat that."

Ryuu frowned. "You never eat anything."

"If we're going to fight Bautix, I'll need all the energy I can get," she said. "Bautix has made me into an enemy of the Steels. And me avoiding capture? Well, that makes me his biggest threat. Without all the people he's blamed for his crimes in prison or dead, people will be free to point the finger at him."

She beckoned them closer to hear the rest of her plan.

Later that afternoon, an hour after Aina had finished brewing a new, faster-working paralyzing poison with supplies purchased by Ryuu, they all gathered in his library.

Upon entering the room, the tapered cedar wood ceiling rising above her, Aina's eyes immediately trailed toward the shadowed area behind the bookshelves where she'd first attempted to kill Kouta.

She glanced at Ryuu, who stood at the edge of the table in the sunken center of the library. There were bags under his eyes that hadn't been there before Kouta's death.

Her heart sank when she took him in. Whatever connection had been between them before was gone now, after her betrayal. He'd never send a shy smile her way or brush his hand against hers again.

He nodded at her as she approached, then turned back to the drawing he'd made of the Tower's basic layout, with the subway blueprints underneath it.

Once Ryuu finished going over the plan again, Teo said, "So, Aina and I are going through the prisons again."

Teo kept his face expressionless, just tapped his fingers along the table. His other hand moved toward the stitches on his forehead, the skin around it still bruised.

"If we do this plan right," Aina told him in a reassuring

tone, "we'll cause enough trouble that they'll barely catch a glimpse of us."

Raurie reached over then, to point at a spot on the blueprints where Ryuu had drawn the prison's corridors juxtaposing the subway tunnels. "So, you'll go through the same vent . . . but you should start at a higher floor. You need to be as high up as you can get. Why not start at the seventh floor? The seventh, eighth, and ninth floors are where the Inosen are held, after all."

"That's a good idea," Ryuu said. "While you two go through the prison, I'll assist in presenting the black diamond to the princess at midnight exactly. Raurie will keep an eye out for Bautix while pretending to be my date."

"I'm glad we're all on the same side this time," Raurie said, grimacing at Aina and Teo. "We can't expect to fight people like Bautix if we're fighting or lying to each other. Now maybe we can make an actual difference."

Teo nodded once. "It's a good plan. If we stop Bautix from hurting even one more innocent person, then it's worth the chance of getting caught."

And it's worth the fear of going back into those dark tunnels. She smothered the thought for now. She'd deal with that fear when the time came.

When Teo and Raurie left to prepare their supplies, Aina stood alone with Ryuu in the library.

A tense silence hung in the air that made it harder for her to speak, broken only by the rain lashing against the window. He rolled up the drawing and the blueprints, taking a bit longer than was necessary.

"How are you doing?" she finally blurted out.

He turned to face her with an odd expression, which made her wish she hadn't asked at all.

What kind of question was that? she berated herself. *His brother just died. Of course he's not in a good mood.*

Instead of answering her question, he said, "All these years, I've been saying I'm not afraid anymore, but I still am. I say that I know how to defend myself and that I'll be safe, but that's not actually doing anything about the terrible things going on here. That's hiding, and letting it all happen because it's too frightening to try to stop it. But now I want to end the things that scare me."

His words sent a chill through her as more memories from the other night returned to her. She remembered why she'd gone to Kohl's in the first place, and her shock when he'd told her the truth about her parents' deaths. She could never forgive him, so there was no point in seeking an apology. There was no way he could bring her parents back to life. The only thing she could do was seek revenge. Try to hurt him like he'd hurt her.

I want to end the things that scare me, Ryuu's words repeated in her thoughts.

"We will," she promised him in a whisper, then raised her voice to add, "I can't bring your brother back to life. I can't make up for how I lied to you. But I promise you, I'm going to stop Kohl."

"Don't do it for me," Ryuu said, his eyes softening a little. "Whatever happens, I hope you do something you're proud of. Something you want to do instead of whatever your old boss would want. If killing him is the answer, do it for you, not me. Killing him won't bring my brother back, after all. But after this is over, we probably shouldn't see each other anymore. I don't forgive you for what you did, but I understand why you did it, and that makes it hard for me to hate you. Even if a part of me really wants to."

She almost asked, *Is there a part of you that doesn't want to hate me, then?* But she kept silent as he walked past her. Anything else she said might hurt him more, and she didn't need to know the answer to that question.

She was no longer just a Blade that Kohl had fashioned her into. She could make something more of herself. Whether Ryuu ever forgave her or not didn't matter—what mattered was stopping Bautix's plans and cutting Kohl out of her life for good.

38

Four hours before midnight, Ryuu and Raurie departed
for the Tower in a carriage. After packing her supplies for the
night in silence, Aina joined Teo in the entrance hall of the
mansion.

The sun had set by the time they set out, leaving them in
near-darkness. A light rain cascaded onto the grass as they
crossed the fields to reach the entrance to the sewers.

It was her first chance to speak with Teo alone since their
conversation on her parents' rooftop. She considered what
to say on their way to the sewer entrance. When they finally
reached it, their boots crunching in the gravel near the shore
of the river, the words came out easily.

"You were right," she said in a low voice.

"I'm right about a lot of things, so you'll have to be more
specific," Teo responded with a wink.

She brushed wet strands of hair out of her face, hoping
her hand would block the heat rising onto her cheeks. She

wondered if this warmth she felt around him had always been there, hiding under her connection to Kohl, or if it was something new. And if it was new, how could she trust it? He was her best friend. She couldn't ruin that.

"You were right about me," she said. "I owe myself more. And you were right about Kohl. He really made me believe he cared. Some part of me is still convinced he does. Why didn't he kill me last night? It would have been so easy."

"That's how he works, Aina. He hurts you and then he twists it, so it looks like he's helping you. Don't let yourself fall back to him again." He looked away from her then, his gaze trailing across the river. "You deserve better than that."

"I know," she said, swallowing hard. "He told me he's the one who killed my parents. He said he saved me six years ago because he felt guilty, but really I think he just wanted to own me."

After a long pause where Teo took in what she said, he placed a hand on her shoulder, and she relaxed under his touch. "All you need is to be brave, like you always are, with everything. Kohl taught you how to kill, but you taught yourself how to live. Don't forget you survived on your own for years, even if it was hard. Now you have to prove to yourself that you can cut him off too."

"I will," she said, her voice growing stronger.

After lighting her flare, Aina waited for Teo to lift the handle in the gravel and descend the ladder. She followed him to the sewers below, and once they were there, they kept their voices and footsteps as quiet as possible. Aina found the entrance to the Inosen's secret passages she, Raurie, and Ryuu had used last time and led the way. Every few hundred feet, they left flares propped against the walls to mark their path.

Soon, they approached the wide cavern where construction

on the platform was still in progress. A few workers were gathered, but their loud shouts and the drill they were using covered the sound of Aina and Teo sneaking along the opposite platform.

They reached the same door Raurie had found when they came to break out Teo. It opened easily, but when Aina looked through it, she shut it quickly and stepped back onto the platform.

"They've posted guards there now," she whispered. "Probably to watch out for intruders since we broke in last time. I bet there's more security all over the prison now, so we'll have to be careful."

Teo shook his head, then withdrew his gun. "Well, we don't have time to find another route. We've only got about three hours before Bautix strikes."

She nodded, then slipped into the corridor, keeping her footsteps and breaths quiet. One of the guards was pacing away from her about twenty feet down the hall and under the ventilation shaft they needed to reach. The second guard had gone down a perpendicular hall, but straining her ears, she heard his footsteps nearing the corner again. Any second now, he would turn down this hall and see them.

Beckoning to Teo, she led the way to a spot halfway down the hall where a fuel tank sat in an alcove surrounded by a metal fence. Hiding on the side of the fence covered by shadows, they held their breath and waited for the guards to reach them.

When the shadow of one guard reached their view, Aina jumped out and tackled him to the floor. At the same time, Teo leapt from cover and shot at the approaching guard, the bullet hitting his arm and making him drop his weapon.

Aina slammed her fist into the face of the guard below her.

He tried to throw her off, but she forced him around, pressed his face into the cold floor, and placed her arm around his throat. A few moments passed as she increased the pressure. He stopped struggling and passed out.

Teo had knocked out the guard he'd shot, as well. Not wasting another moment, Aina gestured for him to follow her, and they left the guards behind. They walked down the hall and slowed under the ventilation shaft she, Ryuu, and Raurie had entered before. A new grate was in place with a heavier lock attached.

"Give me—"

Teo was already passing her the explosives and a match before she finished the sentence. He squeezed her other hand as he did so. "I can do it if you want."

"No, I've got this," she said with a small shake of her head, hoping she sounded braver than she felt.

A moment later, she climbed the handholds into the darkness. Reaching the grate, she tied the explosives in place with a length of rope, then climbed back down to light the match. As soon as the flame hit the string, she and Teo ran for cover around the corner at the end of the hall.

The explosion went off, shattering the grate to pieces. The drills in the tunnel beyond covered the noise. But a different sound came with it now, like nails scraping on a sheet of metal. But it faded away just as quickly, most likely a noise from the construction site.

Aina led the way to the handholds in the wall and moved first, with the flare gripped between the smallest fingers of one hand. It provided a reddish glow of light as they made their way up the shaft.

But then, the same scratching sound she'd heard before came again from above them. Little scraping noises followed it, growing closer with each passing second. Hair rose on the back of her neck as a suspicion struck her.

Her breath caught in her throat when she looked up. Yellow pinpricks stared down at her.

Eyes.

39

Claws as sharp as her blade and the length of her forearm appeared in the red light of the flare.

Then a leg appeared, twice as long as the claw and covered with thick brown hair. More legs and then the massive body of the cave spider appeared. The beast threatened to take up the entire width of the ventilation shaft with its body. Teo swore loudly below her.

The image of the dead cat wrapped in a cave spider's webbing slipped through her thoughts and made her hands turn clammy with fear. Her first instinct was to leap off the ladder and hope she landed without breaking her legs, but there was no time for that.

Instead of fleeing, she squared her shoulders, tucked the flare under her arm, and withdrew a dagger.

"Let's see how this spider fares without its eyes," she whispered.

She slashed at the spider, scraping one of its legs with her blade and drawing dark blood that dripped on her.

It crouched back into the shadows, then jumped.

With a sharp intake of breath, she slammed the hilt of her weapon into its head. Horrible clicking and sliding sounds echoed around her as the beast struggled to regain its tread on the walls.

One of its claws swept underneath her, piercing Teo in the shoulder. She risked a quick glance down to make sure he was still on the ladder. As the claw moved away, Teo took out a gun and fired at the spider.

The bullet pinged off the wall and ricocheted toward a spot a few inches from her fingers. She dug her fingers into the handhold. The dynamite in her pack weighed her down, making her clench her jaw with the effort to hold herself on the ladder.

"Don't shoot anymore!" she yelled down to Teo. Her voice echoed, joining the clattering sound of the spider's claws against the walls.

Just then, one of its long, hairy legs wrapped around her shoulders. The breath left her body. Her grip on the handhold loosened as the beast tried to tug her off.

She tightened her grip again, knuckles straining as she fought against the spider's force. With her other hand, she lifted the dagger again and swept it across the leg holding her, barely missing her own neck. Then she buried her blade deep into one of its bulbous yellow eyes.

It jerked backward, releasing her, and her feet slid with the sudden movement. She cried out as her hands grasped for purchase on the ladder, but as she did, the flare tucked under her arm fell—breaking with a loud crack on the tunnel floor below.

Shadows fell around them.

For a moment that seemed to last hours, she simply clung to the wall and wished she could disappear into it like she'd used glue to detach from her body, her fears, her memories.

She couldn't see Teo, she couldn't make out her blade in front of her, and her own hands were invisible in the darkness.

The only light came from the spider's yellow eyes. Its legs scratched against the wall, its eyes moving closer to where she clung.

If it got another leg around her, it would rip her from the ladder, and she would fall to her death.

She'd join her parents in the mass graves. Kohl and Bautix would win.

With a sharp exhale, she ripped her dagger from the spider's eye. It jerked wildly. One leg dealt a blunt hit to her face. A claw scratched her elbow. Warm blood cascaded down her arm, but she hardly felt the pain.

Aina swept her dagger across the spider's face. It lost its balance, legs scratching against the walls to try to grab onto something. She swung out her blade again, and it connected with a hairy limb.

Gritting her teeth, muscles straining, she sawed her blade through the leg until it detached. Blood drenched her arm, hot and thick.

Then the spider fell, crashing onto the tunnel floor a moment later. Its shell broke with a resounding crack.

Aina sucked in air as if she'd just come up from underwater. She imagined hundreds more spiders descending on her from above and she froze on the wall, fingers clinging to the handholds so tightly, she feared they might break. A cold sweat broke out on her forehead. The blood from her wound trickled down her arm, but she felt no pain. Her pulse still pounded as loudly as the spider's claws had scratched against the wall.

"Did it hurt you?" Her voice echoed, oddly loud in the aftermath of the spider's attack.

"It clipped my shoulder, but it's nothing that won't heal. Are you okay?"

"No," she said immediately, then winced. "Wait, yes. I'm fine. It just scratched me."

She shook her head to clear the image of the spider crawling toward her. She'd beaten the monster. And if she had to, she could do it again.

"I'm fine," she repeated, believing herself this time. "Let's go. That took too much time."

In minutes, they reached the landing of the prison's fourth floor. It was nearly pitch-black except for a shred of light pouring through the crack of a window set in the door at the end of the hall. Dust motes swirled in its silver streak.

Before moving any farther, Aina reached into her pack and withdrew bandages, passing some to Teo.

"The last thing we need is a trail of blood following us through the prison," she muttered before wrapping a bandage tightly around the wound on her arm.

It was hard to work in the darkness, but they managed to bind their wounds within a few minutes, and then moved on. Thick dust on the floor helped mask the sound of their footsteps. Past the door ahead, a staircase wound up the opposite wall toward the higher levels of the prison.

Instead of going through the same door as last time, they took the staircase. They climbed quickly, and for a few minutes, the only sound was their measured breaths. The windows and cracks around doors on each landing provided a bit of light as they climbed higher and higher.

But when they approached the sixth floor, hair stood up on the back of Aina's neck. There was a third set of footsteps. They were nearly soundless, but still audible between the quick beats of her pulse. Someone else was sneaking through the prison's outer corridors.

Glancing over her shoulder, she saw no one and nothing except the worn stone of the stairs behind them. Where the staircase curved back down to the lower floors, there were only shadows.

But the sound had been unmistakable. Someone was following them, likely a Diamond Guard.

Tapping Teo on the shoulder, she whispered, "I'll handle this. You go up."

He left with a nod, his footsteps fading away toward the seventh floor.

Keeping her own steps light as the sound of the person following them grew closer and closer, Aina raced to the sixth-floor landing, then shrank into its shadows.

She withdrew a dagger, and waited.

Their breaths grew close, and then they were mere feet away.

She lunged out with her knife, but just then, a hard punch hit her in the ribs.

With a sharp exhale, she dodged the next strike on instinct alone, brushing into the attacker as she moved. She slammed her knee into their stomach, threw them into the wall.

Her attacker grunted in a familiar voice. Silver and sapphire flashed in the dark as they moved again.

It wasn't a Diamond Guard.

It was Kohl.

40

A footstep sounded on the stone to the right.

Aina shifted, moving left, and struck out into the darkness with her blade.

He moved with a sharp intake of breath. Her strike missed, and she hit the wall instead, her knuckles scraping against stone.

She tried to listen for him, but he moved without a sound. And then his hand wrapped around her elbow. She tried to jerk out of his grip, but he wrenched her backward.

His leg swept under hers, and she fell to the ground, her elbows and knees slamming into stone.

Before she could roll out of the way, he grabbed her. One of his hands hooked under her jaw. He was going to break her neck.

At the last second, her shoulder shifted to block the movement. She shoved his arm away and spun out of his grasp, then punched forward into the darkness. A sharp crack sounded as her fist collided with his face. Blood dripped from his mouth onto her hand as he stepped back, the shadows enveloping him further.

He was the one who'd taught her how to fight to kill, how to protect herself, how to survive on Kosín's streets.

But the biggest obstacle to her survival had always been him.

She took advantage of his injury now and fought like she'd never fought anyone before, using all the skills he'd taught her.

Bringing out a knife and keeping her other hand free, she worked with the sound of his footsteps. They shifted around each other, striking out with fists and blades, their movements a blur with quick breaths, careful footsteps, and flashes of steel in the dark corridor.

She wondered why he hadn't shot her yet, and why he hadn't killed her when she'd confronted him at the Dom. Even something about his movements now felt hesitant.

He took another step to his right. She shifted to her left and struck with her blade. It slipped, scraping against his side rather than stabbing into flesh, but he still hissed in pain.

Before she could attack again, he sped past her, his footsteps flying down the corridor.

She followed for a few steps, then stopped, panting heavily from the fight. Her pulse pounded as loudly as his footsteps fading away.

The Blood King had never run from a fight before.

She could go after him. But this was bigger than a fight with Kohl. If she continued on to meet Teo and got back to the job, they could free the Inosen who'd been imprisoned for nothing more than wanting freedom. They would take down Bautix and Kohl in one shot.

She turned and sprinted up the stairs. When she reached

the seventh level, she peered through the small window set in the door.

The seventh floor of the prison was identical to the lower floors where they'd broken out Teo. A narrow walkway lined the four inner walls of the prison with a pair of stairwells winding up and down to the other floors.

But now, all along the walkway, Diamond Guards were lying in the corners. Five in total, they were paralyzed by her poison darts that Teo had used. Uniforms had been stripped from two of the guards, leaving them in white undershirts. Her eyes flicked to the cell doors. Each had a stick of dynamite tied to one of the bars. A collection of wires led out from under the door she stood in front of and traveled up the stairs toward the upper levels.

She raced up the next staircase to peer through the window of the eighth floor and saw the same thing. When she reached the ninth-floor landing, she found Teo standing right outside the door, holding the rest of the explosives and the rope.

"You work fast," she whispered, walking up to him.

"So does your poison," he said with a grin. "Was it a guard following us?"

She shook her head as he handed her the uniform he'd stolen from the guard below. "It was Kohl."

He scanned her once, as if searching for injuries. "Are you okay?"

With a stiff nod, she said, "I think he's working for Bautix to take out the princess, so he ran before either of us could do much damage. I stalled him at least, but we only have a couple of hours left. Let's do this fast and catch up to him."

She threw the shirt over her head and checked that the badge was still pinned on. The shirt was big, so she tucked it in and made sure her weapons were within easy reach, then took several of the dynamite sticks, tied together by long wires, along with rope and a set of matches. Then she loaded her own blowgun with a poison dart and placed the other darts within easy reach.

With a quick nod to each other, they walked through the door onto the ninth floor as if they owned the whole prison.

She turned left, and he turned right just as the floodlights above shifted to the lower levels, leaving them with only the dim orange lights spaced out along the walls. The less light, the better.

A guard stood at the corner. Aina nodded at him. Before he could do any more than turn to look at her, she lifted her blowgun and fired the dart.

Before it even struck his skin, she pivoted, catching sight of the next guard halfway down the balcony. The guard's eyes widened, and she raised a whistle to her lips, but Aina fired a dart into her neck and she dropped to the floor with a dull thud.

Moving quickly, she shoved both guards into the corners of the walkway where the floodlights' beams wouldn't fully reach.

On the opposite side of the walkway, Teo had just taken out the last guard and shoved his unconscious form into a corner. When he glanced over, she signaled to let him know she had also finished.

She began unraveling the sticks of dynamite, counting out ten, which would cover half of this floor's cells while Teo took the other half.

Separating the dynamite to only place one stick on each door would still result in a strong enough explosion to shatter the cell doors, but hopefully not strong enough to collapse the entire walkway like last time. The prisoners would need the walkways in place to be able to escape.

The floodlights shifted then, nearly exposing her. She twisted out of the way and held her breath for a few seconds until they changed once more.

Approaching a cell door, she knocked lightly on the bars. It was nearly pitch-black inside, but she could make out the slight shift of a shape near the bars. The prisoner lifted his head, eyes widening when he saw her.

"We're breaking you out," she said in a low voice. "Stand back before this dynamite blows, then run to the fourth-floor south stairwell. You'll find a ventilation shaft leading to the subway tunnels. Head down the tunnels and you'll find flares lighting a path to an exit east of the Minos River."

She repeated the message at the entrance of each cell, not waiting around to see who listened. Most prisoners were awake, and she had no time to rouse the ones who weren't. The explosion would rouse them and, if they were smart, they'd run.

All of them would stand a chance, and that was what mattered. Those who managed to escape could expose Bautix for what he was.

Even if all of them were recaptured, the explosions and the breakout would cause a distraction and hopefully draw Bautix's attention away from the Linasian princess.

But she wanted the prisoners to escape. She had no idea how many of them might be imprisoned simply for being Inosen, or how many of them might be people Bautix had gotten blamed for his own crimes. Saving these people wouldn't negate all the lives she'd taken, but freeing them would at least avenge her parents, who'd only died for their own freedom.

Life is precious, like her parents had used to say.

Within five minutes, she and Teo regrouped near the door they'd entered from. He passed her one of his guns wordlessly.

Her fingers shook around the handle as she recalled all the times Kohl had made her practice shooting and reloading, regardless of her asking to stop, no matter how strongly the memories of her parents' deaths flooded back.

Back then, she'd swallowed her fears and convinced herself that Kohl was doing her a favor. She'd taken all his lessons and honed herself into a weapon, another thing to plunge this city into darkness.

Maybe monsters could be made, like her and Kohl, but they could also be unmade—they could choose to work against corruption and terror instead of with it.

She and Teo moved to stand at the walkway railing and gazed down at the courtyard nine floors below. A few guards stood on the glass-covered floor of diamonds, talking in low voices, while others sat in chairs in the center of the courtyard. All of them were oblivious to what was happening above.

Aina and Teo nodded at each other, then struck a handful of matches each and lit the wires, their hands moving at the same steady pace. The wires were connected to all the sticks of dynamite lining the cells of the ninth, eighth, and seventh floors.

It would take a few minutes for the flames to reach all the cells, but the ensuing chaos would at least give the prisoners plenty of cover to get out.

They stepped away from the wires, withdrew grappling hooks from their packs, and tossed the hooks upward to the landing of the tenth and highest floor. The hooks latched on with dull clinks.

Then they raised their guns and aimed at the round floodlights above. The lights shifted within a breath, leaving her and Teo covered in shadows. They fired.

41

Glass shattered, falling to the courtyard below. Darkness cloaked the whole prison. Guards shouted below and above, but it was too late for them to figure out what was wrong. The dim orange lights on the walls were hardly any help without the floodlights from above.

Amid the shouts and scrambling footsteps, the flames along the wires surged toward the sticks of dynamite and struck them one by one. She cringed as explosions shattered the air, one every other second.

Smoke began to climb up the walls of the prison. Orange flames curled along the cells below, their light guiding the prisoners to freedom.

Aina and Teo jumped onto the ropes hanging from the grappling hooks, then aimed their guns downward. Ears ringing from the explosions, she could hardly hear the shouts from guards and prisoners. It all blended together in one wild cacophony.

But guards ran frantically on the floors below, their shadows thrown against the walls by the bright flames. Their footsteps clanged on the metal balconies, joining the din.

She avoided aiming for the guards and instead fired at the glass-covered diamond floor of the courtyard. The glass shattered with just a few shots from her and Teo.

The guards below tried to take cover, but the glass floor collapsed beneath them. They all fell into the pool of diamonds below them, and the diamonds began to swallow them like quicksand.

As pandemonium rose around them with prisoners and guards shouting on all ten floors, she and Teo climbed the ropes toward the landing of the tenth floor. They slipped onto it and joined the fray of scrambling guards, their stolen uniforms covering them as they raced across the balcony.

The guards ran, some nearly falling over the railing in the confusing darkness. Explosions below still sounded, spaced just moments apart.

Aina raced between the guards, but as she neared the corner of the walkway, a hand latched onto her shoulder.

"Stop there!" the guard shouted, pushing her shoulder so she spun around to face him. "I saw you come up from the floor below. Who are you?"

She slammed her fist into his nose. He fell back toward the wall, blood pouring down his face from his broken nose.

Another guard slammed into her as Aina turned to run, and she fell, her hands grasping for the railing to stop herself from flying over.

For a moment, she imagined herself falling to the floor and bleeding out on the diamonds.

Shaking her head to clear the image, she stood and raced around the balcony, pushing past guards in her way, and reached the other side where Teo waited for her near a set of wide double doors.

She passed him his gun. Before heading through the doors, they both glanced back once. The guards were all too busy running toward the explosion and the fleeing prisoners to pay them any attention.

Teo pushed open the doors to a wide hall, bright with fluorescent lights. A voice called out to them, but they sprinted down the hall without looking back, their footsteps echoing loudly. This hall would lead to the rest of the Tower, and from there, they would reach the reception ballroom.

Another wide door faced them at the end of the hall, with a padlock. Teo withdrew a large set of keys that he must have stolen from a guard.

"Ryuu isn't the only one who can open doors for you, is he?" he asked as he tried a few different keys before getting the correct one.

She let out a shaky laugh as he pushed open the door. The sounds of the pandemonium in the prison were still too close for her to relax. As they shut the door behind them, some of the din died down.

Half of her, whatever was left from her parents' faith, was tempted to send a quick prayer to Kalaan and Isar for the prisoners to get out safely. But the other half knew that people had to save themselves in Kosín. She hoped the prisoners would escape, whether the Mothers listened to any of their prayers or not.

Her heart ached as she thought of her own parents, Ynes, and Raurie's and Ryuu's parents—all those who hadn't escaped. There was nothing she could do for them. But if even one Inosen returned to their family safely tonight, then she would feel like she'd done something to honor the parents she'd lost.

42

They'd reached the levels aboveground by exiting from the tenth floor of the prison, but the Tower itself rose roughly thirty stories into the air, and the nearest path to the ballroom was still a few floors up.

They ran, orange lights on the walls flicking past in a blur. They took cover behind corners whenever Diamond Guards sped by them in the opposite direction, toward the prison. Time ticked by steadily, and each time they had to hide from a guard, Aina cursed with impatience.

Soon, an alarm went off. A cacophony of bells rang above and below them, blending with the sound of guards running toward the prison. Every few feet they ran, she expected a guard to appear and shoot them where they stood.

As they raced up another flight of stairs, yet another bell joined the din, this one rhythmic instead of resounding.

"That's eleven," she shouted to Teo as she counted the chimes. "We only have an hour."

With Ryuu's voice reciting the Tower's layout playing over and over in her head, Aina led the way, picking up the pace. There were so many twisting corridors and stairwells that it would be easy to get lost, but she kept replaying his words and focused on reaching the ballroom where Ryuu and Raurie waited for them.

In the eastern wing of the building, they ran up a spiral staircase through one of the Tower's many turrets. Torches were spaced along the walls. The orange flames made their statues gigantic on the stone steps as they ascended. Alarms continued blaring, but soon they were high up enough that the noise was smothered under the thick floors, and all she could hear was their footsteps and her own racing pulse.

At the top of the staircase, they skidded to a stop, panting heavily to catch their breath. A new hallway extended ahead of them, the walls lined with paintings and statues. Three chandeliers hung from the ceiling, their gold light gathering in small pools along the hall.

Aina beckoned Teo into a shadowed alcove. A pair of Diamond Guards stood in the center of the hall, off to the sides, working iron pulleys like the ones Aina had seen in Ryuu's mansion.

"Looks like they're closing off this part of the Tower," she said as, seconds later, a heavy iron gate began to slide out of a crevice in the ceiling. The metal screeched, setting her nerves on edge as it lowered to seal off the next part of the Tower. "Do you have any more darts?"

When Teo shook his head, she pulled out a pair of knives. There was no time to waste looking for another route, and no time to be merciful.

Without another thought, she ran toward the guards with Teo right behind her. Her footsteps pounded across the stone floor, but the screeching sound of the lowering gate was so loud that the guards didn't even turn around.

Ten feet away, she threw her knives one by one into the guards' necks. They died almost instantly, collapsing on the pulleys in front of them.

But the gate still fell, threatening to close off their route to the rest of the Tower.

"Go!" she shouted, sprinting now.

She pulled her knife out of one of the guard's necks, but there was no time for the second one. Covering her head, she slid under the gate. Teo followed right behind her. The gate slammed shut on the floor inches away from where his fingers had been a moment ago.

She wanted to stop and catch her breath, but they had to keep moving. Rolling to their feet, they followed Ryuu's directions the rest of the way. A window flicked by her view as they ran, revealing a heavy rain pounding into the walls of the Tower. They managed to hide from guards most of the time, except once when Teo had to put one into a sleeper hold before the man could shout for backup.

The next hall opened. A narrow corridor with a marble floor extended before them, its surface so polished they could see their reflections in it. Soft yellow lighting in cages of gold vines were spaced along the left wall. On the other side was a line of doors, swinging open and closed every few seconds as a flurry of people went back and forth carrying trays of appetizers. The workers were so busy, none of them even glanced at Aina and Teo.

Scents of meat and spices reached her, and she couldn't help her stomach growling as they approached. Pots and pans clattered inside the kitchens, blending with the voices of chefs and servers shouting to one another.

They slowed down as they neared the kitchen doors, their gait casual as if they were guests for the party rather than two wanted outlaws who'd just incited a massive prison escape.

The kitchen doors swung open again. Two waitresses pushed out a cart loaded with champagne bottles and flutes. As the doors swung, Aina caught a glimpse of the kitchen.

At least twenty workers were in there, cooking meat on the large stoves, chopping vegetables on the tables, and setting up trays of food.

"Too many people," she whispered with a shake of her head.

Teo nodded toward another door farther down the hall, open by a small crack.

They walked toward it, and Aina waited, listening. Inside, people were rummaging through pots and pans and speaking in low voices. She swung open the door.

Three kitchen workers stood inside the small pantry, but they were too slow. Before they could do more than look up, she and Teo had each grabbed one of the workers, putting them into holds that made them lose consciousness in seconds.

The third worker had flattened herself against the pantry wall and looked too scared to do anything other than stare at them with an open mouth.

As Teo removed the jackets, aprons and hats of the two unconscious employees, Aina placed the tip of a dagger at the third one's jaw.

"You saw nothing," she whispered. The woman gulped and nodded, then winced as the blade clipped her chin with the movement.

They tossed aside the Diamond Guard uniforms and donned the kitchen attire, Aina stuffing her scarf in the apron's pocket. All three employees they'd attacked were women closer to Aina's size, so while the uniform fit her well enough, Teo had to squeeze into the blouse and apron, ripping one of the sleeves in the process.

Fighting down a laugh, she asked, "Are you off to bake some cakes? Maybe an apple pie?"

He shook his head while tugging on the tight sleeves. "Shut it, or I'll bake you into an apple pie."

They left through the same door and made their way down the hall. According to Ryuu, if they walked straight for another few minutes, they'd reach a stairwell two floors above the balcony that surrounded the main ballroom where the princess would receive the black diamond.

A pair of Diamond Guards rounded the corner as they went. They both nodded politely at the officers, but the two were engaged in such a low, rushed argument that they hardly noticed the kitchen employees walking by them.

As Teo walked on, Aina dropped to a crouch and pretended to tie her shoes. Straining her ears, she caught snatches of the conversation.

Once the guards disappeared, she caught up with Teo and whispered, "They know there's been a breakout. Apparently, they've taken most of the Diamond Guards out of the main part of the Tower to try to get the prisoners back."

"At least there will be less of them around to notice us."

She nodded stiffly. "You should go meet up with Ryuu and Raurie. I'll find Kohl."

"I'll go with you, then. Let's take him out for good."

But she shook her head. "I want to fight him myself."

He opened his mouth, about to protest. But then he took in the determined expression on her face and pulled her into a tight hug instead. She wrapped her arms around his back, and for a second, she wanted to stay here—safe from the threats, with someone she could always trust.

"I've always known you could take him on," he said in such a nonchalant voice that she knew he meant every word. "But I'm still allowed to worry about you. Where will you look for him?"

"I think he'll be in the balcony above the ballroom," she said, pulling away. "If he's going to shoot her, that would be the best vantage point."

They set off, then, and in moments they reached the staircase that Ryuu had told them about. Two floors down, a landing extended to the left and the hall ahead disappeared into shadows. Aina waved to Teo, and they split up. She took that direction, wondering how much time was left, while Teo continued down the stairs to the ballroom itself.

As she traversed the hall, dimly lit with yellow light bulbs hanging from the ceiling every few feet, she couldn't deny her fear at heading on alone. She'd done everything on this mission with Teo, and telling him to go on and leave this to her made the task ahead even more daunting.

Touching the hilts of her knives for reassurance, she took deep breaths to gather as much energy as possible.

She'd need all she could to fight the Blood King.

She ran down the hall now, afraid that if she paused for even a moment, she might hear his voice telling her she needed him, that it was stupid to think she was anything more than his weapon. But she was done thinking what he told her to think.

He'd taken almost everything from her, but she still had her knives, and she knew how to use them.

She picked up the pace, running down the hall, accompanied only by the sound of rain lashing the outside walls of the Tower to her right.

Halfway down the hall, a figure stepped out of an alcove directly in her path. Aina skidded to a stop.

It was Tannis, her gold eyes shining like beacons in the dark hall.

43

Aina flung up her knife arm by instinct, almost slashing through Tannis's throat, but she stopped at the last moment. Tannis watched her with a raised eyebrow. Neither of her hands had flicked to weapons.

In the dim light of the empty hall, they stared each other down, inches apart, waiting for the other's next move. The only sound other than the rain was their steady breathing.

Killing Tannis was what Kohl would want her to do. Spark more enmity between his Blades, so one of them would take out the other and he would own the survivor.

But something was off.

Kohl had killed Kouta, not Tannis. And though Tannis had attacked her when they'd last met, now the other girl showed no sign of wanting to fight. Throwing stars still glinted at the holsters near her shoulders, but she kept her palms facing outward in a peaceful gesture.

"What are you doing here?" Aina finally asked.

After a beat of silence, Tannis tilted her head toward Aina. "You need to know the truth."

When Aina frowned at her, Tannis beckoned her into the shadows of the alcove where the light failed to reach them.

"What truth?" Aina snapped. "Did Kohl kick you out too?"

Tannis shook her head with a grimace. "I'm on *your* side, not his."

"You have a strange way of showing support." Everyone in Kosín was split between sides or lying about what side they were on, and she was sick of it. Whatever Tannis was doing had only caused more problems. "Prove it."

"Who do you think stopped Kohl from killing you last night? I took a tip from you—I kept a paralyzing dart between my teeth and blew it into his neck. Then I used a smoke bomb so none of his people would see me taking you away. I hid you in an alley, and then, once they all left, I brought you to Hirai's." When Aina went silent, she continued, "And who do you think sent Kouta Hirai the documents with information on Bautix's political murders?"

"How did you know about that?" Aina asked. Her first instinct was to dismiss everything Tannis said as a lie, but that was what Kohl would want her to do.

"Kohl never goes to Rose Court, but he's been attending secret meetings there for a while now. He thinks we're so scared of him that we'd never go through his things, but I got curious." Tannis shrugged. "Right before he gave you the Hirai hit, he went out again. I went through his office and found the documents about what the general is doing, and that Kouta Hirai was the next hit. I also found out that Kohl has been helping Bautix with these murders for years and hiding Bautix's connections to the city's arms sales. Kohl has funneled money from arms sales through the other tradehouses for years, to private accounts Bautix owns under different names. I knew they had history with each other, but I never knew how much until I found all this."

"History? Why would Kohl work for a Steel?"

"Kohl only does what benefits him, you should know that by now. And because of their partnership, Kohl gets away with almost anything in the city. Besides, they're afraid of each other."

"Afraid?" Aina let out an incredulous laugh. Of the million people who lived in this city, Kohl and Bautix were the last two she expected to be afraid of anything.

"Didn't he ever tell you how he got out of prison?" When Aina shook her head, Tannis sighed and said, "Our old boss smuggled money and weapons to the rebels, but he was playing two sides—he also gave information to Bautix, who was rising up in the military at the time. Kohl caught a glimpse of Bautix, but didn't know who he was until he was in prison and Bautix came to inspect the cells one day. Then, after Kohl killed someone in prison, a riot broke out. He escaped in it and ran all the way to the top floor of the Tower where Bautix's office is. I don't know exactly what happened, but it sounded like he almost killed Bautix too, and threatened to reveal that Bautix was selling weapons to both sides during the war—to the Steels and to King Verrain's fighters. Bautix let Kohl go free and caught up to him a few years later."

"What happened then?" Aina asked.

"All I know is that Bautix asked Kohl to put together a group to spy on a worship service and take out some Inosen. I think Bautix wanted a favor from Kohl, for letting him out of prison, and after the war, all Bautix did was focus on getting rid of Inosen. I was part of the group Kohl put together."

"That's where he saw me and my parents," Aina said in a low voice. "He killed them for that job."

Tannis's eyes widened. "I didn't know that. You mean he still recruited you, after killing your parents?" When Aina nodded stiffly, Tannis said, "I'm sorry, Aina. I really didn't know. But it doesn't surprise me. Did you know, I had friends here that died during the war for being Inosen? So I hated doing that job with Kohl. I thought their partnership was temporary, just for that job. But this information I found a few weeks ago proves they've been working together all this time. Bautix lets Kohl get away with almost anything, and Kohl helps him launder money from weapons sales and takes care of his dirty work whenever Bautix asks. I sent Hirai copies of what I found. I thought he'd be rich enough to do something about it. But he's dead now, and Bautix is still getting away with his plans."

After a lull of silence, Aina asked slowly, "So, when you were telling me that going after Kouta was an easy way to get myself killed—?"

"I was trying to get you to stop, obviously," Tannis said, letting out an exasperated breath. "Should have known you were too ambitious to read between the lines of your dream job. I knew you were loyal to Kohl for the most part, so I couldn't say anything and risk you ratting me out to him."

"If that's true, then why did you try to kill me in the alley later? You said Kohl gave you the job instead."

"That was a lie. I knew Kohl would hear about our fight if I confronted you in public, and that would prove my loyalty to him. It worked, since he never doubted me until last night. And I thought that if I fought you, maybe injured you and made you think Kohl didn't want you on the job anymore, you would stop trying, but . . . I have to admit, I admire your stubbornness." She flashed Aina a quick grin. "Mazir, on the other hand, he tried to play the game. But he failed."

"What does Mazir have to do with Bautix's plans?"

"He was Kohl's Shadow, one of the best spies in the city, so I'm sure he figured out what our boss was up to a long time ago," Tannis answered. "But he got greedy. He told that baker you killed what Kohl was up to and got the baker to sell the information to the Jackals. Mazir knew the Jackals might go to Bautix to try to steal the job from Kohl. He hoped the Jackals would pay him for this, but one of Kohl's informants in the casino overheard the conversation and told me what was going on. I told Kohl, and he sent you to silence the baker."

"And then you told him it was Mazir?" Aina asked, remembering her old colleague's glassy eyes staring up at her in the alley.

"I had to or else he wouldn't trust me," Tannis said in a quiet voice. "The Jackals tried to move in on the job. Kohl couldn't stand that, so when he let you go, he knew the Jackals would come after you and that you would kill enough of them that he wouldn't have to worry about them for a long while."

Aina crossed her arms and scoffed. "You're saying he cut me off because he knew I would end up doing his dirty work for him?"

"Yes, but I doubt he knew it would end up this way. If you looked at the reports close enough, you'd see a job or two that I was sent on. But I killed my marks and no one saw me, so Kohl had no reason to cut me off. Bautix still blamed 'a murderer from the Stacks,' but he didn't investigate any further because the job was done. All that mattered was that no one connected it to him. But then when Hirai survived . . . Bautix had to keep up the search for you, at least until Hirai was killed, and I bet he was putting pressure on Kohl to finish the job. I think he knew you would manage to kill Hirai eventually, but Bautix wanted the job done before the princess arrived."

"So then Kohl killed Kouta himself, but didn't even notice that Kouta had the note in his pocket that would doom Kohl and Bautix's entire plan." Aina let out a bitter laugh at the irony. Kohl's confidence had finally derailed him instead of helped him.

He hadn't turned everyone against her. Maybe together, she and Tannis could change things.

"Before you came to fight Kohl last night, before I turned on him and saved you . . . he asked me to be his backup to kill the princess right as she's given the black diamond at midnight," Tannis said, glancing over her shoulder down the hall. "There's not much time left."

"What will you do instead?"

"Stop him," Tannis said immediately, her gold eyes flashing in the dark hall. "Let's fight him together, but I'll let you have the killing blow. You deserve it for what he did to your parents."

Aina smiled. "Looks like we finally understand each other."

44

They traversed the next fifty feet of the hall in silence. Aina's eyes flicked to every dark corner for a sign that Kohl might be here.

Voices rose nearby as the stone balcony appeared on their left. Laughter echoed and glasses clinked from the ballroom below filled with unsuspecting guests. On the right, a wide-open window curved toward the ceiling with only a knee-length ledge separating them from the edge. The view showed the grasslands behind the Tower. Rain fell in steady torrents outside, sweeping diagonally and pattering steadily on the window ledge and the first foot of space inside the hall.

Cold wind cut through the window and ruffled the thick black curtain that hung on the inside of the balcony. A thin crack of light shone through the center of the curtains to reveal a sliver of the ballroom. It was the perfect place for an assassin to wait with their target in sight below, and the perfect amount of space for the barrel of a gun to slide through. She imagined Kohl there, still and relaxed like he was before every kill. She wondered if he'd look so calm when she was the one pointing a dagger at him.

Tannis held up a hand. Their footsteps slowed to silence. Then, Tannis crouched down next to the curtain and peered underneath it, while Aina searched the shadows of the balcony for any sign of Kohl. Her pulse raced with nerves.

They had to find him before he carried out this job and sank the country into war. She had to find him and confront him for what he'd done to her parents, what he was trying to do to the city all for his own benefit.

When she stood again, Tannis whispered, "Everyone's down there, including the princess. I don't know when Kohl—"

Just then, the air shifted behind them.

Kohl's dagger swung toward them. Aina dodged the strike with a sharp intake of breath, but Tannis was caught off guard. The blade clipped her arm, and she hissed in pain.

Taking out her dagger, Aina shifted behind Kohl. A throwing star appeared in Tannis's fingers, and she and Aina locked eyes over Kohl's shoulder for the briefest second.

They both struck at the same time, but Kohl moved so fast, he became a blur in front of them. Aina, lunging forward, stumbled and barely missed the hiss of Tannis's throwing star passing by her neck.

Aina caught herself from falling, but then a tight grip latched onto her wrist and twisted. She gritted her teeth in pain as her weapon clattered on the stone floor. She raised her fist, but Kohl caught it in midair, then shoved her toward the balcony so hard, her feet left the floor.

She grabbed onto the balcony at the last second, her twisted wrist slamming into it to stop herself from going over the edge. The wrist cracked, and she bit down on her lip to avoid crying out in pain. She whipped around in time to see Kohl's fist flying toward her throat.

Dodging it by an inch, his cold knuckles scraping against her collarbone, she kneed him in the stomach. The next moment, Tannis stepped between them.

Aina retrieved her blade from the floor, but her dominant hand ached from slamming it into the stone balcony. It was too stiff to be as dexterous as she needed it to be. She switched the dagger to her other hand. She'd trained fighting with it plenty of times and was good enough, but it was still a disadvantage.

The rain pounding on the Tower walls reached her ears as she straightened. Kohl and Tannis fought fast and hard, quick blurs of steel flashing across the dark hall.

Tannis cried out suddenly and fell back a few steps from Kohl. A knife was buried in her abdomen. Her gold eyes widened, her face paling as she gripped the blade's handle. Blood leaked from the wound and coated her hands. Kohl moved toward her like a vulture circling its prey.

"No," Aina whispered under breath, and in two quick strides, she reached them. As he lifted his blade to deal a killing blow, Aina kicked him in the back.

He fell, but twisted around and swept his feet across her ankles, so she went down with him. Tannis had scrambled toward the open window, clutching her wound and leaving a trail of blood. Kohl knocked Aina's wrist to the side, and her knife skidded across the floor.

His knife flashed in the moonlight. The blade fell toward her chest. With all the strength she had, she jerked upward, forced his leg aside, and rolled out of the way.

But as she did, a searing pain reached her arm. His knife had cut right through it, missing her heart but wounding her nonetheless.

When Aina pushed herself to a stand, blood poured from her arm, making her head spin.

Then Kohl's fist collided with her jaw.

Her teeth clashed together as she fell back and slammed into the nearest wall. Her knees shook, and she dropped to the floor, blacking out for one long second.

When her vision wavered back in, she tried to roll away, but stopped in place when Kohl raised a gun and pointed it at her head.

All thoughts, rational and otherwise, fled to be replaced by a numbing fear. All she saw was her mother's head turning red in front of her and her father's body knocked back by the bullets striking his chest. Nausea rose through her. She was going to die the same way they had, by the same man.

The Blood King's voice softened as his finger settled upon the trigger. "I'm just doing a job, Aina."

45

She counted down her last seconds, the cold barrel of the gun the only reality she was reduced to.

With a clatter, the gun landed on the ground ten feet away. She blinked rapidly, trying to make sense of what had happened. He'd thrown the gun to the side. He hadn't shot her. The breath returned to her lungs in one ragged inhalation that sent a searing pain through her head.

Kohl shook his head slowly. One of Tannis's throwing stars was buried in his shoulder, but he didn't bother to remove it. Sweat poured down his face and blood trickled from the wound, but he didn't even seem to notice it.

"I tried to give you what you wanted, Aina. Don't you understand? I got you off the streets. I taught you everything. I agreed to let you open your own tradehouse. I was hired for the hit on your parents, but I didn't know you—"

"And you're still working for the same man who hired you

back then!" she spat, gesturing toward the ballroom where Bautix was sure to be.

Kohl faced her with a pained expression, as if he truly didn't understand why she was so angry. "I've given you so many chances, yet you can't see why your mistake almost cost me everything. I need to protect my own interests too, Aina, and I thought you were smart enough to understand that, but here you are fighting me."

Before he finished speaking, she was laughing. "And what? Do you think I owe you something just because you showed me decent human kindness when you saved me from that bombing? Even that was a lie. You saved me because you felt bad for orphaning me, and you gave me up the minute you saw me as a threat to your reputation. You don't get to have me and push me away whenever you want. You don't get to kill my parents and then expect gratitude for picking me up off the streets you put me on. I owe you nothing, Kohl."

Before he could say any more, Aina lunged to the right. They moved at the same time, but she swung around first and kicked at his ribs.

He dodged the attack, then aimed a punch at her face. She stepped toward the window, pushing his arm away to deflect the hit.

Blood flowed from her injured arm the whole time, but there was nothing she could do about it now. All that mattered was ending him.

As if reading each other's minds, they brought out daggers at the same time and moved toward each other in one swift step. Metal scraped against metal and iron flashed in the dark as they fought.

Aina leaped backward to avoid his next strike, which missed her by a hair's breadth. That was another moment, like with the gun, where he could have killed her, but he missed or took a second too long to deliver the blow. She'd never seen him miss before.

Whatever this hesitation was, she could use it against him.

She swept her dagger across Kohl's side and jumped past him. He inhaled sharply at the cuts.

A smile lit up her face, and she beckoned him forward. They came at each other again. Aina swung underhand with her daggers, aiming for his side, when he caught them in place with his knife. Her arms began to shake. A small intake of breath told her he was finding this fight exhausting too.

She pushed upward with a loud grunt. His weapons flew in the air and clattered on the stone floor.

But he jumped out of the way of her next strike and grabbed his gun off the floor, lifting it faster than she could blink.

Paralyzed with fear, her only hope was that the Mothers would protect her for once.

But when his finger met the trigger, there was a pause of one second that seemed to last forever.

He fired.

She moved. The bullet missed her head by inches, but she stepped back toward him and swept her blades across his unguarded chest.

The smoke of the fired shot invaded her nostrils, filled her lungs as she watched him falter. She twisted his wrist so his gun dropped to the floor.

"Aina," he said, backing up toward the window. His hands frantically tried to stop the flow of blood, but there was too much. He looked at his abandoned gun, but she blocked him from moving toward it. "Please. Listen—"

"I'm done listening to you," she hissed, cutting off his words. She forced him toward the window so his knees hit against the ledge. He caught his balance right before falling over, but she didn't stop. Rain fell onto them in wild gusts as she forced him to lean farther back.

As she pressed her blade under his ribs, he said in a rush, "You really think this will stop Bautix from getting the princess killed?"

She paused, the knife on the verge of piercing his heart. "You let me worry about Bautix."

Taking her pause as an opportunity to continue, Kohl whispered, "What's one thing an assassin always makes sure to have?"

"A backup," she whispered instantly. He stared her down without blinking, but a slow smile spread on his face. She pressed the knife in a little deeper and the smile dropped. "Who is it? Where are they?"

Kohl laughed despite the blade pressing into his skin. "It was Tannis at first, but she turned on me, so what makes you think Bautix would trust me to pick a new backup? All I know for sure is that your time is running out."

As if waiting for his words, the first chime of the midnight bells rang out.

Aina stepped away, her eyes racing across the balcony. Kohl slumped down near the window.

He was wounded. She could snuff out his life in seconds.

The second bell chimed. In its wake, she whispered, "This isn't over."

Three bells rang as she sped around the balcony, skidding to a stop to stare through the folds of the curtain. Hundreds of people were in the crowd below, gathered around a stage. Teo must have been among them, but she couldn't pick him out from here. Bautix stood on the stage with the rest of the Sentinel, Ryuu, Raurie, and the Linasian princess. Ryuu glanced over his shoulder as if he could sense something was wrong. Would Bautix try something himself if Aina managed to kill the sniper? Would Ryuu get caught in the line of fire?

Four bells. She whipped her gaze around the balcony surrounding the ballroom, searching for the best vantage point where another sniper could be hidden, but everything looked exactly the same except for a few statues poised at the corners of the balcony and the large, golden clock hanging above the crowd, embedded in the opposite wall. The backup sniper had to be here somewhere on the upper level. Five bells.

As she ran, six and seven bells ringing, she couldn't help it; she heard Kohl's voice the first night they'd spoken to each other. *Do you want to know the secret to survival?*

Eight bells. She skidded around the corner, on the far end of the hall.

You count and you look.

Nine bells. She heard Kohl's voice in her ears again and whipped her head around as she ran, expecting him to fire at her from a corner.

You count everything and you look at everyone.

Her eyes widened. The clock. Its incessant ticking raced in her ears as the tenth bell rang, blending with her footsteps pounding down the hall.

Are you paying attention, street child?

She swung open the low door behind the clock and jumped down onto the narrow wooden platform next to Bautix's backup—a boy with a jackal's bared jaw tattooed on his arm.

It was Olaf, the same boy she'd spared in the warehouse. He carried a rifle on his shoulder, but turned at the noise of Aina landing on the wooden platform next to him in the base of the clock. Electric yellow light enveloped them from under the wooden slats, highlighting how his eyes widened when he turned to face her.

Eleven bells. Applause rose up in the audience. Olaf fired at Aina, who flattened herself against the clock face, letting the bullet blast through the side of the clock. She shoved the end of his rifle aside, leaving him open.

Twelve bells—she swept her blade across his throat.

46

Midnight passed while Aina stood in the silence of the clock, breathing heavily as Olaf died before her. His blood trickled through the wooden base of the clock to dot the yellow lights underneath.

Turning from his body, she stared between the clock's numbers toward the balcony across the ballroom from her, where she'd left Kohl. What she'd whispered to him came back to her now: *This isn't over.*

Pushing past Olaf's body, she lifted herself out of the clock and onto the stone walkway of the balcony.

Her footsteps slowed, echoing slightly as she rounded the corner. Tannis was still seated near the window, her head resting on her chest. Kohl was gone.

"How is your wound?" she whispered as she approached Tannis.

Tannis had ripped off the sleeve of her jacket to wrap it

tightly around the wound on her abdomen. The blood flow had slowed, though her face was still drawn and exceptionally pale under the bright blue waves of her hair.

"You got better at fighting than the last time I saw you," she said with a tight grimace. "I'm sorry I couldn't stop him from leaving."

"Wait here," Aina said, squeezing Tannis's shoulder. "I'll get help for you."

When she nodded, Aina turned and retreated down the hall. Kohl was nowhere in sight, but that didn't matter now. She had to check that Bautix wouldn't try anything else once he realized his plans had been ruined. As she walked, she took her scarf and tied it around the wound on her arm.

She soon reached the staircase where she'd split up with Teo earlier, then walked down until the entrance to the ballroom came into view. A few Diamond Guards stood at the entrance, but she hid the blood on her clothes as best she could and slipped past them with a quick nod.

The idea that she'd fought a deadly battle in a dark hallway only one floor above this place made her head spin. The voices of hundreds of people in the ballroom rose louder than the pounding of the rain outside. It would take a few minutes to reach the opposite end of the ballroom by walking, it was so large. It extended two stories above in a dome-like shape, the ceiling black rock, like a cave. A broad gold chandelier hung at the arc of the dome.

Like the courtyard in the prison, this floor was glass-covered with thousands and thousands of diamonds buried beneath it. Guests in thick furs and silk dresses moved in groups toward a platform set up at the back of the ballroom. Their dresses swayed above the floor, blocking her view, but nothing could hide all those diamonds. The death toll in the war had been tens of thousands, but only now, seeing the gems held here, did the number truly strike her.

The balcony where she'd fought Kohl lined the back wall of the ballroom, with the black curtain spread behind the stone banister. She cast a quick glance behind her at the clock. The outline of Olaf's body was visible slumping against the clock face, but no one else seemed to have noticed yet, so she turned away and continued on. A band played on classical instruments in the far corner, but the music slowed as someone on the stage clinked a utensil against a champagne flute to call for the crowd's attention. Keeping an eye out for Teo, Aina slipped between the chattering guests, her bloodstained clothing brushing against their fine dresses and suits.

As she approached the front of the crowd, she noticed the five members of the Sentinel gathered on the stage behind a dark plinth. A velvet cloth covered the top of the plinth and a gleaming, ruby-red box sat in the center of the cloth.

A contingent of Diamond Guards as well as additional guards the princess must have brought from Linash surrounded the stage. The princess, Saïna Goleph, waited off to the side and in front of Mariya Okubo and Raurie. Ryuu stood closest to the plinth at the front of the stage. He smiled politely, but Aina could see the tension in his shoulders as his eyes scanned the crowd and the balcony surrounding the ballroom. She willed him to look at her as she neared the front of the room, and just then, he caught her eye. He let out a breath and a cautious smile tugged at his lips.

General Bautix stood on the stage too, with pearl-coated épaulettes and a crimson sash resting on his fine gray suit and clashing with his red hair. His beard was held at the end by a silver clasp that matched the cuff links of his suit and the watch at his wrist, all of them engraved with Sumerand's sword-and-pickaxe symbol. His eyes kept flicking up to the balcony, but his face was unreadable otherwise.

Aina caught sight of Teo standing near the front rows of the crowd. She stepped between the guests until she reached them, tapping Teo on the shoulder.

"You're okay!" he said, pulling her into a bone-crushing hug next. "I knew you could handle Kohl."

She shook her head. "I injured him, but then I had to stop Bautix's backup assassin. One of the Jackals, Olaf, was ready to shoot if Kohl failed. I killed him, but Kohl got away by then. Tannis fought with me—"

"*With* you?" Teo asked.

"Long story, but she's on our side. We need to watch Bautix. I took care of his backup plan, but I wouldn't put it past him to have another ten."

As Raurie left, Mariya Okubo stepped forward and tapped her champagne flute again to catch the audience's attention. The voices in the hall began to die down. Someone dimmed the lights, leaving the room dark except for the candles on the chandelier and a spotlight that shone down on the stage.

Okubo went on about how the Linasian princess's visit was a sign that both countries were ready to move out of the past and toward the future, this alliance between them sure to hold strong for many years. She then announced Ryuu to a roar of applause. Ryuu stepped toward the plinth at the front of the platform with Okubo, Raurie, and the princess right behind him. Aina's eyes flicked to Bautix. One of the guards had come up onto the stage and was whispering to him just outside the circle of light. Bautix's face grew paler by the second.

Ryuu pulled a string at the top of the red box. It fell away, ribbons fluttering to the floor. A glass case was revealed, and inside it, the black diamond sat atop a silk pillow, so large she could see it from here. It glittered like the night sky with the spotlight shining down on it. A gold chain was laced through its tip to form a necklace.

The princess lowered her head for Ryuu to drape the necklace over her head. As the crowd applauded, the musicians picked up their instruments and played a new, upbeat tune.

"I think Bautix is finding out his prison isn't as secure as he thought it was," Teo whispered.

"Maybe they found Olaf's body too," Aina replied with a smirk.

Bautix nodded once to the Diamond Guard, then whispered something back with a scowl on his face. As the crowd applauded, he began to walk slowly, stiffly, off the stairs on the side of the stage.

"No," Aina said under her breath, one hand going to her blowgun to fire a dart into his neck.

But Teo grabbed her shoulder and muttered, "Wait, look at Raurie."

Aina's eyes flicked to Raurie. She had pulled Okubo a little to the side and handed her a sheaf of papers. As she flipped through them, Raurie spoke in a rush, her eyes flicking to Bautix, who continued toward a door in the back of the ballroom with a small group of Diamond Guards surrounding him. Okubo turned to watch his retreat too, her mouth flattening to a hard line. As if sensing her gaze, Bautix looked back once, then walked faster toward the exit.

"Stop him!" Mariya Okubo shouted suddenly over the applause, the chatter, and the music. She pointed at Bautix, but most of the Diamond Guards hesitated. Okubo could command them, but as the general, Bautix was their highest authority.

The lights flicked back on when Okubo shouted again, and at the same time, Bautix's guards pulled out their guns. The audience seemed to gasp all at once.

"Jackals," Teo hissed. Then Aina saw it. One of the guards' sleeves had rolled up past his elbow when he lifted the gun, leaving the jackal tattoo visible.

One of them aimed toward the stage, right at the princess, who froze in place. The shot fired. Ryuu jumped toward her, pushing her out of the way.

Aina bit down a scream as the bullet hit Ryuu instead. As shouts rose up in the audience, she looked for him on the stage, but the princess's guards ran onto it, blocking Aina's view.

Crouching low, she took out her knives and moved, Teo next to her. Shots fired everywhere as they wove between the fleeing guests. Teo shot two of the Jackals posing as Diamond Guards, but before they could reach the rest of them, they began to slip through the back door.

One of them turned around, and his cold blue eyes locked with Aina's. It only lasted for a second, before Kohl followed Bautix through the exit.

The remaining Jackals fired at the real Diamond Guards, taking out a few near them. Okubo shouted for more backup, but Kohl and Bautix had already fled.

Pushing past the ball attendees, who were shoving their way toward the main exit, Aina and Teo reached the fight. She threw a knife that pierced the neck of one of the Jackals while Teo, the Diamond Guards, and the princess's guards shot at the others.

In minutes, most of the Jackals were dead on the floor. Kohl, Bautix, and more Jackals had left through the ballroom's back door. Guards were running after them, but Aina had a sinking feeling they wouldn't succeed in catching them. She turned instead toward the stage and breathed a sigh of relief when she finally saw Ryuu, who sat on the stage, clutching his upper arm. The bullet wound was still bleeding, but he was alive.

Most of the reception guests had fled, their wine glasses and champagne flutes abandoned on the floor in their rush to get out. Under the stark light, with red wine spreading across the diamond floor, it looked like blood.

The remaining four members of the Sentinel were speaking to the Linasian princess, who looked shaken, but unhurt. Her own guards gathered around her like a shield.

Raurie met Aina and Teo at the foot of the stairs leading up to the stage.

"You're both safe," she said with a cautious smile. "I saw Teo come into the ballroom without you, Aina. I thought you might have been in trouble."

Aina shook her head. "I almost was, but I had help. Tannis, another girl from the Dom, was on our side, not Kohl's. She fought him with me, but he injured her. She's on the balcony, and she's alive, but she's bleeding badly. I need to get a healer to her."

"Let's go help her," Raurie said, then cast an anxious glance toward the stage. "I don't want to leave Ryuu to have to talk to the Sentinel alone, though."

"I'll go with you and help get Tannis to June," Teo said, then turned to Aina. "Meet us there with Ryuu once you're done with this?"

Aina nodded, then stepped between the guards and climbed the steps to meet Ryuu. His face had gone a little paler than usual, but his wound didn't seem to be deep. He and Mariya Okubo spoke in a low voice.

He nodded at Aina over Okubo's shoulder. "This is Aina. She's also a victim of Bautix's plans. But she and two of our friends helped expose him tonight, and she took down the assassin who was supposed to kill the princess."

Okubo acknowledged Aina with a quick nod, then turned back to Ryuu and asked more questions about Bautix's plans. As she spoke, Aina walked toward Ryuu, removed her scarf from her own wound, and tied it around his.

"Thank you," he whispered.

"No, thank you," she said when Okubo left him to speak with the princess. "If you hadn't pushed her out of the way, she would have died. I didn't like that, watching you get shot. But you did what you had to do."

Aina watched Okubo speak with the princess out of the corner of her eye. The conversation didn't last long until the princess shook her head at something Okubo said, and the Linasian guards stepped in front of her. They stepped off the stage and walked toward the ballroom exit without a glance back.

Aina didn't know what would happen with the alliance between their countries, but she hardly cared when there was more to worry about now; what Bautix would do next, how Kohl would come after her, how many of the Jackals still lived and would work for Bautix.

As the room continued to empty out, she sat on the edge of the stage next to Ryuu. Giving her a soft smile, he pulled her into a hug and rested his chin on her head.

"I didn't like it either, when Teo showed up in the ballroom without you. I was afraid for you. I thought something bad happened."

She held back a smile as Okubo walked back over to them, presumably with more questions.

"Maybe we were both afraid," she said, "but we didn't let that stop us."

47

Teo's apartment was emptier than Aina had ever seen it. They'd spent the day packing, had bleached the floor to clean the blood stains, and planned for someone to fill in the bullet holes near the window. Most of Teo's belongings were lined up in boxes near the kitchen window, but there was still his mother's room to be packed, which Aina, Ryuu, and Raurie had assured him they would take care of while he went to get more boxes.

Aina tore her eyes away from the simple paintings on the wall of Ynes's bedroom. Some of the paintings were of the Linasian countryside and others were of their falcon god. Most were coated in dust since it had been more than a week since Ynes's death. Ryuu admired the paintings too, in between folding handwoven blankets into a box. She tapped her fingers along the edge of the box in front of her, wondering what to say to him. This was the first time they'd been alone since the day in his mansion when he'd said they shouldn't talk to each other anymore.

But he'd spoken to her first after Bautix had fled.

I was afraid for you, he'd said.

Clearing her throat to get Ryuu's attention, Aina reached into the pouch of darts at her belt and picked out Kouta's diamond-and-ruby ring among them. It caught the sunlight pouring in from the window in the kitchen.

Before Ryuu could do more than widen his eyes in shock at the ring she held, Aina walked over, took his hand, and slid it onto one of his fingers.

"Is this my brother's ring?" he asked, looking at her with a spark in his eyes that made her cheeks warm. "When did you . . . ?"

"I took it that first night, in your library."

"And you held on to it?" He held it up to the light. Rainbow colors filtered through the diamonds and onto his face. "I thought you would have sold it."

"At first, I forgot about it," she said with a shrug, "but about a week after we found your brother on the train, I remembered it. I should have sold it. I was starving. But it was sort of like holding onto a piece of you." She averted her eyes from him then as a blush crept up her cheeks. "And I told myself that if I found a way to give it back to you, I would, and I'd apologize."

"Thank you. Our parents gave it to him as a present on his tenth birthday. It was the last one they celebrated with either of us." Grief flickered across his features for a moment, but then he smiled warmly. "I have something for you too, actually."

He walked to a nightstand near the door, where he'd left a folder that he'd brought with him this morning. Earlier, she'd watched him take out leases for new apartments from that folder. One for Teo, and one for Raurie and her aunt, with the first three months of rent already paid.

Aina hadn't felt left out. She assumed Ryuu must have overheard her conversation with Tannis once they'd all reached the safe house and realized that their plans wouldn't include a new apartment. The next day, when Ryuu returned with the leases for Raurie and Teo, she'd listened to him telling Teo that he knew how painful it was to live somewhere with memories of those who'd died.

As she watched him riffle through whatever other documents were in the folder, her heart sank. She'd always thought he was lucky that he still had a mansion and servants to return to after his parents' deaths. She'd never before considered that his parents' and brother's ghosts haunted every hall, every library and study, each statue and chandelier.

"There it is," he said, pulling out a small stack of pages. Holding it upside down, he passed it to her wordlessly. When she turned it over, she saw a bank statement for an account she was unfamiliar with. "I overheard you and Tannis last night."

After they'd spoken to Mariya Okubo, they left the Tower to go to the Inosen safe house and take care of their wounds. Tannis, Raurie, and Teo had already been there. Raurie had managed to bandage Tannis well enough before leaving the Tower, and June used magic to stop her from bleeding out once they'd arrived at the safe house. But she'd still moved gingerly and winced as she sat next to Aina. In a way, Aina had already started thinking about the plan Tannis had proposed next, and she knew they would do it best together.

They would hit Kohl where it hurt the most.

She shook her head and scanned the paper once more. Then she saw the names of the account holders: Tannis Bayen and Aina Solís. She gasped and dropped the paper like it was on fire.

"There's a million kors in there!" she choked out. "What the—"

Ryuu laughed, brown eyes lighting up as he took in her incredulous expression. "Remember when we were waiting to break into the prison to rescue Teo? You told me your old boss took all your money. I didn't know you very well then, but I could tell you were terrified." His smile faded slightly. "I could tell you'd lost a lot. So I used my connections at the bank to get some of his money transferred to this new account. I spoke to Tannis this morning before she left the safe house, and she told me she was going to open a joint one for you."

Her eyes widened. "This is all of Kohl's money?"

"No, I can't get into all of his accounts," he said, shaking his head. "But Tannis told me she'd seen information on this one from her snooping through his office. It was one of the fake accounts he had set up to filter money to Bautix from his arms sales, and based on the statement, it looked like some of the money from Pavel's own business went through there as well. You heard Okubo last night, she said she would reward you for your help in bringing down the princess's attempted assassins. I'll tell her about this and ask her to lift the price on your head. That should be reward enough, right? I told you, my name can open doors." He lifted his shoulders in a casual shrug, as if this had been no more difficult for him than a stroll through a park. "In this case, it was the door to one of Pavel's safes."

She let out a small laugh, then folded up the paper and tucked it in one of her jacket pockets.

Maybe they shouldn't talk to each other, after all the betrayal between them. But within their betrayals and their separate goals, he'd shown her his truths and fears, and she'd shown him some of hers. If there was anything they did well together, it was challenge each other to dig a little deeper into their own truths. If a friendship was anything, it should be trying to make each other see how good and brave they could be they tried.

Before she could think of something to say in reply, Raurie suggested they take a break. They gathered around the same table where Aina had seen Ynes sit hundreds of times, blankets drawn around her, prayers muttered under her breath.

To distract herself from those thoughts, Aina reached for the newspaper at the edge of the table. The headline read: "General Alsane Bautix's Betrayal." It didn't list the details of all Bautix's crimes, but it covered his murder of the late Hirai mine owners and their eldest son. It also mentioned Ryuu and how he'd been a key part of the effort to stop the attack on the visiting princess and to catch Bautix in his corruption.

A few minutes later, Ryuu brought over cups of tea for them. Reaching for one, Aina placed the paper back on the table.

"Are your aunt and uncle headed to your new apartment yet?" she asked Raurie.

Raurie shook her head. "I spoke to them this morning before I left. They'll go there later, but all the older Inosen wanted to have a meeting about how we're going to move forward after what happened with Bautix. Some of the prisoners you broke out last night were recaptured, but most escaped. Some went to the safe houses and told their stories. They were arrested for praying, or having relics of the Mothers, or speaking in the holy language. With Bautix's crimes exposed now, it's the perfect time to question all his other actions. The Inosen think we should present a case to the Sentinel to decriminalize our religion and free anyone imprisoned for it."

"I'm sure they will," Ryuu spoke up. "You heard the Sentinel last night. They're really grateful for what we did."

Aina grimaced. "The Sentinel did nothing to stand up for the rights of the Inosen for years. In a way, I can see why they were afraid, after everything King Verrain did in the war, but that should have stopped after he was dead. I'm not going to trust them anytime soon. They have nearly fifteen years of crimes against Inosen, and ignoring the conditions of the poor in this country, to make up for before I trust them. They're grateful we stopped the princess from being assassinated and a war from happening, and they'll pay us as thanks, but that doesn't mean they'll actually change anything."

Raurie nodded once in agreement. "We'll still try. We'll never stop fighting for our freedom. But we're not going to be naive either. I'll believe they've changed only once they prove it, and right now is the best time to test them."

As Raurie's voice faded away, Aina recalled their conversation with the four remaining members of the Sentinel last night. They'd been so shocked by Bautix's crimes and the attempted assassination on the princess—who had left to return home at once with no word on the status of the alliance between their countries—that Aina wouldn't trust any of them until they could get their heads on straight. But she also thought the Inosen were right—now was a good time to strike, when the Sentinel was willing to question everything Bautix had ever supported.

Ryuu had given them most of the information about Bautix's crimes last night, and he nearly said Kohl's name—but then he'd looked at her and she'd shaken her head. There was no point putting any kind of arrest warrant on Kohl. If he were in prison, he would simply break out again. She also preferred to handle her problems herself. Kohl's murder of her parents, and how he'd tricked her since she was a child, were problems *she* wanted to punish him for. She couldn't let the Sentinel do that for her.

After finishing her tea, Aina left Teo's apartment. She stood at the doorway for a moment, shielding her eyes against the bright sun. Teo was walking toward the apartment with a stack of folded-up boxes under his arm.

She stepped out and then leaned against the wall in the alley between his apartment and the next as he walked up to her. They'd moved into the shade, but the sun still sent a streak of light across the other side of the alley. Voices from the main street and from Lyra Avenue a few blocks away managed to reach them here.

"Are you going to meet Tannis?" he asked, leaning on the wall next to her, their shoulders nearly touching as he did. When she nodded, he asked, "How are you holding up, after everything that happened with Kohl?"

After a pause, Aina let out a heavy sigh. Thinking about Kohl was a headache, but she'd have to deal with him soon.

"I'm glad I know the truth. And I'm looking forward to what Tannis and I will do. But it still feels like"—she paused again, her eyes flicking to the shadowed reaches of the alley—"every corner I look at, he'll be there waiting for me. Either to save me or kill me."

"You don't need him to save you."

"I know that," she said quickly, brushing loose strands of hair behind her ear. "Thank you for always telling me that, even if it took me a while to realize. But I've only ever known him as someone who saves me and hurts me at the same time. Someone I tried so hard to please. The man who killed my parents. How can I forgive myself for that?"

Teo turned to his side to face her, one of his shoulders still leaning on the wall. His eyes looked darker without the glint of the sun on them, umber instead of copper, but no less warm. He was tall enough that if she tilted her head to the side a few inches, her head would be resting on his shoulder.

"You can't blame yourself for something you didn't know," he said. "It makes sense why it took you a long time to see that he wasn't good for you. But that doesn't mean you don't deserve good things or can't recognize them when they come. You'll find someone who treats you the right way, and you'll deserve it."

His voice drifted off near the end. Tears pricked the corners of her eyes as he spoke. Averting her gaze, she scuffed her boots on the pavement, trying to think of something to say.

Then he said, "When my mother died and I was taken to that cell, all I could think of was her final moments. All I pictured was myself standing over her and holding the gun that killed her. I'm not the person who killed her, but I'm no better than them. I deserved to be in that cell, if not for my own mother's murder then for every mother's child that I've killed."

She was already shaking her head before he finished speaking. "Teo, you're the most honorable, trustworthy, loyal person I know. Who cares if you haven't always been the politest person in Kosín?"

"Not the politest person in Kosín?" He let out a loud laugh. "That's some understatement."

"You know what I mean. You've killed and stolen and spied because you were good at it and you needed to be good at something if you were to provide for your family after your father died. I don't judge you for the path you've chosen. Ryuu and Raurie don't. Your mother never did, and your father never would. Who else do you even need?"

"No one at all," he said with another laugh. "What I'm trying to say is that I'm glad I stuck through this. At first, this job seemed too good to be true. I felt for sure we'd get caught. But maybe it wasn't really that I was afraid of getting caught, but that I was worried I'd become an even worse, more dishonorable person because of it. But then, when you, Ryuu, and Raurie got me out of prison, and I started to think about what I really want, to stop all the terrible things that keep happening here, all the people like my mother dying for no reason . . . We accomplished something, Aina. I'm proud of that."

As he finished speaking, he reached down to take her hand. His eyes were slightly averted from her, as if he were nervous, something she'd never really seen in Teo.

They held hands for a while as Aina tried to quiet the storm inside her—half of it blazing and hot, telling her this was where she should be, the other cold and roaring in her ears, giving no hint as to when it would ever leave. For a moment, she felt like she was falling, weightless, into something unknown.

"I don't know what I want, Teo. And until I do . . ." She squeezed his hand once and let go.

He crossed his arms and cleared his throat. "That's for the best, then. As long as you're away from him, I'm happy for you."

She gave him a small smile, hoping she could convey in it all the feelings she could hardly describe to herself.

She'd fallen for Kohl, wrapping her life around his to the point where it nearly killed her, all because he'd shown her some kindness. He'd promised her the world, he'd promised she'd never fall again—and then he'd removed the world from under her feet so all she could do was fall.

And now she was reaching, like she always did, for something or someone else to cling onto and comfort her. It might be Ryuu, Teo, or even Tannis now that they were on the same side. But if she gave into any of her feelings too soon, she might hold onto someone who wasn't right for her. She might once again confuse kindness and favors with owing someone her life and loyalty. Until she made sense of what she truly wanted, she would guard her heart. Even against someone like Teo, who she knew would never hurt her. The last thing she wanted was to risk losing his friendship if she gave into these scattered emotions too quickly, so she would hold back even from him until she was ready.

"I'm worried about what you're going to do now," Teo said then, breaking the awkward silence.

"I'll be fine," she said with a shrug.

"You always are, aren't you?" Teo asked. "I know you can handle anything. But just in case, you know I'll be there for you."

"And I will for you," she said with a smile, then waved as she left.

48

The scent of grass fresh from the rain overnight mingled with the smoke belching above the train station. Aina stepped along cobblestone streets that soon grew choked with people, always the same crowds and hectic clamor she'd grown up with in Kosín. The square with King Verrain's statue opened wide, packed with workers on their way to the factories as the sun rose above them.

Everything had changed overnight, though it still seemed the same. Maybe she was imagining it, but she felt the city brimming with some new energy underneath—maybe it was hope, or a growing will to fight.

When she descended the muddy hill leading into the Stacks, it still felt as if daggers were pointed at her from all directions, but soon enough, everyone who mattered would know that she'd nearly beaten Kohl. News traveled fast, and if she needed to provide a leak, she would: how she'd held the Blood King at knifepoint, how he'd begged, how he'd fled and joined a Steel rather than face her again. All the fear and respect she needed to protect herself would be handed to her once everyone knew.

She passed by her parents' old house, glancing at the closed door that shielded a new family inside, and at the rooftop where she'd hidden from the world so many times.

As she stalled in front of it, she began to hear faint gunshots in her head, and saw her parents falling to the floor, the memory having replayed in her head thousands of times. But new details came back to her now. Her father's arms held out as if he could shield her and her mother with his arms alone. Her mother's hand stretching back, fingers spread, like she was trying to force Aina farther away from the man who wanted to kill them.

With the news of Bautix's corruption getting out, and Inosen rallying to stand up for their rights, maybe more people would be confident to proudly practice their faith. Her parents still had no justice, and they wouldn't get any. She didn't know if she could accept Kalaan and Isar into her own life like her parents had, but she wanted to believe in something—the right to freedom that everyone should have, and for the future of the city that had taken so much from her, but that she'd give everything to protect.

Her parents would be proud of her for doing whatever she'd had to do in life to obtain her own bit of freedom; they'd done the same, after all.

She remembered her father laughing and telling stories, her mother sleeping next to a copy of the Nos Inoken every night. There were so many things worth fighting for—the warmth and happiness she'd felt at her parents' side, and the happiness she felt now with the people she cared for—but most of all, standing up for something. Believing in something. Hoping for something more.

After staring at the house for a moment, she continued on her way to the southeastern shore of the Minos River.

The Dom loomed on the bank, its shadow covering her as she approached the manor without fear. She supposed she should stop thinking of it as "Kohl's tradehouse" and start to think of it as . . . *mine.*

For the first time in ten years, she breathed air that felt free.

When she entered the Dom, she found Tannis, Mirran, and the three young recruits Kohl had brought in sitting together in one of the second-floor bedrooms. Aina's eyes flicked to her own bed once—the last time she'd slept there, she'd still been under Kohl's rule—then waved at the others. Tannis had been speaking, explaining the events of the past few weeks to the others. At the sound of Aina's footsteps, Tannis turned, her gold eyes brightening with a smile instead of a glare.

"Tannis said Kohl is gone," Mirran said with a shocked expression. "You fought him?"

"I almost killed him," Aina clarified. "Tannis and I will be in charge of this place now. You're all welcome to stay if you want, or you can leave. We won't stop you."

Without waiting to see what they decided, she walked the length of the hall. Memories of training and living here with Kohl hit her with every footstep, leaving a bitter taste in the back of her mouth and an uneasy sensation in her stomach. They'd taken Kohl's tradehouse from him, they'd taken a lot of his money, they'd stopped his plans with Bautix, and they were on the verge of ruining his reputation. Her head spun with the thought—had she and Tannis just guaranteed their own deaths?

But she shook the thought away. He had nothing left to scare her with, and in the end, she'd gotten what she'd wanted: a place to call her own and people who respected her. She'd even gotten Kohl to see her as an equal, if the fear in his eyes and the plea on his lips when she'd fought him were any indication. She'd taken the Dom for herself rather than simply accepting whatever was left for her. She'd kept her promise, the silent one she'd made to other kids who slept on the street—that she would rise, and she wouldn't fear falling again.

The fear itself was greater than the thing I feared, came Ryuu's voice into her thoughts. She clung to those words and wrapped them around herself like armor—maybe fear would come sometimes, but she would face it when it did.

Footsteps sounded behind her, and she turned to see Tannis. She still had bandages wrapped around her stomach and she walked gingerly, but she would recover quickly enough.

"Ryuu got some of Kohl and Bautix's money transferred to a new account for us," she began slowly, wondering how Tannis would react. "It's a lot. More than we need. I want to give some of it away."

"To who?" Tannis asked, brushing a loose strand of blue hair behind her ear.

Aina shrugged. "To an orphanage, I was thinking. When I was a kid, there were only a couple around, and they were too full to take me. Maybe they could use the money to expand and take in more people."

"That's a good idea," Tannis said. "And we won't have to worry about the other bosses. I went to one of the other tradehouses this morning, told them how you fought Kohl and he ran, and now he's cozying up to Bautix. Maybe Bautix used to grant Kohl certain protections in the city, but Kohl never extended those to the other tradehouses, so they're not particularly happy with him for turning on us all. The boss I spoke to said there are a few Jackals left, but they're hiding now. I assume Bautix and Kohl are with them, and that they're all working together, but I need more information to be sure."

"We'll get to work tonight," Aina said. "We need to spread the word as much as we can and recruit a few more people. Show that we're strong without him. We need to look as united as possible or someone else will come to take over the Dom."

"We won't let that happen," Tannis said in a cutting voice.

"We won't," Aina agreed. "I still want to stop Bautix and whatever new plans he might come up with, now that he's got the Jackals working for him. But I'm going to find and kill Kohl too."

She would hunt him down not only because of what he did to her, but for her parents, for Ryuu and his brother, and for anyone else he'd hurt. She couldn't rid herself of the blood staining her past, but she could stop Kohl from gaining power and influence again.

No matter what happened next, she was grateful Tannis was on her side—no one else knew their business as well as the two of them, and no one else knew Kohl better either. They'd be a good team in whatever was to come. A bit of hope bloomed in her heart as she shook Tannis's hand—like a door was opening, rife with possibilities inside. Like she might be able to trust people again.

"By the way," she asked slowly, "if we're going to work together as equals, you should know I sell rough diamonds on the side."

"I know," Tannis said with a shrug.

"What? How? Did Kohl know?"

Tannis pursed her lips. "He might have, I'm not sure. I was doing a job in Rose Court once and saw you walk into a jeweler's. You came out and double-checked there weren't any Diamond Guards nearby. People who don't know you wouldn't be able to tell, but I could see the nerves on your face." She let out a laugh when Aina glared at her. "I know it's risky, but you can still do it if you want. I know how important it is to take freedom where you can find it."

As they walked down the stairs and turned toward Kohl's office together, Aina remembered how she'd held Kohl at knifepoint in the Tower. He didn't have to tell her about the backup. And he hadn't been gravely injured. After all, he'd managed to escape. Why hadn't he gotten up, retrieved his gun, and killed her before she could locate the backup? And a better question, why hadn't he shot her when he'd held her at gunpoint? Instead, he'd thrown his weapon to the side and asked why she couldn't understand him.

Maybe he'd been truthful when he said he'd taken her in and trained her to make up for the guilt of orphaning her. It would never make up for how he'd treated her over the years, but it might have been his weakness in their battle; something that made him spare her when he could have killed her. She couldn't imagine Bautix had been thrilled with the outcome, and that meant there was probably already strife in whatever partnership they had. That was where she and Tannis would stand stronger.

When they entered the office, Aina's eyes fell to the desk. She inhaled sharply and stepped back, one hand reaching for the wall.

"What?" Tannis asked, throwing stars already in hand as she searched the corners of the room.

"Kohl left that here," Aina said with complete certainty.

She walked to the desk, where her mother's tiny porcelain horse statue sat, the pink ribbon around its neck too bright and cheerful for this office. Aina swallowed hard, looking left and right, as if she expected Kohl to fall out of the ceiling and shoot her.

A note was held in place by a string tied around the horse's body. With shaking fingers, she slipped out the note and had a sudden vision of Kohl shoving a book in front of her. *Read.*

She unfolded the paper and scanned the words a few times. It was only a couple of sentences, but each time she reread them, they pierced her more with fear and anger.

Enjoy your stay in my house while it lasts, Aina.

And keep this good luck charm your dear mother left behind.

You're going to need it.

She thrust the note at Tannis, then curled her hands into fists at her sides. It was easy to let the note scare her, but she held it together. Kohl wasn't as invincible as he thought. Their fight in the Tower had proved that. Now she only wondered at his weaknesses and how she might use them against him: his tradehouse, and her.

He'd abandoned and threatened her because he cared about his tradehouse and reputation too much. Then he'd spared her because some part of him, however twisted, felt guilt toward her and wanted her to live.

And now, she'd taken his tradehouse from him.

The question was, *Which of us makes him weaker?*

Tannis folded up the note, then looked over her shoulder. "He's going to come for us."

Aina turned to face the doorway that led out to the hall. She'd left this office countless times with Kohl's threats and ultimatums hanging over her, his promises that if she just did one more job, or listened carefully enough to his words, she'd be safe. Her hands tightened around the hilts of her knives.

"Let him come," she whispered. "He won't escape my blade this time."